Face grey, filthy black hair over his eyes and button nose, but the three little scars on his cheek from the wild dogs that had plagued Fort William when they were kids, made it impossible for him to be anyone else. He looked sick, stumbling on the churned earth. But it was Alex, as sure as Warren knew his own face. "Hell." The world roared to life with machine gun fire shredding the air and plugging his brother like iron hornets. Warren screamed as the soldier fell back, out of sight. Warren began clawing his way out of the shell hole. Before Tik could stop him from charging into No-Man's Land, the thunder of artillery filled the air, consuming all sound in its wake, including Warren's guttural scream as he chased his dead brother.

Harvest of Of Blood and Iron

JASON RIDLER

"It would be much more practical to fight modern wars with mechanical robots than with men. But then, men are cheaper ... From the point of view of efficiency in war, the trouble is that men have feelings; to attain the perfect soldier, we must eliminate feelings."

Richard Aldington, *Death of a Hero*, 1929.

PRELUDE

July 15th, 1914

Queen Victoria's visiting chamber was among the most secret of Buckingham Palace, a shadowed corner of the hallowed grounds where her family had wielded power since Elizabeth united the country. It was lit by weak candles, for that was her optical preference.

One attendant wiped her exhausts clean, another fed coal into her scoop, which retracted into her wide carapace where her remaining organs, braced by brass, wood, and wire, pumped the life back into her, while the third powdered her face. The room appeared as bare as an inquisition's cell, but hidden within its walls were what Mr. Wells had playfully called "counter measures" should any try to do what time itself had failed to do and end the age of Victoria.

A knock. A fist drowned. Ripples long past their center.

"Who?" she said, and her body vibrated like a wax cylinder echoing the symphonies of a lost age.

"Minister Churchill," said Lord Barrett. "As requested."

"Enter."

The attendants retreated into their alcoves. Dim light sliced away the dark with a wide arc as the fit, small man with ruddy face entered, bowler in his hand, grim lines in his young face. She was glad smell was lost. For he looked to smell of cakes and ale.

"Majesty," he said, the soft lisp of his meager royal blood annoying her gears. "I fear the earliest reports by wire were true. Our mage was shot—"

"Killed?" She inhaled. "Wells?" Each word punctuated by pain and a plume of steam. "Killed?"

"Nearly. The assassin's bullet was arcane. It avoided others in Piccadilly Circus like a mosquito which craved one victim's blood. After working with Scotland Yard, I have no doubt that our assassin was sent by … the German side of the Society."

"Outcasts," she said, wishing her words would flow as did Mr. Churchill, minus his ignoble lisp. "Judases."

"Of course, Majesty. There is no longer doubt that the Kaiser's self-appointed exile from the Theosophical Society has led to a first strike against our talents. He is preparing for war, thinking he has the advantage of chaos, first from taking his country from the Society, then our dear Mr. Wells. We have not had this much discord since our last ... rupture."

"Bonaparte," she said, disgust vaporizing with the effort, the lingering nightmare of the Corsican demon coming into the bedrooms of her children, Boney coming to get them. "Russia?"

"They are onside, and stabilized. I have finally convinced your great nephew that their maji is a cancer and not an asset, though the Tzarina is less sanguine. Thus, the mad monk lives, but is now contained in the *katorga* of Siberia. So long as mighty Russia holds, Rasputin is no threat."

"Heathen. Death."

"I concur, but given that Russia keeps Germany in check with the largest army in Europe, I believe we should allow the Tzar to punish his rogue the way he sees fit. Contained he will no longer speak of the might of flesh over machine, of corpse magic, of the unholy power of the damned. The creature was replaced by Monsieur Fabergé."

"Acceptable."

Churchill nodded. "And our focus must now be on the war to come. I suspect they will turn this Balkan debacle into—"

"Wells? Alive?"

"After a fashion, Majesty. He sits in Dorset under the finest care with our most talented healers, I assure you. Alive but unresponsive and, even if he returns from wherever that great mind is lost, he may... not be able to move again. The bullet's damage to his spine, I fear, is beyond our best hands. I fear only Mr. Wells had the facility to bring himself back whole, as he has served with you."

Steam hissed out of her back.

Churchill cleared his throat. "I can report that all houses of the Society are working toward breaking the Germans for their insolence, and returning the balance, as the Society has for centuries."

"Understood."

He nodded, turned, and then walked toward the open door.

"Minister."

He turned.

Her metal teeth shook. "Prevail."

"Always, Majesty. The alternative is unfathomable."

CHAPTER ONE:

THE TROGLODYTE WORLD

In the cold basin of a muddy shell hole, Warren Bishop inhaled the fetid scent of death that covered all of No-Man's Land. What is this death scent doing to my innards? Did the mangled remains of so many rotting dead hunks of soldiers leave a wicked curse or spell in the living? A grim magic fouler than the eerie march of mustard gas or the hellfire of a creeping barrage?

Was there a hint of Alex in the air?

Guilt chiseled his dead brother's face into the mud before him. And even in the numbness of soggy clothes and boots which sank into his flesh with a damp regret, he could still feel the echo of Alex's slap at the train station three years ago. The word his younger brother had branded into his mind still stung as hard as the open palm shot.

Coward.

"Hey, Qimmiq," Tikani Joe whispered, his Eskimo voice hard and jagged as the brutal landscape above the lip of the shell hole, but strong as the shark tooth that hung around his neck. "Eyes up. Stop staring at the earth. Plenty of time for that when we're dead. Eyes up and on the Bosch." Lieutenant Christopher, that prissy prancer who acted like he was a British-born member of the ancient Queen's family, had yelled at them both when word got around that they were the only snipers who talked while stalking a Hun. Neither Warren nor Tik cared. What would he do? Send them to war if they got caught?

Warren smirked. "Good thing I got better eyesight than you then, huh, Tik?"

Tik picked more mud off the barrel of his Ross rifle. The moonlight was strong enough for Warren to see his old friend's smile. Tik's reputation as a sharpshooter had killed all the dirty-Indian jokes in the platoon, and those that didn't know his rep ended up eating their teeth by Warren's hand; it was sure as sunrise that if Tikani hit a white man, he'd end up on some suicide mission to nowhere all by his lonesome.

"How many Bosch you up to?" Warren said.

"Thirteen," Tik said. "Bad number. Need to add another notch or I'll have bad luck for seven days."

"That secret Eskimo superstition?"

"Catholic wisdom, you godless shit. Now keep an eye out."

Warren took his filthy periscope, cleaned the lens, and covered the top with dirt and a shattered branch, and slowly lifted it above the rim of the hole. Then, there it was, a reflection of No-Man's Land.

Christ, he thought to himself each and every time he forced himself to look. Alex had called him a coward for not signing up in '14, but how could anyone blame you for not wanting to run headfirst into hell's shithouse? And, apparently, joining the Experimental Flying Corps in the West didn't take guts, as if breaking the laws of nature and heading into god's country on a flying gas tank was for sissies and mollycoddles. Not everyone had to die in the trenches to prove themselves.

But Alex did.

"Anything?" Tik said.

"Wait," Warren said. "Yes."

Tik loaded his rifle in two movements with barely a hint of sound.

"Yes, there's a hole in the earth. And ... movement."

Tik began to rise.

"Wait!"

Tik froze.

"My God. It's a skeleton army rising from the ground, killing every man, rat, and Eskimo in its path, consuming the earth in its wake, like a tidal wave from hell!"

The rifle butt jarred Warren's back hard enough to kill his chuckles. He fell down laughing in the mud and sludge.

Tik shook his head. "You read too many dime novels, Qimmiq." That was funny, since Tik didn't read at all. Instead, he took great pleasure in harassing Warren to tell him tales he'd stolen from Burroughs, Kipling, a stray penny dreadful or a bawdy story he'd picked up in Edmonton on the Flying Farm, where he'd heard the news that Alex was dead. "Combat is not for jokes." Warren had enjoyed the listless life of a thousand jobs and loud women before scratching out stories while those American experts of aviation sent their consultant to Edmonton to teach the foolish and criminal and otherwise unfit for duty to fly in contraptions that he was sworn to keep secret.

But Tik? The Eskimo had been a warrior without a war. Ever since they were kids, Tik had been looking for a good fight, bad fight, any fight until there were no more critters on two legs that would test him, so he wandered with Warren and started his own trouble until he found out Europe was in need of fresh corpses while Warren saw the sun go down while flying like a dust mote in the face of god.

Until he got the letter about Alex, hit the canteen, and so too tight that the next thing he knew he was in a night sky, trying to reach heaven in a Sopwith Camel that the Corps claimed had been invented by Thomas Edison himself, a flight so light that you'd think it ran on good intentions. But heaven was closed, Alex was gone, and Warren still didn't know if his crash landing was intent or accident.

Neither mattered. Alex was dead. And now, kicked out of the Flying Corps, the only thing he could do was punish himself on the Western Front.

But with Tik, he kept on living.

"So, is this combat all they promised?" Warren spit dirt and set his scope back up. "How long they been at this shit now, three years? This ain't some storybook war of daring and courage and glory. They turned Europe into a bleeding graveyard. How many dead now? Can we even count that high? All of it for some king they've never seen, safely tucked away in his castle. Any idiot who gets caught in this whirlwind deserves his fate."

Tik's face stiffened. "Even Alex?"

The last word stung in his back like he'd fallen on a hornet's nest. Alex, five years younger and five years smarter, hadn't waited until he was eighteen. He had bribed the doctor for a medical with a fake birth date and steamed it across the Atlantic to London, then France, in 1914.

Dead three years later. At Vimy Ridge. Great victory, they all said at the Flying Camp Barracks, the American advisors and the British instructors and the Canadian meat packed into the winged coffins. What a hero, what a soldier, what a guy, they all said. What good is being a hero if you're dead and buried and no one can slap your back, buy you a round?

No one said that.

Mother had sent him Alex's Victoria Cross, just to rub iodine in his sour soul. It arrived while he was still on a drunk about Alex, working tables at a tavern in Edmonton, stealing sips and tips while the last of his sprains healed. The whole bar, old drunks and young soldiers, cheered the boys of Vimy when they saw it. Victoria Cross in his tight fist, Warren had knocked five down and nearly strangled a brash soldier to death before he was arrested, beaten, and jailed.

When an MP came to see him swollen in shackles, and asked if indeed he was the brother of war hero Alexander Bishop, Warren showed him the bloody VC and traded jail for the Western Front.

Tik spoke low while dark winds caressed the air above. "Sorry, Qimmiq."

"It's fine."

"No, it was a dirty punch."

"Forget it, okay? Let's just focus on not dying tonight."

It sounded good for a lie. But Warren saw no point in this goddamn rich man's war besides keeping his friend from heading off to the afterlife.

"Okay," Tik said. "You want the rifle? I could use the dummy head?" The dummy head sat in a sack with a couple of boards and other sniper junk to fool the enemy into giving up their position. They'd named the dummy head Christopher after their lieutenant, who seemed to think dispatching raid after raid would get him noticed by General Currie. Once he heard about the dummy head, Warren and Tik ended up lead snipers on the next raid. And the next. And the next.

Prissy shit couldn't take a joke in a war that was nothing but absurd. "Nah," Warren said.

"You sure? You're almost as good a shot as I am."

"Almost?" Tik had taught Warren how to hunt, shoot, and live in the wild, something that drove Mother crazy. Unlike Alex, Warren wasn't latched to the idea of the cozy home of Mother. Too much blood on the floor, even if Alex had never seen it. "Hell, I tied us up last raid with two kills."

"They don't count."

"Why not?"

"Because those Germans were fat. Too easy. Like hitting a wall with an apple." He chuckled and Warren did, too, feeling nothing. Tik always did this to keep Warren trying, practicing, striving to do better, trying to beat the mighty Tik. Mother hated the Eskimo for teaching him about hunting, about woodcraft, about how to fight like it's your last act in a deadly play.

But here, Mother's disgust and the sting of her rod were fading from memory. Warren would find death here, he was certain. And with it, maybe rub the stain of his brother's disgust from his mind.

"Thanks," Warren said, scratching the louse-itch on his neck. "But I'm fine being your eyes tonight. Let me get the lay of the land before we get Little Christopher out of the bag." The perpetual gloom of No-Man's Land was easing with a bright summer moon, as patches of clouds swam the sky like ghostly sheets on a window. Looking through the periscope, Warren wondered how many moments he had left for peering over the hills to hell before the devil found him. Focus, he told himself. Just focus. You never hear the one that gets you, anyway.

Their goal was simple. Scope terrain. Make notes. Run back with the specifics, then get back to the hole and wait for the raid to start. Once it did, and the enemy gave up their machine gun nests, put as many holes in them as you could.

Somewhere, hidden in the cracked landscapes like ants in their caves, the Hun sat. And, if you believed the trench papers, they polished the skulls of the dead Canadians and used them for toilets.

God, he thought, the trenches were full of macabre stories far worse than magical monkey's paws or chatty ravens or any other wild maelstrom of monstrosities that rose out of Poe's head. In the filth and the unyielding stench of death came tales of crucified soldiers on church steeples. Of the Germans harvesting corpses for their dreaded tallow machine to churn humanity into grease for artillery. And the most sensationally bizarre of them all, the tale of the Lost Battalion, soldiers who abandoned both sides to live, fight, and die in No-Man's Land against anyone and everyone until the war was finally over.

I wonder if they're hiring, Warren thought as he blinked away the sweat itching at his eye. He ignored the aches in his neck and joints, the lice down his neck, the fear that rats were chewing through his boots when he wasn't looking, the mercurial shiver that every night was the night that his number was up, and that he might snuff it just because Lieutenant Christopher couldn't take a goddamn joke.

Fact was, Christopher didn't consider Tik and Warren real soldiers.

Real soldiers were the ones who signed up when King and Kitchener called, not the ones who hightailed for some wild experiment on the prairie, riding planes against the winter sunlight, dressed like flying Eskimos, planes that could withstand cold better than a man covered in seal blubber. No, these pilots were freaks and remittance creatures who had no value on the front and were turned into flying lab rats.

Real men, like Alex, died when asked and did not make fun of their superiors. White and proud. Tik at least was a warrior born, probably served in as many battles as …

Alex. The bitter look on his face, the hard crack of his soft hand. The branding word of coward.

It infected Warren, awake and asleep. To be a coward and shirker to the one soul you tried to do right by, tried to teach, the one who followed in your footsteps and avoided Mother's rod and tongue because you took the blows first. The good son.

Rotting in a mass grave in France. All Alex was, all Alex ever would be, was that bitter face inside Warren's head. Haunting him like a frozen ghost against the Western sky.

The cracked landscape was unshifting, and after a while his mind wandered again. War was an awful dream, he thought. And no one is waking up anytime soon. Clouds rolled over and the blue moonlight was snuffed, only returning in splinters and small waves.

"Qimmiq," Tik said, back to the shell-hole wall, holding his rifle as if it were Excalibur. "Tell me a story."

"Thought you didn't like my dime-novel mouth?"

"Not when you're lying to me. Tell me more about that place like this. The Earth with an open wound."

He adjusted the periscope, and the mirror world filled with pock-marked fields blossoming with barbed wire and lumps of ruined earth, mangled trees like the bones of shattered giants, and busted sandbags filled with spare body parts. If the Hun was out there, he was hiding better than a snake in tall grass. "You mean the hollow earth? Sure you don't want me to tell you about Tarzan?" He smirked, but cut his breath short when he saw ... something.

"You keep your noble savage stories and shove them up your ass, Qimmiq."

Whatever he'd seen move, it vanished.

"Forget that hollow earth," Tik said. "How about one of your own stories?"

The beaten earth held shadows in the silver moonlight that stayed still and quiet, though the sound of vermin was everywhere. "You might find this surprising, my warrior friend," Warren said, "but I haven't had much time to type things up in the parlour."

"Bah, the best stories are told, not read. What about that one about the duelling pilots?"

"Winter Knights?"

"Tell that one."

"You're not sick of it?"

"How can I be? It ends with you crashing on your ass!" Tik laughed.

Warren mumbled. "Well, it was a lot less funny when I walked away from that mangled heap of wood and wire." It was a strange thing, desiring a profession your mother hated and yet supported. She'd made sure there were buckets of books in the house, but as soon as Warren told her he wanted to be just like Edgar Rice Burroughs, he had the dream beat out of him. Almost. How quaint and strange that she found it odd he didn't want to stay on the farm.

But that dream was eaten by the moths of war. He'd barely saved enough for a Remington before the drunken brawl he'd started at the Lonely Horse, Victoria Cross in his hand. And if he survived, what then? After this kind of hell, he thought, how could you write about adventure without it drowning in the red shadow of combat? War is just a grave for the brave, and the spoils of victory go to the snakes.

His thoughts snapped.

Through a low fog, movement on the rim of a shell hole. His eyes focused with an icy precision.

A rat? Too big. Dog?

No, wait ... a ... head. Someone was out there. Maybe this was the machine gun nest.

Warren whispered quiet as a church mouse. "Tik, get ready."

Shoulders.

"No joke?" Tik said.

He shook his head, eyes unflinching in the viewer.

Torso.

"Ten o clock over my shoulder. Ready?"

"Ready."

Clouds ran by, then moonlight returned, and what blood was left in Warren's face fled to the soles of his boots and into the grave dirt of Europe.

Emerging from the shell hole, dragging another body out.

Face grey, filthy black hair over his eyes and button nose, but the three little scars on his cheek from the wild dogs that had plagued Fort William when they were kids, made it impossible for him to be anyone else. He looked sick, stumbling on the churned earth. But it was Alex, as sure as Warren knew his own face.

"Hell."

The world roared to life with machine gun fire shredding the air and plugging his brother like iron hornets.

Warren screamed as the soldier fell back, out of sight. Warren began clawing his way out of the shell hole. Before Tik could stop him from charging into No-Man's Land, the thunder of artillery filled the air, consuming all sound in its wake, including Warren's guttural scream.

"Alex!"

CHAPTER TWO:

A LADY OF INVENTION

Hazy afternoon light flittered in through the window of the hospital where Vasilya sat, waiting for word of Monsieur Fabergé, for almost three hours. His ragged cough had all but dissipated from the barred hallways where he was kept, until there was nothing left but an echo of a memory.

Wait until we hear from my contact, Oskar, he'd said, before collapsing on the rail platform and those soldiers in long coats and hard, German faces dragged them to the nearest hospital.

Across from her was a German soldier in battle dress, head bandaged, face covered in bubbled flesh. Mustard gas. Three years of war had consumed the world and there was no end in sight. Vasilya tried not to stare at the soldier, tried not to hate him and everything he and his uniformed kin had done to Russia. War was the enemy of creation, Monsieur Fabergé had said. And she'd never agreed with him more. It twists the progress of industry into a forge of hate and has a bottomless appetite for all that is good in the world. And it was destroying Monsieur Fabergé and his family, and tearing her away from Russia, casting her into the heart of the enemy.

God, she thought. Here I sit, staring at my worn summer boots, hoping no one notices my Slavic features, or French dress, torn, dirty, but nicer than any cloth on the thin women of Berlin. To be Russian, let alone a pacifist, in Germany's terrible capital … this was tantamount to suicide. Mother had screamed as much when Vasilya told her she was going with M. Fabergé, and that she could not stay in Russia as it collapsed in on itself with that awful revolution, tearing the royal family to pieces and staining the streets with their blood. Dark whispers followed Vasilya from St. Petersburg. The Tzar was dead. His wife murdered. The children butchered and the corpses hanging outside the Duma.

She held her thin hands in a still and perfect pose. Bolsheviks, she ruminated, were monsters and barbarians seeking to use the talk of progress into sending Russia into a new dark age where the peasant mobs ruled instead of those suited by birth and ability. Vasilya wanted no part of such a nightmare. Even if she wasn't a royal, but only the bastard daughter of the Tzar's jeweler.

So, here she was, sitting quiet in the heart of the German Empire, with her protector now ill and vanished. She was as lonely as a star in sunlight, invisible and distant, but it would keep her from harm. Temporarily. How long would she be sitting here in the open? Monsieur Fabergé had not said. Questions produced the worst coughing from him, the kind tinted red. She simply trusted his word that he had a way out of Russia, and away from the lynch mobs of those who served the royal house. And she believed him.

Her only suitcase lay across her lap like a writing desk. Inside, Click and Clack, her greatest creations yet, slept like real mice after a long meal, though she was grateful they did not leave a trail of droppings wherever they went. Monsieur Fabergé had called them "magnificent creatures," his kindest word yet on her meagre, independent efforts, and none could have been possible if he hadn't seen the talent in her, worthy of his attention. It was her proudest moment, since after she'd shown him their mechanical hearts, he'd again asked her to work with him on the next Egg. The Tzarina's Easter Egg.

Her last Fabergé egg.

Also hidden inside her case was a worn Tom Swift book she ached to read, to transport her mind away from war and the sallow looks of the people everywhere, to a place where genius saved lives, where invention trumped savagery, where science was a savior. Mother had destroyed her copies of H. G. Wells, for fear they would be found by the Red gangs who were breaking into homes, searching for any reason to drag you away, including books by "foreigners."

Peasants, she thought. Mindless, thuggish peasants. She'd saved her Swift books while Mom was tossing Wells in the fire.

The great man had been in a coma for three years, another visionary destroyed by German savagery, or so everyone said in St. Petersburg. Wells was too visionary to keep alive, so some kraut assassin had silenced his mind to prevent another far seer from telling humanity there was a future that did not involve ruined cities, ruined earth, and generals and revolutionaries with bloodstained hands.

She caressed the locks on the case … Click and Clack always returned a glimmer of hope to her heart that she could make things of wonder, that maybe, one day, she too could take part in the Fabergé legacy and create magic for the royal family, maybe even rise to the premier jeweler of the nation…

No, she thought as her flight of fancy began to drag with the harsh grip of reality. I would remain in the shadow as Monsieur Fabergé's sons took the family business while I toiled in the workshop he had provided, where he would teach me his secrets, because while they may lay claim to the name Fabergé, they did not have their father's gifts. Not like I do.

You must be strong, Monsieur Fabergé had said in low whispers to keep himself from coughing on the train. *We are noble servants of the Tzar, and we remain so. We do not coddle weakness. Be strong and patient, my protégée, or else all I have planned for is lost.*

She folded her hands.

"Ms....?"

An ancient nurse with sharp green eyes and not a single iron-grey hair out of place stood beside her, a model of Prussian womanhood. "Eva," Vasilya said, quietly, in practiced German. "Eva Klein."

"Ms. Klein, you may see your uncle now."

Cold rivets of fear sliced down her back. Vasilya stood, gripped her suitcase, and followed the nurse through the antiseptic smell of the hospital. It made her gag.

They walked to a far wing, where the sounds of patients' moaning could no longer be heard. Nor was there a hint of Monsieur Fabergé's demonic cough. "In here," said the nurse, jutting her chin to the door on Vasilya's right, then stalked off with precision steps that would have made a Swiss watchmaker swoon.

She pushed the door open and before her was a screened off portion of the room, shadows lying behind it. The door closed behind her. A sound, like a rusty bellows, heaved in the air. Shadows flared against the wall in time with the wretched sound.

"Hello?" she said in German. "M. Fabergé?"

"Hello," said a voice. In Russian. "Come forward."

She gripped the knob, but the door was locked.

"Unless you have the strength of steel or a lock picking kit in your suitcase, I'd suggest not wasting my time any longer."

Click and Clack could pick the lock, but she wasn't supposed to have even brought them, one of the few times she'd disregarded one of Monsieur Fabergé's commands.

"I won't ask again." The voice was grizzled and curt, as if his lungs had been branded with hot tobacco and never cooled. The shadows rose and lowered with the rusty grind of gears about to spark. "Come forward."

Vasilya parted the curtain and dropped the suitcase in horror.

Monsieur Fabergé lay lifeless on a worn and rusting hospital gurney, arms tied to the sides with blood-stained bandages. A sheet covered his naked form to his neck.

And that's only where the horror began.

His face was a mechanical bug, some iron and widget fly-face with massive dark eyes and a mechanical snout and snorkel made of plastic and cloth that looped over his shoulder and attached to the hideous metal bellows that rose and fell above a metal canister with a series of dials and switches. Another tube led from the side of the canister and fitted upon a bucket filled with a repulsive-smelling, green-and-red liquid she'd seen stained on his handkerchief. Her mind ran over the machine like water, trying to figure out its operating principles.

"Impressive, no?"

She gasped, having just focused on the motionless man behind the machine. His silver moustache was like a broom, each hair cut level with the rest, no nicotine stains, no dirt or grime. The elderly German wore a full officer's uniform, chest adorned with more medals than Vasilya had seen on any soldier in Russia or Germany.

But for all his impeccable attention to detail, two things were missing. An arm and an eye. A folded jacket sleeve revealed the one; an eye patch covered the other.

Her lips trembled, wondering what to say.

"Choose the language you are most comfortable with," said the German. "I speak most of them."

"What have you done to him?" she said in French.

He smiled and returned in kind. "Saved his life. He has influenza. A virulent strain. I suspect given to him by a mutual foe If not for my invention, his lungs would be drowning in his own liquids."

"You ... built this?"

"Only the weak allow their handicaps to stop them," he said coolly.

"I didn't mean—"

"Yes. You did. Vasilya Savorov." He stamped the floor, startling her. "Illegitimate daughter of the esteemed jeweler and master craftsmen Monsieur Fabergé."

The words were cold, factual, and yet her temper began to rise. But Monsieur Fabergé had warned her that just being talented does not give you license to lose your head. "And who are you?"

"Colonel Gustov Balk. The man who is keeping your father alive, and you would do well to remember it. You are swimming in hostile waters, child." The bellows creaked and M. Fabergé's body seized.

"Sir!" she said, gripping M. Fabergé's hand. "You can't die. Help him!" she yelled at the colonel. "Do something!"

"I am and I will, you have my word."

"Then why are you just standing there like a corpse!" Monsieur Fabergé's whole body fought for air, gripping at nothing behind the metallic bug-eyed mask.

"Because I need your word that you will help me."

Her whole body shook. "Help you what?"

He stood back, taller. "Help me win this war."

CHAPTER THREE:

THE PERILOUS INSTANT

The world shook from hell to heaven as Warren's feet touched No-Man's Land. Star shells bloomed in the black sky as planes flew above them with the grace of metallic hornets, while in front of Warren shells returned to earth like god's fists. Streaked with lightning, they rolled toward the enemy lines, churning earth, abandoned corpses, and barbed wire into a mess that could be traversed by infantry or maybe those monstrous ironclads on land, tanks.

When battle came, everything shifted, everything moved, like millions of pieces on the clockwork chessboard. And the horrific shit was internal, too. In a perilous instant, when battle began, but before he could turn his will to action, Warren's heart and soul flared.

And into that fury of fire, metal, and death Warren plunged to save what he had seen, the impossible mirage he could not ignore:

Alex. Alex was there. Alex was hurt, he was dead and hurt and out there.

Legs trembling on the shaking earth, Warren cut across the savaged battleground, breathing dirt and smoke, running into the maelstrom. Questions —Where has he been for a year? What hell is he living in? — stabbed him then vanished as a shell exploded and sent him thundering back in the hole.

Tik grabbed him by the collar. "Idiot! The barrage has just started! We need to get that machine gun nest on the hill that just rattled off!"

Warren shoved Tik back with anger that actually moved the massive warrior. "Alex is out there! They hit him! He's there!"

Tik stared hard.

"I'm not mad," Warren screamed. "I saw him. I know it's him."

Tik shook his head while hell thundered above. "You won't live to find him if we don't take out that nest. Do you hear me, Qimmiq? Listen. I'll help you find him, but we need to do this first. Get it?" He gripped Warren's shoulder. "Do you hear me?"

"Get the fuck off me." He shoved Tik away, and with his free hand grabbed his own Ross rifle.

Tik glared.

Warren picked up the periscope and gazed.

Alex had vanished from the jumbled vision of the battlefield, and for the first time since he saw his kid brother off at the train station, tears swelled Warren's eyes. I'm a fucking coward, he thought, as the wall of burning artillery fire thundered forward. I'm a goddamn coward if I don't get him out of there. Soon, there would be the charge of the battalion, the asshole veterans who hated the snipers because they hadn't bled with them at Vimy, but waited until the war was old before getting thrown in the ranks.

Fuck them, Warren thought, but bit his trembling lip. If Alex is out there, I'll find him. He scanned the rugged ground until he caught sight of blasts of machine gun fire three hundred yards away in a mess of a tree trunk and sand bags.

"Three hundred," Warrens said. "One o'clock from your position." Tik fixed his own scope. "Bet there are three there." Above the parapet of their shell hole was a block of wood covered in filth and slit near the bottom for the barrel to go out and the scope to see through. "You take the shield," Warren said, and unslung his rifle, and pulled down his helmet. "I'll use the naked eye."

"Dangerous work," Tik said. "You take the shield."

"Why?"

"Because I'm less scared to die than you, Qimmiq. Fear can make your hand tremble."

"Bullshit!"

The Barrage crept away. "No time," Tik said, moving away from the base of the shield. "This is our best chance. Go."

They acted in unison like two cowboys fighting a last stand battle with their backs against the Alamo wall, slow and certain and bodies synchronized to one purpose.

They stood, back to the mud wall, and slowly got into position. Warren checked his scope to make sure it was clean, then loaded the rifle in two movements.

Tik nodded, Warren nodded back, and took a long deep breath. One, two—

They turned in unison, slid the barrels into position, Warren with the shield, Tik the exposed shell mouth. Warren focused his sight on the distant head of a German machine gunner, visible between the splintered halves of a dead oak trunk. He fired first and the man's head snapped out of view and the gun died as another man took his place. Another bolt of rifle fire and his head vanished in a sea of red mist. Then another for the next idiot to take his place.

Tik was on fire and smiled when a fourth shot cracked. Tik hit the bottom of the shell hole, gurgling, as if kicked by a mule.

"Tik!"

Warren dropped as bullets cracked into the shield. Snipers. The Germans' snipers.

Blood leaked out of every hole on Tik's face.

"Stretcher bearer!" Warren cried, and Tik shook his leaking head. Because he knew a bearer would be fodder for the sniper, even if it was Florence Nightingale. And Warren saw that Tik knew it wouldn't do him any good.

Tik reached into his shirt and snapped off his necklace, handing it to Warren.

A single shark's tooth hung off braided hemp, the rest having been lost in the muck of the shell hole. Tik's massive fist folded Warren's hand around it and held his hand tight as a crimson smile came across his face.

This is the way he wanted to die, Warren thought. A warrior looking for a war. "You bastard, don't you leave me, too."

But Tik gurgled a laugh, clasped his hand tighter, then stared at the heavens before life snuffed out of his black eyes.

The dead grip on Warren's hand was tight.

But he broke it.

He grabbed his Ross. Then Christopher's dummy head.

He tossed the head in the air and stuck his head above the parapet.

Three shots cracked, all from the same position. Chickenshits, he thought. From a mound of corpses, a hundred yards away to the east, he saw the first German's head, saw his eye wide for a second before he trained his rifle on Warren.

Lightning-quick, Warren aimed and fired, then scrambled up the hole and ran across the mangled landscape, reloaded, and fired at the next bastard's skull, watching its gory plume before diving behind mangled mounds of earth as a shot snapped by his ear. He charged across No-Man's Land like a lunatic past the asylum gates. Screaming nonsense as the last German got closer, as the scope bruised his eye, he fired and fired until another German's face imploded.

Twenty yards away, another one popped up like a mole from the rotten ground. Warren fired again, piercing another Hun's hand. Ten yards, he reloaded, and didn't use the site.

With his naked eye, the pained look of the last sniper's face fueled his anger, his motion, his malice until he stared the last son of a bitch down from the top of the hole he'd fallen in. Warren fired.

The German winced.

Nothing.

The gun, covered in dirt, jammed. Warren seethed. Miserable Canadian-made piece of shit!

The German grabbed his pistol and Warren tossed his rifle at him, then yanked out the spare bayonet from his belt like a sword and dove, screaming, into the hole.

CHAPTER FOUR:

FAUSTIAN BARGAIN

The greenish brown liquid in the bucket smelled like disease itself. But Monsieur Fabergé was sleeping now, and Vasilya was grateful.

And trapped. And terrified.

Colonel Balk gazed at her with the unmoving glare of a Sphinx. She wanted to run, but where? To grab an orderly in the heart of the country that had crushed Russia's spirit into shards so that those Bolsheviks could destroy her themselves?

She'd felt powerless before, disdained in the eyes of Monsieur Fabergé's sons, who hated her so much she wasn't allowed near their shop and had to be content with the one Monsieur Fabergé had built for her near Mother's house. A small, dark sanctuary where she could tinker in peace, where she'd made Click and Clack, and where Monsieur Fabergé sometimes came to ask for her assistance on the Tzarina's eggs …

Like the final one.

Shattered dreams, one and all.

A nurse arrived to retrieve the bucket of foul phlegm. Colonel Balk's one eye had an impatient stare that made the nurse move fast to replace the bucket like it was on fire.

The door closed.

"Is he saved?" Vasilya said.

"For now," Colonel Balk said. "This machine is expensive, and experimental. There are many sick people in Germany, heroes of the front, who could use it. Heroes who will die choking on their own fluids before the night is through."

Vasilya cringed. "What do you want of me?"

He marched slowly around the bed while Monsieur Fabergé slept beneath his bug mask, the bellows rising and falling with the rhythm of his chest. "I want to make your dreams come true, child. I want to give you your own workshop. All the materials you could need. And all I ask in return is that you do everything in your power to end this war."

This German is a fool or a madman; how could Monsieur Fabergé stick me with him? "How can I end a war?"

"I know about your talents." She took a step back, towards M. Fabergé's machine, as Colonel Balk rounded the bed. Her suitcase lay between them but she was too scared to pick it up, to hide Click and Clack from possible exposure. Colonel Balk stared her down, and the eyebrow rose above his eye patch. "You have your father's gift for creation. Intricate machines, such as the last egg for the late Tzarina. The Constellation." There was malice in his smile. "You finished it for him."

"No," she said, looking at her suitcase. "I just helped with—"

"He told me." His boots lay at the foot of her suitcase and she worried he would crush Click and Clack with his stampeding German feet.

"I don't believe you."

"Believe this. My codename is Oskar."

She froze her surprised look and remained perfectly still.

"You are right to be suspicious," Colonel Balk said. "But we do not have time for games, so I will make this clear. Carl was going to help us end the war in the West. In return, the German empire would save Russia from the Bolsheviks and restore … a suitable royal line. One that had not failed in its duties …" Then maybe it was true, Vasilya thought, that the Tzar and his family were killed. "Carl and I have known each other for years. We both collect … unusual machinery." He kneeled down. "I have been to his private workshop dacha, child. I've seen the toy army. Before Lenin and his creatures burned it down, the fools."

Blood ran out of her face and the smell of Colonel Balk's breath was almost as vile as the liquid in the bucket. What the colonel was talking about was something she'd only heard in whispers and caught only once, when he was forced to take her to his shop because the dynamo he was working on was too small and fragile to move. And she saw them. A wall of dolls of all shapes and sizes, faceless but to scale, and large holes in their chests. She was sworn to secrecy, though she had only a glimmering of what they were. "Yes," the colonel said. "I know all about his automatons. I sold him parts for the last project, the replica of Descartes' fabled fortune-teller. Though I must say when he was finished it looked more like you than anything." He smiled, and nicotine teeth revealed themselves above black gums. "We were friends, child. Your father was trying to help us."

Lies! she thought. They were toys, just toys, not an army. Toys for the Tzar's youngest, once he was well enough to play with them. "He … was a pacifist."

"All parents lie to their children. He served the Tzar and his idiot family in many ways, but when the Bolsheviks infected him with the influenza currently killing him, he saw the light on who to side with."

"They did what?"

He stood. "They are crafty vermin. And some are trained in dark …
medicines, similar to your talents. They had served another master until
he was killed. Now, they are Lenin's alchemist. They tried to kill your
father and make it look like illness."

Words shot past her lips faster than her mind could stop them. "Then
perhaps your nation should have stopped him from returning to Russia.
Or is it a lie he received free passage from the kaiser, himself a crafty
vermin?"

Regret stained her lips bitter as the colonel held her gaze and the reality
of her place in this world threaded into her nerves with precision. "If your
tzar had not mobilized his army in an ill-fated attempt to intimidate us,
his country would not have suffered such defeats and he would still be
alive. We had no desire of war with Russia, and there are older bonds
than nationhood that your fair Tzar ignored because he was convinced
his mighty army was invincible. He put his hope in a demon who he then
had to kill…" The colonel exhaled hard. "Listen. You have a free tongue.
I suggest you chain it before I have to cut it out. You'll kill your father
with such asinine outbursts." The fact that he was right annoyed Vasilya
to no end. "Mistakes are made in war, child. Which is why we must end
it, sooner, not later. Pacifism is a luxury no one can afford today." Colonel
Balk straightened his back. "Monsieur Fabergé was to help us end the war
quick, but the sickness curtailed his efforts. The Empire has poured sacred
treasure into his work and now has nothing to show for it. Except you. His
greatest protégée."

"You are mistaken," she said, ignoring the word "father." "His sons are
master craftsmen."

"Yes, though most lack the uniqueness of your talents."

"What talents?" she said, anger rising. "I make toys, not armies. Just
stupid, childish toys."

He nodded. "Animated ones."

She leaned against the rail of M. Fabergé's bed as Colonel Balk kneeled
and picked up her suitcase and handed it to her.

"Like something from one of your Tom Swift magazines. Though I
would keep those terrible books hidden. Such foreign literature might
bring suspicions." How fitting that the Germans were just as barbaric as
the Bolsheviks, she thought. "But in your own workshop, you will build
marvels so wondrous and sublime that they would make Mr. Swift jealous.
Creations even the late Mr. Wells could not dream, Build for us, and we
will continue to pour our efforts into saving your father. After all, at war's
end, I suspect that you will be the one to inherit his empire of marvels.
And the new Tzar will need a jeweler."

She held the suitcase close to her chest, fighting tremors. No, this was
a dream, a nightmare, a mistake, a cruel joke.

But it was as real as the phlegm staining the white bucket. As real as Monsieur Fabergé, finally sleeping peacefully, the wheeze in his chest lessened, but still sticking to his lungs.

She took a long deep breath. "What do you want me to build?"

The door swung open and a young German officer in spotless uniform and shaved face glared at them. "What the hell are you doing, Balk? That machine—"

Colonel Balk's face puckered. "You forgot to salute, Captain Stenner."

Stenner swallowed the sneer emerging from his face and saluted. "That machine was not to be moved. We have soldiers dying, Colonel. German soldiers."

The hate radiating from his presence made Vasilya grip her suitcase as she had once held a pillow as a shield against nightmares, until she heard Colonel Balk's voice bite back with iced words. "Do not presume to remind me of the hardship of soldiering, Captain. I've lost more in war than you've ever had in your short life, hiding damn far from the front!"

Captain Stenner was shaken, but held his ground. "The machine is the property of this hospital."

"And the hospital is under the command and behest of the Army, who, I remind you, paid for this machine, and will use it as they see fit." His gloved hand took a sheet of paper from his breast pocket and handed it to the captain. "Or would you prefer to tell Ludendorff and Hindenburg that you think their orders are out of line yourself?"

Slowly and methodically, Captain Stenner read the note, seething. His words were cool and low. "When you fail, Balk, when whatever idiotic scheme you've planned turns to dust, and all the money the high command shoved into your monstrosities vanishes, I'll be the first witness at your court-martial. And the first to pull the plug on your sacred friends." He scrunched the note in his fist, glared at Vasilya, then stormed off, but the last words stung the air. "Baltic German toad."

The door closed.

"Doctors," Balk said. "Think themselves gods among sheep."

"Will he hurt M. Fabergé?"

Colonel Balk snorted. "Not now. But he'll not be idle. Stenner has friends in high places who play chess with the home front and we must be a few moves ahead. Or I fear your father—"

"Don't." Vasilya said. "Don't call him that." He'd never allowed it. Not in Mother's home. Not on the street. Not in the secrecy of his late-night visits to her tiny workshop. Even long past midnight as they had pondered, experimented, and unraveled the mechanical secret of the Tzarina's egg, Vasilya's hands thrumming with instinct as she refined his design for the heart of the motor into a smooth whole, it was still Monsieur Fabergé. No matter what she did to please him, how smooth the gears ran, how silent the motor; no matter how bright the illuminated glass and the movement of the ornate figurines; no matter how deep she listened to his every word, studied his every move—even when the praise of his word and the sun in his voice made her feel happy and safe and loved …

He was always Monsieur Fabergé.

"Captain Stenner won't rest until he has this machine for himself." Colonel Balk said. "If we are to save … Monsieur Fabergé, you need to help me win this war. Or else, we're all doomed to a fate far worse than we can imagine."

Vasilya hugged her suitcase, as close as she could be to Click and Clack, and looked at M. Fabergé. A cough burst form his sleeping form, and the machine chugged hard and long until the bucket began to fill again.

She swallowed. "I'll do it."

CHAPTER FIVE:

FRESH FLOWERS ON AN OLD GRAVE

Blood, dirt, and fire—the whole world was made of it, destroyed by it, reborn of it. Whirling against the jagged edge of the enemy shell hole, Warren and the German waltzed with a bayonet, while a symphony of the assault filled the darkness, the familiar music of a battalion chasing the wall of fire toward the German line.

Bright blood pulsed out of the German's hand, Warren's shot having gone right through. Their tussling had painted them both with shiny redness, but Warren had not been able to disarm or kill his enemy.

The bastard knows how to fight for his life, Warren thought. Time to show 'em the rough-and-tumble ways of Fort William.

He charged and their arms locked up for a tussle like in a wrestling match, each bayonet eating some flesh, but Warren had to close the distance and make this count before a shell or stray bullet killed any chance he had hunting for Alex.

Hard and fast, he nailed his forehead against the kraut's nose. A nostalgic "crack" echoed through Warren's head, and he may as well have been in a saloon brawl with Tik. The kraut's grip loosened some, and Warren let go of his shoulder, yanked the bayonet out of his other hand, and jammed the blade under his neck, pressing him hard against the shell wall and staying there while the kraut's life burst from his muscles, trying to hold him back. Blade and skin touched with shaking force as each man pushed the other.

The kraut whispered words of prayer, of begging, of mercy in the brutal, broken tongue of the Germans. He slipped, losing leverage and the blade inched into his neck.

"No!" Warren screamed, pushing forward. "You killed Tik, you killed Alex. Twice! Before I could even find his goddamn ghost, you rotten son of a bitch!"

Dirt slipped from under his foot as pain gored his balls. The German's knee nailed in to his crotch. Pain shimmered and everything contracted, before Warren was shoved to the ground. The German stomped Warren's left hand and the bayonet rolled out as Warren rolled to the side, breathless, and leaned against the shell hole and scrambled up while the German, bayonet in hand, charged. Eyes wild—

Just like an idiot at a saloon fight.

Old habits flushed fresh in his reflexes. He ignored the pain and the urge to run, to drop, to get the hell out of danger's path, and let the bastard charge him.

The screaming face came closer, the same look he'd seen in countless brawls, so familiar it was sickening, and the moves Tik had shown him years ago ran like instinct.

He raised his arms. The Hun stabbed. Warren shucked right, the blade tearing into his uniform, then dropped his elbow down on the hand that held the blade. The wrist broke. The kraut pulled back in fear and Warren tore the bayonet from the kraut's hand and drilled it into his neck.

He yanked the blade back and fell backwards on his ass while the kraut twitched in a spewing fit of blood and gurgles. It was a long while until he passed out and died in a heap next to the ammunition case next to his two dead comrades, pistols still in their holsters. "That's three, Tik," Warren said, huffing air and then cackling in the dark. "And none look fat to me."

He touched his sides and hissed. The blade had taken a chunk out. Not too bad, but it was covered in the fetid soil of Europe and that meant infection. He tore his old handkerchief from his pocket and pressed against it, then tried to regain his senses as the lightning-quick adrenaline ran out.

A cold, dark wind pierced Warren until he swayed like a willow. The strings that had driven him to act as the battle had surged … had snapped. Alone with the dead, bright blood running down his muddy skin, Warren held his knees before the men he'd killed by gun and hand.

And around them, worms. Sickly creatures, mindless monsters of the ground that he'd detested since before he could remember, even killing them on a hook brought no relief. He stabbed them until they were mulch, but more were coming. A million more to eat the dead and inherit the butchered world.

He dropped the bayonet and held his knees hard, rocking back and forth to work up the strength to climb out, on to the new world the war had made, a landscape void of life. All the rotten worms would inherit were machines and corpses.

His fingers trembled, then shook. He hardened his grip. "Steady," he told himself, "Steady. You ain't the first man to kill another, you won't be the last, and not all killers have gone mad."

But that's what he was.

He'd been a scrapper for years. A soldier for months. And he'd killed men in battle, but always at a distance. Like a game. A deadly, vicious game. But he was surprised at how easy it had been, through a scope, well hid.

But with your own hands ... the sensation possessed him like a thunderstorm on Christmas.

Tik had killed men with his bare hands. But he'd never shared the dark wisdom of how to live with it. What would Tik have told me? Warren wondered. Anything useful? Or would it be some Catholic Eskimo wisdom on each man needing to go his own way, or some riddle about blood and the snow his grandfather had taught him?

Now, instead of a snort or laugh from his only ally in this world over the past ten years, there was nothing. Tik sat in his own shell hole, a warrior who finally found a war grave that fit him. Son of bitch left me alone, Warren thought. He's probably laughing at me for being such a goddamn weak-kneed, mollycoddle white man.

But I bet Tik had never been this alone

This abandoned.

Lost.

Alex, Warren thought. Think of Alex. You saw him, you did, he was there, before the machine gun burst lead into him so he danced like ice under heat ...

The image of Alex faded, and he could not call it back. Stains of mud and blood covered his eyes as he blinked them away, away, away. The war above was raging without him. Forgotten.

If it was Alex.

Oh lord, I'm cracking. Shell shock. Battle grind. Slipping into darkness—

Alex. You did see Alex. Least you could do is give him a decent burial. Walk through No-Man's Land, just like he did, bring him back home. "Yeah," Warren said, voice breaking. "Then try calling me a coward." That is, if I can find the guts to get out of this festering hole.

Think of Alex.

Memories would not stick. And he couldn't think three seconds ahead. Past and future blurred like dirt on his eye skin and Warren sat in the perpetual now of the war as it burned on and on toward Judgement Day. The tether to the lunar world above snapped and his bones became anchors as his hands shook against his will. Despair, fear, and rage were old friends. He had a bottomless well for lust and laughter and dodging the world's blows. And he'd seen death since—

The image of Dad's broken head, the bullet hole still in the wall, slapped him before vanishing.

He swayed as star shells faded in the night sky. Dawn was coming. And soon, anything topside would be so much meat for the butcher's bill.

Better choose, he thought. Die on your feet or your knees. Let fate pick the shot. I've always been good with dice and cards. But waiting here, waiting in a grave with these goddamn Huns. No.

He dug into his front pocket and tore out the folded red cloth that hid the medal he'd carried with him from Canada. He removed Alex's Victoria Cross and held it in his left palm. With this right hand, he took a German's officer pistol. A small, square gun.

The world grew quiet.

Both items weighed the same in his hand as Warren closed his eyes. Should I flip the medal like a coin? Lion's I go forth into the breach, hunting ghosts and burying bodies. Backside, I take my last ride out of here, on a bullet.

Silences coloured the darkness.

He tossed the medal in the air like a silver dollar. It landed in his palm.

Swallowing dryly, he opened his eyes.

And stared at a lion.

He stood, weak, but able, resigned to his fate.

"Warren."

On the mouth of the shell hole, Alex stood. Pale face just as young as ever, minus the little scars, his chest clothed in a shredded uniform, rifle gripped by both hands.

"Alex? My god, Alex! It's you! I was coming for you."

Alex nodded, and smiled. As dawn's light infected the sky, a hideous smell filled the air that had become jaundiced mist. The smile cracked with sadness. "Hello, Warren."

Before Warren's face could register his horror, Alex shouldered his rife and fired.

CHAPTER SIX:

A WOMAN OF INDUSTRY

Rushing from hospital to private car to secret railway carriage with Colonel Balk, all Vasilya wanted was the hard, strong voice of Monsieur Fabergé, telling her what to do next, assuring her of the colonel's honour, and the need to stop the war by helping the hideous Germans.

Instead, she sufficed with the images around her as she raced through Berlin. The sunken faces of Germans in long lines made the great capital seem like a hovel for wretched beggars and peasants; smoke laced the city as much as the countenance of starved children, the heavy sound of industry pumping out the engines of war that consumed the earth for no reason but the pride of old men and older maps.

The order of things is being ruined, she thought. And what will replace the grandeur of our nations, even the barbaric ones, if revolution creeps into the hungry eyes of the poor here? She shivered. It was rotten to contemplate. She hated Germany, but respected it. But a Germany of beggars and thieves in the garb of a Leninist revolution? Disgusting.

She was quickly brought to a different rail station, littered with soldiers, and was actually grateful that the colonel's presence seemed to keep her beneath even the shadow of suspicion. The rail car was itself modern, sleek, and well maintained, and she wished she could examine the engine and undercarriage to unlock some of its mysteries but was shooed into a private car.

She adjusted herself on the plush red seat as the train pulled away from the station, still gripping the suitcase with Click and Clack. "Where are we headed?" she said in slightly stilted German. Monsieur Fabergé had long tried to get her to speak it smoothly, but it was such a vulgar language compared to French or Russian. Even English, that claptrap of a thousand different bits, was effortless compared to the harsh vocals of the Teutonic people.

Colonel Balk gazed out the window. "To a private workshop, outside the city limits. For your protection."

She laid the suitcase down, ignoring her fears, and tried not to stare at the arm flap where Colonel Balk's right arm should have been or the patch over his eye. "Who would want to hurt me?"

"Only a few million French and British. And an unsavory character who taught the magic of disease"

Vasilya frowned. "The demon you mentioned?"

"Don't scoff, child. You're about to change the fate of nations with talent you have. A talent few possess and fewer control."

"Sounds like you failed to control this demon."

"That was your Tzar's failure. When his government fell, the Bolsheviks released the demon from Siberia, but not before forcing him to teach them a … darker art than you currently practice."

"Where is this demon?"

Balk looked out the window. "He is not your immediate concern." He tapped the glass window with his left hand as they passed by threadbare strangers on the platform. "It is the regular civilians we must fear. They're weak. From hunger. From a long war. From the constant stream of tragedy that comes home from the front, disguised in the rhetoric of valour. They are seething. And I fear that even with our victory in the East, a revolution is brewing."

The word revolution plucked strings of fear in Vasilya's heart that became all-too- familiar images: broken glass and screams cutting through the once peaceful quiet of night, strange men with guns but no uniforms, looking for enemies and friends and Vasilya never knowing which one was which.

His white eyebrow arched. "You're staring."

At his arm. And, now, at his eye patch. "No, yes, I mean I didn't mean to."

"But how could you not? Such things are magnets to those who are still wholly flesh and blood."

She nodded. "Did you get them in the war?"

The arch softened. "You're a brazen one. Asking a soldier about his wounds."

Her face furrowed. "I thought you'd want to talk about it. Isn't that what your kind does? Brag about scars and injuries and cheating death?"

Colonel Balk lifted his chin. "So. You have no love for soldiers."

She clasped her hands in mock love. "For all the wondrous things they've done since nineteen fourteen? For the museums they've blown up, the cities they destroyed, the architecture they've used for kindling, the harvests they've burned? I did not realize these were gifts." She silenced when the cancerous look in the colonel's one good eye almost popped it out of its socket. But she would not apologize. All the wonder that she had known, the Tzarina's eggs, the cathedrals of St. Petersburg, the marvelous world of the royal family caught at a distance but still shimmering, all of it had been torn down by the war and the revolution that was born in its many coffins.

The train chugged along, buildings devolving into countryside. It was a bitter silence, only broken when the colonel was done wiping down his moustache until it was even as a comb. "I fought in France in 1870," the colonel said, finally, eye staring at no fixed position as trees with leaves still green on their branches rolled by. "Under the great Marshal Von Moltke and Chancellor Bismarck, with the Kaiser himself on the field of battle, fighting for Germany to be one country, free of division, strong enough to call its own destiny and to be let into the concert of Europe."

"And join the Theosophical Society, no doubt."

If it were possible for Balk to stiffen even more, the mention of the M. Fabergé's favorite society did it.

"And what do you know of such things?"

"I know they have members throughout the world. Even America. And they shared knowledge."

Balk snickered. "Is that so? What also did you glean from reading letters that were not your own?"

Vasilya stiffened in return. "How dare you say—"

"Spare me the outrage, Carl knew that you had broken into his safe years ago. So, tell me what you've read from a box only one other person on this earth could open?"

She hugged her suitcase. "Every major government had membership. They shared ideas about science, engineering, and other developments that emerged from Britain and their revolution in industry. Japan had been made a member, despite Russian protest. There was talk of China joining." She recalled the fine script, always in cursive Latin or Esperanto. "But there was an argument."

Balk smiled. "And who started it?"

"My government. About older knowledge …" Letters retreated from her mind. "I am sure I read them."

"I'm sure you did. The reason you are forgetting is the ink that was used. It plays with your memory. And the words you read in Latin and the idiotic Esperanto were the surfaces of a much deeper story about the Society."

"How was Russia responsible? What older knowledge?"

A military porter came to the door and knocked. The colonel waved him in. "Sir," said the porter, "there's an urgent message for you in the wireless room."

"Who is it?"

"Freitag. There's been another … accident. They want your orders."

Colonel Balk waved him away and the door closed. He pinched his nose and stood. "Stay here. And don't speak. Your German is thin gruel, indeed."

When he'd vanished down the hall, Vasilya, making sure the coast was clear, undid the latches and entered the proper code on the numbered lock before taking out the key in her pocket and opening the suitcase.

She inhaled the heady scent of well-oiled metal, leather, and the bite of paper and glue. There, on the cover of the magazine, sat Tom Swift, decked out in a fine brown suit, and gazing into his amazing invention: the photo telephone. He was the missing link between Thomas Edison and H. G. Wells, not that Mother approved of any of those men, especially poor Mr. Wells. "Too busy writing nonsense about the future. We have problems here and now. Why doesn't he turn his supposed amazing mind to those, hmm? No money in it."

Edison ... Wells ... the Society mentioned them, but ... confound it! It was as if it was erased from parchment in her mind as soon as her memory re-wrote it.

But Wells stayed on her mind. She never agreed with her mother. Wells was no idle hand, but a true giant of the mind. He'd predicted so much that sadly came to pass. The war in the air, those dreaded tanks he'd called the Land Ironclads. Chemicals used to kill soldiers with poisoned gas. He'd cried, shouted loud and hard in his stories for man not to abuse science and the mechanical arts to create new engines of destruction. But none heeded the call. And then his great mind was silenced for good by some Hun barbarian's bullet. He could have made Swift's invention real, she thought, if he had the proper backing, the proper support.

Like me.

But my backers are the agents of destruction.

She'd turned seventeen two weeks before the guns of August fired in nineteen fourteen. And like so many other things that summer, her dream died before it could blossom. Russia crumbled around her. No last chance to show Monsieur Fabergé that she was good enough to work at his private shop, to be one of his great jewelers, that his ... affair with Mother could not stop the truth of her talents and their value to making the Tzar and his wife happy. The plans she had made for the next Egg, a Wells- inspired design that showcased Russia through the ages ...

Such dreams were dangerous now. Diversions from the task at hand. Straying from the path before her could mean death for Monsieur Fabergé.

I finally have the chance to build something wondrous on my own, she lamented. And it's purged and replaced by this rotten and insidious war.

But I will not let Monsieur die by my negligence.

Beside the well-worn magazine was a Chinese puzzle box Monsieur Fabergé had made of cherry wood and oak. She'd kept it well oiled, and knew the secret combination of pushes and turns on the structure for her to hide her most precious creations. She threw a casual look up, then risked it.

She traced the edge of the combination lock in the familiar pattern of M. Fabergé's rare nickname for Vasilya: Dove.

The box unwound itself and became a place mat upon which sat two silver mice, one with red eyes, the other with green, both dull as they slept. Click and Clack.

She caressed the cone ears of each. "Good morning, my friends." The red and green eyes sparkled, and their sharp noses wiggled back and forth. The thrum of their tiny engines and gears made her smile. They moved, humming in her hand, heads roaming around. "We're no longer at home, dear ones. We're … we're going to build you some brothers and sisters. And you will help. Won't that be fun?" Click nodded, but Clack was still scanning the room, nose tweaky and eyes sharp.

Vasilya faced the cabin door.

The military porter was outside, staring in. She snapped the suitcase closed and Click and Clack squeaked. She pressed the locking mechanism.

The porter smiled, and then opened the door.

"Cute pets," he said. In his hand was a pistol. "Hand over the case."

She pressed the emergency resort button. "No."

He shut the door behind him and pressed the pistol to her ear. "It wasn't a request, you Russian shit."

White fear blanketed her skin. Her thoughts raced through the permutations any action might take, but it was clear that handing things over would lead to death and with it the death of Monsieur Fabergé.

The factors boiled down to a single possible action.

Nerves shaking, she held the suitcase on her lap. "Please, I'll do as you say, just don't point that thing at me." She called up tears as if it was her last hope, though it made her sick to look so weak. But girls cried. Even in Germany.

The pistol slowly retracted, and pointed at the ceiling. "Smart Slav. Perhaps you don't all have Asian brains. You might live for a while longer. Now let go."

She did. Smug and proud, he gripped the handle of the case … and a snap of direct current flooded his body.

The pistol fired into the ceiling light as he hit the ground, limbs at all points like an electrified Vitruvian man, shaking the case until the discharge ended.

Commotion filled the train and panic told Vasilya there was one thing to do: run.

After kicking away the porter's gun, she hit the trigger's release for the electrical discharge with her boot heel, grabbed the suitcase, and ran into the corridor.

But which way?

Toward where he'd taken Colonel Balk?

Was the colonel in on sending this thug? No, she thought. He would not have gone through all the motions just to have some assassin hit her.

And if Colonel Balk fell to these villains, what would happen to Monsieur Fabergé?

She opened the case.

Click and Clack scurried out, slight smoke coming off their hides No doubt the charge was painful.

"I'm sorry, friends. It was necessary. But I need you to be brave now," she told them, and the sound of her voice calmed their servos. "We must all be brave."

She placed the mice in the inner pockets of her dress and their warm hum calmed her nerves. "Be brave," she told herself again, closing the suitcase, and marching toward where Colonel Balk had walked.

Be very brave.

Pain gripped her shoulders. A harsh voice spat in her ear. "Good voltage." The porter squeezed. "But not good enough."

CHAPTER SEVEN:

FROM THE ASHES

Worms filled Warren's mouth with a deep, woody flavour of dying fire and burning shit. At least his scrambled mind thought they were worms, gooey burrowers inching down his throat, gunning it into his chest, and snagging his heart.

He screamed and gagged, fingers digging into his mouth to tear the carrion eaters from him. Air rushed in and tasted vile. Each breath was pregnant with the stink of ash and rotten eggs. Cold slivers ran up and down his body as if his veins had been torn out and replaced with barbed wire and then doused in kerosene before someone jammed a flare in his heart to set him off like a powder keg.

"Fuck!" he screamed, until an iron hand clasped his maw.

A harsh voiced whispered into his ear, then a gas masked was shoved on this face. "Shh! You're not supposed to tear it out. Oh, damn it."

On his back, Warren glared at his stretched out legs. The air was thick and foggy, turning the world into a haze until his eyes focused through the yellow.

Mustard gas!

He struggled, and an arm hugged him stronger than Tik.

"Calm down. You're fine. Can't say the same for the rest here."

He wore layers of Germany cloth on all of his exposed skin. Above and beyond the edge of Warren's boots were the dead Germans. Boils and malformed flesh ran across their faces like cancerous worms, eyes bleeding puss and blood as the festering boils continued to grow in the searing mist.

"The gas is heavy," said the voice behind Warren. "And it stays in the holes, so no one will come near here for a bit. Winds calmed down, too. We have a little while before day makes it impossible to move. So if you promise not to scream and let every Tommy and Hun in Europe know we're here, I'll let you go. Ok?"

Warren, stunned, nodded.

The arm released his chest.

Warren shoved himself to the side and in the sickening haze he saw …

"Alex?"

Alex smiled, still a kid. Still alive.

"But you're dead. You're supposed to be."

Alex nodded. "Guess it was a good death, huh?"

"What?"

Alex tossed him his VC, which Warren caught in a gloved hand. He handed it back to Alex, who pushed it back. "I'm well beyond the good grace of Queen Victoria by now, Warren. Besides, I saw what you did, storming this nest. You've earned it. Though not sure if it should be for bravery or stupidity."

"I don't want a goddamn medal," Warren said, tossing it at Alex, who caught it, sitting in mustard gas as if it were light rain. "I want to know why you lied. Where the hell have you been? How come you're … alive? Including now!"

He looked at the shredded jacket Alex had been wearing when the machine gun burst found its meaty target. Warren pushed the strands away.

There was no wound.

No blood.

Just the soft muscle of a boy who left home too soon. "Alex, what the hell is happening?" The mask steamed with his words.

Alex grinned. "I'll let you know, ok? But we'll have to move soon." His face crinkled. "You … you came back for me, didn't you?"

Warren wiped his nose. "Alex."

"I called you a coward, and you ran across hell to save me. Thinking I was dead, or a phantom, and you did it anyway." Alex gripped Warren in a strong embrace and cried so hard and painfully it bruised Warren to the core. "I'm sorry, brother. I am so sorry for what I said, for … everything. I hope you'll forgive me what I've done. Somehow, someway."

Warren hugged him back. "So you're real? Not some shell-shocked ghost I've been chasing?" He gripped Alex's shoulders and pulled him back to gaze at him. "Really real?" There was a bloodstain on Alex where he'd touched Warren's chest.

Right above his heart.

Alex's smiled, then grunted, as Warren's fingers traced the hole on his chest.

"You … you shot me."

"Well, yes. I had to, you wouldn't survive if—"

"Bastard!" He collared Alex and tossed him to the ground, trashing him with a few empty fist haymakers like when he'd found out Alex had broken Mother's favourite lamp, knowing full well he'd be getting blamed to save his little brother from the rod. "'Well, yes,'" he said in a mock impersonation. Alex struggled, but Warren hammered his fists down on his brother's shoulders. "What kind of answer is that?"

Alex grunted. "You have to believe me, there was no other way. The gas was coming. If I didn't, you'd be just like those Huns, roasting into monstrous shapes." The haze embraced them like an ethereal monster, flesh hissed and bubbled from the Germans, but it did not wrench and scar Alex or Warren. "I know, okay? I know it makes no sense. I can't explain it well, either. But I know someone who can. And we must go, Warren. I'm already late and ..." There was that same old rabbit fear on Alex's face when he'd broken that stupid lamp. "Trust me. I can keep us alive. I might even be able for us to find a way out of this war. But you have to trust me. You have to believe in me. Please, Warren. I didn't want to shoot you. But if I hadn't, you'd be as dead as those Huns."

Warren got off him, crouching low. Alex stood, slung his rifle, and climbed out into the piss yellow landscape while a stillness crept over the land. The mustard gas was exterminating everything. Rats. Men. Even the lice had stopped itching on Warren's hair and skin.

At his feet was the VC.

He stepped on it, climbed out ... and might as well have awoken upon the surface of the moon. The upturned world of No-Man's Land was a dead place, the only sound the crackling of flesh as it transmuted into repellent forms on corpses. Daylight was breaking, but the world swam in poison mist. And only Warren and Alex stood alive.

"Come on," Alex said, running like a wild elk over the rugged, ruined terrain. "The stormtroopers might be trying to reclaim this in the wake of a counterattack, and they've got solid gas protection."

Warren followed, and heard something jingle. He pulled Tik's shark tooth necklace out of his pocket. It slipped off his hand and, kneeling, he wasn't sure if it was a good or bad luck charm—

—when burping machine guns filled the air. Cries in German followed in the distance.

"Run!" Alex said, disappearing into the yellow mist. "Follow me!"

Warren grabbed the tooth and charged, knowing full well the bug-faced stormtroopers would soon get another bead on him. Alex darted off, almost out of sight. The jackrabbit was always a fast one, and he was sure the little shit's heart wasn't hammering him like—

His heart was still.

It beat. Slowly.

"Warren! Come on!"

Running over churned barbed wire, stray limbs and pock-marked earth, Alex finally jumped into a hole in the ground. Not a shell hole, more like a well. Tiny. Just about the size for a body.

Warren stole a glance back at Tik's grave. So long, bud. This war won't be the same without you.

"Warren! Hurry!"

Warren jumped into the hole while machine gun fire gutted the sea of gas above him, and descended into the unknown.

CHAPTER EIGHT:

SPIES AND MONSTERS

The porter shoved Vasilya back in her cabin so hard she stumbled to her stomach, suitcase flying, as the train chugged on and on.

The door lock clicked.

"Clever one, you are," he said. Whiffs of burned hair and smoke choked the air. "Too clever to allow you to do what you're planning." The pistol made a "click" and she gasped. "Deactivate that suitcase. All of its traps and triggers, or I'll give you good reason to scream."

"Please," she said. "Please don't hurt me."

"Do it!"

She did.

"Open it."

She did.

"Now put those two marvels of engineering back in their cage."

She closed her eyes and turned over, gun starring at her face. "No."

"I do not have time to argue. Either you do it, or I rip open that pretty dress and take them from you." He smiled and sickness filled her.

She grimaced, humming a staccato sound. A few bars, complete with spaces. S. O. S. Click and Clacks hummed, then revved. "I don't take orders from German swine."

He snarled, then gripped the front of her dress,

"Defend!" she said, in Russian.

Click and Clack shot up his arm like two bullets, reaching his eyes before he could blink. He released Vasilya and tore at his face with his free hand, gun hand swinging wild. "Get them off me!" Click wrapped around his finger and flared with red fire as Clack dove into the eye socket, then flared green.

Vasilya covered her ears as the German wailed briefly, then silence returned as he hit the ground. The acrid stench of death infected her. "Desist," she whispered in Russian, sickness growing in her stomach.

Click and Clack strolled away from his body, both stained red, and the stench of death clung to their silver frames.

Slowly, she regained her composure. With patience against fear and sickness she had never previously known, she picked up her suitcase and took out a small belt of cleaning tools.

"Come," she said.

The mice crawled up her leg and onto the soft cloth on her lap, staining her dress some. The world melted away as she picked up her thin driver and steam wrench, working them over before unveiling the cleaning acid and oil. She could almost smell the old workshop, the burning of magnesium, the sharp taste of arc light, the way her sweat balanced on the edge of her stub nose, shaking as she worked a motor with tweezers for the Tzarina's egg …

She cleaned Click and Clack with a vial of water and special soap, freed them from the sticky grime of human foulness. As she put them to bed, the compartment door slammed open.

Colonel Balk arrived with three soldiers, pistols drawn. He stared at the body, face contorting. He holstered the weapon, then lifted the body off the ground with his lone hand, displaying a strength that would have been impressive if Vasilya gave a damn about such things. He tossed the corpse to his guards. "Get this maggot off my train," he growled, scaring the otherwise stout guards. "Then put the head of security under arrest with my personal guard and inform him his destination is a firing line as soon as we stop. And if anyone comes near us who does not have my password, you are to shoot them on sight, and if you do not, I will hang the lot of you myself with my last breath." His gloved fist shook. "Do I make myself clear?"

The guards nodded, saluted with shaking hands, and took away the dead assassin. Colonel Balk walked across the blood stained carpet and kneeled before Vasilya. "Are you injured?"

She shook her head.

"But there is blood on your hands, your dress."

She nodded. "Now I'm no different than anyone else in this world."

"How did you … subdue him? His face was—"

"I have many traps. I am no fool." She wiped the blood from her finger. "He wanted the suitcase," she said, accusingly. "Why?"

He stood. "Open it and see."

"There's nothing in there he could want." Except Click and Clack, but she refrained from sharing their existence unless she was sure the colonel knew of them. Indeed, she was not keen to touch their clean bodies until her own hands were clean.

"Look closer, child," said the colonel.

She hated the way he said "child," with that smug sense of superiority the Germans said everything, as if because he wore a uniform it gave him license to boss her around and tell her which way the sun rose in the morning.

He towered over her, bending down and said again, firmly. "Look."

She grimaced, then opened it.

And there sat Tom Swift, just like before. "So your enemies are fond of children's literature. How quaint." Then she noticed it. Something bulging within the folds of the worn magazine.

She opened the cover and flipped through the pages until she came to a piece of drafting paper, folded. She looked at the colonel, who sat stiffly opposite her, boot in a bloody puddle. He nodded.

She unfolded.

And within the folded paper was a monstrous drawing. She thought of the Hunchback of Notre Dame. Of the sad creature in Mary Shelley's novel. Of the hideous phantom below the Paris opera. Of the Morlocks that hid in the future.

But this ... creature was made of wood, wire, and iron. A form of life not yet in existence. A mechanical demon littered with engines of war, cannon and barrels and bayonet blades. It stood before a human body for scale and dwarfed it like a mansion to a cat. An industrial nightmare torn from the mind of some mad man.

Not a mad man, she realized, looking at how well constructed it was, how intricate, ornate.

"No, please no."

But the drawings flared with the gentle hand of its creator, a talent for beauty that made such a horror ... it was almost too much to bear, to believe. But the notes and schematics etched at the side, and the signature at the bottom, destroyed any illusion of this drawing's maker.

"Fabergé."

"He was to build it for us," the colonel said. "At last, a war-winning weapon. We have the materials he requested, but he kept his plan to himself."

"Plan?" Vasilya said, as if the word were made of spoiled meat. "This is a sketch. A prototype, an idea on paper and nothing more. He would have made complete design plans and schematics and patterns and kept it—"

"What?"

"Fire." She gripped her head, mind casting back to the last days in St. Petersburg. "There had been a fire at his workshop not long after the revolution. When the Bolsheviks hunted him. And he hid with us. Only his ... real family knew where he was." She traced the outline of the mechanical beast. "He must have hidden it here. Just in case." She shut the suitcase. "Was he really going to make this ... thing?"

Balk sat straight back on the plush seat. "His obligation is now yours. With this weapon, we could win the war. End the fighting. Return to peace. Without it, I fear our enemies will drive into Berlin, slaughtering us all in our homes. With the Americans now throwing their bodies into the fray, they have a bottomless supply of fodder for our guns. We'll run out of bullets before they tire of dying against us."

"So," she said, bitterly. "I suppose your great offensive in March didn't mean the end was nigh."

They glared at each other.

Coldness infected the low words the colonel uttered. "The West will not free your country of Bolsheviks, child. Nor do they have means to keep your father alive. Build me a weapon of victory on Germany's terms, and you will have both a free Russia and a living father. Fail me, and I will have no recourse but to send you to the firing line. Believe it."

What little affection she'd accrued for the wounded man who was keeping Monsieur Fabergé from death's door iced and broke in the wake of these words.

She opened the suitcase, stared at the monster inside, and despite being unsure where its head was, Vasilya was certain that the monster was staring right back.

"So be it."

CHAPTER NINE:

THE LOST BATTALION

Once Alex had given him the sign, he'd taken off the mask. The subterranean crash was hard, the air rotten, but Warren enjoyed that the war above him was muted, as if God had shoved a rag in its iron mouth.

"Hurry," Alex said, vanishing down a dark tunnel just big enough for a body to run crouched. "I'm already late."

"Late for what?" Warren said, feeling like Alice's rotten big brother had been shoved down the rabbit hole. "Wait up!"

Beneath the sky, below the war, Warren chased Alex like two bullets down the same barrel, and to his astonishment his eyes adjusted to the cavernous dark as if soft gaslight flecked in the air. And his heart kept its same, slow beat.

Deeper they ran, and the war softened to a distant thrum, a storm in a faraway land. The tunnels they dashed through were just big enough for men, but not clear of debris. Stray limbs and shiny rat eyes littered the path as he chased Alex without a heartbeat to his name, running faster than a deer from fire.

Some of the tunnels were old trenches with the remains of soldiers and stray concrete, smashed skulls and fat rats. Others were rounder, like the ones for the London Underground. They burrowed deeper into the earth.

Another world, Warren thought, I'm down the rabbit hole and running into another world. Perhaps Edgar Rice Burroughs wasn't so wrong after all, with his drilling machine to the hollow earth. What fresh nightmares bred in the belly of planet? Good god, Warren thought. Tik said I'd find enough stories in war to last me a lifetime and I think I've already had my fill.

Deeper into the belly of the world they ran, but fears trembled through Warren as he ran harder, unsure of what it was that fed his body its strength. His heart ... those worms in his mouth that ran against his gag...

The thought eclipsed all others: worms in his belly. He dropped to his knees and rammed his fingers down his throat.

A single black worm slapped the dirt at his knees, burrowing fast into the earth.

"Warren? Come on! We have to keep moving!"

"No!" Warren shouted, wiping bloody and muddy spit from his torn lip. "Get them out of me!"

Alex's footsteps returned. "Get what out?"

Warren clawed at his belly. "The damn worms! Get them out of my guts. What did you do to me?" He gripped his head like it would crack without the pressure. "I'm running like a wild dog, but my heart is slow. What the hell did you shove down my throat?"

"Jesus, Warren. It wasn't worms. I'll explain, but you can't tarry—"

Warren stood. "The hell I can't!"

"No, you can't! There's going to be an—"

A distant rumble. The thunder echoed, then grew, and charged. Warren turned and the tunnel shook.

"Run!" Alex said, yanking Warren to his feet. And they did, faster than he'd seen any beast run in the wild, toward an opening of a larger cave. Explosives cracked in the air, shocks ran down the tunnel with the force of a buffalo stampede. Out of instinct, he leapt, and the wave crashed into him, sending him spiraling like a rifled bullet until he slammed into Alex and both brothers lay face-first in a larger expanse. The tunnel they had come from was now filled with dirt, and from above earth sifted on them while the world creaked.

Alex kicked him away, spitting dirt. "Idiot! Do you want to spend your life crawling out of graves? Why do you never listen to me?"

Warren shook the loose filth from his head, wiped his eyes, and pulled himself up. "Well why didn't you say there were sap charges behind us? And how did you know they would go off?"

"They always go off when I pass a check point."

"Check point? You mean, there are others ... down here?"

"Others and then some," came a British voice. On the far side of the cavernous room was a Tommy wearing a hodgepodge of uniforms. A French greatcoat, a German helmet. "You're late, Alexander," said the Tommy, cockney accent thick and annoying, though not as repugnant as the high accent of the posh officers that Lieutenant Christopher thought he was. "And I can't believe you brought back a tourist. Boss won't be happy."

"I'll deal with that, Graves," Alex said.

"I look forward to seeing that," Graves said, "especially if you wasted your precious cargo on some poor air-sucking git in No-Man's Land."

Warren strode toward Graves. "Wow, I didn't realize Limey cocksuckers burrowed this deep, unless it was for a bit of sodomy." His hand caressed his bayonet handle.

Graves sneered. "If you're so eager to die twice, hero..." He made a come-hither motion with his hand. "Keep it up."

Alex stood between them. "Don't. Warren. This isn't some saloon in Fort William. There's something big afoot."

"Like I give a shit," Warren said as Graves thumbed his belt. An officer's pistol sat in the holster.

Alex glared at him, all puppy dog eyes. "You should. There's a new war brewing. A war we can win. Now, ease off."

A pain in his chest birthed. He grunted, and took a step back. The pain receded, but the memory lingered with the sting of moonshine. Alex sighed, and then turned to Graves. "Where's Rasputin?"

"His Majesty awaits your humble return in the lounge," Graves said, then bowed. "Oh master of the dead root." He rose, snorted, and spat on Warren's boot. "Come on, before he has all our heads on pikes."

Warren snorted, ready to launch a phlegm bomb in Grave's eye, but Alex shook his head. Warren swallowed the bomb for later.

They marched across rough churned earth to what Warren thought of as a cramped, underground street. Handfuls of soldiers cleaned weapons by mild light coming from tiny fires, eyeing the two brothers and laughing darkly.

All were pale. Some wounded. Holes in chests. Some were missing hands, arms. All had their legs.

But the voices stiffened Warren's fears.

German and Italian … then Russian, French and English whispers cut across the darkness between them. All had mismatched uniforms, like Graves. Patchwork clothes rifled from the dead. They all wore thick metal helmets like bizarre knights from a King Arthur tale.

My god, he realized. This … This is the Lost Battalion … that trench rumour of soldiers who'd abandoned each side of the war to fight against both sides.

Alex is one of them

And … they're all dead.

They had to be. The wounds of the broken ones alone were enough to kill a man, but left untended, many of them should have been rotting with gangrene and filling the air with a putrid stench of a clearing station. But the wounds were just grey shreds of flesh.

His mind frosted at the thought, and the chill ran down his spine but did not touch his heart … that beat like a monotonous drum no matter his ire.

We're all dead, he thought, coolly and absently. Beneath the earth. Oh sweet Christ, this couldn't be happening.

"Better take care of your sibling," Graves said with a snort. "Looks like he's about to crack like an egg under a boot."

Instead, Warren giggled.

Then laughed.

Then cackled.

The soldiers stilled and their countenances turned perplexed, as if he were stark raving mad. And why not? It was absurd as tits on a bull, and yet it made sense, so why not? He was down the rabbit hole like Alice, and everything else was topsy-turvy. In this rotten Wonderland, below a war without end in the tomb of Europe, why wouldn't there be a misfit army of the dead, damned, and doomed? It was logical as the Somme, if not more so. He half expected the Mad Hatter to ride in on a horse, blaring a bugle, and declaring war on the Dormouse's Brigade. "Now that is a fight worth fighting!"

The soldiers looked at each other while Warren cackled, gripping his knees.

"Warren?" Alex gripped his shoulder. "Warren, you need to snap out of it."

"Oh, so this is a dream?" Warren said. "If so, I think I ordered the wrong one, 'keep. Mine tend to have barmaids with thick rumps and breasts fit for milking, not a gaggle of dead soldiers hanging out in Morlock country." Warren howled, throwing his head back. "But I guess you have to dance with what brung ya, so hello, Lost Battalion. Hallowed be thy name. From Kingdom Come, until Armageddon, on earth without a heaven!" He laughed so hard his eyes shut tighter than a virgin's snatch.

Pain sliced across his cheek as Alex slapped him so hard his face hit the tunnel wall.

"We don't have time for madness," Alex said. "Come on," he said as he put a hand on Warren's shoulder, "we have—"

"Grrrah!" Warren swung and nailed Alex with a haymaker that drilled him straight across the cavern and stumbling to the ground, a blow that should not have been possible, a righteous, battle-ending shot … that barely gave Alex pause as he massaged his face.

And his heartbeat flared. He hissed as a bruise simmered, then vanished, like a freshly cleaned stain on Alex's face. "That's it, you ungrateful bastard."

"Donnybrook!" said Graves. Alex pulled himself from the floor, eyes wide, and then charged.

The men surrounded them, smiling with gritty, sharp teeth, goading them on with pumping fists as if this were a lumber camp brawl. Alex came at him, collar and elbow, and before Warren knew it they were tearing at each other's arms, gunning for a good hook to wrench each other apart. They spun, boots across the mud, trying kicks to shin and knee, two whirling dervishes without a single heartbeat between them.

But Warren was always bigger, if not faster, and he tossed Alex hard into his dead colleagues. Again, his heartbeat punched back. He grit his teeth.

"So much for the mighty Alexander Bishop," Grave said. "Hero of Vimy and runt of his litter!"

The crowd laughed, and shoved him back in.

And Warren's hate focused on Graves. He hawked back his phlegm than spat so fast the Limey didn't get his hand up in time, nailing him in the eye. "Talk shit against my kin, you shit heel, and I'll feed you your fucking teeth."

Graves grimaced, the snot-shot dropping like a muddy tear. They locked eyes, but out of the periphery came a blur. A hideous punch clocked Warren on the side of his head.

The pain was thick and muddy. And the force of the blow was like an anvil being tossed at his head by a circus strongman. He spun to the ground, but got up, pain receding as fast as it had engulfed him.

Fists tight at his side, Alex shook with a bitter cadence, a harsh grimace both foul and feral. "Don't move," he grunted.

And, despite his new strength, Warren was frozen.

And the sucker punch that Alex now launched into him, a hellish right cross, drove Warren's head into the muddy wall where it stuck.

His body might as well have been drowned in molasses because he couldn't move a lick: his arms would not go up in a guard, legs would not run, and Alex approached.

"I don't need your protection!" Alex screamed. "You need mine!"

A hushed tone enveloped the crowd of soldiers. But Alex leaned back to drill him again.

"Be still," said a quiet voice.

And now Alex froze, mid-punch.

The circle parted. Walking to the centre, a wild black-haired man, like the homeless vagabonds of Fort William's rail yards, gripped their attention. A grey uniform hung from his wiry frame. Sleeveless, his arms were knots of muscle and strange tattooed symbols mingled with dirt to give him the etched features of a circus geek who'd escaped his cage.

"Alexander," he said, an accent lacing his words that held the cadence of the Ukrainian day labourers that occasionally worked on their farm. But this tone was more sinister. "Your mission was successful?"

Alex was still locked in place, just like Warren, grimacing, grunting. "Yes." Warren struggled. His finger trembled, but could move. The ice in his blood thawed.

"And you spent your bounty on this … man?"

"Yes, but he coughed it up. It didn't take root. I'm so sorry."

"Be free."

The punch fired and Warren ducked. Alex's fist went elbow deep in the wall before he yanked it out, turned, and saluted. "I'm sorry, Rasputin. He is my brother."

"Damn well should be," Graves said, but was silenced with the wild gaze of Rasputin eyes.

Warren, getting a grip on himself, stood next to Alex in the thin firelight as Rasputin approached "I do not see the resemblance."

"I've got the milkman's eyes," Warren said with a snort.

"No time for jokes!" Alex said.

"He is the older," Rasputin said, eyes glassy with a greenish-grey centre, glare digging into Warren so hard he wanted to tear out those thieving orbs with his own fingers. "The first born. The one who had to learn everything without a guide." Rasputin tilted his head, hands wringing each other as if in some contorted prayer, his accent chewing the words. "Yes. The hard road. Trial by fire. Mistakes punished. A childhood of blows to harden you to a life without a father."

Warren's actions snapped before his thoughts.

Fast as rifle shot, his gripped Rasputin's throat, a muscled mass that resisted his grip.

None of the men moved.

"I warned your bootlicker Graves," Warren growled. "And I'm warning you. Talk ill of my kin, and you're worm shit."

Rasputin's eyes focused. "Tell him," he said, voice clear, quiet, and soft.

"Let go," Alex said.

His fingers resisted his thoughts.

"I said," Alex boomed, "let go. He ... can't die."

The fingers peeled back.

Rasputin smiled and walked back to the centre of the circle. "You have a strong will. No doubt it kept you alive in the topside Armageddon." He turned. "But you are no longer what you were. Nor are you like your brother. Your heart is beating until its final drum ... and until then, you are an abomination. Strong, and you can endure, but unlike my chosen your candle is burning bright, I can see you dying before my eyes. A doomed little warrior. You may join us."

Warren flexed his fingers, seemingly back under his control, and glared at Alex. "What, the Lost Battalion?"

"No, Warren. Be a foot soldier in the only army that will win this war," Alex said.

Rasputin smiled. "Truly said. And soon, we will emerge from our cocoon, a leviathan of vengeance for the dead. And you," he said to Warren. "Will be on the side of righteous retribution, for the eternal slaughter our father nations have produced. Welcome to my Draug Army, Warren Bishop. The army of the dead." Constantine grinned. "And now, the dying."

CHAPTER TEN:

LADY FRANKENSTEIN

Vasilya could taste it as much as smell it from behind the large door: the dust and the rich, smoky scent of shaved and polished wood, the metallic tang of copper wire, and also iron and steel, each laced with a flavour of expectation. She enjoyed that moment, in the darkness of the evening, nerves finally calmed from the horror of the train, as Colonel Balk unlocked the door to a large building the size of a munitions factory, hidden from view behind a majestic mansion and surrounded by oaks whose branches bled into the starless murk of night.

"This is your new home," said the colonel and opened the door.

The darkness welcomed her, and the rush from the aroma of a workshop. Thoughts of home pierced her mind. Dear Mother, she thought, will you survive long enough that I may see you again? Or are the memories the best I can hope for?

In the dark, such memories danced. Of visiting Paris before the war to see *The Rite of Spring*, and Mother's comical disgust for its "modern" butchery of the art of ballet. Mother's art, betrayed by the tide of progress. Vasilya hadn't cared for it either, but her disgust was for the riotous crowd that littered the streets after, and how Mother held her tight on the way to the hotel Monsieur Fabergé had paid for them, the grip of safety and protection as fierce as her mother's glare.

A switch flicked. Warm and electric hums fizzled from nothingness. High above, light bulbs slowly burned away the dark sea into an island of shadows and shapes that, slowly, widened Vasilya's eyes.

"Mother Mary," she said. "What creatures and contraptions are these?"

Within the long deep rows of the workshop were not just the instruments of creation (workbenches, lathes, piece fittings, forges and torches) lining the sides of the cavernous room, but other … objects. Marvels she'd only read about or heard Monsieur Fabergé speak of while she practiced the art of lapping, grinding, or drilling. Her fingers almost danced out of their skin to touch them.

"You recognize them?" The colonel walked with sharp, sure steps.

With her index finger, she tapped her lip "Some. Not all."

"I would hope not." He walked by an ornate wooden figure, scaled the size of a man, a Turk in oriental garb sitting before a magnificent oak and rosewood chess board. "You see before you the largest private collection of magical devices, automatons, and mechanical oddities in Europe. Fabergé and I were something of ... rivals, collecting them, back when we met. Him for their beauty, me for their secrets. Our collection the finest in all the Theosophical Society. Come. Let me show you."

He led her past strange machines, bizarre dolls, contraptions and machinations whose purpose her own mind started to peel apart, layer by layer. "Most came from auctions. Some from ... less reputable means."

"Stolen?" she said.

He threw back a dead glance from his eye patch. "Rescued," he said, then continued. "Including what I hope will be a most inspired source for you as you begin your journey."

Amidst the marvels at the centre of the room, the colonel stood before a large bookshelf littered with volumes of books in a dozen languages. The entire shelf was immaculate, with a rich dark finish and well-sanded edges, and each book looked in wonderful shape. "You read French as well as you speak it?"

"*Oui.*"

He grunted, removed a large book with oiled leather cover, and handed it to her. Vasilya held back a rather gruff grunt of weakness as the heavy tome sat on her arm. She opened the warm cover and read the title.

A Conjuror's Confessions.

Her lip trembled once. "This ... this is the biography of the magician Robert-Houdin," she said breathlessly. "Monsieur Fabergé spoke of him as if he were Merlin himself."

"Not quite," said the colonel. "But he had been among the greatest inventors and detectives of the Society, a great advisor parading as an entertainer as he sought knowledge to share with us all, before this war cut of all communication. Thus, it is a prized part of a now rare collection. This is the original, unpublished biography Robert-Houdin wrote for his friends in the magician's community, not the tawdry adventure story he sold to the rabble. Here he spoke of the true magic of our age. The kind that is in your hands. Like you, his work is one of a kind."

Awestruck, she closed the book. "How ... how did you ever come across it?"

The colonel placed his sole hand on the bookshelf, gloved fingers tapping the spine of each book. "During the war with France. My regiment came upon his home, shortly before he died."

"You stole from a dying man?" The disgust contorted her face. "How very German of you."

The colonel's fingers stopped tapping. "If I had not taken it, the men I was with would have set the place on fire. The dunderheads did not know Robert-Houdin from Wagner. No, child, I did not steal. I—"

"Rescued. Like you did with me? I see the German members of the Society are far more enlightened than those who only fill the ranks of the Kaiser's army."

He tore the book from her hand and returned it to the shelf with such violence that Vasilya gasped and held her suitcase like a baby with its blanket. His voiced burred with resentment tangled with anger. "I've been too easy on you, what with the attempt on your life, but that ends, now. There is work to be done. And I suggest you get started."

He marched off, leaving her alone with the assortment of shadowed oddities and a few hundred questions muddling her head. So she blurted out what her fatigued body was whispering. "But ... it must be two in the morning."

"Tell that to my countrymen dying in No-Man's Land. I suggest you get busy," said the colonel. "Start making me my war machine. If I do not have results to show the Kaiser in a month, we're all as good as dead."

"A month!" she screamed. "That's not possible, even for Monsieur Fabergé."

"Is that so?" The colonel stopped by the door. "Then why not make your peace with god and go to sleep. Because you have but two choices here, child. Death or victory. Me? I've had my fill of the former."

He slammed the door, as she knew he would, then the familiar click of a key's bit engaging the tumbler. Too easy, she thought, until a more industrial sound followed. So, they've improved their locks, perhaps one of the "pick-proof" ones she heard Theo Fabergé claim the Americans had invented.

She was tempted to test that theory when hunger gnawed her stomach, reminding her it had been days since she'd left Mother's stew, her dark bread, and the thin vegetable soup her mother had taught her to make, days since Mother's sour face grew too tired of arguing and told her to go, leave, abandon her to the wolves.

Loneliness coiled around her hunger, and nausea followed. Then get to work, she thought. Industry focuses you, and can keep the hunger at bay.

And, hopefully, memories.

On a massive oak work desk, she opened her suitcase and entered the code on the puzzle box. Click and Clack slept.

She caressed their silver hides. "Wake up, my friends."

They did, eyes alight and scurrying. Clean as the day they were born, as if the horror of the train had never happened. "All right. Enough rest. It is time we take inventory and start up what we can. Monsieur Fabergé needs us." But the secret image buried in her heart was of returning to Russia in the wake of a fresh victory, one that would return royalty to government. With it, a new age, a new family, a new need for beauty to fill the hearts and minds of a Tzar and his Tzarina.

The image burned bright in her mind. Of a new egg. Dark as opal, but within it a golden phoenix.

She shook it from her head. Such a future is dead if we do not make progress today in this vile world of war and weapon, she told herself in a harsh, reprimanding tone. She swallowed a rotten taste in her mouth, then removed the schematic Monsieur Fabergé had made. The hideous war machine. "Oh Sir, how could you turn such wonder in your mind to a monstrosity?"

But it was a monstrous time.

And the clock was ticking.

"God help me. I am becoming a Lady Frankenstein."

She began to list the components she could see on the creature, and hoped some of them were in this chamber of mechanical creatures.

A scent gripped her. Strong, sharp. Coming from her suitcase. Under the cover of the Tom Swift magazines.

Fear gave way to hunger, and she tore away the cover. She found a hole, cut through the stack of magazines, a hole that hid a bundle encased in the old kitchen cloth with embroidered chamomile, the yellow dull and the green stem worn. She unwrapped the bundle. Half a loaf of bread, and old cheese, dried and salted beef. About all that was left in the cupboards. She tore into the bread, and saw a small scrap of paper. On it, a handful of words in Mother's elegant script.

"God keep you from harm, my daughter. Love, M."

Tears welled as Vasilya softly chewed a last taste of home.

CHAPTER ELEVEN:

QUEST FOR DEADROOT

Warren cackled, hooted, and grunted his mirth into his hard fist until Alex silenced him with a "Quit it!" But the laughter bubbled in his dead chest. Army of the dead? he thought. Jesus, Alex, this Rasputin looks like a career drunk on an epic tear, and talks like a penny dreadful.

"We are a lucky few, as yet," Rasputin said, a hand on the shoulder of a gaunt faced man in French uniform, moustache like piss-stained straw. "A true band of brothers."

God, quoting Shakespeare? What's next, juggling? Swallowing a sword? Warren crossed his arms, unimpressed.

"And once we have gathered our strength," Rasputin said, gripping the Frenchman's shoulder with greenish hands more akin to talons. Then he walked in front of his whole battalion. "I attempted to avert the coming of this war. I served as arcane advisor to the Tzar, but my pleading against the growing toys of the Royal Families of Europe were ignored. They wish to keep you all chained to factories, feeding industry with human blood and sweat, turning you to tallow, and never revealing their true nature."

"And what's that?" Warren said.

"They are a cruel family who have ruled for centuries by controlling those of us with gifts. Wild talents who could shape metal or bone, create wonders and machines of power. Architects of cities whose very bones influence how the people think and feel. The Theosophical Society and its inbred nobility harvested us with talents to serve their ends. What do you think has led to Victoria's continued and wretched clinging to life? She is no more flesh and blood than a steam engine now."

Warren glared as Constantine rolled on.

"I uncovered the German plot to start a war to harvest these talents. I implored the Society to stop. To let me try another way to contain Germany. But they feared what I knew: they wanted this war for the same reason. For you see the talented are no longer seen as seers, as advisors, as guiding stars.

"We are tools to be used, and locked away when no longer valuable" Constantine stared at the earthen roof. "Though not all prisoners are bound by the laws of nature." His gaze fell on Warren. "Now, we are small, yet vital. We shall seek vengeance for all the dead." He faced Alex. "You wasted what deadroot you found on this sibling?"

Alex nodded.

"He wasn't dead when you service him."

"Close," Warren said. "German sniper." He tapped his chest. "Must have been born with eagle eyes. Most krauts can't hit the broad side of a city hall with an apple." The slow thump of his heart made him sick.

The men in Austrian boots and German helmets grunted. Rasputin put his arms behind him. "Then you are no draug, Warren."

"Yeah," Warren said. "That's me. Lucky Warren Bishop. Must have a rabbit foot."

"Then you've failed in your mission," Rasputin said to Alex, and he drew a pistol from behind him. "And you know the price."

Without thinking, Warren covered his brother. "Easy!" Phantom echoes of a panicked heartbeat filled him, but there was just a steady drum. "What price? He didn't do anything wrong."

Rasputin shoved the pistol to Warren's head, voice curled from a low timber to a hard scream, eyes wide like a circus freak and wild as a drunk lumberjack. "He wasted the most sacred substance of the deadlands! He has defiled our cause by bringing back a loved one instead of a proper soldier! And not even a draug, but some half-lived wraith. His own root is now forfeit."

"The hell it is!" Warren gripped his bayonet, but Alex pulled his hand back.

"I'll give it, Sir."

"Don't listen to this shit heel," Warren said.

And, fast as a mule kick, Alex slapped Warren so hard the lights dimmed, and Rasputin pulled back the pistol and pointed it at the ceiling of dirt. "You still don't get it, do you?" Alex said. "This is bigger than us, Warren. This is something that needs to be done. This war will not end unless we end it."

Warren wiped the shock from his face. "Oh, come on. It's not going to go on forever."

The legion laughed, black spaces between their teeth giving them the cavernous countenance of skulls.

"He doesn't believe," Rasputin said. "When, boy, did you arrive here?"

"Last year," Warren said. "After sniper school."

The laughter of the legion became angry grunts.

"We have fought here since the beginning," Grave said. "While turds like you waited for us to die for victory."

"Sat back like cowards," said the Frenchmen in broken English.

"While we died like cows in the slaughter pen," said a German with small eyes beneath his thick helmet.

"You dare tell us about this war?" Rasputin growled, walking forward, pistol again at accusing angle. "I have seen horrors the likes of which would drive you mad."

Warren didn't doubt it. There was a zealous energy in those eyes. Like a mad preacher, or hunter who'd spent too many nights alone in the wild, or a native elder who'd drunk too much rotgut and, as Tik would say, "gone off the rails of his spirit journey."

Tik.

Dead.

Real dead.

And yet here Warren was, trapped in a macabre dime novel below the war, below where his friend drowned on his own blood. Dying the way he wanted.

As the pistol's barrel glared at him, Warren put his hands in his pockets and held the shark tooth necklace. "Maybe not," Warren said. "But I don't know how much hell you have to see until you can call yourself a resident." He pushed his forehead against the gun barrel. "I've watched good men die for no reason, and I ain't got nothing to go home to but a house full of hate, and a future that stinks of corpses of friends. So tell me what you can take from me, Preacher?" He pushed harder until the pistol was shaking against his forehead. "Guess that head shots can take out this magical army of the dead. Look in my eyes. You think I'm scared?" His teeth gritted. "I've fought tougher clowns at the goddamn fair, so you can knock off the medicine man scare show because it can't work on me. Oh, and in case that wasn't clear enough for you, Fuck you, fuck your army, and go fuck yourself with the devil's prick."

Rage shook him and the pistol as Rasputin's mad glare tried to penetrate him like spikes through his eyes. His heart beat punched at its steady, slow rate.

Then, beyond all reason, the mad Russian relaxed, and smiled. He lifted the pistol up. "So. You're not as useless as Alex has told us. Maybe there is a place for you amongst us after all."

"Who said I signed up?"

"I do," Alex said. "Sir, I can find more deadroot. I'll go now. I don't care if its daylight. Let him stay behind and learn the importance of what we're doing here."

Rasputin scratched his beard with the gun barrel. "I'm afraid we do not have time to coddle your older brother for our cause." He pointed the gun at Alex. "He is bound to you. His failures are yours, and vice versa. Now go. Go before I regain my sanity!"

He fired at the ground and everyone laughed as Alex and Warren danced away from the bullets back down a rotten corridor.

The tunnel walk was a silent march on muddy ground. Warren coughed. "Thanks. For sticking up for me."

"You'd have done the same," Alex said. "Right?"

A bitter taste of memory, Alex's face at the train station, stung his mouth. "You tell me."

Silence resumed its bite.

They came upon a fork in the corridor. Down one alley of darkness was a deepening hole almost too dark for even Warren's new eyes to see. "This isn't an old trench," he said. "It's like that other one, shaped like the underground in London. Don't tell me there's a subterranean train to hell you guys are using?" Alex grunted. "How are you making them? Can't be a handful of men there, and didn't look like many were sappers."

"These tunnels weren't made by men," Alex said, a hint of fear in the words.

"Well then, what? Badgers? Beavers? Rasputin's pet groundhog?"

"Worm."

Twitches ran across Warren's lip. "Worms did this? You've lost what's left of your mind!"

"Not worms. Worm."

Warren snorted, shaking his head. "Funny, Alex. And here I thought I was the one with the runaway imagination."

Alex's face betrayed not a hint of sarcasm, of wit, but maintained the solemn, joyless look that he'd carried with him through most of his life as the dutiful son. "Rasputin calls it Charger. It lives deeper in the earth. But he can summon it after long meditations, and hold its will, direct it like a puppet until it breaks free and burrows home."

Warren coughed in his hand but couldn't hide his mirth. "I think Rasputin is reading too much Burroughs. Next thing you tell me, Tarzan is in your air corp."

"Shut up!"

"Maybe I should steal that bit for my own book."

Alex spun, face contorted as it tried to remain calm against the swell of rage making his hands flex. "Shut your cake hole and listen for once, Warren. You're not in command here. You're not holding my hand and leading me to market. You're in the rear, dead last, and if you don't pay attention you'll be dead for good. Just accept that for once I know better than you, ok?"

Warren raised his hands. "Whatever you say, brother."

"You ungrateful toad! Don't get sarcastic with me. You'd be a mustard gas corpse if it weren't for me, and what did saving you almost earn me? A bullet in the head. Mother was right, you're the most selfish, self-absorbed critter on two legs to ever waltz out of Fort William and I swear to god that if you do not wise up to the fact that you are not the hero, not the smartass, but a coin toss away from being rotting flesh in the shithouse of hell, I will kill you myself! Again!"

He stalked off, and Warren followed, finger rubbing the shark tooth in his pocket until the anger and frustration in his silent chest eased. It was harder to gauge when to speak when he couldn't hear the ragged breath of Alex ease between the steadying beats of his heart. He counted to fifty, then spoke. "So. What's the story? I mean besides finding this deadroot stuff." Silence responded. "Okay, all right. You're right. If I'm going to walk out of here alive … or whatever … I guess I'd best know what the hell is going on. What happened to you?"

Alex marched on. After a while, Warren could almost hear the guilt greasing the gears in Alex's mind as he sighed. "I died at Vimy."

I know that, Warren thought, but kept his trap shut. Let it roll out of him his own way, he thought, like a drunk finding a lost soul to chew the fat with. Give them silence and they'll fill it with their biography.

Alex marched as he spoke, harder, faster. "We'd practiced the assault for weeks until it haunted our sleep. Taking the Pimple, a fortified knoll. The barrage was nightmarish. Never heard anything like it since the Somme. But our idiot commander went light on shelling the route we were to take. We hit No-Man's Land with some of the kraut line intact. It was like we hadn't learned a damn thing over the past two years. The platoon was eaten by the Hun's machine guns and I knew we'd never make it out alive if it stayed."

Alex stumbled.

Warren caught him but was soon shrugged off, until Alex fell on his ass, shaking hand covering his face. The tremors shot through the rest of him until he was shaking like a sick wet dog.

"I … took it out." He nodded. "Killed three of them with my own hands." His hands shook before him as he put them into fists. "Did the heroic thing, right? Saved my mates. Killed all the bad men. Just like we're supposed to do. Right? That's what the hero does, he kills the villains. Right, Warren?"

Warren fought the reflex to touch him. Men in Alex's condition could snap. And since he wasn't even alive, he feared what might happen. "Right, Alex."

Alex nodded, lip shaking as he massaged his chest. "I never saw the last one until the dagger came out of my chest." He lifted his head. "And guess what was the only thing I could think of, as death tore into me? Where's Warren? He wouldn't have let this happen. He'd have protected me." His face puckered and then a dark, tight laugh creaked out of him in jagged sniffs. "Can you believe that? Two years of war, and I was still a Mother's baby boy, crying for help." He punched his face. "Baby." Again. "Baby, baby, baby!"

Alex wailed on himself until Warren's hand had gripped his wrists. "Easy."

"I hated you so much." Hands shaking in Warren's grip, Alex sobbed without tears, just a cadaverous sadness etched in his countenance. "I hated you … and there you were, hunting for me. You were late, Warren. Why are you always late?"

Warren released his grip, and held Alex in a bear hug as madness and grief turned his body into a whirling dervish.

"Late! You're always late!"

He held him tighter. "I know, Alex."

"I hate you!"

"I know!"

He held him beneath the earth. Above, there was a distant rumble of thunder.

Warren inhaled dirt and filth and exhaled a promise. "I'm sorry, Alex. I'm sorry I didn't get on that train with you. I'm sorry you suffered alone. And I'm sorry we're in this mess. But we're in it together. I'm not going to leave you again. Whatever happens, I'm here."

The tunnel shook but stayed firm, sending a dusting of filth upon them.

"I'm here."

CHAPTER TWELVE:

WORLDS OF WONDER GONE ASUNDER

Strewn about Vasilya were the ugly toys of wood, copper, and clockwork hearts; the biggest and most accurate sat on the table glaring back at her with a faceless countenance of smooth pine. She had not named the mechanical beast, for she feared giving it a humanity it would not deserve. So, she called it Nameless.

And Nameless might as well have been a euphemism for worthless. Despite her best efforts and Colonel Balk's angry tantrums, the creature was but a bipedal husk of gears. A tin man stuffed with straw instead of a brain or heart. And what of the final trinity of Oz, she thought. Where would courage lie in such a tool of destruction? But whenever her mind drifted, Colonel Balk's angry brogue ate through the revelries with the strength of a torch on flesh. "Do you realize how many are dying for every day we fail?" he would scream, chastising her slowness, gruffly handing over her dinner of cold meat, rolls and a rare tin of carrots.

"Did I start this war?" she'd say, taking the tray. "Those deaths are not on my hands."

"One will be," Colonel Balk snarled, then slammed the door.

A merciless week had commenced, of making models from soft woods and tin, like Monsieur Fabergé taught her, before even thinking of greater scales.

But all her little Nameless models collapsed under their own weight.

Glaring at the faceless creature, Vasilya finished the last slivers of cold tea that tasted of oak leaves and a hint of pine, and something sparked in her mind.

She'd been focused on the core of the being in the sketch. A single piece. Sometimes, with puzzles, it was smartest to get the outline, the full form, and this might impose the structure in ways that starting at the centre would miss.

She considered Monsieur Fabergé's sketches on the drafting table, pinned up like some industrial nightmare from Goya. But past that, deeper than that, she could make out a complexity, a layering of texture, that formed a small link in her mind, one that needed another.

When she'd wandered around the room of wonders, of magical contraptions and unmovable creatures … there was a connection, but it was lost, like a piece of Morse code torn in half.

She ran to the small shelf of drafting materials, grabbing some waxed paper and a large pencil, then ran back to the drafting table. She fixed the paper on top, and began to trace.

"To imitate is to create," Monsieur Fabergé had said one dusty morning in her tiny, private workshop, a rare moment while his steady hand worked on the glittering egg and turned the tiny screw of the Constellation's dancing gears into place with the ease and grace of a maestro conducting a silent tune, and his eyes sharpened, and his mouth loosened from the cadence of instruction and sharp critique. A softness, like warmed gold, came from him. "It is a beginning, not an end, but we must all start somewhere. Do not believe the lies of geniuses who tell you they appeared fully formed with greatness, like Athena springing from the head of Zeus. Such nonsense distorts our progress. We begin by imitating our inspirations. And soon, when we've unlocked the secrets of our heroes, we search out our own mysteries."

She'd read such words in the letters shared between him and others across the world, the Theosophical Society's membership reaching London, Paris, Geneva, Hong Kong, Tokyo, Cairo, Constantinople and even Washington, DC, and a place called Ottawa. She had known these letters were coded, as they were far too banal for men of M. Fabergé's intellect, but sometimes they were written directly with the vigor of seekers, seers, and scientists of the unknown.

Now, in that cold German evening, with a thick engineer's pencil in her thin, strong fingers, Vasilya missed the sense of adventure amid the horrors of the toyshop that was her prison. She outlined the creature Nameless, his jagged contours, his unwieldy arms and legs and growths from the back like a mutated hunchback.

And there, in that strange growth that she assumed was some sort of cannon, she dropped her pencil.

On each shoulder were what appeared to be wings. Small, sharp, yet majestic and full. Not like a bird, but … a butterfly.

"Eureka," she whispered, then ran from her bench, grabbed a mighty tome from the bookshelf, and charged through the throng of machines while hideous light from weak bulbs in the ceiling forced shadows from the automatons, painting the floor like posters for the wretched Grand Guignol Theatre, until she stood before the mechanical orange tree of the famous magician Robert-Houdin.

The box was Brazilian rosewood with Belgian velvet patched on each side. Brass work lined the edges and at each corner lay four tarnished spheres. A crankshaft sat in the back, to wind up a tree that, like Click and Clack, was clockwork. The orange tree was planted within a cherry wood box, green leaves thin and covered with dust.

"Fake," Vasilya said. The leaves would have long been dust themselves left alone in his workshop, and the trunk would be a withered dead thing.

But it was not.

Nothing in the workshop was dead. Or alive. But immortal in their own materials.

And soon, Vasilya thought, they'd be dissected and resurrected. If I am right.

She approached the faux orange tree, and searched around the base. There lay an ivory box the size of her forearm. Inside, an ornate pistol with a ridiculously large barrel, and a handkerchief.

She reread the section of Robert-Houdin's book, though it was a ridiculous account from a self-important man who liked to weave his life's story like a fairytale adventure.

"For the trick was not a trick at all, but a covenant made between myself, the gun, the tree, and the ring I'd placed in the muzzle. For years, sleight-of-hand artists have tried to remake and revise my fondest work and none have accessed the secret of making the butterflies rise, and release. But if you've ever witnessed me perform, the truth is self-evident!"

"Well, that was a pleasant load of nonsense," she said to the tree. "He talks in meandering circles." Click and Clack came near her feet while she traced the edge of a sharp leaf, recalling the reviews she'd read of Robert-Houdin's act in journals of magic on the bottom of the book shelf.

She traced all the leaves, ran her fingers across crack and seam, pressed and knocked at the base for a dusty hour as Click and Clack's bright eyes cast the box in Christmas shades of red and green. "There must be a trigger here," she said, tapping her lip with a dusty finger, "a way to release what's inside this tree. Because if I'm right, then I may have unlocked M. Fabergé's code."

But this was no toy, nor a simple puzzle box. This was the grand theatrical wonder of the world's greatest magician, one who prided himself on secrets and misdirection, of leaving the truth in plain sight and hiding it before the open eye. There were no hidden latches or buttons, hollow points, slip triggers or catches. It was a box. A box by some friend of Balk.

And hidden within it were two mechanical butterflies. According to his book, Robert-Houdin's coup de grace with the orange tree was this:

A jewel was taken from a lady of high station in the crowd, placed in a handkerchief that was fixed in a glass case while Robert-Houdin presented the magic pistol, which was then stuffed with the handkerchief and ring.

The owner was then asked to fire at the orange blossom tree. When the handkerchief was removed, the jewel was gone. The magician would then crank the box's ratchet lever. Not only did this move an internal disk with raised bumps against the metal comb, producing the same tiny but animated tones of a music box, it would also initiate the magic of the tree: blossoms emerged, then, actual fruit, real oranges, appeared as if hidden by the leaves. All the oranges were real, save for the one on top, which would split apart and, from within it, two mechanical butterflies would flutter into the air, carrying the handkerchief and, tied with a bow in its centre, the ring from the audience member.

It was a dazzling combination of sleight of hand and mechanical wizardry. And those butterflies were the key to M. Fabergé's drawing, Vasilya thought.

She turned the ratchet lever. One revolution, two ... but there was no music, no butterflies, just the rusty resistance of old gears.

"Charlatans," she said, then leaned against the silent life-sized figure of the Flute Player, resting her hands upon the automaton's knees. "Charlatans and chicanery."

Sleep pulled her, and the little lights of Click and Clack faded like dying starlight as the two creatures scurried on their own missions, hopefully having more success than she did.

"I'm sorry," she said, thinking of Monsieur Fabergé, face drained of sickness by a metallic mask. "I'm so sorry, I just need a little rest."

Boots cracked on cobble stones outside. She woke right before the door opened, and she startled back from the smooth and comforting lap of the Flute Player.

Colonel Balk strode in and Click and Clack hid amidst the creatures. "Sleeping while the rest of the world toils in darkness?" He walked fast through the workshop. "Days have costs, child. Every day I have to fight for your right to be here, the right for you to eat when German families starve. This is no vacation where you can rest when you want to! Days I've been fighting for you and what have you produced? Nothing! Nothing! Nothing!" He stamped his feet until fear replaced sleep in Vasilya's mind.

"I've been working," she said.

"Playing is more like it." He kicked the little nameless dolls on the floor hard enough that they vanished into the dark museum of lost contraptions. "Then where is my machine?"

"I've been here for days, just days..." she said, astonished.

There was a jagged anger in his voice, as if he had been stepping on tacks with every stomp. His voice lowered and chilled. "This war will not wait for you to build some fancy egg for a dead royal, child. And if you cannot produce a result soon, you, and the man who fathered you, will both be sharing the same grave. Now, show me something, anything, that can hold back the high command from ordering you dead for failing the state's trust in you!"

The warning made her blink, and despite herself she did not cower but stepped forward, breath even and words assured. "I've not slept an hour since I've been here. You've surrounded me with riddles. With creatures of smoke and mirror, of lies and subterfuge to build a creature that I've only barely begun to decipher."

"If you want pity," Colonel Balk said. "Find a church. Show me something. Anything, my god, anything!" His boot smacked the workshop floor. "Now!"

Her hands tensed into tiny fists. What's left? What else can I do? Her only hope was in that stupid box.

Fine.

With steps as stiff as any Prussian soldier, she marched back to the orange tree. She retrieved the pistol and the colonel grunted. "I doubt you'll be able to kill me with that."

"I need a jewel."

"We do not have time for games as you try to master Robert-Houdin's masterpiece."

"Time is wasting," she said, curtly. "Sir. A jewel."

The air between them tasted frosty in the morning glom. "I have no jewels," Balk said.

"Nor do I. And there's nothing here that fits."

"Child—"

"Maybe one of those proud medals on your chest? I cannot do the trick without something in the barrel. Trust me, it won't be damaged."

He grimaced.

She pouted. "Or should we let the war rage on another minute because you care more for your uniform, than the lives of proud, young German soldiers?"

His moustache twitched. Slowly, deliberately, his gloved hand removed the largest and sharpest looking metal. "This is the Iron Cross."

"Impressive." She plucked it from his hand. She wrapped it in her handkerchief and shoved it into the gun's large barrel.

"No," he said, surprising her. "No. It's not." He straightened up, adjusted his uniform, and nodded. "Let us see what secrets you've uncovered. And I hope they are resplendent, child."

Me too, she thought.

She turned toward the orange tree, but her mind was thrumming back to memories of her tiny workshop, of the very first birthday of Click and Clack, of how her hands hummed as she made the final adjustments to their tiny clockwork hearts, after weeks of watching their jewelled eyes fail to brighten, fail to … come alive.

In your hands. Monsieur Fabergé's voice rippled in her mind, the same hard tone he'd used to keep her at the work desk, focused and clear and unmoving as a statue until a calm came over here. It's all in your hands. Work past the pain, the ashen taste of failure. Focus and cradle your talent in your heart and mind, and let it run through your fingers, like a current in search of the infinite.

She pointed the pistol at the orange tree, cocked the pistol, and pulled the trigger.

She winced, but there was no bang, no pop, not even a crack.

Nothing. Not even the morning birds outside stirred away from their song thanks to the useless pistol.

"Unfortunate," Colonel Balk said. "I thought Carl was overstating the case of your … abilities. It is a shame he was wrong. For it will cost him." He turned and strode toward the door. "I will tell Captain Stenner he can have our machine. I can no longer let friendship control my judgement."

She cocked the gun again. As M. Fabergé's words echoed in her head. "The world is a puzzle. Every piece has its part, every part has its piece, and the picture is made of all of them. The trick is to see the picture as it should be, and then with your hands bring the pieces together. It's all in your hands."

She focused.

Like she had the night Click and Clack were born.

And she saw the pieces.

The world was a jigsaw scramble of parts and the jagged lines were etched in secret across their skin, invisible to the naked eye of most of the world. Untouchable but to the fewest hands.

"I am sorry, child," said the colonel, walking to the door.

The lines emerged, grey and white and thin in the air, but visible like the wire skeleton of an X-ray. And, there, hidden within the base of the orange tree's box, she saw … wings.

"Your father will be missed."

She held the gun with a warm hand. The handle melted into her skin, and locks and tumblers rolled out of their slumbering places to release the trigger, chamber the round.

"He was a good man."

She fired.

Thunderous force shattered the windows and the morning birds scattered with wild abandon into the morning's murk. Alarms sounded and were followed by Colonel Balk yelling to shut them off.

But Vasilya stayed still, a dark smoke from the pistol vanishing and revealing the orange tree. The jigsaw lines were gone. It was as it had been … though a tremor in the air tasted of something new.

She lowered the pistol, hand cold and sore.

Movement twitched from the orange blossom tree, and the plunk and plink of a music box disc fed Beethoven's Ninth Symphony into the air. White flowers bloomed from stalks, delicate as tissue and ornate as snowflakes on one's eyelash. Slowly, a fresh scent ate through the dust and wood, a natural freshness unlike sawdust or tinder, a citric aroma both sharp and sweet. From behind thick leaves, oranges appeared, one, two, three … a fourth one on top sat like a crown that split in half, and rising out of its innards …

A flutter of wings with the cadence of a music box.

Two butterflies held the cloth from the gun.

"My God," Colonel Balk said.

In the centre of the cloth, sat the Iron Cross.

"The drawing was a map," she said. "The components for the machine are hidden within these other machines, like matryoshka dolls." She took the medal from the cloth. Gently, the two butterflies landed on an orange.

She handed back the medal. "Is this enough to keep him alive?"

He took it, placing it back on his chest. He nodded. "For now, child. For now."

As guards rushed to the door Colonel Balk's angry voice barked at them to fix the glass immediately, and that if they weren't ready by the time he got back from Berlin they'd be hanging from the oaks as a feast for crows.

Vasilya approached the butterflies perched on the oranges. "Good morning, friends," she said, and lifted her hand to one. It flew into the rafters, and the other one followed. She was terrified it would vanish through the broken windows.

The last orange fell, the supposed real one. It sat there like a golden sun of treasure. She touched it, and it slipped and shattered upon the workshop floor, turning into a foul green dust. "Just as well I didn't enjoy a bite," she said, then jumped back. Something dripped down on the dust.

Oil from the butterflies, she thought. Could they be leaking?

But the colour was bright, and crimson.

She touched her nose and sniffed. Blood slicked her fingers. She wiped her nose with a handkerchief as both butterflies fluttered around the room, and landed on her shoulders, heavy as a five-pound sack of ball bearings. They were dusty gold and etched with fine designs she'd never seen. Their colours changed to electric blue. "Amazing," she whispered, looking at one, then the other. "Not even Mr. Wells or Tom Swift had such companions as I do. Robert-Houdin, you were truly the last great magician of your age." She lifted her hands to them, and each weighty marvel rested upon wrists.

Click and Clack ran up her dress, perching on her shoulders, staring at the butterflies, eyes blinking with anger and curiosity. "Do not be alarmed. These are our new friends." She sniffed. "And I think our strange family will continue to grow." She cleared her throat. "A family hidden from the world." That is, until one of the members was sent out to win a war.

Both mice hummed, then descended her skirt, as Vasilya returned to Monsieur Fabergé's drawing to see the hidden parts. Both butterflies flew up into the rafters in chaotic, electric circles, then vanished in the dark.

But she knew they would not leave.

CHAPTER THIRTEEN:

ALL WAR IS A STAGE

For Warren, the war had been a timeless slog of boredom punctuated by abject terror, but hunting deadroot with Alex convinced Warren he'd died on the battlefield and woken up in some strange land like John Carter on Mars.

For where else but on Mars would he be scourging abandoned battlefields for a flower that, according to Alex, sprouted out of the dead chest of the wounded, a white flower with a black bud. The flower he'd torn from his mouth, with roots like worms.

Madness makes more sense, Warren thought as he trolled through smashed trees, shooing flies with one hand, the remains of part of the Somme. This chunk of France was as barren as a dead whore's womb and just as rotten, but at least what was living couldn't hold a rifle. Void of value, the armies had fucked off to conquer another square inch of hell. Rats feasted on old corpses until their bellies were about to burst, so they paid Warren and Alex no mind until they punted them off the ruined remains of what looked like a British platoon.

"Like trolling through a cemetery," Warren muttered, amazed that he wasn't sick to his stomach as he kicked rat after rat into murky puddles. The smell should have made him gag, the sights should have torn his mind asunder, but it was horrifically normal. Banal, even.

"If not for such trolling you'd be dead," Alex said, pushing over a corpse whose entire backside danced with maggots.

"So you have a magic dead flower where your heart should be?"

"Yes. And you would, too, if you hadn't ripped it out. Now I don't know what you are."

Flies blurred his vision, so he swatted them. "And Rasputin thinks he can find enough of this flower to raise an army to beat both us and the Germans?"

"There is no 'us,' Warren. I may have died for the Canadian Corps, but I live now for the draug."

God, he thought, he sounds like a recruiting poster. Warren wanted to shake Alex's head clean of all of Rasputin's claptrap, but now was not the time. He was ignorant as shit about this whole freaking mess and if he was going to pull Alex out, he needed to know what he was dealing with. "How in the name of the Holy Ghost does a Russian end up on the Western Front?"

Flies swarmed Alex, who, unblinking, ignored them. "He was a soldier in the Russian Expeditionary Force that came to France a few years ago. Dragged from his home in Siberia and shoved in the Tzar's army to fight on even more foreign soil."

"And when did he eat a bullet?"

Alex looked at him as if he'd grown another head. "He's not like us. He's human, but other. We're … something else, really."

"And could you enlighten me about what that is?"

"Draug." The foreign word broke across Alex's lip like his mouth was full. "Undead creatures. Stronger than the living. Tougher too."

A trail of spent German 77mm shells, each bigger than a child's coffin, gave Warren focus. He followed them like dots on a scared treasure map. "But not tough enough to take a bullet in the skullcap."

"No, but just about anything else, we can walk away from and heal. Like you saw when I found you."

"And shot me."

Alex shoved a blasted tree trunk to find a mangled body that had turned to little more than bone and grey meat, little scars upon the top sockets where the eyes had long since been taken away by rodent teeth. "And saved you. But I'd never done dead root. So I couldn't change you, like Rasputin changed me."

No wonder his sense of obligation is so damn high to that Slavic conjuror. He regretted reading Alex only Westerns and not enough outlaw stories, stories where the villains are smart enough to see that honour and gratitude translate into slavery, and loyalty was often betrayal in waiting.

"He wants to end this war," Alex said.

"So do Generals Haig, and Ludendorff, and Fat Hindenburg. What makes Rasputin think he'll succeed where the bastards of Europe have failed?"

"Because he's not a politician," Alex said, coolly. Careful, Warren told himself. He's getting that puffed-up look when he'll have a tantrum. "He doesn't want more territory. He doesn't want revolution."

"What does he want?"

Alex glared at him as if he were an idiot. "Peace."

"Ok, peace. I like peace. I'll fight for it," and anything that gets me the hell out of here, he thought. "But, Alex, how is he going to get it? What's his angle?"

"The Army of the Dead." He pushed Warren's shoulder. "That's his *angle*. That's his goal. We get our army, we take out the others, and we tell those idiots in London and Berlin and Paris that it's over." There was a look in his eye that made Warren wince, the same kind Alex got in church when the preacher would be filling their hearts and minds with brimstone and damnation if you even thought about touching yourself or a girl, and the pot of gold just behind the gate of St. Peter if you died a sin-free and joyless slug. Alex was strong, smart when it came to lessons and copying whatever the schoolmarm taught, but he was a sucker for a grand story that made him part of some quest for a grail. He didn't see the way Father Gillies drooled at the young girls while discussing the specifics of sin, or smelled the rye on his breath when he was warning them about the demon alcohol. Warren had learned fast and quick that those most willing to cast aspersions on others were doing so to cast eyes off themselves.

Mother's rage had taught him that.

Poor Alex, he thought. You're downright enchanted with this mad fucker Rasputin. How the hell am I going break the spell and get you the hell out of here?

"Don't look at me like that," Alex said.

"Like what?"

"Like you did when I told you I was signing up, like you were searching for a polite way to tell me I was stupid or crazy."

"You're neither. I just don't get—"

"Don't get what?"

He dragged the edge of his boot on the mouth of a dead shell to scrape off the muck. "We've been out here for days, hunting for this stuff. How are we going to find enough to make an army? You'd told me deadroot, once found, needs to be planted in a freshly killed soldier." God, he thought, this shit coming out of my mouth ain't worth a dime novel. "If it takes weeks to find one, how can you find enough to make an army?"

Alex's mouth was about to spout off, but his face bunched up. "You just have to trust me—"

"Shit, he hasn't told you, has he?"

"—like I trust Rasputin, Warren. Has he lied to me about being what we are? What we can do? About deadroot and his … pet below the surface? No! All of it is real! Real as this nightmare that has us trapped. So stop looking at me like I don't know what the hell I'm doing! You're not the one with all the answers, you know."

And, against all odds, in their own, private patch of hell, Warren laughed.

"What the devil is so funny?"

"You are! You make it sound like I just told you Father Christmas didn't exist when, truth is, you told me that he does. That's funny, Alex."

He laughed and laughed until finally, against the odds, Alex began to fight a smile. "I'm sorry. All of this is overwhelming. And to think that … life can come of death. It's astounding."

Alex nodded, swallowing his smile. "And so is Rasputin's temper. We should get back to work."

Grey night became grey morning. On they foraged, Warren being gentle with his questions. Amidst the field of crows and rats feasting on the mutilated dead, Warren looked in shell holes. "Say, if you wait too long after death, you can't give anybody deadroot. Timing is kind of important?"

Alex flicked stray maggots from his fingers. "Yes. It must be moments. Why?"

In Warren's pocket, the shark tooth warmed his filthy palm. I'm sorry, Tik, he thought, then muttered a godless prayer, hoping he was okay in whatever afterlife his people believed in. If anyone deserved to keep fighting in this war, Warren thought, it's you, big man, not a second-rate lumberjack and remittance man who socked a soldier in a drunken rage and was given no real damn choice in the matter. "No reason, Alex. Come on. This magical root won't find itself."

They hunted, fruitlessly, but talked.

Warren discovered that Graves was Rasputin's second-in-command. The second to be brought back with deadroot, after Alex. He'd been a British dock worker. "He likes to fight," Alex said. "And even Rasputin has a hard time controlling him."

"Controlling?" Warren bristled at the word. "How? You said he's not a draug or whatever."

"No. He's more like a sorcerer."

This was getting insane, until Warren recalled his body freezing when Alex had given him a command in the tunnel. "How does this sorcerer control folk?"

Guilt washed over Alex's face. "The one who brings you back to life has an … influence. On you."

"Is that right?" Anger coiled, then snapped like a match below dry kindling.

"Warren."

"So, you have been influencing me?"

"Just to save your life."

"Or make me look like a fool? Make me do anything you want?!" He grabbed Alex hard. "Now I'm a goddamn slave?" Terror washed over Alex's eyes. "I was better off dead!"

"Let go."

The two words ran through him like mercury. "Nnn. Nnn. No." Warren fought back, and his blood itched then burned.

"If you keep fighting, you will die," Alex said, gently, sadly. "Please, Warren. Let go."

Grey froth covered his lips and tasted of mud and ash. Shaking, Warren swallowed the hideous fizzle when a dagger-edged scream cut through him. He fell in a heap at his brother's feet, every nerve crippled.

"I'm sorry, Warren, I don't like this—"

Warren wiped the grey froth from his mouth.

"I promise, I won't—"

And, like a primed and ready mortar, Warren's big right hand shot up and cracked Alex under the chin. When Alex staggered back, Warren charged over the jagged mud, tackled his brother and scrambled his knees on his brother's shoulders, and covered his mouth. "Listen, and listen good. You so much as even think of 'influencing' me, as you call it, and I will tan your hide, hell and heaven be damned. You got me?"

Alex nodded, eyes caught between angry and sad. Warren took his hand off his mouth. "Jackass," Alex said, then shoved him off like tossing off a pillow.

Warren hit the mud, two feet away. "Yeah, but a free jackass. And don't you forget it."

Alex dusted himself off while anger and righteous pain dissipated from Warren's sore body. Thoughts calmed, and a truth emerged from a buried plot in Warren's mind. Rasputin. He'll have an army under his influence. A sorcerer's command. He could lead them all into suicide battles and none of them could retreat. As shitty as Lieutenant Christopher was, he knew a hopeless mess when he saw it and would pull them out of the grease fire before it was too late. And somehow Warren didn't think Rasputin would be "leading from the front."

"Warren! I found it!"

Alex had run to a knotted tree of crooked branches. Broken and mangled on its limbs was the corpse of a soldier, a strange puppet with its strings tied to give it an inhuman show. From his chest, above his heart, was a beautiful white flower. At the centre sat a black bud with a silver pattern that Warren swore was a skull.

Alex smiled.

And a shot cracked through the air.

CHAPTER FOURTEEN:

HIDDEN TREASURES AND SECRET TRAPS

Sleep was a long-lost relative Vasilya could barely recognize by name. In a hot haze, as the moon chased the sun outside the workshop, she began the sad art of dismembering the world's greatest inventions, Click and Clack on her shoulder, jewelled eyes providing the light by which she worked. They cast the entire world into a strange Christmas relief despite the stuffy summer weather. And high above, the ornate iron butterflies of Robert-Houdin fluttered and chased each other. Vasilya had long given up any fear that they would run. They'd become attached to her as she had to them, distant but close until she allowed Click and Clack to sleep before winding them up.

As the mice slept, the butterflies would flutter, gentle motors carrying the hum of metallic hive, and dance around her head, each one a marvel of skill that almost rivalled that of Monsieur Fabergé. But there was little time to enjoy them, knowing that, sooner or later, they would be used by her hands to create something monstrous.

Furiously, she worked to unravel the secrets of the mechanical beasts, automatons, and magical works before her, and she let her hands do the guiding.

"It's in your hands now," Monsieur Fabergé had said, voice a wet rattle as she led him to the hospital with their documents, terrified for his health and of the stares of the Germans. "Let them be your compass for the work ahead. They will lead you past where all others fail." It was a crumb of a compliment, but she'd devoured it as if starved.

Stop daydreaming, she told herself. We have work to do. Sighing, Vasilya rubbed sweat and dust from her forehead and then resumed letting her fingers trace, tamper, caress and prod the mechanical wonders from around the world.

And then began an orgy of disassembly.

Hesitant at first, the unlocking of mystery gave way to the joy of discovery, to the uncovering of hidden masterpieces, of wonders laid bare before her eyes and hands in a rush.

From the Turkish Chess Player, there was a mechanical mind, a puzzle brain of a thousand brass gears.

From Psycho the dancing midget, there lay an impressive dynamo heart, a prototype of an internal combustion engine that took up his entire belly.

But that morning, as blood itched and teeth chewed nails to ragged, bloody stumps, Vasilya uncovered the string that would tie them all together.

She stood before the silent Flute Player. Her perfect figure, smooth beauty and graceful poise would have impressed even Mother.

Vasilya lifted her hands, gulping hot air and blinking away the sweat, sniffing in what she'd hoped was not blood.

Her fingers formed a square. Focus, she told herself, focus. She'd tried this trick a few times with smaller pieces, but the Flute Player was almost as big as the Turk. And she had long suspected that, despite the refutations of investigators, the secret to the Turk's genius lay not with sleight of hand or a pygmy within the chess table at its feet, but within his mind. A bullet hole in the Turk's spine, perhaps from Colonel Balk's overzealous compatriots, had allowed her to access the trigger for releasing the puzzle brain. But the Flute Player was as fine and whole as when she'd been first crafted, a sculpture seemingly carved straight out of soft white wood.

Concentrating her attention, ignoring her own ragged breath, Vasilya focused her mind's eye within the folds of her fingers, a prism to block out the rest of the moving world, and let her gaze soften into a heady glare where all that was before her was the Flute Player's beautiful face.

Then, her breath dampened.

Sparks filled the little square, as if lightning bugs had become trapped on a screen. One small bristle of light. Then a bigger flash. Then two. Until the square was abuzz with the radiance of burning magnesium. Click and Clack scattered into the folds of her stained work apron, but Vasilya peered through the curtain of bubbling light:

There stood the Flute Player, illuminated as no other human being had seen it. She was alive in that sprightly lit screen, a creature of wild beauty and silent movement, a Cinderella of sparks.

Beneath her frame, sunk within her polished body, emerged a system of wires the likes of which Vasilya could not have dreamed. A spider web of copper tubes leading to a black space where her heart was …

"Gone," Vasilya said in clenched teeth, and tasted blood before the screen shook. "No, not now!"

Her body tensed, face dribbling bright dollops of blood on her apron, but the sparks faded, the little stars died, until her finger snapped back and she fell before the Flute Player.

She wiped a red smear from her nose across her forearm. "So the pretty thing thinks she can hide her secrets from me." She stood, swaying. "Enjoy your little victory, princess. I don't think I need your heart anyway."

Vasilya stumbled to the work table to examine the dynamo heart of Psycho and compare it to the fragment she'd traced of the original drawing for M. Fabergé's nameless war machine.

The glass encased clock on her work desk ticked louder than usual. She normally never gave it a thought, except as a warning bell for the colonel's daily visit.

Which was about to happen in three, two, one—

The door did not crack open.

She coughed. "Well, maybe this clockwork Prussian wasn't forged at the Krupp factory after all," she said, laughing a bit louder and longer than normal. She gripped the jagged heart of Psycho, the dancing midget.

It was a fool's heart. Meant to look like a technical marvel of gears and servos, a phoney dynamo. Because Psycho, like so many of these worlds of wonder, was really manipulated by a complex of tomfoolery, sleight of hand, ignorant audiences, and air tubes.

But in Vasilya's mind and hands, as per M. Fabergé's instructions, they were becoming part and parcel of a creature greater than the sum of their parts. Maybe even this faux heart could be a tool of creation.

I can make them work, she thought, caressing the dead heart of the lifeless midget. "I can make them live. Like Frankenstein's creation … oh god," she dropped the heart and gripped her leaking nose. "I must be going mad." The butterflies fluttered down before her. "You'd tell me if I'd lost my faculties, wouldn't you, my friends?" They swam in the air and retreated to their dark nest when the door swung open and Colonel Balk appeared.

"You're late," she said. "I worried that the world was tilting out of control."

His countenance, usually as tightly wound as a coiled spring, was twitching like he had palsy. "General Hindenburg wishes to see a demonstration by the end of this week."

Laughter cackled from her and fresh blood ran down her face. "I hope you know what day it is, because I don't!"

"It does not have to be complete. The armaments can wait. But if we cannot show him—"

She waved away his words with a trembling hand. "I know, I know, you'll kill Monsieur Fabergé. And me. And what will it bring you? Nothing. Not victory. Germany will be in the hands of the French you've been murdering for four years, along with my people. So stop thinking you have me crushed under your thumb, Colonel. No one can build this contraption but me. It's in my hands, after all." She smiled, then made the box with her fingers and gazed at the colonel. "I wonder if you have anything of value hidden behind that rotten moustache I could use. I mean, what's left of you. One eye, one arm, if I take too much your symmetry would be as ugly as a squashed egg." She sniff-laughed.

The colonel raised his chin. "You're sick."

She dropped her hands, wiping away more blood. "I don't have time to be sick, Colonel. I have a war to win. Now, if you'll excuse me, I have to gather my materials for the general." The colonel's face was covered in swarming mosquitoes. "I think we have a hive in here. Why don't you shoo them away, huh? Goodnight, Colonel."

She turned, and her body turned to steel. In gravity's grip, she fell to the floor as mosquitoes swirled around her vision, blocking it like her sparks did.

"Child?" she heard the colonel say, tiny and distant. "My god, what have I done?"

CHAPTER FIFTEEN:

A WAR OF ONE'S OWN

Warren and Alex hit the jagged ground and scrambled for cover amidst the corpses and churned tree trunks, using them as sand bags while more rifle rounds crackled over them. Thank god this shit was a lousy shot, Warren thought as he shoved a bunch of bodies up to block the incoming shots.

Alex was lying flat on his back, gripping his chest.

"Shit," Warren said, "are you all right?"

Alex nodded, then shoved two fingers into the gory would in his chest, and yanked out the crunched round. "Lee-Enfield."

"The fucking British are shooting at us?"

"Must be a raid recce," Alex said. As he patted down the wound, Warren's jaw hit the ground. The damn thing closed up as if it were a button hole that vanished into the grey flesh.

"Fuckers probably have rifle grenades," Warren said. "We can't just sit here. Can we?"

Alex shrugged. "Never been hit by one. Don't much care to try my luck now."

They scanned behind them for a retreat line to the wormhole they'd emerged from. Fifty yards of open hell and bad running ground looked back at them.

"I think we can make it," Warren said. "Maybe use these old boys for shields."

"You think like one gory penny dreadful, you know that?"

"Do you have a better idea, Alex? I mean, besides getting shot, again?"

Alex grimaced. "I'm not going without that deadroot. And we can't waste time. They don't last forever."

"Then think of something, you're the hero, remember?"

Alex looked at him as if he were the dumbest son of a bitch to fall off the turnip truck. "Surrender."

Now he was talking common sense, Warren thought. Then another thought bit him. "And then what?"

"They're not our army anymore, Warren."

An emptiness sapped Warren's strength. Alex's face was rock hard sincerity and stupidity. Warren had no love for the British. They could be either the dumbest shits who ever played cards, or the most arrogant bastards to be tossed out of Oxford. But they were allies.

But not to Alex.

Clearer than his words on the subject, Warren realized the cold hard truth that Alex was in a darker war. It had its own rules. Its own enemies. Rasputin spoke of secret societies and royal powers and it all sounded like a bit much, but here he was with his dead brother, wandering a patch of hell, the earth having rumbled with the movements of a creature beneath the roots of the earth.

And something about the way his brother had looked under the gaze of Rasputin made it clear that this war, their war, was one even worse than the one Alex had died for, the one Warren had ignored. There was no return home.

Unless that Russian shit heel was buried deep. And it would be a good death to free Alex from the little Caesar with the mesmeric glare.

"Fine," Warren said. "But let me handle it. There's likely two of them. Follow my lead, ok?"

Alex's face soured. "It's my plan. You follow my lead."

Dirt and corpse meat exploded before them. Warren coughed out what he swallowed, and before he could change his brother's mind, Alex had torn a handkerchief from inside his jacket and was waving it shouting. "Surrender! We surrender! Canadian Corps members. We surrender!"

Amazingly, they didn't blow him to shit. Instead, a Scottish accent filled the space between them. "Both of you, hands up, move forward. And fast, huh? Go!"

Warren stood. They marched slow, past the corpse tree with fresh deadroot blossoming from a corpse chest, hands up like highwaymen captured by the constabulary in a dime novel. Whatever Alex had planned, Warren knew death would follow. The cold assuredness in his eye spoke more than he could ever say.

They approached a pine casket, torn up like a dog's chasing stick. "That's far enough," said the voice from the casket. "Stay right there."

Seemingly out of the ground itself emerged a Tommy, Lee-Enfield trained on them. It was a slit trench, built for one. But the voice was pure Glasgow. "So why in the name of damnation are two colonials fucking around on my stage?"

"Lost from our battalion in a raid," Alex said, earnestly, like when he was trying to lie to Mother. "German shell in the ground, we thought it was a dud, but it went off. We woke up here."

The Tommy trained the gun on Warren. "So you woke up and decided to start pulling apart the dead for a bit of sport? I nay think so." He pointed the gun at Alex. "And you took a rifle shot that should have killed a wild hart." He laughed. "I know the dead when I see them." The rifle shook in his hands. "You're turncoats, hunting corpses to feed the tallow machine."

Shell-shocked son of a bitch, Warren thought. The tallow machine was one of the nightmare rumours you heard in the trenches. With the British blockade, the Huns were low on supplies of everything. So, they were taking corpses and melting them down to oils and fats to use for their artillery. It was macabre nonsense to scare the stupid and exhausted.

And it was obviously reality for this shell-shocked lunatic.

"Bastards!" said the Scot "I leave for one minute and you've torn my new theatre to shreds! I should kill you where you stand!" He loaded the chamber so fast Warren thought they were goners. Alex can't deal with the mad, he's too damn earnest. This lost soul won't let us close enough to finish him.

Mad logic was close to drunk logic, and Warren had talked him and Tik's way out of enough bar room brawls and alley fights to play this hand they had been dealt.

"Theatre?" Warren said, looking back at the corpse tree. "That was your theatre?"

The Scot nodded. "And you ruined it!"

"I had no idea. It was so lifelike. Better than the Grand Guignol."

"Sacrilege!" said the Scot. "There is no better theatre!"

"Shut up," Alex whispered.

"I meant no disrespect to the great circus of the macabre," Warren said. "I'm an admirer. I saw it once. A six-play show that ended with a version of *Titus Andronicus*. It was a nightmare come to life!"

The Scot nodded. "I ... I played the gravedigger in the *Rape of Juliet*."

Sick bastard, Warren thought, but kept a smile. "I'm afraid I missed it. And I am sorry we ruined your new theatre. Are you still performing?"

"Of course!" the Scot screamed. "I won't let the Hun ruin the greatest show in France! Help me get my work back in place and I'll show you colonials what real theatre is all about!"

CHAPTER SIXTEEN:

THE WOE OF TALENT

She swam in a sea of sparkles. Above her, rings of light ran over a wire. She gripped a luminescent ring, and her body charged through the crackling sea like a steed, everything electric and wild, the rush of energy through her skin, flesh, and bone. Never had she felt so alive. Never had she wanted just to run so fast and free. Fast as a lightning bolt, quick as a current, powerful and free amongst a world of glowing stars.

A forge roared behind her, a ballast-scream unlike anything she'd ever heard. As if an entire factory was consumed with fire and bellowed out the dead through a hole in the wall—

Vasilya turned her head.

A black speck in the far distance was charging itself through the stars. Its movements were simian, but the body mechanical, and huge. A monster that grew as it surged up the wire Vasilya was racing. A nameless beast.

She turned, and swam with one hand, but she could not increase the speed of the ring she held.

The creature was closing.

And there was no mistake about its hideous form.

It was the Nameless beast, tearing through space, a rancid monster of metal and wood. Its hands swung on the wire, climbing forward as its fists sparked wild with current, an industrial roar from its belly. The twin butterflies sat on its massive shoulders, fluttering hard to give it speed and direction.

Its massive gauntlet reached for Vasilya.

"No!" Her hands shook on the brass ring.

The gauntlet enveloped her body, closing in around her neck.

"Release me!"

The grip was total.

"Let go!"

The world hummed like a Tesla coil before darkness flashed into light—

Cold and hard, the world rushed, than settled in: she was on a cot, immobilized as if wearing an iron lung, and Colonel Balk was gripping her forehead, fingers like a massive spider. The glove was off.

"Colonel—"

"Silence!" But on the edge of his word was concern, not anger. "Be still. Just … be still."

Coolness descended, like the first snow of winter, gentle dusts of relief that kissed her skin and eased deeper into her mind. A coil of nerves in her spine, one she had ignored through the hard nights and days, began to relax. Each breath softened from the iron-flecked wheeze she'd woken with.

"That's it," Colonel Balk said, voice strong and deep but low like a distant current, spider grip still on her head. "Let each breath strengthen the other. Taste the air. Let it run deep in your roots."

She did, until the aches and pains that had become her armour since arriving in the workshop rusted away, leaving her weak, but free and light.

"Now," he said. "Take a long, deep breath, as if your belly were a bottomless well, and then breathe out as hard as you can until I say stop."

She did as instructed, fearing she'd cough on the slick taste of blood that had dripped down her throat the past few days.

But the breath was long and rich and tasted like dew and warm herbs. So strange was the sensation that he had to remind her to keep breathing. She did, and, when she'd filled herself up, she exhaled.

"Good," said the colonel. "Be strong with that breath. Keep going."

Pain nagged her throat and she grunted.

His voice hardened. "Don't stop."

She was coughing outward and didn't want to continue.

"Keep at it."

She shook her head and his fingers became like iron rivets.

"Do not stop! Harder, breathe out harder. Don't be a coward now. Breathe!"

Malice and pain rocked her, but she'd show him. She pushed until her face was a red balloon.

Stabbing pains filled her chest, as if something was tangled in there and was becoming unravelled.

His spider grip tightened. "That's it!"

Yellow smoke passed by her lips that tasted as foul as a corpse smells.

"Keep going."

Gagging, she pressed forward until the yellow smoke emptied itself from her lungs.

His fingers detached and she gasped. He covered her mouth with her weak hand. The yellow mist swirled, searching, descending. "You don't want to let that poison back in. Cover your mouth!" She did.

Colonel Balk's old, scarred hand grasped the yellow sickness dancing in the air like a jellyfish, his face bitter and angry as always, while he muttered strange words beneath his moustache. Words that carried a distinctly non-German cadence. The yellow swirls entangled his fingers like thorns of smoke, when the colonel snapped his fist closed and muttered a word. The smoke shook as if it were a strangled snake. "Next!"

He opened his hand and the smoke sparked, and vanished.

He exhaled hard himself.

"What was—"

"Poison," Colonel Balk said. "And a rather insidious one at that."

"Language?" she said, gasping for air. "That was a Baltic language … Latvian. But you're Baltic German?"

He blew off invisible flecks from his hand, thick ropes of scars around his own flesh like chords of hemp. "My family only moved away from the Western Russian Empire fifty years ago, during the famine of Courland." He fixed his tunic. "My mother was Latvian. Anyway, my family tree is of no importance now. We have an assassin on the grounds, one who clearly knows of your existence and talent. I've arrested the guards and had them replaced. When I find the backstabbing coward who did this—"

"Where am I?" The room she was in was almost too small for the both of them. "Am I still near the workshop?" Oh god, she thought. Click and Clack were probably ruining her work without her there to keep them in line. And the butterflies. She pulled the rough wool blanket off her, but it made her arm shake.

He placed it back. "Don't be stupid."

"I'm not stupid," she said. "I'm the girl who will win the war." She laughed.

"You're exhausted," he said, then fitted his black glove on, pulling it in place with his teeth until it was tight and smooth and hid the mighty scars. "And light-headed, and talking nonsense."

"And I suppose what you did was scientific common sense."

The sound out of him was a stifled growl.

"What is happening, Colonel?"

He wiped down his moustache with his shiny black hand. "Someone dusted my collection of mechanical devices with a poison. Odourless. Tasteless. I've had it removed but—"

"It made me bleed?"

He sighed. "No. You did that. All talents have a price, child. And yours requires payment in blood."

She pulled the wool closer to her chin, as pieces fell into place the way a puzzle made of rain became a clear, reflective pool. "So, it's your talent keeping Monsieur Fabergé alive?"

He nodded. "And the price is quite high, as well."

"That ridiculous contraption was just a ruse?"

"Made of derelict gas equipment and a spare magic box from Robert-Houdin, with some welded dials and tubes for good measure."

Her whole body sighed as whispers escaped her smile. "You're a magician and charlatan, too?"

He smiled back with smug satisfaction. "It fooled even the talented Vasilya Savorov."

She grimaced, until a thought dawned. "You're keeping him alive," she said. "Why didn't you just do what you did—" And it was clear. Why the colonel needed the illusion of the machine. "If the army knew of your talent—"

He raised his hand. "The Reich Akademie, The Germanic wing of the Theosophical Society, recognized my talents and removed me from the front. However, to keep the army from abusing what they view as a strategic resource, a ruse was needed. And my people crave what you have far more than I, the ability to meld life and machine. A man such as I, a healer? If the army knew of my talents, they would lose sight of the bigger picture and drag me to the front, or to a Faber laboratory where I'd be, more or less, a rat for testing in a medical prison, trying to wield what I can do to machine and man."

He shook his head.

"They tried?" she said. "They tried to use you like me?"

He shook his head. "I was not used. I served the Academie. And the results were … unsuccessful." He coughed. "But I did not survive the battle of La Manse to have my remaining pieces torn apart by men with no inkling of what they are messing with."

"You heal?"

"And you build. And someone tried to poison your efforts, perhaps to reveal mine. We've come close to the edge of failure, child. For a moment you were lost even to what little art I have left."

The compassion in his voice surprised even her. The colonel read her expression and replaced concern with the armour of duty. "Vigilance is now our standard. And yet we must obey the law of depreciating returns. I cannot risk losing you to over-exhaustion again. You'll be supplied with a specially selected labourer to ease the burden." He swallowed hard. "I informed the general that we were delayed for a month, but we could soon—"

"Colonel," she said, fatigue fighting with the image in her head. "I can build it. In a week."

"Don't be mad, child. You almost died with—"

She shook away his concern, breathing easier, head clearing as she focused on the hideous image in her mind. "I will draw up the specification for others to weld. You can give them each such a tiny piece that they won't know the sum of their parts. Then I'll put the pieces together. Can that be done?"

He calculated things behind his eyelid for a half dozen heart beats. "Yes. But I still insist you have help in the workshop."

"As you wish, Colonel." She yawned. "But I'd rather start sooner than later." More time spent in that workshop, with the thing in her mind that she would turn into reality ... the idea bristled with dread.

Colonel Balk strode off to a painful-looking wooden chair in the corner of the small, windowless room that faced a door. "Sleep. Rest. Tomorrow we start again."

He drew his pistol, eyes on the door.

Sleep claimed her before she could say anything else, and the thank you for saving her life drowned in the onslaught of sleep.

CHAPTER SEVENTEEN:

BEHOLD THE GARDEN

Warren was skating on lies as thin as dimes talking to the Scot called Marlow about the Grand Guignol, while Alex was itching for a moment when the shell-shocked soldier would finally drop his guard.

"I spent three seasons as master of the eye poke trick," Marlow said. "Hunting Parisian butcher shops for the very best goat's heads. We used their eyes, you know."

"We all thought it was real!" Warren said and Marlow laughed, eyes flittering from brother to brother as they approached the desecrated graveyard the loony had turned into his own theatre. "Rumour was, the police chief in Paris allowed you to use criminals as the victims."

Marlow howled. "Grand, that! We sold the illusion as reality too well! But I've got something even better in store. Something that will make them regret ever firing me! My own Theatre of the Macabre! Here, in No-Man's Land. We'll hold performances under the stars, and for all the snipers to see. Vignettes taken from the classics made real! Because our bounty of corpses will never run dry!"

Alex's hand gripped the bayonet.

"But first we need the bouquet," Marlow said, "and I'll wager I'll need your hands and arms to harvest them."

"Bouquet?" Warren said, shooting Alex a glance to steady his killing hand.

"You know, the one you boys were staring at before I shot you!" He pointed at the tree-hanging corpse with the deadroot coming through its chest. "Lovely, aren't they? And the smell is hypnotic." He pinched his nose twice. "My first scene is a wedding and I need flowers and those damned ones are the only kind I've found."

Warren said quickly. "You mean, there are others?"

"Hell yes! Scads of them!"

Alex's hand retreated from the handle and dove into his pockets. "Where?"

"Oh, that would be telling," Marlow said, chuckling. "Come thither, my thespian soldiers. And I will show you the harvest of war the likes of which will make it the eighth wonder of the world. Come thither!"

He ran across the scared battlefield as if it were a grassy knoll, and they followed, far enough behind to whisper each other.

"He's insane. And he's dragging us away from the deadroot."

"He might be leading us to more."

"He doesn't know what he has, and Rasputin is waiting."

"Do you want us to go back telling him that we passed on the opportunity to find a harvest of this stuff? Do you think he'll hand out a medal for that?"

Alex grunted. "The bastard shot me."

"You shot me. At least he didn't kill you, which, as you might have noticed, doesn't seem to bother him. Come on, Alex. He's as lost a soul as there is in this world. He'll be dead in a few days from mucking about with gangrene corpses."

"Soft spot for a lost soul, huh? Why do you care?"

Warren gritted his teeth. "I see me in him." It was true. The more Marlow talked, the more Warren smelled a kindred spirit, a remittance man and wanderer, living by wits and small crimes, master of his own destiny even if it led him nowhere but the next hot meal or a cold stone bed. And gutted and lost on the plains of battle.

"You can't save him," Alex said.

"That doesn't mean I need to kill him."

"You're not weak like that. He's a rabid dog," Alex said, voice harder, sharper. "He let the war ruin him. We'd be putting him out of his misery."

"He doesn't look miserable to me."

Alex shook his head. "I'll follow him for now, but he's dead for what he did to me. And he won't come back."

There was a stubborn streak in Alex that was as strong as his body and Warren stopped wasting his breath. Fine, little brother, be bold and talk like you've read Darwin and know how the whole big bad world functions. "Remember that, brother, when someone stronger than you thinks they know what's best, and puts a knife in your back and calls it a favour."

He ran harder, chasing Marlow, and Alex stayed a few steps behind. Warren hoped his point had stuck in Alex's thick head, and prayed he hadn't shouldered his rifle to prove his point.

Following Marlow, the world seemed to cool. Corpses and rats began to disappear from the landscape. Churned earth led to the shattered remains of a forest, a ring of broken trees. Acrid stenches the likes of which Warren had no memory of filled their noses until Alex ran up beside him ... and they both covered their mouths.

Marlow stopped before the ring of trees and sniffed in deep. "Ah, c'est *magnifique!* Glorious. Can you taste it, boys?" He cleared his throat. "The flowers that sleep by night, opened their gentle eyes and turned them to the day. The light, creation's mind, was everywhere, and all things owned its power."

Warren stopped, Marlow on his right, Alex on his left. "Shakespeare?"

"Dickens! Good god, man. Don't you know the masters when you hear them?"

"No," Alex snorted. "Unless the master is Edgar Rice Burroughs."

"Burroughs." Marlow glared at Warren with rank disgust. "I thought you were cultured."

"A childhood favourite," Warren said, and let Marlow look away before drilling Alex's shoulder.

"Behold the Garden." Marlow inhaled deep, then turned and gripped Alex's shirt. "Promise me one thing, my thespians. You won't tell anyone else about this place. It's truly a wonder and I just know Bloody Haig and the Bosch would love to trample it down."

Alex crossed his heart. "I promise. Haig will never know of this place." When Marlow turned, Alex's face was pure malice.

Marlow's hand rested on Warren's shoulder. "Promise."

"I promise we won't let your flowers fall in the wrong hands." Marlow's jaw was shaking spit from his brown teeth. The mad old hermit was holding on by a thin tether. "I promise. No ill will come of your kindness to us."

He smacked Warren's shoulders twice. "Grand! Now, my fair guests, allow me to introduce to you, the greatest wonder of the modern world." He walked between the dead trees, brittle branches crunching under his torn boots. They followed.

And emerged at a crater.

"May I present to you, the Swollen Garden of Abaddon."

It was the size of a hundred shell holes, as if an entire battery had targeted this spot to obliterate a pit from hell.

But it wasn't filled with water and mud.

Bodies, hundreds of them, stuffed the crater.

"No smell," was all Warren could mutter at the mutilated, silent picture of rotting humanity that spread out before him. It should have stunk for miles, there should have been vultures circling and a stench so foul it would waste away a man to shadow, a decaying stench of a slaughterhouse gone to seed, but there was nothing. Just a wild sweetness.

"It's the roses," said Marlow, smiling. "Look. Over their hearts." And, sure enough, emerging from the chests of the dead were lines and lines of deadroot, scores of it, amidst the carnage of shattered skulls and once-human material. Remains of tents, and what looked like mutilated bedpans, littered the scene.

"It was a hospital," Alex said. "They shelled a hospital." But his eyes were transfixed by the deadroot that blossomed below, enough for a small army.

Marlow nodded, and for a moment, staring at the macabre scene, he stopped shaking. "Clearing station. But swollen like an infected limb. I was in No-Man's Land. Stretcher bearing for the first fallen when I heard the mouth of hell scream. We'd just received a massive amount of casualties. Everything was blood and cries and maggots and by the time I got back … dead. Everything. Everyone. Just me left. Just me and the garden for my theatre. Which reminds me."

Marlow drew an officer's pistol and shot Warren point blank in the shoulder. The pain was uncanny as he snapped back on to the ground, unable to move. Another shot fired out and hit Alex in the back, shoving him over the lip of the crater.

Marlow's shaking hand snaked around Warren's ankle. "It seems only fitting, since you ruined two of my actors, that you become their replacement. But I think you need to swell some for the coup de grace I have planned. Guh!" He tossed Warren like a sack of flower into the air, descending into the pit of Abaddon, crashing into a bloom of corpses, the smell of deadroot like wine in his nose. Alex was already arm deep in the corpses. "Welcome to my troupe, boys. Be ready for our first performance at midnight, by the light of harvest moon."

Marlow whistled a hymn and vanished from the pit's edge as Warren struggled in pain to move. "Alex," he grunted from clenched teeth. "Alex, are you—"

"Fine," Alex rejoined. "No thanks to you. Falling for this mad hermit. I swear, your sympathy for the shit heels of the underclass—"

"Shut up! Can you move?"

"Not yet. Our hearts are prone to shock and pain but I'll be moving soon. And when I can, I'm going to tear out that madman's kidney and—"

Then, they heard it. A scurry beneath them like an army of tiny feet marching anywhere and everywhere. "Jesus," Warren said. "Rats."

Alex snickered. "So what? Let them chew us for a while. We're draugs."

"I'm not! My shoulder's on fire!

"But my flesh will just grow—"

A dozen beady eyes burst from torn, swollen bellies, darted from dark holes in skulls, scurried past exposed rib cages like thin convicts from jail. The feral eyes were multiplying. Dozens became hundreds, hundreds grew into thousands. Warren and Alex sat in a rat feast, paralyzed. "We won't have anything left to grow back if we don't move now." Warren struggled, fingers twitching but arms still stuck, as the black hole in his chest mended. A rat jammed its nose in the wound and chewed. "Ow! Miserable shit!"

Anger and instinct burst and he dug his teeth into the coarse, muddy fur and flesh, shaking his neck like a wild dog with prey, then spitting out the foul greasy flavour.

"One down," he screamed, "a million to go!"

Alex thrashed, as if his body was starting to respond to his brain while rats poured over each other to the fresh meat. Warren followed suit, limbs starting to move as a dozen teeth sunk into his flesh. "Goddamn it, you didn't say we could still feel pain like this."

"Stop being such a woman!" Alex said, tossing a handful off, only to have another handful on.

Warren rolled on greasy, red corpse meat, hoping to lose them off his back, but their teeth and claws were sinking in like barbed wire. The army of rats was relentless. Shortly, Warren and Alex were covered in rat skin coats, dead blood dripping from a hundred wounds.

"I won't die like this!" Alex said, tossing around in anger, rats flying free and new ones taking their place. "Gah!" he slipped and a mass of vermin covered him. Squeals of the fetid creatures filled the air like merciless grind of a rusty wheel.

"Alex!" Warren yelled, and dove for his brother, tearing at the wall of rats that seemed to have no bottom. They thrashed hopelessly. The rats drowned their heads and dug into soft cheek, mouth and eye—

A guttural roar made the pit and prey tremble.

The sickening symphony of a million squealing rats filled the crater as the critters ran for the edges with mouthfuls of Warren and Alex. Warren gripped his mangled head as sickly flesh began knitting itself back into place, like bugs were working his wounds over. He gave Alex his arm, but Alex refused it, scuttling to his feet on his own, both men covered in gore.

"What the hell was that sound?" Warren said.

"Who cares?" Alex shoved fistfuls of dead root into his torn shirt. "Grab as much as you can!"

"Or we could get out of this pit and come back later."

"Ah, there's the coward I know and love. How droll."

"Did you hear that sound? What the hell can scare an army of rats off a free meal?" Then he saw the wound in his shoulder stop leaking but hang their liked a gored slab of meat in the butcher's window. "I should be bleeding to death—"

Alex fist clenched Warren's throat, a torn eyelid zipping itself back. "I will not go back to Rasputin empty-handed. Either help or—"

An acre away, the corpses were moving in a gentle wave like a freshly disturbed sea of mangled flesh until, from the rotten centre of the pit, burst a mouth and scream, howling against the sky of clouds.

A rat the size of a tank, fur slick with gore and crimson eyes shining, howled like a freshly kicked hornet's nest. Its mouth was jammed with dirty razor teeth the size of bowie knives, and limbs jammed between their jagged edges, rats, and something white and black.

Alex grunted. "It's mouth. It's full of—"

"Deadroot." Warren whispered.

The beast snarled at invisible predators around the crater, then sniffed and turned.

Warren grimaced. "Shit."

It dove for them, ragged mouth charging.

CHAPTER EIGHTEEN:

PRELUDE TO CREATION

Lemony fresh scents and the aroma of well-scrubbed floors created an atmosphere of healthy return as Vasilya sat at her drawing board, finishing the last of her component sketches while Click and Clack chased the mechanical butterflies.

The long days didn't hurt so badly now, as good sleep, a cleaned workshop, and Colonel Balk's spider touch had removed the last of the poisons. But she had now developed the rude habit of touching her nose at regular intervals.

Just to be safe.

The morning sun was burning into the warmer stages of the afternoon as she finished her tea and stared at the final sketch, which she called "The Swift Automatic Nervous System."

On it, she'd drawn the dynamo heart of Psycho, the brain of the Turkish Chess Player, and, connected to each of them, the nerve wire of the silent Flute Player.

Everything else, the frame, the hydraulic arms and legs, the joint system, all of the components on their own were being constructed in secret warehouses outside of the shop, round the clock, with each component to arrive by the end of the week. She'd give instructions on which automatons to disassemble and how. All that was left was a handful of lost-cause magical devices: a disappearing closet, a water torture device, a wooden duck that was supposed to defecate, and other useless scraps that offered her no value. But she had kept Psycho's dynamo heart, the Chess Player's puzzle brain, and the internal wires of the Flute Player …

… and the butterflies. They needed a hand gentler than that of a thuggish German labourer.

Despite the Nameless creature's future ugliness, she'd grown a proprietary sense for its existence. This was not some artillery piece, not some mass-produced German rifle that anyone with a sliver of education and hand-eye coordination could make. It was a tool of destruction, but it was also a piece of art, perhaps the last one to bear the Fabergé name, and she would not allow all its secrets to be shoved into the hands of inferior talents of mass production before she tried to make Nameless come alive.

But it was so many lumps of coal if her Swift System failed.

"All based on a dream," she said to the strange drawing. "Is that not how they all start, though, Monsieur Fabergé? Wasn't that a line from one of your letters to the Theosophicals?"

"Excuse me?"

"God!" Startled, she snapped back out of her chair and into someone's arms. She scampered away with swinging elbows, turned, and adjusted her dress. "Who the devil are you?"

Before her was a rough-looking boy with coal-black hands and a filthy summer shirt missing a button. The stench of coal and sweat was awful. Fatigue bit his face hard, which was topped with a cap of a labourer. He leaned on one foot. "Felix, Ma'am. Felix Hilt. Colonel Balk sent me." His voice was rough, wheezy, as if he had a chest cold and smoked too much, the cadence of the working poor in the so-called heart of Europe. The accent, though, was softer than that of the colonel, or most of those in Berlin. Perhaps he was a lazy Bavarian.

"As I am not running a coal mine," Vasilya said, "I doubt you'll be of much service. Now, if you don't mind, I have important work to do." She turned back to the sketch, trying to cover it with her body.

Felix coughed. "I've only been working in the mines because of the war. I'm good with woods and metals."

Confused, she gazed at him over her shoulder. He was young, and not in uniform. All of them were in the war, or dead. He was a rare thing, even if covered in industrial mess. "Why you?"

"Pardon?"

"I was expecting an engineer of distinction to help me with this ... project. And you don't look old enough to have had more than a year of shaving under your belt. Why you?"

"To beg your pardon," Felix said. "I told you. I'm good with wood and metal. Building things." He coughed again, softly, as if not to disturb the fluid in his lungs, then his face bunched. "Odd things."

So. Here also was a "talented" young man. Like her? Like the colonel? Like M. Fabergé? How many, she wondered. How many were there with gifts just a bit wondrous? The engaging thought was snuffed out by the picture of the sketched nameless creature from her mind, one that would soon terrorize the battlefield where millions marched to their doom, and then to Russia to abolish the nightmare of revolution. Years would pass before a semblance of normalcy emerged, where people of talent might be free of the yoke of conflict...

Not free, she realized. Gone. Whatever talents this world had, they've been the minority amidst the masses, and no doubt they've been churned into nothing by the war like everything else. Crushed before their roses could bloom, or courted to make weapons. Were there talented people in London scheming against her? What of Russia? Were there wild talents serving Lenin to keep the nation burning?

Pain thrummed through her heart as she recalled the smashed glass and screams that was left of her once beautiful city, bloodied boots crushing jeweled eggs under their heels in the name of progress.

The tremor of a tear began to swell.

"Ma'am? Are you all right?"

She swallowed grief until it tightened her heart into a stone. "I'm not all right. We are behind schedule. Have you seen what happens when the colonel is angry, Felix?"

"No, nor do I care to. He scares me worse than the coal bosses."

"And so he should. Come." She pulled a fresh roll of paper over the Nameless drawing. Everything had been secrets and shadows and hidden treasures so long that sharing her knowledge all at once was as reckless as a game of chance.

Felix sniffed and walked over, dragging his foot some.

Clubfoot, she thought. Well that explains one reason you're not dying for your nation's conquests. He stood beside her, the smell of industry ruining the freshness of the workshop she'd so enjoyed. "How much do you know of our project?"

"Just that it's a vehicle. A big one. Like those monstrous Land Ironclads I've heard about in France."

"Tanks, those are called tanks and … wait, Land Ironclad? That's from H. G. Wells. The English writer who is in a coma."

Felix went white. "I wouldn't know anything about that. Just thought they were like battleships on land."

She smiled inside, but kept stern. He's a little more interesting than I assumed. "What I am about to show you is a national secret and we'll both be sent to the front if it gets out. Understand?"

Felix nodded.

She lifted the paper dramatically, revealing the sketch of the three components. "Have you ever seen anything like this, Felix…?"

"Hilt. Felix Hilt …" He shuffled forward and leaned in. The smell was dark, the oil and sweat almost too much. "I … that's a dynamo," he said of the heart, "but the strangest shape … how does it…" He shook his head. "That thing above it." The Turk's brain. "It reminds me of an Arithmometer."

Vasilya let him take the seat, giving her a moment to steal some fresh air, but soon everything around her stank of Felix and she found herself touching her nose again. "Of course it's an Arithmometer." She nodded, hands at her sides. "And what is that?"

Felix scratched his cheek. "Japanese adding machine. My father … brought one back to Germany, about the time I was born. He worked in the Tokyo rail yards as an engineer, for the man who invented it, a great Japanese inventor. Father built the parts; he was a natural pattern maker. Said the Arithmometer was like a mathematical brain for doing rail tables. But this is more … ornate. And I can't see how it works."

Because it doesn't, Vasilya thought. Not the way it's configured, to dupe folks into thinking it was an illusion. That was the great secret of these three automatons and their mysterious makers. But she was impressed. This Felix had an eye for the mechanical arts. But he stank like factory waste.

"Oh, god, I cannot stand this!" Vasilya said, finally pinching her nose, glad it was not red and wet. "You must grab a shower and come back clean. Not mine, but there's one behind the workshop, I've heard it running." The last thing she wanted was him staining her little bath and washroom with his filth. "I'm sure the guards can help you."

"But the colonel said I had to help you right away. And, it's freezing out there."

"I can't work if I pass out from the stench of you!" Vasilya said. "Now go, be quick, or I'll tell the colonel myself you were wasting my time."

And like that she made Felix, clubfoot and all, run.

Her whole body itched from shame and no position on her stool felt comfortable. Click and Clack were at her feet. She picked them up. Their eyes glared at her. "Oh, don't be so sentimental. I didn't treat him that poorly," she said. "But he needs a leader. He needs direction." Click looked at Clack, then they both stared at her. "Monsieur Fabergé would not tolerate kindness and slovenly attitudes and deportment, and neither will I. There is no time to waste on pleasantries."

They stared at her.

"Fine, he smells awful and I hate it, and his accent is annoying and weak. But I can't be soft, friends. Not now. We need to work like fiends if this is going to work. Now go, shoo, and stay away from his feet." They scurried and she sat at her desk, contemplating the heart, brain and wires of the Swift System. The hiss of the outdoor shower made her think of rain in St. Petersburg in March, how cold it was, how the only warmth had been in her cramped workshop, hands aching until they began moving and she fitted screws or twined wire for an engine.

A dream, she thought. That time, that place is now vanishing in the wake of my experiences here. I'm standing on the back of a train filled with these oddities, and my past is disappearing behind us into the distant horizon. Only I can't reach the engine room to see where I'm going.

But I know where I'm headed, Vasilya thought.

She tapped her nose, the nameless pieces of the creature glaring back at her.

It won't end with one creature. With this invention done, the Germans will do what they always do: mass-produce it. The inventor will become irrelevant if they can make it on their own. And what will then happen to me? To Monsieur Fabergé?

And, yes, even the colonel?

The shower's shimmering sound stopped.

Today, we build the monster, she thought. This is not how Victor Frankenstein felt, she remembered. He was elated, in a fever dream and at the height of his powers, defying the laws of nature.

But I know what he created. A creature of sadness and violence. A dark shadow of his creator's intent. I have no illusions of hope to cling to. Only the desire to keep … Monsieur Fabergé alive. The dream of Russia free of revolution in the wake of such a creature at the vanguard of a German army? What was to stop them from taking it all?

Nothing.

"I don't want to do this … Father." The word dropped from her lips in near silence. "But I can see no other way to save you." She looked at her fingers, grateful they were not crimson. "It truly is in my hands."

She wiped away a cold tear as Felix knocked on the door. "Enter." She sniffed and tied her hair back tighter.

He stood at the door. Ill-fitting soldier's clothing was rolled up around his elbows and ankles, and he now had on boots that were too big. "They said I had to burn my old ones because of—"

"Lice." And Vasilya caught a sad and fleeting bit of whimsy in her mind as she looked at the clean Felix, a childish wish that he would indeed be a handsome boy in the garb of an ugly duck.

He was not.

He was a clean, misshapen boy with bad posture and teeth. About as charming as a street urchin. His one redeeming feature was his hands. Strong, long fingers, callused, as thick as leather. They would be good for what they had to do.

"Are you ready?" she said.

He nodded. "At your command."

She disdained and enjoyed his near-subordinate attitude. "All right. Let us build a monster."

CHAPTER NINETEEN:

OF RAT AND PIT

As the sea of corpses churned, the monstrous rat charged at the only two-legged creatures alive in the pit. "Move, now!" Warren yelled, shoving Alex as far as he could as the rat roared, mouth a jagged gap of teeth, limbs and deadroot.

Warren drove his hand in to the human soup around him, hoping for a rifle, but came up with a maggot rich bone. Damn. He swung back, maggots dancing across his knuckles, ready to meet his maker, when the rat careened to his left. What looked like the jagged edge of wooden bed leg was jammed in its head. Its nose crashed into the shell wall behind Warren.

"Eye!" Alex screamed, the other half of a broken bed leg in his hand.

And Warren thrust the bone into the red eye of the beast. It went right to the wrist.

A demented snarl rang out before the rat's nose thrashed Warren in the gut, cracking ribs and launching him skyward until gravity tore him back. Flailing, he crashed, chest first, on the edge of the crater, arms scrambling to pull himself up, using a handful of roots. A familiar pair of boots walked at his eye level. Warren craned his neck and looked up.

Marlow smiled, rifle in his arms. "Met Oliver, I see. Denying him his meal. I shan't be so cruel. When he's done with your brother, he'll want some dessert!"

The boot nailed Warren's face, but Warren gripped his ankle.

"Hey! Hands off!" Marlow lifted the rifle to his eye, but Warren yanked as yard as he could, hearing the ankle snap and Marlow stumbled. Warren drove his elbow into Marlow's gut as hard as an upper cut, and the lunatic's body swung into the pit. Warren shambled up in time to see Oliver the Rat turn his one good eye from Alex to Marlow, and then dove.

The beast ate deep, as Marlow's grisly screams chewed the air in Gaelic, then, finally, stopped.

But not Oliver.

Alex sloshed his way toward the edge of the hole faster than a greased pig. Oliver growled, nose twitching, mouth still grinding the remains of Marlow. He'll cut the distance and Alex in half in less than three heartbeats, Warren thought. Oliver charged as Alex reached the crater's edge.

Shit!

Warren ran and launched himself from the edge of the hole and grabbed a handful of the greasy fur and flesh, pulling Oliver back so he could get a grip and try and rein the rodent in like a horse. The rat's hide was harsh and slick, but Warren's grip was iron. Wild shakes and violent turns attempted to toss him, bashing him against the hard and rough surface of the giant rat's hide.

"What the hell are you doing?" Alex screamed.

"I don't know!" The rat thrashed. "Just get out!"

And, despite telling his brother to do so, Warren felt sick as he saw Alex climb over the lip of the pit and vanish.

And I'm the coward, he thought, before a violent jerk tore his grip and rat hide from Oliver's back and his body tossed in the air, crashing into a heap of degenerating corpses so foul they even made his draug stomach turn.

Oliver shook, Marlow's head jammed in his mouth, the lunatic's eyes glaring into the abyss. The critter snarled, one eye filled with a broken leg, the good one focused, nose twitching to find him.

From the graveyard sea around him, Warren tore another rotting arm. "Come on, you shit. C'mon and try me again!"

Oliver roared and charged—

A crack of thunder, then Oliver's head blew apart like a ripe melon dropped on a hard floor. The rat slumped, and lay still. It was only a breath before the pit began to seethe with sound.

The sea of a thousand eyes emerged from the muck and descended on the corpse of Oliver in frenzy. Warren dropped the arm, and looked up.

Alex stood there. Pistol in his hand.

"Where did you get that?"

"Flew off of Marlow when that beast finished him."

"Nice catch. Now get me out of here so we can tell your general where this hell pit is!"

Using both their belts, and working against the rampaging flow of rats feasting on Oliver, Alex pulled Warren up just as a thick rain began to fall. They walked, letting nature rinse the unholy mix of blood and death from their bodies, but Warren feared there was no substance alive that could wipe clean what they'd just bathed in.

"Thanks," Alex said.

"You're welcome. Uh, for what?"

Alex's hair was covering his eyes, rain dripping off him in a thin stream that broke and then reformed itself. "I'd thought—"

"That after I'd made it out, I was running off."

"Yeah."

"Like on the platform in Fort William. When you were heading off to this grand adventure."

"Yeah."

"Tell me straight, little man. There ever going to be a time when you don't think I'll take the coward's way out?" Silence. "Well, thanks for saving me, too. I guess I can always count on you to be the hero of the family. Next time you see a whisper of cowardice, why don't you use your 'influence' on me to keep my spine from going yellow. Because, after all, only a real hero does everything he's told regardless of what he thinks, like a good little Marconi receiver, never questioning, never standing up for himself, never having a goddamn free thought in his head no matter how much the rest of the world hates it!"

Warren stormed in front of his brother for about a mile until he turned around.

In the distance, Alex was standing still, like a scarecrow.

"What is it?"

"Warren? I got hurt ... in the pit ... I'm sor—"

He fell like a leaf, and crumpled into himself.

"Alex?" Warren ran and kneeled before his brother who was sprawled on his back, eyes milky. "Jesus, Alex what happened ..."

He cupped Alex's head and the body shivered as his hand went wet with blood. "... Alex, roll on your side." Warren helped him do it.

And forced a look.

The back of the skull was gone.

The brain ... was black. And scarred. Slow, deliberate movements followed as Warren spoke clear words and undid his shirt, ringing it out carefully. "Alex. Listen to me. You have to keep listening to me. I need to bandage your head. It's not bad, but you shouldn't have a wet head. Just like Mother said—a wet head is a cold waiting to happen. You remember that?"

Alex shivered, but nodded. Warren took off his shirt, rung it out, began to wrap Alex's head to cover the fist-sized hole.

"Is it ... bad?" Alex said, voice a mere tremor.

"Nah, worst you'll get is some bed rest, I'm sure."

"Warren, I don't feel good ... I haven't felt this bad since ... Vim, Vim ... Vim—"

"Easy, brother. Easy."

"I'm scared." The milky white eyes blinked. "I forgot I could be scared."

"We'll have you back, good and healthy, soon." But there was no hospital other than the graveyard they'd survived. No clearing station. Not even a spot of morphine. "Rasputin," Warren said, bitterly. "If he wants you to fight, he's going to have to heal you first. Can you stand?"

Alex shivered in response.

The rain fell in thick sheets and the craterous earth began to fill with water, creating thick polders.

"No worries." Warren grunted as he dragged his brother up with one good shoulder. The bullet hole from Marlowe looked sickly, and it hurt like an anvil was pressed against his flesh, but he could move.

"The deadroot," Alex said.

I'll grab a handful, Warren thought, and that Russian charlatan better know what to do with it or so help me god I'll kill every last member of that Battalion with my own hands.

On he marched to the wormhole as a distant battle commenced in a war Warren no longer recalled fighting. All that mattered was keeping Alex from dying in his arms.

All else was madness, folly, and lies.

CHAPTER TWENTY:

OF STILLBIRTH, STEAM, AND SADNESS

At three in the morning, even the loudest of the creatures outside the workshop lay still while the bulbs inside burned brighter above Vasilya and Felix.

The inspection was but ten hours away.

The week had been consumed into a single long day of sawdust and soldering and frustration and tempered hope.

The shyness of Felix burned away in his work as his hands took tool and material and proceeded to build the chamber where Vasilya would place the heart, head and nervous system of her creation.

Felix's chamber was akin to a human chest made of wood and iron. Vasilya toyed with the Chess Player's puzzle brain, but her eyes were drawn to the speed at which Felix could work. It was hypnotic. Time slowed as he turned the lathe, and shards of wood for the internal brace, which needed some give, flew into the air like feathers from darting doves.

When he'd look back, she'd shiver. Ugly features calm, happy in the throes of his work, the kind of ugly that would never grace the Tzar's palace … she laughed to herself, because such a thought was not completely true. Only in her dreams were the royals and their kind as beautiful as their mansions and dachas. When Mother had taken her to the Bolshoi, Vasilya had seen too well that the rich were not immune to the ugliness of natural selection, and inherited Hapsburg lips and weak chins and red eyes from countless years of cousins bedding cousins. And it was this elite that had made this so-called Theosophical Society, whom she'd read about in fits in starts from Robert-Houdin and others, mentioned in passing as if it were merely like the Royal Society in England, but Vasilya began to picture them far more as an alliance of aristocrats who were using people like her for their own ends and purposes, far removed from the public or newspapers, diplomacies and deals and stratagems amongst themselves, and this war, this stupid horror show made real, were responsible. Whatever reasons or demons ran in this world, the blame was at their thrones.

Felix was about as far from these creatures as you could get. Ruddy-faced, broken body, and yet when the torch was in his hand and a welding mask upon his head, and sparks filled the air like stars, there was a kindred spirit. A magic, like her talent, to see design. But where she could translate it on the small scales, he worked with an effortless speed to turn paper ideas into steel truth. He was a wizard of forge, fire and torch. Of wood, nail and joint. Transfixed, she bore witness as he turned her drawing into a hulking reality. The spell was only broken when the torch was out, and the mask pulled back.

Ugly Felix of the clubfoot was sweating so hard his chin dripped. He wiped and turned and she felt silly and glared at the Chess Player's brain. "I believe that's it," he said, huffing. "Just need to let the joints cool."

"Well it's about time," she said.

The chamber was a skeletal sphere the size of a rotund man, and sat upon a re-enforced wagon that could bear its weight, iron braces on each corner kept it from rolling away. Even without armaments, it was heavy enough to crush anything under it and Click and Clack and the butterflies had wisely hidden while they worked on it. Ragged sets of wires prodded out from four cylinders, one for each limb. Within it, the dynamo heart of Psycho the dancing pygmy sat in the centre of an iron web. Within that heart was a magnet, one that needed to spin if its own magic was to be released.

"Are you sure," Felix said, "that it can alternate currents?"

"Positive," she said, thinking of her dream, of being chased by the creature along a direct current to her destruction. "And I will thank you not to doubt my work."

He raised his hands and lowered his head in surrender. "No, I just don't want that heart to burst if it can't handle the charge and the changes. Edison said AC was killing people who thought they were getting—"

"And Mr. Tesla proved them wrong." She'd asked the colonel for as much reading material on the two men's arguments in the old copies of the Theosophical newsletter, known as the *Codex Arcana*, as he could find. Vasilya found herself agreeing with the Croatian wizard more than the Magician of Menlo Park. "And we shall prove Edison wrong again. I finished the control box yesterday." She took the large oak box from the table, the dials and switches so fresh and new they positively dared her fingers to touch them. "Are you sure that every single one of the wires is insulated?"

"Yes," Felix said, shuffling toward her. "I've followed your diagram exactly."

The confidence in his voice was reassuring, but his emphasis on it being her diagram was bracing. Vasilya nodded. "All right. Let us put this doll together."

Felix nodded, then slowly pulled the massive chamber toward what Vasilya referred to as the Hanging Garden of Prometheus.

In a cleared-out section of the lab they called Test Ground A, two chains hung from the reinforced tracks in the ceiling, and on their bottom run swung the mighty arms of the creature. Like a human limb void of skin and blood, they were skeletal limbs of iron and wire, of wooden braces and rivets, hydraulic tubes at their core that, if the engine's pump worked as she'd hoped, would allow those swinging arms to move.

Below them was an even more impressive duo: the iron legs, complete with reverse bended knees so that it could rest its hideous weight without cracking the metallic bones and wires. The space between the legs and arms was just right for the final component. Hanging down, ready for the chamber, was a massive chain and hook.

Slowly, Felix dragged the chamber toward the Hanging Garden as dawn softened the blackness of twilight outside. And with it, fatigue and nerves waltzed in Vasilya's blood. With the scrape of the wheels on the scuffed wooden floor, the rush of her mad life seemed to gain weight and step forward as the end began to dawn.

Soon, I'll have made this creature.

Soon, it will do things to other human beings I cannot contemplate. I will be releasing a wild weapon into the human landscape.

Tom Swift would not approve. But she began to doubt the same could be said of the lost Mr. Wells. The *Codex Arcania* carried his initials on letters of sturm and drang with Jules Verne, his French rival for the imaginations of the world. Wells, she had found, saw the world in far less human terms, and she wondered what secret war he was fighting on behalf of Queen Victoria … whose long life, attributed to the growth of her empire, Vasilya suspected had more to do with "talented" people bled dry to keep the fat royal alive. She pictured a clockwork Victoria with a black heart, as the children of the empire were fed into her mouth like Turkish delights, keeping her gears wet.

She laughed, the sound hidden beneath the echo of the chamber's journey to the Hanging Garden, until tears swelled. She was glad Felix was too exhausted and focused to see the weakness leaking from her.

You're saving a life, she thought. You're saving one. You did not have a choice.

No choice. It was a no-win situation, an impossible circumstance, an accident …

"Child!"

They both swung to see Colonel Balk, face greyer than usual, storming into the room. His uniform was disheveled and buttons undone, eyes wild and moustache ragged. "He's here."

She wanted to say "who" just to buy more time, instead she yelled at

Felix to hurry, then turned back to the colonel. "How long do I have?" she said.

"His car will arrive shortly."

"General Hindenburg?" Felix said, standing like a midget beside the giant leg. "But we haven't tested ... anything."

"We don't need to," she said. "It will work. Just get the chamber attached to the limbs and make sure all the wires are connected."

As Felix attached the hook and began to crank the chain on the far war, Colonel Balk walked toward the creature, his steps for once soft under the sound of the great chain until he stood before it. With the chain locked, and Felix climbing a ladder to begin the connections, words dropped from the colonel's mouth in a tone void of emotion but not power, while his one gloved hand got his uniform in shape.

"'For by Art is created that great Leviathan called a Commonwealth or State, which is but an Artificial Man; though of greater stature and strength than the Natural, for whose protection and defence it was intended; and in which, the Sovereignty is an Artificial Soul, as giving life and motion to the whole body.'"

She stood at his side. "What was that? Clausewitz?"

"Hobbes. One of the earliest British members of the Theosophical Society, and the last one who made any sense." He exhaled hard and the bristles of his moustache waved. "It may take a monster to defeat the hell we've unleashed on ourselves, child. I do not doubt that, should this ... creature work, there will be those who will call you heretic, a mad Daedalus, including from the Society. But they will do so from the garden of peace you provided by ending this war. So, should I not remember to say so—" He turned, his one good eye red. "—thank you."

She stood beside him, heart breaking into tiny bits because of what she now had in mind. She believed the creature would work. It would be a moment akin to Prometheus handing fire to humanity.

And in the process, she would let it burn.

Hindenburg will have his monster, Vasilya thought. And it will tear that general to pieces. And with his death, the war would be over. And the beast would be dead. An accident. That is what is needed. An accident that killed two birds with one evil stone. Let the Society and Academy and whoever else conspires to ruin creation collapse under the weight of their own monstrosities.

And what of Monsieur Fabergé?

It's a risk, she thought. But seeing the creature come together, knowing what it might do ... the risk of its evils was too great. An accident, she thought. Maybe it would get her shot, but it might save his life in the long run. The risk was worth it.

I am sorry, she said with a prayer. The colonel placed a gloved hand on her shoulder and she clenched herself tight as a coiled wire inside the dynamo heart. She lifted the controls and waited for the end of all she had known.

I'm sorry, Father.

CHAPTER TWENTY-ONE:

BENEATH THE WAR-TORN SEA

It was hell not to run, but Warren couldn't expect his makeshift bandage to hold forever, and he was sickened with every step at the thought of losing Alex to a savage misstep.

As Warren marched the barren earth, black birds circling above, Alex whispered and muttered, but sense and word were beyond him. Warren retraced his steps as best he could, glad for the sense of direction that years of running, hiding and hunting had provided, until, in the midst of thundering rain and darkness, he came upon the mouth of the wormhole from Rasputin's Charger.

"If the madman can make worms his allies, he can heal you up, brother."

He entered the dark maw, and slipped before he could regain his balance. Alex grunted. Apologizing with every step, Warren found himself in the dark world beneath the war, eyes adjusting as if this were his natural home, more than twenty feet under.

"Qimmiq."

Fear glazed his nerves, but Warren kept walking, even though it was clear as day that beside him, big as life, was Tik. "You … didn't find some deadroot on your own. Did you?"

"No," Tik said.

"So you're really dead, the old-fashioned kind?"

"Yes."

"So does that make me crazy, or am I seeing beyond the pale thanks to the worms he shoved in me?"

"You tell me, Qimmiq."

"Why don't you tell me something only Tik would know? Maybe something even I don't know."

"The amount you don't know could fill the halls of hell, heaven, and everywhere in between."

Well, it sounded like Tik. Warren shook his head and just tried to walk with his dead friend as if he were still with him. Let an alienist and witch doctors decide if that was batshit lunacy. "I'm sorry, Tik."

Tik shrugged. "Not your job to be sorry. I got the death I wanted, Qimmiq. Did you?"

"No. I guess not."

They walked slow and steady down the unholy tube cut by Rasputin's beastly creature until the silence ate away Warren's patience. "Why are you here, Tik?"

"Why do you think?"

"Don't answer questions with questions, it was annoying as hell when you were alive and more so now."

Tik laughed. "Why is that?"

"Tik!"

Alex groaned and Warren shifted Alex on to his shoulders in a fireman's cross.

"He didn't get the death he wanted either," Tik said.

"Got the Victoria Cross for it. I thought that was what he wanted."

"Not that death. The one that's coming."

Warren stopped. "What do you mean?"

Tik crossed his arms. "You're traveling with some bad company, Qimmiq. Dark stuff in the air, like a cancer. This—" He motioned at Warren's entire body. "—It's stealing from death. And Death will want its cut back worse than a drunk hunting for a stolen pint."

"I know."

Surprise took Tik's face. "You do?"

Warren licked the grit from his teeth and spit into the darkness. "I'm playing a cheating hand. I know it. I feel it. It isn't right. Not that I'm looking to die anytime soon. You've always been way too comfortable with the afterlife for my tastes."

Tik smiled. "Same old Qimmiq."

"But for all the strength, all the wounds that heal—" He swallowed. "It comes tied to this madman's hand like puppet strings. He's got these lost souls hoodwinked, Tik. But if he's right, if he starts an army ... he could win." He shook his head. "I don't want to know what I know, what guys like me can do. But a division of unkillable men, men who know how to fight, who want to kill that which killed them..."

"Damned," Tik said. "That's where they are headed."

"Even if they win?"

"Especially if they do. Think two moves ahead, Qimmiq, like you're playing chess or cheating a gambler out of his coins. They win. Then what? They take the long journey into night? They lay down their arms before heaven?" Tik shook his head. "What do you think they really want?"

"I don't know," he said. "And I don't much care. Alex is close to the end of his rope and the only man that can bring him back is this nutcase Rasputin."

Tik gripped his belt. "You know what to do."

"Shut up."

"Let Alex die."

"Shut your gin hole, you igloo-making shit!"

Tik let the insult bounce off him like bullets on a tank. "I've been your friend for almost as long as your brother has hated you. I walked a long, crooked mile to tell you what you need to hear because you were a friend and died to avenge me. So listen up, Qimmiq. Let him die, or you're going to be tied to this war worse than anyone. Ignore this advice, and you're rolling the dice against a dark house that will not stop until you lose everything you've ever cared about. Mind, body, family and soul. With Alex at rest, you'll have a better chance or coming up box cars. If he's alive, you've got to make seven the hard way."

Warren shook for a long time as his dead friend's eyes began to fade into the tunnel wall out of reach and out of sight. "Tik. I can't."

"Don't worry," Tik said voice like smoke. "I have faith you'll somehow fuck up your own stupid plans. And when you do, the right thing will be there to hold. Good luck, Qimmiq. I'll keep a bar stool warm for you."

"And would that be in heaven or hell?"

Tik laughed. "See you around, Qimmiq."

Long, jagged miles of earth passed under Warren's boot heels until there was the familiar garrulous laughter of soldiers. Even the dead ones jibed as if life was a carnival and they were all confidence men with an ace up their sleeves.

"Shhh! Someone's coming!" said one.

A dozen rifles loaded as Warren approached the main cavernous room where he'd first met the Lost Battalion, firelight birthing long shadows of dead bodies that still moved.

A handful had been playing cards on a crate next to a weak fire. Graves stood in front, smiling, fists flexing. "So, you did come back. Empty-handed and with your brother in a sling. Nicely done."

Warren let Alex's feet hit the ground until he was standing, leaning forward like a willow against hard wind. "He's hurt. Get me Rasputin."

"You don't outrank me, little rabbit," Grave said. "And I'm sure in time young Alexander will be standing tall."

Warren's anger cooled. He could not drop Alex to feed Graves a fist, no matter how sweet the taste. Save it, Warren thought. That iced rage, that bitter need to hurt, save it. Tuck it hard into your chest like a jack-in-the-box and when this smug, worm-faced son of a bitch is laughing at the wrong moment—pop goes the weasel.

Warren helped Alex to the ground where he sat with outstretched legs. He leaned forward, and Warren undid the homemade bandage around his heads. Snickers silenced and Grave's face dropped its smug cadence. "His brain is damn near falling out," Warren said low. "This hole ain't healed since I started us back." He stood, slow, hands like iron pendulums swinging at his sides. "Either get me Rasputin, or this little rabbit will tear off your head to see if it grows back."

Grave's lips curled, but he backed off. "Lads, wake the boss."

Shortly, Rasputin emerged, shadow leading the way in the torchlight, tattooed arms folded across his chest and smelling like burning hair. He shot Warren a hard look. "How did this happen?"

"Some critter, a rat the size of a tank, took a chunk out of him. While hunting for your damn deadroot."

The slap was so fast and hard that Warren swallowed a molar before the stars in his eyes twinkled.

"How could you let this happen!"

Simmer, Warren told himself, unflexing his fists to empty hands at his sides. "What can I say? War is hell. Can you save him?"

Rasputin grunted, then leaned to examine the hole in Alex's skull. "Brave little warrior," he said, then closed his eyes and shook his head. "The root is torn, holding on by a sliver."

"Save him."

Rasputin blinked at the cracked hole in Alex's skull and the dark jelly of his brain buried within. "He ... is beyond help."

Warren had lost too many rounds of poker not to see a tell-twitch when it appeared. "You're lying."

Rasputin stood, and a backhand came at Warren again like the devil—

But he caught it.

The room fell silent as rifles were raised. But Warren held on to the iron wrist.

"Release!" Rasputin said.

Warren grinned. "No." A ripple of anxiety flooded the room. "Save your commands for the fools who owe their life to you, because this miserable son of bitch ain't one of them. I am not under your goddamn spell." Rasputin's wrist shook but Warren twisted it hard until he was behind him, Rasputin in a hammer lock, and Warren's left hand cinched under his neck. "Struggle and you'll just choke yourself. I've gone catch-as-catch-can with Inuit who wrestled bears for sport." Every rifle was trained on Warren's head. "But before your boys roll the dice on how well they can blow off my head while leaving yours clean as a baby's wiped ass, I'll make you a deal. Save him. And I will show you where all the damned deadroot is that you could want."

Rasputin motioned for the men to lower their arms. "You ... found—"

"We found a goddamn orchard full of the stuff. Only two people have seen it. The one you're not saving, and the one your men want to kill. You want your army of the dead, you better save his life first." He tightened the choke and Rasputin grunted. "Your move."

The flicker of dying flames whipped the air around them until Rasputin nodded. "I will try."

Warren released him and every rifle was at the ready—

"Down!" Rasputin yelled and the rifles dropped like a line of chorus girls dropping their legs. Graves's arms were shaking, trying to bring them back up. "I said down!"

Graves grunted, wet ooze coming from his nose, until he gasped and his arms hung dead at his sides. "Bring Alexander to the healing room and keep his brother in the shackle until I am done."

"No way," Warren said, yanking the pistol from his belt and digging the barrel into Rasputin's chest. "I'm going to be there. No way you pull some fast shank and end his life and call it an accident, then give me some Russian tragedy about how you tried but it made no difference. Where he goes, I go, and if he dies …" He put the gun to his own head. "… so does your dream army of the dead."

Rasputin nodded, bitterly. "You are playing a dangerous game, boychik. And it will bring a savage harvest."

"Save the prophecies for your disciples and go save my brother."

The hate in Rasputin's eyes was thicker than lead. "Patience," he said, as if to nobody, then gave his men orders.

As they lifted Alex, Warren kept close to Rasputin, pistol in his back. No way on this earth is the last thing my brother sees going to be this madman's face.

Behind him, came a scraping sound.

Graves was sharpening a bayonet on a stone. Same kind Warren had used on the Germans who killed Tik and Alex.

The road to madness had become his trail. And Rasputin knew the way.

CHAPTER TWENTY-TWO:

OF BEASTS AND GENERALS

No official pictures were allowed, so Vasilya had Click and Clack take small ones from the mirror box Vasilya was hiding in, for it was a momentous occasion on the horizon: the accidental death of General Paul von Hindenburg.

For when he'd come into the room, the general was bigger than life, a hulking figure with a square head, a thick man stuffed into an officer's clothing that bristled with more medals than Colonel Balk. Standing next to Hindenburg, Colonel Balk looked like a thin shadow. With his moustache trim and long, the general appeared like an exotic offspring of a bear and a Walrus, a blustery presence, and eyes like two raisins rammed into dough, though his voice had a weird timber.

"My time is limited, Colonel," he said, cutting his way through the workshop as if he knew where he was going. "General Ludendorff should not carry the burden of the war effort alone."

Vasilya and everyone had heard those two names, synonymous with the defeat of the Tzar's armies. For it was Generals Ludendorff and Hindenburg who had turned the tide of the Russian advance at Tannenberg and, as everyone suspected, were the real authorities running Germany.

"Of course, Sir," said the colonel, trying to keep up, a pain in his face like he'd swallowed a mouthful of tacks. "Our entire focus has been to provide you a tool that could—"

Hindenburg silenced him with a look. "The German army will win this war, Colonel. Whatever wonder you've constructed will only speed their final victory."

"Naturally, Sir."

The squat smugness in the general's face gave way to wide-eyed surprise as his thick neck craned up to see what Vasilya and Felix had forged together as fast as they could.

"General," said Colonel Balk with a cool edge. "I introduce you to the new armament for the German Army. The Juggernaut of the Reich."

Juggernaut, Vasilya thought with a cynical bite. What an appropriately German name for this colossus of destruction.

And it was a sight, as, suddenly, Hindenburg was no longer the biggest thing in the dusky light of the room. Instead, a monstrous form, the size of a small house, hunched over on inverse bent knees.

Closer, Vasilya thought, tapping the control box gently. Closer.

The general puffed up before the Juggernaut, meaty fists on the hips of his great coat. "I hope it does more than stand idle while sucking at the teat of the Reich's Treasury, Colonel."

"We can demonstrate it—"

Hindenburg raised a hand. "Who made it?"

"The limbs were constructed by Krupp, though the armaments and armour are rudimentary."

The general turned fast. "So it is unfinished?"

The colonel pursed his lips. "Full weapon field trials were unavailable because of the exercises of the new armies. Sir. We thought it unwise to have all our eggs in one basket until then."

It was a good lie, and probably true, and Hindenburg simply turned back to the beast. Vasilya's finger hovered over the controls. One button, and the dynamo would start, the beast would flail, and crush the brains of the German war effort, leaving only Ludendorff in command. And, from what Felix had told her, that the general had gone mad when his March offensive had harvested nothing but more corpses and no end to the war in sight, let alone a quick German victory. The strain of the war was killing him, said Felix. And the war would be over. If the fat general who was not a lost soul would only come closer.

Hindenburg did, inspecting its skeletal steel arms and copper screwed joints. "Who designed it?"

"A team of—"

Now—

"Nonsense!" The general marched back to bark at the colonel, and Vasilya's finger rose. Damn him! Stay still, your corpulent thug! "No team designs such things, Colonel. They execute the will of the mad tinker who came up with this. And before I allow you to switch this … contraption on, I want to know who it was that built it. Who is responsible?"

Damn it! Vasilya thought, already knowing what would happen, the same reason she was hiding in an old magic box instead of standing by her monstrous child. Such bigotry should not have startled her, but it had. And it hurt worse than she let on when the colonel spoke—

"Felix," the Balk said. "Come here. Now."

Felix shuffled forward from where he'd been standing stock-still amongst the remains of the mutilated automatons: Psycho's wounded chest, the Turk's empty brain, the Flute Player's long scars where once had been her veins ... and in his hand, a fake controller made of spare buttons Felix had welded to a Chinese puzzle box in record time. The air still carried a whiff of the torch's white flame.

"Yes, Sir?"

"This is Felix Hilt," the colonel said. They all stood in a close circle, the colonel and general like two trees, a pine and an oak, surrounding the dirty little sapling of Felix. It couldn't get worse, Vasilya thought. "He is the son of railway engineer."

"Master Engineer Marcus Hilt," the general said. "Your father was critical to our successful mobilization." He leaned back as if to take the whole of Felix in, which was stupid, given how little he was. "It would appear some of his talent has been passed on to you."

Felix nodded. "Some," he said, softly, whole body shaking like an itch he could not scratch. Vasilya was furious at someone taking credit for her work, but such dishonesty actually looked to be making Felix sick.

Part of her wanted to jump out of the magic box and yell at the dunderheads that she had deduced Monsieur Fabergé's secrets, teased out the system of heart, brain and vein for the beast's life to exist on more than paper, turned a picture into a monster come to life...

Only it hadn't.

Not yet.

They'd only assembled the pieces with scraps and clanks and bruised and cracked finger and busted skin, before Colonel Balk's ridiculous order to hide, and for Vasilya to "disappear."

"You've restored some of my confidence, boy," the general said, sausage fingers on the boy's shoulder. Indeed, he was the fattest German she'd seen in an otherwise starved country. Rank certainly had its privileges. "Now, show me what it can do."

And they stood there, together, as if welded on the spot. And Felix pressed a big button on his fake controller, and waited for Vasilya to use the real one, the little Marconi she'd worked on all week. His finger sat jammed on the button and his lip began to twitch, waiting for her to do her part.

Three lives. She would take out three lives and save millions. That was a calculus for success, even if they discovered it was no accident.

"What the hell is going on, Balk?" said Hindenburg. "If you've failed—"

Vasilya finger hung above her own ignition button.

I can't, she thought. I can't let this thing live. And I won't let Felix die for my mistake.

The Juggernaut remained lifeless.

Felix jammed the button again.

And the general's hand gripped the colonel's shoulder so hard he winced. "Do you have any idea, Balk, how many might die if I am gone longer than I should be? And do you, boy, understand the penalty for wasting my time?"

I can't do nothing! she yelled at herself. "Sorry," Vasilya whispered, then pressed the button.

She gasped.

Nothing.

Fear triggered a bolt of tremors inside her—

A whirling sound … picking up steam and speed.

The generator fans in the back of the command chamber kicked in and the floor at their feet was alive with dust. The watchers covered their faces, until it was clear.

But Vasilya barely noticed. Thrumming inside her was a current, rich and sharp and growing with a fever in her blood. But unlike the poison sickness she'd survived, it was pure, without worry, a golden heat that tingled her extremities as she placed her hand on the controls and breathed.

The fans flared.

The golden richness hardened. She tasted metal. Strength flooded her bones and reached for her heart.

"Well?" the general yelled. "I hope it does more than clean dust."

Vasilya snorted, tired of his booming voice. And gripped the controls. How about this for a display of strength, you fat pig!

The hands of the Juggernaut flared out and everyone stood back. Its body creaked and swerved. Weakness poured into Vasilya's knees as she struggled to maintain her composure.

Gentle, she thought. Gentle and safe.

The general walked forward. "It's a shambling mess. Artillery will chew it up in its swaddling cloths if it moves slower than those blasted tanks. I cannot believe you've wasted my time on a puppet show! This operation is over!"

Over.

She could not let that happen.

Monsieur Fabergé—

The general strode off and the beast's hands opened and grabbed him like a doll so fast the only thing the crowd could do was gasp. The colonel glanced around to see where she'd hid.

Felix was covering his mouth, fake controller in his hand.

The guards fired.

Something bit into Vasilya's skin, a little more than a mosquito's sting.

Oh god, she thought … I'm feeling what it feels.

She looked at her left hand. It was a crooked fist.

The beast held the general as he screamed "Stop firing!"

The acrid stink of gunfire filled the room as the beast held the general.

This is it, she thought. The war is in my hands. I just have to squeeze—

"Hilt!" screamed the general. "Get me down or so help me I'll drive you to the front myself!"

Felix played with the control box.

The golden feeling flooded her heart until it was so heavy she thought it would tear through her chest. Everything hurt.

Just close your fist. Just close it.

"Hilt! Now!"

She nodded.

The beast's hand lowered itself and released its grip with the hiss of steam and the whirl of fans. Vasilya cried. Emotions took shape and strangled themselves within her bosom while she swallowed gasps and sobs and the general coughed and cleared his throat, shoving his guards away from him. "That hideous thing hasn't harmed me."

Vasilya shook her head. The golden feeling leaked out of her while the Juggernaut's dynamo heart slowed … then stopped. Weak, shaking, tired to the bone. It was all she could do to stop from being sick upon herself.

"I've seen enough," the general said to the silent room. "You've accomplished something, Colonel. You've got my attention. If your toy is ready for war in a month, we will have it tested. But fully armed and armoured."

"Sir!" said the colonel, proud as a new father. "Shall I tell command that we will need the field outside of Dachberg for the exercise?"

The general folded his arms across his barrel chest and the look of disgust was like a stain in the air. "There will be no exercise. Have it ready for battle."

"Sir…" the colonel's mouth strained for the words. "We need to train it with infantry, and we haven't even selected a division and support staff for it serve with, and—"

"And it will be in the order of battle in a month, Colonel. Or it dies in the toyshop where you birthed it. Victory is at hand. The only real test will be if it can hasten that victory. Understood?"

Vasilya clenched against the storm of pain in her stomach and bit down on her lip.

The colonel's face contorted. He nodded. "Yes. Sir." He saluted.

The general saluted, slowly.

When the door shut behind Hindenburg and his entourage, sickness rushed from Vasilya's stomach, through her mouth and past her hands. She shoved open the magic box door as wet vomit splattered the dusty ground.

Felix ran awkwardly, tossing the fake controls and helping her out of the foul box.

"Get away, I'm sick," she said.

"I smell like a burning coal mine," he said. "You can't make me smell worse." With a strength she had not supposed he had, he carried her with an awkward gait to a work bench, laying her down. She rolled on her side, mouth hot and throat burning.

"Thank you," Felix said, kneeling.

"Don't thank me," she said, wiping spit from her mouth, then covering it to hide acidic stench. "We're doomed anyway." She clasped her hands and nestled them at her heart. "It doesn't work."

"But the hand—"

She shook her head.

He whispered. "It was you."

Tears swelled in her eyes. "It's the heart. The engine won't work unless I … let it feel my heart. Connect with it. We had no time to make a really good one." Like Click and Clack, like the engine in the Tzarina's last egg—

He took a cloth from his overalls and wiped her lip. The stain … was dark. Grey.

"Don't move," he said, and ran toward the Juggernaut as the colonel walked by.

"Don't lecture me," she said, gripping her knees for comfort. "I'm not in the mood."

"No lecture," the colonel said. He lifted his gloved hand to his lips and hard, little teeth. "Do you need … assistance?"

"No."

"Do not confuse pride with stupidity."

"And do not throw moral *bon mots* at me as if I were still in diapers."

There was a whirl, a sound of gears twisting and steam venting.

"Colonel!" Felix yelled. "Colonel, we have … a problem."

Vasilya strained to get up and despite her protests he helped her with his one arm and slowly they made way toward the Juggernaut.

The command chamber was open. Felix sat inside, legs dangling. In his gloved hand was the steaming dynamo heart. Black drips fell off the tips of the rivets. They landed on the ground in thick drops.

"Is it leaking oil?" said the colonel.

"No," said Felix, wincing, as Vasilya predicted the word that would come out of his mouth. "Blood."

CHAPTER TWENTY-THREE:

WORMS OF LAZARUS

Graves assisted Rasputin as they laid Alex, stomach first, on a waist-high slab of clay. In the torchlight of the chamber, Warren stood, pistol out, ready to blast Graves's head into the far wall.

Alex was still mumbling his fever talk. Skull exposed like a cracked egg, blackish brain visible. It was a sickly sight but transfixing.

Flames flickered from wall torches as Rasputin's tattooed arms began some medicine dance above Alex. The Slavic words and mumbles made Warren wish whoever had started this war had given him a manual on dealing with Russian magicians and their carney stooges.

"Each of you," Rasputin said, walking to the foot of the clay table. "Hold one of his arms. He will struggle."

Slowly, Warren holstered his pistol, Graves smiling as he did. "What are you going to do?" Warren said to Rasputin.

"Make a believer out of you." The Russian gripped Alex's ankles and held them together. "You must pull his arms out, as if on a cross."

"Crucifying your brother," Graves said. "Very Judas of you."

Cold, Warren told himself. Stay cold. He grabbed Alex's wrist and pulled it out as Graves did the same, then both put their free hands on to Alex's shoulder blades as an anchor.

"Do not let go," Rasputin. "No matter what you see. No matter what you hear. It is an ugly but delicate dance. If it works, he'll heal fast. Return to us as he was."

"And if not?" Graves said.

"Shut up," Warren said. "Just get it done."

Rasputin nodded, then his eyes rolled behind his lids, and rollicking Russian words slithered out of his mouth. His neck twitched and jived as if his daddy had been a cobra. Warren blinked in the smoky firelight. Rasputin's tattoos, they'd stopped being solid etchings on skin, and … blurred. They swam with the same movement, swimming across his skin.

"I've seen snake charmers from the Raj work a cobra into a belly dance, but I'll never get used to seeing this," Graves muttered.

Similar snaking movements stained the cavern walls around them, shadows dancing to the pied piper Rasputin.

Until the entire cavern was alive with movement.

Worms.

"Christ," Warren muttered as own skin began to crawl.

The legions of night crawlers slithered, dropping like maggoty rain. Right on them, and Alex.

Hissing breath through clenched teeth, Warren gripped Alex even harder. Rasputin's arms flexed, tattoos still swimming, as the worms moved from all of them to the centre of Alex's back.

"Urozhenets," said Rasputin, and the pool of worms began wriggling into each other until—

"Grim and ghastly, this shite is," Graves said.

"Hold his fucking arm!" Warren said, and Graves did.

The grey-skinned thing on Alex's back was a ball of worms. It inched up his spine with the movement of a dozen worm-like legs, to the crack in his skull, and Warren's resolve was near-famished. The horrors of this world rivalled that of any mad creation in Burroughs or Kipling or the penny dreadfuls. If we should survive this nightmare, he thought, I'm only going to write tales of love and romance.

The ball of worms reached the crack in the skull.

And though Warren had not eaten in days, and had nearly forgotten he even had a stomach, he felt the urge to wretch as the worms entered Alex's skull.

Alex screamed and pulled his wrists forward towards his head with a fierce, savage strength.

"Hold him!" Rasputin yelled.

Graves did, with equal viciousness.

"Hold him or he's beyond my help!"

Warren yanked his arm back as Alex's screams consumed the chamber. "They're inside me! Help me, Warren! Get them out! They're tearing me apart! Warren, please!"

"Hold!" Rasputin yelled as if Alex were a ship in the grip of a violent gale.

Alex twisted his face, and black eyes screamed at Warren. "Coward! You were supposed to protect me! Protect me!"

Warren took every insult as it rolled out of Alex's screaming mind and mouth, body resisting like a mad seizure, yanking one side as Graves pulled the other, a ghastly smile on his face as Alex raved about everything.

"I know you stole Dad's rifle and sold it for whiskey, you miserable thief! I know, I know everything! Mother told me everything!"

Sympathy faded.

"I know you killed Father!"

"Shut it, you ungrateful shit!" Warren screamed.

"Do not listen, just hold him!"

"You killed him. You killed him."

Warren yanked harder. "That lying witch! She killed him, you idiot! She killed him when he was on a drunk so bad all he saw around him were goddamn Boer commandos, riding horseback into Fort William to kill him." He tore Alex's arm so hard Graves hit the clay tablet. "He hit her bad enough she can't hear much in her left ear and I tried, goddamn it, I tried to kill that son of a bitch but he was too big, too strong, and … he kept hitting her until I stood in his way."

Alex seethed, but his arms were still. "Coward and killer!"

"I took every shot he had, until she fired one he couldn't get up from. You woke. She said it was a burglar. And then she started drinking worse and hitting me more because she knew I could take it. Take whatever she had, and I wouldn't fight back. Leaving her precious Alexander without so much as a spanking."

Rasputin let go, then Graves.

"She said every mistake you made was my fault. Every spill, every broken toy, every stain in the rug. Tore it out of me. But I'm done paying. I didn't kill him, you stupid, ignorant shit. I tried! I fucking tried!" His fist came down like a hammer, breaking the clay table. Alex spilled to the floor. The crack in his head was filled with a grey substance. "Let me show you how well I can dish it out now!"

Graves grabbed him and they struggled hard until Rasputin's voice commanded the room. "Stop! Look!"

Alex sat on the floor, legs sprawled within the rubble, head low. The edges of the crack on his skull grew, covering the hole. Alex covered his head just as the hole vanished. He looked up. Blackness retreated from his eyes.

"Alex."

Alex stood, as if the march from Marlow's pit had never happened. Graves let go. Alex placed a hand on Warren's shoulder, smiled. Then drove his fist hard into his gut, breaking ribs that soon cracked back.

The pain was fresh and tremendous.

Then he picked Warren up, and hugged his crouching form.

"It is done," said Rasputin, breathing harder and heavier than a horse after a race. "I've held my part of the bargain. You will be true to yours."

Alex smiled.

Warren smiled back, then stood straight. "Yeah. Time for a long walk to hell."

"He must mend first," Rasputin said. "Rest, and then we march."

He put his hands in his pocket, and caressed the sharp edge of Tik's shark tooth, before Rasputin gathered a handful of men with sacks to begin the long march back to Marlow's pit.

Warren Bishop, who had never given a damn about this rich man's war, had only gone to make his dead brother proud, had now become something so big and rotten that it had the word doom stamped on the back of his eyelids. He was a soldier of the Dead.

Somewhere in heaven, hell, or wherever the Inuit tormented the living, Tik was laughing and shaking his head.

CHAPTER TWENTY-FOUR:

ENGINE OF WAR

Time slipped hard and fast in the silence that followed Felix's discovery. Vasilya's sore heartbeats punctuated each terse moment as all three of them sat at the workbench and stared at the floor, or the mangled wonders they'd destroyed to make the beast none could look at.

She'd rebuffed the colonel's healing hands, and slowly her sore heart eased. But there was a phantom pain that lingered, one she held on to. The pain that it took to make the monster move … it was a lesson she wanted to be reminded of, even if hurt. Giving life to a monster, it could take her own.

"I don't understand," Felix said. At his elbow sat the massive dynamo heart and a blood-soaked rag, dark and filthy, that made Vasilya sick. "It should have worked. We had enough gasoline. The specifications—"

"Had never been tested," Vasilya said, tapping her lip with her smelly finger. "We'd done nothing to guarantee its success. We rushed. We were sloppy. We cut corners in the name of speed and expediency like a peasant plumber. And we paid the price for it."

The colonel brushed down his moustache.

"What will happen," said Felix. "When the general comes back?"

"Nothing serious," said the colonel. "I'll just be tried as a war criminal for wasting millions of Papiermark on a useless enterprise. You'll be lucky to be sent back to the Ruhr, if not the front, as he promised. And our little inventor will be accused of being a foreign spy and hanged. Besides that, our fate is clean."

Vasilya sneered, three fingers over her lips. "I suppose you wish I'd destroyed myself again for that wretched thing? Torn out my own heart and shoved it in there to save your precious vision?"

The colonel exhaled slow, controlled, and frigid. "He is the brainchild of your patron, child. Do not forget that. And, yes. For the end of a war that has consumed a generation thus far, I think a life is worth it."

"Then why not tear out your own damn heart and put it in there!" she screamed, fist hammering the crimson rag. "You can talk all you want about the nobility of death, Colonel, but you are wasting your breath. It is people like you that have killed those generations. Not me. I build, I create, and so when you've found no way to stop the war you've let run like some perpetual motion machine of agony, you force me to create that … that hideous beast!" She pointed at the Juggernaut, then her fingers went crooked as spikes of thick, sharp pain flexed in her chest, as if her heart had become a ball of broken glass.

"Vas!"

Weakness took her to the ground, but Felix's iron hands caught her beneath her shoulders.

"Lay her down," the colonel said, bringing his black glove to his mouth to remove it.

Felix stood back a few paces. "No, she needs rest. Real rest. And not just so she can get back to work. She needs time—"

"We're wasting time with your petty romance," the colonel said. "Do not forget your place, Hilt. She's part of the royal court of the Tzar. If we manage to bring back her beloved Russia from the brink of revolution, you'd be no more wanted there than she is here, and don't you forget it! Now, put her

"If I do, you'll be the next one to hit the floor." The steel in his voice came with a tremble in his body. "Send me to the mines. Or to France. But if you lay that hand on her against her will, just so you can shove her back in a box to work a miracle for this war, you're dead."

"Boy," the colonel said.

"You're right, Colonel. I'm just common kin, not the son of the Junker class. And most of my kind would be all too happy to follow your commands" He moved back, awkwardly, clubfoot dragging. "But, as you can see, I'm abnormal. You neither scare me nor impress me and unless you want to see what a coal miner can do with his bare hands, then get out and let her rest. Now."

Vasilya hung in his arms, exhausted and dumbfounded. She did not want to be protected, she did not want to need rest, she did not want anyone on earth to be her soft place to fall…

But the relief, in that moment, overwhelmed her heart and mind. The colonel tightened his glove on his grey teeth, turned, and marched out. He made a point of locking the door as loud as pots and pans being dropped.

"I can sit," she said,

"I know, but you should lie down." His face was grim.

"Felix, I'm all right." She blinked, fatigue shaking her as she tried to move. "I'm … all right."

His voice softened, though was still strong. "Rest, Vas. You've more than earned it. I'll watch over you. You'll be safe"

His grim, ugly face did not yield, nor did his arms. And, in a moment of weakness, grief, and exhaustion, she nodded gently and began to feel the thick, warm hum of sleep within the strength of his arms.

Deep, dreamless, murky sleep followed. It left her frazzled body feeling like it was wrapped in a warm cocoon. How long, she was uncertain, but the fears of the return of General Hindenburg stirred her to wake like a splash of ice water in winter.

Felix gently helped her back to her cot. It smelled of clean sheets, and despite herself, the oily tentacles of sleep consumed her.

And the longer she slept, the stronger her heart became. She broke from slumber in fits and starts, and each time she breathed easier, longer. Sometimes it was night, and others it was day.

And in one dream, above the mangled wonders of the shop, she thought she saw Felix and the colonel, talking in the shadow of the Juggernaut. She strained her head to see two stern faces. But the exhaustion was total, and her efforts led her to collapse.

She woke to the steamy smell of beef broth.

"Time to eat," Felix said. His hand was dripping, and in it was a small bowl. "There is beef, and potato, and carrot. A real harvest this time." He took the spoon from the bowl.

"Enough," she said, and with supreme effort, swung her legs over the edge of the cot. "I have not been spoon fed since I was a baby, and if I ever do find the means to go back in time I would surely stop that Serbian terrorist from shooting Franz Ferdinand before going to my days in diapers. Give me the bowl."

He did.

It shook. Tremors ratcheted up her arms, to her spine. She gripped the blanket across her lap and peeled it off. It seemed to weigh an iron ton. Then the smell of soup caused ripples of hunger that focused her exhaustion on one goal. The spoon was heavy with meat, but she managed to bring it to her dry, cracked lips without making a fool of herself.

The broth was thick. The meat, too. And the carrot, as rare as a Fabergé egg, was sweeter than a cake. She tried eating slowly, but soon burned her mouth as she devoured the whole bowl.

Felix chewed on a crust of hard bread. "Appetite's a good sign you're on the mend."

She exhaled steam. "How long was I …"

"Not long."

"Don't lie. You're too earnest for that."

"Three days."

She felt the look of horror freeze on her face before anger gave her the strength to rise above the cot and slap him across the shoulder. "Three days? I should bash your ugly face with this bowl. Three days behind an already delayed schedule ..."

His hands were on her shoulder, easing her back to the cot. "Three days you needed. You're wasting away to shadow."

"Now I can live well enough to have Hindenburg kill us all. Delightful."

Felix put his hands in his pocket. "I don't think so."

"Why? Has he got a fate worse than death planned for us?"

"He died."

"What?"

"That's what the colonel said. Seems like we did some internal damage that crept up on him after all."

The ramifications were huge, but all Vasilya could think as she chewed the weak beef was to say, "And how does that save our life?"

"Colonel said only his guards know about the machine. When they told Luddendorf about it, he ignored their protests that anything was wrong. I think he's gone mad."

That explains a never-ending war, she thought to herself. "But ... but what does that mean for us?"

Sadness bit Felix's face. "Nothing. Everything. No one wants the machine. So, the colonel is sending me back to the Ruhr."

She tapped her mouth, playing a silent and melancholy tune on an invisible instrument. "Of course."

"And the colonel said you'd go to see your father."

"When?"

"Midnight. The last train to Berlin. Colonel is occupied until then."

Two hours.

"That's barely enough time. We should get started," she said, polishing off the soup and slowly getting up, and this time he helped her.

"Started on what?"

Her face contorted in shock. "On taking that beast apart so these filthy merchants of destruction can never use it with an alternate heart." She rubbed hers and tasted a faint flick of silver.

Felix's hand left her side. He turned and began his shuffle walk. "Funny. I figured you'd want to spend our last minutes together covered in grease and grime, tearing down what we made." He kept his sad walk. "Luckily, I foresaw that."

He hit the far lights and the creature was not in sight. She walked as fast as she could, until she saw its assorted pieces lying in hunks on the floor. She'd slept through the sound of dismemberment.

"My god, it's—"

"Done," he said. "All but a final step. Come."

They walked to the work desk. It was clean and clear except for two objects:

The dynamo heart and a pair of welding pincers.

"I thought you should have the honours." Felix lit a strand of newsprint, then walked to the forge standing like a cement and steel fist emerging from the workshop floor. He shoved in the flaming paper, then turned the gas: Deep orange and yellow flames roared and dark, rich heat washed across her face as he released the paper and it burned to quick smoke and ash.

She picked up the pincers with a grunt. It shook, and she could see the look of longing to help in Felix's eye. She grunted, gripped the dynamo heart, remembering the open cavity of Psycho the automaton, and the shattering pain in her own chest four days ago. I pray that I am not still attached to this thing—

With both hands, Vasilya carried the dynamo heart towards Felix and the forge. But it was slipping, and even against her glare, relief flooded her blood when Felix's hands gripped the pincers and they walked together the last few steps.

"It ends tonight," she said, the heat oppressive and yet welcome. "The nightmare ends tonight."

They stood together, and rammed the heart into the forge's maw. Flames ran wild and thick as the metal heated overtime. With hypnotic grace, the flames ate time as the complex, intricate and splendid heart became a ruined, misshapen mass of metal.

Felix's face twitched.

"Are you all right?"

He nodded. "The heat ... gets to me."

They pulled out the mangled mess of a heart and dropped it into a water bucket. Violent steam erupted like a volcano and the air tasted foul. Fans were switched on and when the acrid stench cleared, Felix was walking away.

And Vasilya's heart hurt again. Deeper, and cleaner, but no less painful. "Where are you going?"

He walked off, into the centre of the mangled wonders. "To find tonight's entertainment."

A scratch and a hiss cut through the last sounds of steam before the entire workshop filled with the most magnanimous notes of music.

A sweet word escaped past her lips and the fingers guarding their entrance like prison bars. "Chopin."

"Nocturnes," he said. "I thought you might like it. Since you're Russian."

"He's Polish."

Felix scratched his head. "Sorry. I'm not as cultured."

"Never mind that," she said, taking steps as quick as her heartbeats. She took his callused hand and shook it thoroughly and gravely. "Thank you, Felix. For everything. For ..."

Tears dripped off his thin lip. He nodded.

She'd never seen a man cry. Let alone an ugly man. Let alone ... a friend.

It was infectious. And she despised it, and him for being so weak. She had to do something or else she'd break down as bad as him. "Felix."

"Yes, Vas."

She swallowed the sadness. "Dance with me."

His eyes widened. "I ... I can't."

"I don't care. I don't care if we look like fools to the rest of the world. I don't care about anything else right now because right now, tonight—" A wet sliver from a single tear cut down her cheek, offering relief from the heat of the workshop. She sniffed to keep the rest at bay. "Tonight, I want to dance. With you." She put took his right hand in her left and raised it to begin a waltz.

Felix nodded, grimly. "Ok, Vas. But you lead, all right?" He smiled and the tears dripped. "You're good at it." Then, he chuckled.

She smiled and laughed, too, and with awkward movements they waltzed amidst wonders of the world to the soft and sad notes from the gramophone, transforming an hour into an eternal moment, just for them, the mad world be damned.

A yawn shook her and Felix held her close. Thick waves of fatigue turned the waltz into a slow, gentle turn, before she lay her head against Felix's chest.

"I'm sorry," he said.

"Me too," she whispered, eyes drooping.

"Not as much as me." His voice became distant. "Goodbye, Vas." And despite the spark of will to stay awake, she slept, thick and deep, in his arms.

CHAPTER TWENTY-FIVE:

DEEP WELLS OF HUNGER

Warren marched alone, behind the ragtag outfit that neither wanted nor cared for him. Alex led them, Rasputin at his side. Alex had said nothing since that glob of worms had brought his brain back from the pit it had fallen into. He was strong enough to march, to fight, but speech had been lost. Rasputin said it would come back, in time.

Coming back, Warren thought. Could anything come back from this?

They'd come back from death.

To kill.

And when it was done, where would they go?

What would they do? Return to the pit?

No. They would not.

They would continue doing whatever Rasputin wanted.

And somehow, taking the first train back into the grave did not seem like it was in the cards. They'd keep fighting and fighting … maybe until all that were left were their kind.

A million Graveses and Rasputins.

Their peace would make Europe a living graveyard.

Run, Warren thought. I could run. I did what Alex wanted. My bones won't be worth a damn to the war they're about to wage. Run. Just run like I always do. Running Dog, that's what Tik had called him when they were young, back in the normalcy of a Fort William dice game and rotgut rye, fixing a card game, always ready to run if things went bad …

… but always ready to run into the storm if Tik was in danger.

Alex.

What are you now?

Undead. Draug. Worm brain. Puppet. Brother.

"Get your head out of your ass," Graves said from yards ahead, "we won't wait for you to catch up."

And the legion walked forward, flickers of torchlight giving them dreadful shapes on the walls. Tik used to say you can tell a lot about a man by his shadow, that it was a part of the man who hid inside the other, "the devil twin you keep in line." When Warren asked where he'd gotten that line, Tik had smiled. "Some drunk preacher trying to save my savage soul. It was the last thing he said before he grabbed my wrist and I broke his god-fearing arm and told him I was already saved."

Warren laughed at the warm memories of Tik, of running wild in Fort William, of stealing train rides and having to become a remittance man, and of the books he told Tik he would write. Yarns of adventure, and the macabre, and spicy tales of bordellos classier than any of the whorehouses they had experienced. Tales of monsters and heroes, of guns and grit, pistol-packing whores who fought off drunken lumberjacks.

And Tik always just shook his head. "You're a dreamer, Qimmiq. You talk of writing, but you'd rather live it than stay still and write it."

"Maybe I'll write it if I have an adventure worthy of sitting down and typing."

"You don't even own a typewriter."

"Well, I'll dictate."

"You've been doing that to me, Qimmiq, since before the world was born. And I can't write!"

Those conversations ended up in collar and elbow matches that destroyed tables and windows until they were gouging each other in the mud, nine times out of ten with Tik riding Warren's back, bulk arms around Warren's neck, choking him until the stars in his eyes blackened in what Tik called the hangman's knot.

But Tik was dead. And a hangman's knot wouldn't do piddly to Warren's dead neck. It seemed an awful trade.

Hard, lonely miles stretched under the earth as Warren trailed the Lost Battalion. He cut his thumb on the shark tooth in his pocket, and hated the sick, suckering feeling of the wound closing in on itself as if eating the cut and birthing new, dead skin.

Was it the cruel laughter of the Lost Battalion or the painful throbs in his stomach that Warren heard first? Unclear, but they were marching side by side as they all followed the dark worm tunnel.

Warren grunted.

They snickered.

He swallowed hard and grunted again.

A few stray laughs from the bastards in a dull rainbow of different uniforms.

He gripped the loose earth of the walls as an ungodly pain burst in his stomach. For the first time since Alex had brought him back from the pit of death, weakness gripped his balls and pain seized throughout his guts.

"Somebody's hungry," Graves said. "Say, Alexander, ain't you taught him how to feed?"

Alex looked back, but said nothing.

"Show him, Graves," Rasputin said.

The miserable Brit, grinning ear to ear, took off a backpack. "You'll hate me first, but thank me later."

"Too late on the first part," Warren said, spitting through clenched teeth, hunched over his bent knees.

"No way to treat a gourmet chef." He dug into his back and pulled out a sack made out of what looked like butcher paper. "Now, dear heart, the key to this is teeny tiny bites, chew, chew, chew and swallow."

The smell was ungodly, a plumed stink of rotting meat and spoiled wine, and sickly intoxicating.

And familiar. Same scent that stains the barbed wire of No-Man's Land as you try to pull a mate from the metal teeth holding him like a fly in a mechanical spider web, a smell rich in the air of a casualty clearing station or the freshly-shelled hole of the enemy's forward positions: the stink of human meat.

Haze filled his mind, and he fought the awesome pull to eat. Gripping his shoulders, he found himself unable to pull his eyes away from the slick, sinewy block.

"A bunch of the boys were whooping it up in the Malamute saloon," Warren coughed, covering his mouth, mumbling the line as he pretended the agony in his belly was somewhere else. "The kid that handles the music box was hitting a jag-time tune; Back of the bar, in a solo game, sat Dangerous Dan McGrew. And watching his luck was his light-o'-love, the lady that's known as Lou."

Graves snorted. "Jesus, what are you, a beggar poet? I'm giving you a meal for free, you idiot." He kicked the meat to Warren's feet, and just seeing the dirt start to stain it made him furious.

But on Warren went, reciting the poem, until the worlds dissolved into meaningless gasps of sound, mouth shucking open and closed until every poem, every tall tale, every bawdy song and carney tune in his arsenal had vanished as soon as he thought of it.

All that was left was the thick, sweet aroma of meat.

The last dollop of restraint broke in Warren's frazzled mind. His hand shot into the bag, and shoved the contents whole into his mouth.

Gushes of fresh blood and meat released a wave of relief through his whole body, a heady euphoria he'd never experienced. Neither drink nor the rare opium smoke from the decadent Orient had unlocked such a golden rush. He devoured the meat, eating one end of the piece to the other, half expecting himself to crack the bone for marrow. Relief washed over him as he fell to his knees, about to bite in the far end.

"Good mutt," Grave said. "But I warned you, as soon as you're done—"

The drips from his lip grew as he shook, staring at the end of the meat stick.

A hand.

A human hand.

He convulsed and Graves's iron hand covered his mouth and shoved his head into the dirt wall like one of Tik's straight right hands. "Don't you dare retch it up. I ain't being nursemaid to a baby draug again. Keep it in you."

Warren struggled, but the meat … the human meat … sat in his belly for an instant.

A shock of pleasure filled his squirming heart.

Then he stopped squirming.

"That's it, mutt. Let the meat take hold." Graves took away his hand. "Feel better, don't you?"

Warren pulled himself from the man-sized imprint he'd left in the wall and drooped to the ground on all fours. "Sick, you people—"

Graves kneeled and whispered. "We're your people now, Mutt. If you like losing battles, go on pretending otherwise. But do so on the march and follow us, or the next time Rasputin turns his back I'll drill your skull so hard that not even all the king's worms will be able to put your brain together again." Then he clasped Warren's neck and pulled him close. "And try, just try to wrest a morsel I'd been saving since you returned, and I'll be chewing on your own goddamn arm, just to see if a new one can grow back." He tossed Warren, face-first, against the tunnel wall, and started marching double time. "Time waits for no man, Mutt. Get in step or wait for the Charger to come and find you. Classic law, fear what's behind you more than what's in front!" Graves's dark laugh echoed in the tunnel, his shadow long and lean with hands at his sides like claws.

Warren spit the taste from his mouth that was still ambrosia to his tongue, then stood, leaving the filthy hand behind him.

Cannibals.

An army of dead cannibals.

Other words fouled his mind like the taste on his breath. Ghouls. Vampires. The monsters of myth made flesh.

So this was the price for immortality, he thought. Devouring the lives of others.

And it clicked.

There would be no end for creatures like this … like him. They were a maw of human suffering, worse than the war. Because a war had an end. Peace would return. Or at least it could.

But not for these men.

There would be no peace for those who dine on the living. They would always need more.

If Rasputin gets all the deadroot he needs … then maybe the war would truly be eternal.

A pair of hands lifted him from the ground as the far torchlight stopped moving.

Alex smiled, but his eyes held worry.

"It's all right," Warren said. "I'm all right."

Alex swallowed a sad thought. Warren figured it was about this little price tag for immortality. "I'm all right."

Alex, childlike, nodded, and took Warren's hand, leading him to the front to walk with him and Rasputin, who was clearly upset.

"Alexander, we haven't much time," Rasputin said.

Alex nodded, and the three of them continued, the Lost Battalion singing songs of victory in Russian, German, French and English, a strange cacophony that prickled Warren's ears.

Marching on, Warren truly feared what was in front of him more than what was behind him.

But he would not run.

Whatever hell awaited, he was going to protect Alex from it. And hell was coming. The only question was, would it be hell on earth? Surrounded by the Lost Battalion, guts filled with the flesh of the living, it was beginning to be easier to believe that if God had existed, he'd abandoned them for good.

He sucked the warm, sweet taste of flesh from his teeth. Tik, he thought, I hope I have the strength to fuck things up like I always do.

CHAPTER TWENTY-SIX:

OF MICE AND VENGEANCE

I'm sorry.

Vasilya was stumbling off her cot, to her feet, shaking the thick sleepiness that had filled her head for a silent eternity.

Her bowl was besides her cot. With a supreme effort, she lifted it to her clearing sight.

A hint of powdered residue was at the bottom.

I'm sorry.

She dropped it and it failed to shatter so she stomped on it with her booted heel until it was broken. Anger began to burn away the sedated sensation in her bones and blood.

Drugged. He drugged me …

She ran to where the Juggernaut had been lying in pieces, Click and Clack at her heels then up and into her pockets, the brass butterflies fluttering in the distant rafters above her. She ran to the Hanging Garden of Prometheus.

Nothing.

Every limb, and the command chamber, even the remote box, was gone. She'd slept through everything.

"I'm sorry."

She froze. The anger in her wanted to burst, but she let it simmer. "Where?"

Colonel Balk walked through the path cut on the dusty floor where they'd dragged the Juggernaut's pieces. He stood by the chain where the arms had once hung. "I had no other choice. And do not think too bad of young Felix. He is a brave German boy who had no choice, either."

She shook the web of sleep from her mind. "Where is he?"

Balk laid a hand on the Turkish Chess Player's head, tracing the hole in the back where they had cut out his mechanical brain. "On the road to ending this war, child."

"Impossible," she said, arms crossed. "Felix's gifts were building, not designing, not controlling. He doesn't know how to make the creature move. I barely do, and I never showed him anything." The colonel's face puckered, and she read the expression like a puzzle. The fear. The regret. The smugness that he was likely right. "Where is Felix?"

He caressed the face of the Flute Player, long wounds where her veins had once been. "You've done us a great service, child." Then he passed the midget Psycho and his gapping, empty chest. And flinched. "I believe the war will be over soon."

The picture in her head completed in vibrant, awful colour, a monstrous vision of matryoshka dolls made of the Juggernaut, each one consuming the other, until all she could see was the small, fragile, baby. "Oh god ... he's not going to control it. He's going to put himself ... inside it." He eyes narrowed. "And use his own heart as the engine! You did that, with your blasted spider hands. Didn't you? Answer me, you monster!"

"I had no choice!" he screamed, but she stood firm. Balk inhaled once, and then the words stormed out with frenetic energy. "I do not have the luxury of not giving a damn what happens if I fail. The nightmares that continue. The ruin that leads to my doorstep. If I had not found a way to salvage the project, we'd all be dead."

"You mean you'd be dead."

The anger boiled in his voice as he slowly leaned down to stare at her face to face. "You think I fear death? What the hell do you know of it?" He walked forward and she stepped back, stunned by what she had triggered. "All my life I have served. Served my prince in his army. Served my growing nation in battle. I've had more than one whiff of grapeshot, and I've still gone forward. When the blasted French mobs organized an army of drunks at La Manse, outnumbering us five to one, when there was no hope but for the iron disciple of the firing line, I did not fear death, even when it came for me." He lifted his eye patch, revealing the skull socket and skin like leather. "Death came for me and I would have gone, and would have put my crippled old body within that wild contraption." He dropped the patch. "But the one thing I could not do was heal myself. I would not survive a surgical insertion." He stood straight. "But I could heal him."

"You mean ensnare him in that contraption." Air pipes and copper wires, digging into Felix's chest like spears and vipers; she could see it, grotesque and clear in her mind. "Stop him."

"It was his choice."

"Stop him, Colonel. I'll do it. Put me inside instead."

"No. If he should fail, we'll need someone to fix the machine."

Her teeth ached as the words forced themselves past. "And get another corpse to ride in it. You're sending him to his grave. You're a murderer."

"The loss of a life, to save a million. That is the final calculus of war that we have used."

She strode forward. "It is the math of a barbarian. And I won't be part of the equation any longer. Take me to him."

He was taken aback at the steel in her voice. "Don't be foolish."

From the door came a creak. The soft steps of feet and cane. A man stood by the doorway, a dark brown suit, complete with gold pocket watch. Thin, frail, but eyes sparkling like blue diamonds, bald head free of fever sweat, beard clean and crisp the way he liked it in summer.

"Besides," the colonel said, "there is someone who wants to see you."

Her anger softened as he tried to smile. "Good morning, my beautiful dove."

Hands dropped to her sides. Words formed on her lip. But which ones? Father? Monsieur Fabergé? Her mind chose the safest one.

"Sir?"

He nodded, breathing hard. "Come closer."

She resisted. She wanted anger to rule this moment, the image of Felix punctured and stuffed inside the hideous beast … but she could not deny Monsieur Fabergé's long suffering an ounce of relief.

She ran, wanting to embrace him, but the look on his face held her back.

"We must talk, child. No room for petty sympathy."

She nodded. But inside she winced. Not even a thank you for working to save his life.

"You worry about this boy?"

She nodded. "He's in that thing—"

"I know. The colonel and I have discussed it."

She swallowed a painful sob. "Discussed?" A spark of hope. Surely, Monsieur Fabergé would know how to save Felix—

"From the beginning, he has kept me abreast of your efforts."

"Wait, you knew? About Felix?"

He gave a quick, stern nod. "I was the one who suggested he help you. I knew his father. He was an amateur collector of automatons, like the colonel and myself."

"No, I mean, you knew what happened to Felix."

"Listen to him," said the colonel, hand behind his back.

She continued to face M. Fabergé. "Listen to what?"

Monsieur Fabergé's face hardened to a diamond visage. "We need Felix to do this, Vasilya."

The sound of her name, coming from his crooked mouth, was like a slap in the face, a surprise so big it hurt. He'd never called her that. Always a nickname. It sounded awkward and sharp.

"We believe Felix will succeed," Monsieur Fabergé said. "And if that happens, we shall have peace in the West."

Vasilya caught the colonel glaring at him. "Peace in the West? Not peace?"

M. Fabergé's glance waltzed the room. "Well, of course, we would use the machine to root out the Bolsheviks."

"We must focus on the immediate concern," the colonel said. "Germany will not go back to fighting a two-front war."

Vasilya steadied her breathing as anger began to roll out from her heart, tightening her body. "What happens after there is peace in the West, Sir? And once the Bolsheviks are done? What then?"

"We leave that to the politicians," Balk said.

It was a fragment of the truth, a jutting piece of honesty that was not complete. But from its ragged end she could see the missing piece.

"I know what she is talking about," said Fabergé, with a smile both wicked and clever. Then he placed a worn, wrinkled and steady hand against her cheek. "It's what she's wanted since I built her first workshop. And it will come true. When Lenin and his thugs are hanged from the highest tree, you will come to work with me at the master workshop for the new Tzar. And together, we shall provide the new royals the magic of wonder that will become the symbol of a new Russia. You will make the first egg, the one you've been sketching in secret for all these years. The Phoenix of Russia."

Vasilya wanted to deny the rich, soothing tone in his voice that caressed her dreams so sweetly she could almost see the grand palace at full bloom for a Tzar's return—

She shoved Monsieur's hand away, to his obvious horror and disgust. "What happens to Felix?"

"Felix sacrificed himself," said the colonel. "Would you deny him the freedom to choose his fate?"

"Choose!" She seethed. "You call this choice? You probably told him I'd be in that monster if he didn't volunteer, and then let him think he was choosing to save me."

"Vasilya, it is done," M. Fabergé said, her name again a bitter barb across his lip, the arrogant tone richer than when he'd chastise her for working too slow, or too fast, or on every stupid question she would ask about the strength of gold, the density of wire, the conductivity of copper. "The wheels in motion cannot be undone. We must accept it and move forward on our own steam. I am sorry for your friend, but there is still hope. He is brave, and strong, and with the colonel's agency ... there is a chance we will see him again."

He reached out again, and she retreated. Hands shoved in her coat, she held on to Click and Clack. "You're right, Sir. There's a good chance I'll see him again." I only have one chance at this, she thought. Father, forgive me.

Monsieur Fabergé lifted his cane and gave the air a tap. "Now that is the triumphant spirit of my dove."

She gripped her mice, tapping a Morse code on their bellies. But realized their hearts were thrumming with hers. No code needed. She tossed them at each man before her.

Balk and Fabergé shrieked and scampered but could not find purchase to the razor quick mice as they followed her thoughts like Marconi receivers. They hid in their jackets.

"Be still." Her voice chilled. "You saw what they did to the spy on the train, Colonel. Don't move."

Both men held themselves as calmly as possible.

"What are you doing?" Monsieur Fabergé said.

"Taking command of the chess game you were playing for me," she said. "I'm sorry … Sir. I no longer want to play this part of marionette and monster-maker and potential murderer."

"You can't save him," said the colonel.

"Nor can you stop me from trying," she said, "unless you wish to lose your last eyeball." She went to Robert-Houdin's magic books, and opened up the last volume. Inside was a pair of iron handcuffs, tattooed with rust. She placed them on the hands of Monsieur Fabergé.

"I cannot believe you are doing this," he said.

She cinched them tight. "I could not believe you drew the plans for the Juggernaut." She led him to a magic cabinet. "The guards will likely notice something is amiss later, and will free you. By then, we should be gone."

She helped him in as his soft face turned stern. "You'd do this to me after all I have done for you? For your mother?"

She placed her pillow behind his head. "What was the first lesson you taught me in the shop? When I started on old watches. 'Finish what you start.' I'm doing exactly that, Sir. And I'm finishing it on my own, without your guiding hand."

He shoved back and sounded low. "You will release me at once. I will not take orders from—"

She waited. "Can't say it, can you? Then allow me. You will take orders from your bastard daughter, the shame of your family, and the only one who is your rightful heir to the talent of the Fabergé name. And you will do so now, and without question, or I will have my greatest creation burn your spine to cinders."

A terse silence.

Monsieur Fabergé grimaced.

And she braced herself.

"Your mother was a dancehall whore. And you are no goddamn daughter of mine."

The words hit, and she let them sink in, because she knew what must happen next.

A thought flittered and there was a horrific whiff of ozone as Monsieur Fabergé's body seized hard and wild with convulsions, blood oozing from his nose and ears until the seizing stopped, his gargled screams fell silent, and he fell into the magic box. Clack's smoking form ran out from the folds of the clothes and into her pocket, the warmth bringing her a small measure of comfort as she slammed the magic box shut, and secured the lock. "Goodbye. Father." The words were frigid. "I'll be with you in a minute, Colonel. Why not tell the guard he should go have a cigarette while you scold me."

She found Felix's old clothes, filthy as the day she arrived. It was awful, and heavenly, and she tried not to let nostalgia run amok. She put them on, bunning her hair into his cap, then smearing her face with grease and dirt from the machines. She stuffed some rags into her clothing to give her a modicum of bulk and less obvious bosom, and stuffed more rags into his old shoes so they fit. When she was done, she looked like a thin version of Felix and smelled like Sulphur and mange.

The twin butterflies landed on her shoulder. "I suspect you don't want to say here and wait for someone else to mangle you?" They fluttered, but stayed put. "Fine." Gently, she took them in hand, and they folded themselves until they were paper thin, a wavy strip of tin to the naked eye. She hid them within the folds of her jacket, but they migrated toward her back, almost smooth against her shoulder blades.

I seem to have become an Arc, she thought, and smiled.

With Clack in her pocket, she walked to the door as the colonel, sweating, opened it. "This is a fool's errand," the colonel said. "How the devil do you think you're going to get to the front?"

"That's for you to figure out."

"I will not—"

"You will, Colonel. Because I have nothing to lose. Take me to Felix, or lose the only one who can fix and manage that monster."

"You forget yourself. We have your father."

She snickered. "Unless your spider hand can raise the dead, no, you don't." Her sarcasm was venomous. "Hurry, Colonel," she said, walking out of her prison, the feeling of freedom, of control, like cherry brandy on her lips. "We have to catch a train."

CHAPTER TWENTY-SEVEN:

PITS AND CIRCUMSTANCES

Hideous light from the battlefield above began to fill the tunnel with a grey gloom as they approached the end of the worm hole, Warren sick in his gut, mind, and what was left of his soul. Rasputin called up a German scout named Dolph, who had gaps between his teeth big enough to pass a baby's fist. They spoke in Hun tongue while Alex smiled at Warren and Warren tried not to bawl or retch. Soon, Dolph returned with a report.

"We must wait for night," Rasputin said. "But we are deep enough in the earth that the creatures above ground will not hear even a gunshot. Dolph believes there is an advance party of Germans here. Snipers and some artillery."

"Why not take them out now?" Graves said. "I'm tired of living like a mole."

"Be my guest," Warren said. "See how that thick head does with German snipers."

"Right," Graves said. "Might end up like poor Alex."

Rasputin's hawkish gaze fell on Warren.

Warren smiled, hands palm up. His hate for Graves was a blizzard in his heart, but he kept it confined.

"We wait," Rasputin said. "We move like worms. We take what is ours, and then return to prepare for the end of this war."

Warren leaned against the wall. It crumbled some on his neck. "Mind sharing how you plan to do that?" Warren said. "For those who aren't already in the know? I mean, what do you know that General Haig and the Huns don't know?"

An odd quiet came across the men. A treacherous silence. Rasputin gripped a handful of dirt, letting it fall through his hands. "We will show them the true face of war. And as each one of their soldiers falls, like the dirt from my hand, he will be born again in the army of the damned."

"Bull," Warren said. "There ain't enough deadroot to do that. That pit, well, it might be filled, but you'd need thousands, maybe millions, not hundreds." The Canadian Corps alone was tens of thousands strong, and it was part of the British Army, and France's and Germany's armies were bigger still. "You're holding back your ace," Warren said. "What is it?"

Rasputin smiled. "I don't play my hand until it is time to win, Warren Bishop. But I'm starting to think you doubt my ability to command this mission." Everyone stepped back, even Graves. Alex's face went taut with worry. "So I give you this chance to change the guard." He dropped his tattooed arms. "If you can."

"What? Fisticuffs?"

"If that's what you'd prefer—"

Instincts snapped as quick as his hand. He drew the pistol and fired at Rasputin's head. The Russian madman flew back and hit the wall.

Shock coiled their attention, but before they could scream or gasp or drive a knife into Warren's throat, Rasputin rolled over, twisted, and stood upright, smiling. Between his teeth was a bullet. He pushed it out with his tongue. "You're a good shot." The smile dropped. "My turn."

His fists were on Warren faster than hornets from a freshly kicked hive, and life became a tidal wave of sharp pain and woozy rebounding. Blocks torn down, kicks blocked with hammer strikes as the light in Warren's eyes dimmed and flickered. He'd only seen Tik fight like this, as if trained to anticipate every move that came, like some dance of pain and instinct.

The ground hit him hard and was followed by a boot to the back of the head that sent him breathing dirt.

As if staring into the blackness of an open grave, Warren thought he saw Tik, shaking his head. "Come on, Qimmiq. You ain't dead yet. How you take out a man kicking the shit out of you?"

Warren nodded to the fading ghost.

"Now stop bothering me," Tik said. "I've got a life here that doesn't revolve around your fuck-ups anymore." Tik laughed and vanished.

Spikes of pain rolled across his back as Rasputin's boots tried to dislodge his organs.

Warren drove his hand in his pocket. He gripped Tik's shark tooth. Then he shoved himself over, gasping for the air he didn't really need.

A boot cracked his ribs, rose, dropped again.

How do you stop a man from kicking the shit out of you?

Let him.

Then—

The boot cracked two more ribs in gushes of pain and Warren gripped Rasputin's ankle and twisted.

The wizard hissed, and pulled it away. When he put it down, he growled, then glared.

Warren pulled himself up, already feeling the bones mend with a sick sucking. Then he faked a left jab and threw a haymaker of a straight right, right at Rasputin's temple—

His fist ate dirt instead of skull as Rasputin ducked and rolled as if made of wind, and was back on his feet. The shark tooth bit into his fist as he yanked it out, warm pain a gentle stream. Warren dropped his guard, grabbing his ribs, and the snake took the bait.

Those cold, iron fingers choked his neck, lifted him from the ground. Warren flailed, hands trying to undo the grip, as Rasputin brought him eye to eye. "See, boy, that you cannot undo that which has been cast by destiny. So, if you cannot face the fate I am about to unleash, then be prepared to be buried deep beneath its fathoms. Plato said that only the dead have seen the end of war. The question is, will you be the dead who sleeps without it, or the dead that brings it to sleep?"

The crowd stood behind Rasputin, a ragged mob of killers whose eyes were glazed with the kind of belief that led to crusades and inquisitions and holy war. The mindless devotion that drowns everything in its wake with redness.

And Alex, sad-eyed, worm-brained … what world will you inherit when this madman has done his worst on the world? Rasputin's voice was a ragged growl. "Choose, or I'll tear your head off like a boil."

The shark tooth burned in his fist, and in the darkness there began a hazy red glow off the staring faces.

"Chief," Graves said. "His hand—"

Thunder rumbled.

But not from Warren's hand.

A shimmer wave of shock was rumbling through the ground, gaining speed and violence until they fell to the floor. Echoes of blasts beneath the ground rode each other. But Rasputin still clutched hard.

"Sappers!" yelled Graves. "We got sappers! We need to get topside!"

"No!" Rasputin yelled.

"Yes!" Graves yelled. "We'll be frozen beneath the dirt, easy pickings for head shots. Chief, there ain't no thinking about it!"

Another blast. A dark, thick wave filled the cavernous hole.

"Avalanche!" screamed a Frenchman.

Finally, Rasputin released Warren. "To the topside!" They all ran up as all around them the world collapsed into darkness and mud.

"Come on, you maggots!" screamed Graves, as if he'd been born for such moments. "Leave the grave for the living!"

They scurried up and out of the hole, ants in the dirt, Warren swallowing and gagging as he fought against the filthy tide, searching for Alex's face in the swim upstream. But all he found was muddy blackness …

… and a warm pain in his fist he could not shake.

The shark tooth was in his hand, sore as hell, and something told him it would not come out.

Crawling toward daylight, Warren burst into the hot vibrant embrace of the war, alive and well and screaming despite his absence. Shells churned the already wounded earth into a quicksand earthquake and he scrambled against the sound of Lee-Enfields cracking shots. Somewhere close by, ruinous blasts of a Bren gun turned the air to lead.

"Helmets on, scatter and return fire!" Graves yelled while lobbing grenades from the tip of a gully littered with broken wagons like wooden skeletons. A German helmet graced his head. Shots cracked around him but he stood facing it with a sneer as he tore open the wrapping around his own Enfield. "Come on, Come on! Cry Havoc, and all that shite! Operation Sleeping Dog! Go!"

And, mortality and death splattering around him, Warren saw Graves in his element. Carnage suited him like scales on a snake. Warren dove behind a mangled black husk of a tank, the beast still stinking of diesel and blood, and slid underneath and out of sight. Graves fired and the hundred troops rallied around him. A shot tore into him and he hit the bottom of the gully.

They all stood firing, helmets on like a brigade of brigand knights, and one by one they fell into the trench like an open grave. Madness, Warren thought … then connected the dots as bullets tore into them, until all of the Lost Battalion lay motionless in the trench.

Sleeping possums.

Cracks of rifle fire stopped as an order was given to hold fire.

Warren knew the procedure for the advancing troops. Leapfrogging, they approached the gully. Warren tucked in deeper beneath the tank. Still, eyes half closed, but focused on the lip of the gully, he watched.

Grenades were thrown.

The blast was awful.

And bodies flailed in the air, landing awkwardly as toys tossed on a nursery floor by a giant.

A few more grenades, a few more charred soldiers. God, how can they stand it? It was agonizing, thinking Alex was in there, but he'd never save him by running out alone.

"Clear!" called the scout, and judging by his puttees he was a Brit. And soon there was a familiar sound of boots thumping dirt, bodies jangling across the scared earth.

Warren went limp. Boots surrounded his tank, carrying a nasally Manchester accent so thick he wondered if it were Gaelic or the lost languages of earth.

"Any Jerries?"

"No, just a dead colonial underneath, by the uniform."

"Jesus, where did he come from?"

"Fuck knows, but I didn't hit him and you can't prove I did."

"Like I have time to court-martial you for being a bloody idiot? Come on."

A cry from the lip of the gully, then a swell of voices. "Hell, what's this?"

"He's no Jerry, that's a Hapsburg tunic."

"That's a French uniform. What the devil is a Frog doing here?"

"Jesus, there's a Tommy here!"

A weak voice. Graves. "Help ... me."

"He's alive! Medic!"

They rallied around the body being dragged from the gully.

Graves, helmet and German great coat no longer on him, stumbled around, acting wounded or drunk. "They ... came from nowhere. Never saw them ... coming. They were a nightmare, the worst bastards you'd ever seen. Came out of nowhere." He stumbled forward and everyone turned their back to the gully.

"Who came out of nowhere?"

Graves fell to his knees, reached into his shirt, and yanked out a grenade with a thick smile. "We did." He yanked the pin and laughed. "Catch." He tossed it in the air and dove.

The blast ate their expressions and Warren jammed his head to the earth. All that was left were smears, limps, and a red mist. Graves had been shot a few meters away, but stood quick, mangled flesh on his tattered back and calves weaving itself back to its grey self. "Fuck the defensive. Battalion, charge!"

And they did.

Warren was beside himself beneath the tank, watching a massacre unveil itself as the remaining battalion of Tommies struggled to stop the madmen who ran on as holes were blasted in their chests, or bayonets caught in their throats, stray shots bouncing from their helmets. Relentless and vicious, the Lost Battalion were dogs who had learned well how to shoot and kill with gun and fist. The kind of stupid risks you never take in battle became their doctrine. A reckless, savage carnage of meat, bone and bullet.

And Alex, the most savage.

Gone was the tranquil silent face.

Instead there was madness and rage.

There was no good reason to think that the old Alex was buried beneath the new, alive in the worm brain beneath his skull.

A fresh platoon charged the elevated hill that the British had run over, heading right toward Alex whose bear hands were cleaving men's jaws from their body. Training kicked in like a forgotten instinct rekindled: Warren shouldered his rifle and fired as Tommies charged Alex, picking them off like a ducks from the marsh, each bullet ending with a punctuated burst of the man's head, taking them off as they emerged. There was nothing else to do.

"Pull back!" Graves shouted, hoarse and loud, from somewhere. "Jerry is here! Jerry is—"

Shells hammered with constant strikes—a creeping barrage. Across the battlefield, to the left of the hill, a curtain of fire and steel roared against the earth. The battalion charged like steeds back to the gully where, to Warren's astonishment, Rasputin stood out in the open.

Warren scrambled from beneath the tank, ran to the gully as the barrage shook the earth, and charged into the trench, only to hear the vile whispers coming from Rasputin. Speaking the wormtongue he'd heard in the hospice with Alex on the slab.

Alex crashed beside him, smiling red, nodding.

Warren smiled back, but avoided his brother's joyous eyes while the thunder approached, knowing that even these unstoppable men could not withstand a full artillery battery that crashed louder and closer and louder until his bowels quivered—

Then nothing.

A heartbeat later, the tremble of a distant tremor and then, a metallic crash.

"Charger to the rescue," Grave said, sucking shrapnel from his teeth, then spitting it out. "Nicely done, Chief."

Warren peered above the lip of the gully.

There was no giant worm. But trouble was beginning to storm. On the field were the advance platoons of stormtroopers. Masters of small infantry tactics that had been causing havoc everywhere on the front. Tough, smart, and armed with flamethrowers. While every one of the soldiers looked fine in their torn clothing, he did not relish the idea of being burned and growing new skin, no matter how fast.

Rasputin's voice was loud, clear, and forceful as a gale at sea. "Finish those Teutonic bastards," Rasputin said. "Let them also taste the scythe we bring."

"Right!" Graves shouted. "Loose formation. Everyone buddy up, Froggy style. Charge!" Graves said, and like starved dogs unchained they screamed murder in a dozen languages, put on their helmets, and followed him onto the battlefield, Alex in tow, and Warren behind him.

Bullets flew as the distance closed with the thunder of boot heels scraping ragged terrain made of scorched earth and dead men. The krauts shouted something. Then Warren saw ... they were all masked.

"Gas!" Warren shouted

Grenades cluttered the air, and a series of dull explosions unleashed a sizzling haze.

Shit, Warren thought.

Mustard gas. Goddamn Jerries have them in grenades?

His skin rippled as it had the first time, but did not burst. They ran into the chemical fog and Warren saw each of the battalion target a Hun. One charged head-on, tearing off the bastard's gas mask. Another ran through the gun fire, tackling a flame-throwing Hun to the floor, followed by a scream and an explosion as flames and heat punctuated the haze. Alex was firing his rifle and jamming his bayonet in another kraut throat, leapfrogging Graves's position deeper into the murky green and yellow battlefield.

A rumble stopped them cold.

It wasn't a sapper explosion.

It wasn't artillery cracking the earth.

Nor the distant rumble of the mysterious Charger.

It was a steady, slow, plodding thud. Boom … Boom. Tiny earthquakes getting closer. When a shadow emerged from the fog, all the blistered and healing eyes dawned upon it.

Bullets whizzed by. Warren's dead heart pushed him across the shaking terrain, the monster on the horizon towering above the ruined stumps of trees.

Right before Alex.

A swarm of pain cut into his side, shoving his momentum of track. As derailed as a drunken train, he tripped over his feet.

On his back, he seethed. More machine gun fire peppered the air above him. Hold on, Alex, he thought. Hold on to what's left of you and I'll do the same.

He crawled, the wound in his side knitting itself closed. Bullets sizzled past and for the first time since he'd started basic training at Valcartier, he wished he'd had that stupid tin hat. Too kind of Rasputin not to issue him one.

Hugging the earth, he scrambled like a crab while the puckering of his wounds made him sick. The bullets were still hot inside him, pinches of metal beneath fresh skin that wove itself over the hole.

Heavier sounds came from above the mustard haze: the scream of shells descending from heaven. The impact shattered and launched him into black air. Pain flashed and vanished as a weightless tear roamed his gut. He spun, lifeless, and saw Alex's bone-white body like a single flower in a garbage heap, yards ahead.

Warren landed, all elbows and knees The impact rattled his bones, scared that his body had been torn in half and he hadn't realized it. He dared a look. All the pieces were there, or so it seemed. Words were muted in the scream of dirt and fire, and all that ran in his head were three simple words—

Fuck, fuck, fuck.

Still shivering, he ran, bullets tearing fresh holes with the impact of brass-knuckle punches, but he sallied forth against their mortal impact and surged forward as Alex stood, gun at the ready and pointed at the thing that had silenced the battlefield.

Warren swallowed hard as the thunder approached through the mist and took concrete form.

Standing before him was a steaming nightmare, three stories tall. A giant man that was half-tank, half-artillery battery, metal arms and legs thicker than redwood tree trunks, and shining with enough barrels and cannon to scare a brigade. Centred in its chest was black glass in a metal frame, giving it the appearance of a spider's cluster of eyes, and at the heart of the black eyes, an Iron Cross. Its massive legs wheezed with steam as it stomped on the spot where Alex stood, knocking him to the ground.

Warren's mind scrambled. Was it a cast-iron Quasimodo? Some creature torn out of a scientific romance? It was as if every dirty idea in creation had been welded together. The cannons bristled. A dozen belts of ammunition were jammed by mechanical grace into their feeding mouths. Soon the air would become a mist of shrapnel.

Warren wanted to run. Find a saloon, the warm arms of a whore, and the safety of a bottle.

A single shot crackled the air. Alex, a gnat before a bulldog, had his Enfield at his shoulder. He fired again.

Each shot bounced off the creature's hide like dimes off a freight train. Then, from inside the creature's arm, emerged a hose.

Warren charged toward the beast, a sweltering heat in his shark tooth hand. Whatever that hose was, it was going to unleash hell on Alex while the rest of the unit hung back like a bunch of cowards. Warren cut the distance in half, then a quarter, eyes on the hose. Something sparked.

Its hand bloomed white, an inferno that stank of gasoline and burning hair.

The world hazed. Alex charged with his bayonet, and the sound of whooshing flames matched the hideous cloud of fire that engulfed him.

"Stop!" Warren yelled—

Alex danced in silent agony, a living pyre, before crumpling to the ground, rolling and writhing as the flames upon him raged.

Warren's scream raged across the battlefield. Despite the smoke, the hideous aroma of burning flesh, the rotting air and the fact that the creature's many glass eyes and burning hand were now trained on him, Warren charged on animal instinct as the flame-throwing behemoth turned to face him down.

CHAPTER TWENTY-EIGHT:

THE GENERAL'S WILL

For a moment, walking down the vast earthen trench network, Vasilya wished she'd never arrived at the front. It was like an ant colony perpetually burned by the spyglass of giants beyond the horizon. A city of men and guns that, when you gazed closer, revealed a horror deeper and viler than she could have ever known. A labyrinth of earth-work trenches lined the horizon, punctuated by concrete slabs where men with machine guns hid. Their faces were as serious as a forge, as locked as a Chinese puzzle box. Gaunt and grim.

The aroma of war was a fetid, ruinous plague on the senses. Ripe and rotten and wet as an open wound, a stench that hung around like poison gas. It took all her concentration as they passed the casualty clearing station not to vomit.

"This won't work," said the colonel, Click's tiny form just bulging under his collar.

"Make it work," she said, curtly, then closed her mouth. After some quick requisitioning, and a painful haircut courtesy of Clack, she had been uniformed and scrubbed to look like the colonel's executive officer. She kept the stains on her face because they hid her Slavic features and reminded her of Felix. We can't fail now, she thought. We've come by train, car, and motorcycle and have not been stopped yet, she thought, the whole miserable trip to the front where, thank god, the colonel's rank and purpose with regard to Project Juggernaut had allowed him access.

They rumbled down wooden planks that lined the trench floor, looking for Major-General Vogel, the division commander who was in charge of the unit Felix and the Juggernaut had been assigned, when a runner charged past them screaming. "Out of the damn way!"

He charged into a dark hole in the earth flanked by two guards.

"That's it," the colonel said.

"How do you know?"

"Runner had his divisional badge. He's bringing news from the front."

"Then onward, Colonel," she said. "Unless you wish Click to find a new home in your body instead of your coat."

They approached the guards, who saluted. The colonel returned it, tired. "Colonel Balk, Special War Projects Division, to see General Vogel."

"General can't be disturbed," said the dead-eyed one on the right.

"Yes he can," said the colonel, handing over a black book. "I have authorization from General Hindenburg himself to see him regarding special projects."

The dead-eyed soldier passed the book to the one on the left, who leafed through it, then handed it back. "No one disturbs the general once battle is on," said the left one. "Especially some crippled straggler from the home front."

No, Vasilya thought, don't cave now, Colonel. But she knew he could. If he wanted, he could shrug his shoulders and even if Click did his dirty work, she'd be found out, ruined, and—

Instead, the manic fire that hid in the colonel's heart seemed to burst. "You dare call me a shirker? Me? I've been fighting for Germany since before unification and before you were a dirty thought in your father's eye!"

The two guards recognized their mistake but fear kept their mouths shut as the colonel pounded his chest where the Iron Cross sat, face the colour of a ruined grapefruit. "I've killed more French bastards than you've ever seen, guarding a general's shithouse! And if you two miserable stains so much as block my way with a finger, I'll have you both back at the front testing old gas equipment during a storm trooper charge! Stand aside, now!"

It's over, she thought. We'll be tossed out on our backsides because of his stupid temper—

They guards parted, saluting, and they strode into the darkly lit corridor leading to the general's general staff and command room. She gave an internal sigh.

The sharp sounds of the war muted against the earth and concrete surroundings. "Thank you," she said.

The colonel harrumphed, a bit too loud. "Most soldiers are fools, especially ones who have not seen death first hand."

"How could you tell?" They all had the same look to her.

"Most of these guards are dullards, craven youth, and criminals because anyone with a brain or a heart is doing his duty at the front."

"So the rotten will inherit the fruit of the brave," she said. "Not a fine equation."

"Letting the war devour another generation when you have the power to end it soon is even worse," he said, sharply. "Now shut up."

She allowed him the illusion of control because underneath his desire to chastise two imbeciles, Vasilya knew the colonel would see things the same way as she: Felix would not survive without her. Maybe, together, they could keep him alive. But she knew his heart, while strong, would not withstand combat in that machine. He must be in agony already, she thought. And I doubt I'll last too much longer. But this is my mess, not his. I'll be damned before Felix pays the price for it.

They came to a room of men using telegraph machines, marking maps, and discussing things at a rapid rate. Standing before a table cascaded in white lamp light was a shadowy-faced man with small eyes and a clean-shaven face, dark hair shaved almost too the skull.

The colonel announced himself. "General Vogel, I am Colonel Balk. Special Projects Division."

The general did not raise his head.

"The inventor of Project Juggernaut."

Surprise bit Vasilya as she winced at the colonel calling himself the inventor. How dare he … but the thought faded.

Colonel Balk's face tightened. "Sir, we may have a problem."

"Tanks," said the general. "My kingdom for some tanks." Then he muttered something in what Vasilya thought was Yiddish. "I asked for tanks. They give me a contraption that required trains, wagon, and horse to drag to the front, then a small brigade of engineers to assemble, and a child as its pilot in a vessel I myself was not allowed to look into."

Felix, she thought. The general had seen him, seem him arrive. Her hand rose to touch her lip, but she bit it instead and tried to look glum and obedient.

"But I did peer inside your dark machine." The general finally drew his gaze upon Colonel Balk. "I do not know what Faustian bargains you are making to deliver me such terrible wonders, Colonel. But I fear for what's left of your soul." Eyes dropped back on the map. "We have employed the Juggernaut with an assault battalion."

"And?"

The general tore into the remains of old cigarettes stubs and removed the tobacco. On a fresh paper, he sprinkled the remains with a sharp, mechanical fashion. "After some initial difficulties, I'm told it, or he, whatever the hell it is, performed well. The British battalion it encountered did not survive."

The swelling pain in Vasilya's chest eased with relief.

"Then why do you look so crestfallen?" said Colonel Balk.

"Because something far worse than the British have attacked us." He rolled the tobacco slow. The nicotine stain on his finger was brownish yellow and led up his hand like jaundice. The general shook his head. "And it has so far destroyed the entire Assault Battalion. Even after the gas attack. So much for the vaunted gas grenade that was to turn every man into a chemical weapon." The disgust in his voice cut the air with a serrated edge.

Gas? Vasilya thought. Oh god, gas weapons. The Germans had used them against us at the start of the war. Vasilya had heard whispers of how they attacked the soldiers, of men choking on a fog of chlorine, then mustard gas blistering them to inhuman masses of sores and rotting flesh.

And Felix stood there, within the Juggernaut. Heart and lungs giving the beast its locomotion. She prayed they'd made it gas proof, used chemical filters to protect his lungs…

"Wait," the colonel said. "If it's not the British—"

The general tore a match from a packet. "I'm fighting ghosts."

"What?"

The general snapped a match between his fingers and a magnesium glow flared against his face. He was young. Younger than the colonel, anyway. He lit the cigarette and inhaled an acrid stench of burning things, then spoke with smoke at the tip of his words. "There's a regiment there. A … mixed battalion, if the observer is right. Germans. Austrians. British. Even the damned French. The uniforms of every nation except those bloody Americans, from what I can tell. And before you tell me that this is bizarre but of no consequence, here is the rejoinder I need inform you of. These men, they won't die. My regimental commanders, who have served me well since Tannenberg, have assured me of the authenticity of the eyewitness reports. They are shot, they are hit with shells, and they stay down just long enough to get up. They survive in the gas without masks and now the only thing standing between them and our line is this nightmare machine of yours that even Goya could not have painted." He blew the burning end of his cigarette so it flared and ashed. "This is hardly the war I signed up for."

"We need to get to him," Vasilya said.

The colonel could have killed her with his glare. "Silence, unless you are spoken to."

"There's no time for useless protocols," she said. "General, you must get me to him or I believe he'll die."

A resigned look hung over the general's face. "Does your adjutant always speak with a hint of a feminine cadence? Or is this some kind of joke?"

"The only ones who will be laughing are those soldiers Felix is fighting if you don't listen to me. The gas … I don't know if what you … did to him, to attach him to the Juggernaut, I can't be for certain that whatever filters were made will hold."

"Why not?" said the general, the jovial tone absent.

"Because I didn't make them! Besides, Felix has his own filters. His lungs. It might … his lungs might be tied to the filters." The colonel froze his expression and she knew he'd done it, tying the fate of that accursed machine to the body of a young man. She sneered. "And if they are, they won't be strong enough."

"That makes him a very expensive target," said the general.

"Not if I can get to him," Vasilya said. "I can ... run the machine remotely."

The general wiped his face, but it twitched. "If it were not for the seemingly infinite number of impossible things that have been thrust on my desk today, girl, I'd have you tossed in a madhouse before you could spit." He turned to the colonel. "Is she right?"

The colonel nodded, hesitatingly. "If the boy fails, she'll be the only one to command the Juggernaut."

The general looked at each of them, then pinched out the half-finished cigarette he'd made out of remnants of old ones and put its smoky remains behind his ear. He exhaled weakly. "I'll have you geared up in gas detail quickly by a matron, so as to be discreet. Sending a girl to the front to face a monster ... I am beginning to think this war has cracked a hole in the world, and the devil himself is playing us for fools until we all go mad. Wait outside until my runner is ready for you."

Vasilya and the colonel marched out into the grey and screaming day.

"I hope you're happy, child," he said, abandoning the pretense of disguise. "You are about to walk into the mouth of hell itself. And should that brave boy die, be assured you'll be taking his place."

They were just words, tiny slings and arrows against her iron will to see it done. Felix would not die if she could help it, and if he did ... she feared what she was capable of in this world of blood and iron.

Focus, Vasilya said to herself, amidst the rush toward the forward trench, the same focus you would have cutting a diamond or putting together the heart of a watch. Focus!

Because everything sought to steal her attention and drown it. The distant cries. The explosions. This world of war where every one of its million parts seemed tied to some invisible motor. This was truly a hybrid world of bug and machine world, she'd thought. Men scrambled like warrior ants to pre-determined roles across the planks in the trench, across the battlefield, in automobiles and rails and horse, their bug faces of gas masks made them grounded wasps in search of hive or prey.

Her own gas mask was tight, stuffy, and turned the world into a shadowy murk she hoped she'd get used to. The sound of her heavy breathing oppressed her with every breath, and each gasp tasted like rotten rubber. The colonel ran ahead, looking stranger than the rest, a one-armed wasp charging toward the launch point of battle.

They came upon a gaggle of husky soldiers, none of them wearing their masks. The thickest one had a shaved head and full beard and looked like an angry bull. Balk removed his mask. "Major Hientz, we are—"

"I know who you two shits are," he said with a low, buzzing voice. "You made that tin can monster that got my men killed. I should toss you head first into the battle for that."

"We did not kill them," Balk said. "But we'll help you kill who did. Just get us close to the battle."

Hientz laughed. "My pleasure, Colonel. Do you want me to carry you, or will your grandson do that for you?"

"These are Major-General Vogel's orders." Colonel Balk shoved them at Hientz's chest. "So unless you'd like to defy an order in front of witnesses, I suggest you shut your fat mouth and let us help you save what's left of your men."

Hientz's eyes were swollen with rage as he gripped the order. "What's left is corpses fit for the fire. One of my best regiments was wasted trying to get that monster to the front, and for what?"

"Last I heard, that monster is the only thing left standing."

Violence simmered in the air between them.

This wasn't going anywhere, Vasilya thought. "Let us help you avenge them."

Slowly, Hientz focused on her. "And what the hell are a cripple and a midget going to do that a regiment of stormtroopers can't?"

"We can keep the machine going," she said. "Get us to the front, leave us there to die if you want, but let us try."

Major Hientz spat against the trench wall. "Fine. We'll drag your carcasses to the battle. Getting you back is the last of my concerns." He barked orders to his men and it was as if a tide of movement had overtaken Vasilya's life as she swam with a violent current, Click still in the colonel's clothes, Clack hiding in her own, and twin metal butterflies nestled across her back as Vasilya prepared for a plunge into a deadly unknown.

CHAPTER TWENTY-NINE:

TWELVE ROUNDS AT ABADDON

The flames from the mechanical beast's arm surged forth like a burning orange cloud, creeping toward Warren at an alarming rate, when a force like a moose kick dragged him out of the line of fire, and the flamethrowers hose blasted behind him, singeing his skin but not roasting him alive.

He hit the ground in a tussle and roll, and found it was Graves who had tackled him. "Flanks, idiot! Don't take it head-on! Shit, it's turning!" They both scrambled up as the gear-popping whirls of the beast signalled its change of direction. "Come on! Try and get behind it! Spread out! Go!"

From the haze of the mustard gas, the Lost Battalion was firing and charging in squads. One group laid down heavy fire that caught the beast's attention but didn't leave much more than a scratch. It flamed a circle to cut off an advancing two-man crew, while another tossed a grenade that sent shocks through everyone.

Everyone but the beast.

It might as well been a can tossed at the shithouse door.

The battalion circled, firing, throwing, and achieving scratch-all since the beast arrived.

Alex still burned, embraced by the terrible jelly-flame. Fuck flanks, Warren thought, and beat his boot heels toward Alex.

"Machine guns," screamed Graves.

A hiss and a click later, the air was alive with Maxim machine gun fire from every possible angle. Lead pummeled into Warren so hard and constant he danced in the air like a mangled puppet before hitting the ground and covering his head, the wounds zipping themselves shut as the bursts faded and the thundering steps returned.

And where was Rasputin? Nowhere. Bastard was leading from behind again.

The beast marched toward a quivering Austrian who swore loud and hard in German, torso cut to mangled grey shreds that attempted to turn his mutton flesh back to muscle and bone. The mighty mechanical arms lifted the top half of the screaming kraut above its spider eyes, and hammered the earth—

There was nothing left but human material that had rotted from within. Brain, blood, meat, bone, and skull … it was all crushed under the creature's blow. All the kings horses, all the kings men, nothing could make that kraut whole again.

With the creature's back turned to him, Warren ran to Alex, who writhed in silent agony as his skin healed only to feed more fire jelly, releasing a burning tang in the air you'd expect to emerge from hell's dungeon: infinite fuel for infinite torture. Warren tore off his shirt to stuff out the flames, and the burning cloth stuck to his hands as if made of molasses. "Goddamn it!" He shook them like an idiot while his shirt burned to ash on Alex, wide eyes pleading his older brother to not be so stupid and save him from the burning. But all his screams were silent suffering as Warren gnashed his teeth and waved his hands.

Meanwhile, the beast crushed the battalion with a massive iron fist. Some were picking themselves up enough to scramble out of the way. Others became permanent etchings of ruin on the battlefield.

The iron fist rose in the air once more, when a mortar exploded on the spider eyes and shook the beast from its final hammer. The central body spun like a globe, turning its right hand into the left to face what had attacked from behind.

And there it found Graves, dropping another mortar. The shell fired as he picked up a massive Lewis gun with one hand, voice rising about the hail of metal. "Retreat!" screamed Graves. "Retreat to Rasputin!"

It bought the battalion seconds to pick itself up and run. The only soldier in the creature's eyes was Graves.

"Come on you shits!" Graves yelled at it. "Run or I'll cut your fucking heads off!"

The iron fist came down with the force of an anvil dropped from heaven, and Grave sidestepped it.

Warren tried to pick Alex up, but his burning skin clung to his hands like tar, breathing flames. "Goddamn it!"

"Bishop! Get the fuck out of here!" Graves rolled away from another industrial hammer strike. "Leave him! He's doomed anyway."

Words sizzled from Alex's mouth. "Hu, hu, hu—"

Warren shook his burning hands, but instead gave birth to fists swarmed in flame like some lost demon. The pain surged, a churning, bubbling agony he sucked into his guts as flesh tried to mend itself and the flame just kept burning, cold and paralyzing.

Graves dove away from another blow as the giant beast dropped both hands to the ground and shook the earth. "Well, Jesus, if you're just going to stand there and burn, do something!"

The beast gripped Graves by the legs and the next sound was the crunching of bone as the mechanical fist rose in the air, then thundered down, cracking his body against the scorched battlefield.

Warren faced the shoulder of the beast, burning hands outstretched. The beast's hulking, mechanical back, a mishmash of armoured guns, piston and steam valve, lay exposed. He bared his teeth, ran, and leapt. Both burning hands gripped thick cables, and he yanked himself up as the beast jerked and whirled and spun. Warren held on as the world went ass over tit, Maxims and fire nozzle turning the air around them to steel rain and lines of liquid fire, trying to dislodge him.

Warren screamed, and dove his hand into the creature's back, yanking and tearing while his flaming hands flickered like torches. He tore inward, pulling apart metal and wire until he saw what appeared to be an ammunition box. He gripped the top with his burning hand, tearing it off.

The shiny rows of bullets for the creature's Maxim guns sparkled at him like finger-long diamonds. Time to turn you into a powder keg, he said. He dove a hand in, just as the massive mechanical fist yanked him away like a toy, flames from his hands licking the underside of the mechanical fist.

It yanked him in front and what seemed like a hundred machine guns snapped from secret caches across it's massive, round figure. The Iron Cross paint job had been torn away by the battalion's bullets, and, this close, he could see the spider glass for what it was: a series of periscopes.

He glared at the creature. "Sorry, Alex," he muttered. "I tried."

"Hey, sunshine!" The guns and Warren's eyes turned to see Graves, broken on the floor, bones mangled and legs cracked in a dozen places. Yet he was smiling, propped up on an elbow, with a pin in his teeth. In his last good hand was a live grenade. He spat the pin. "Catch!"

He tossed the incendiary. A Maxim burst tore Graves away from the earth … including his head. It was a slow horror, despite the speed of bullets. Skin, meat, and bone broke away from any visage of resemblance to a human face until there was just a mash of mess. And when the bullets were finished mangling his form, it stained the ground in a grey tapestry. Through the remains of the skull, a black brain melted into the scarred earth.

All the while, the grenade flew through the air.

Warren got dropped as the massive hands covered up, taking the brunt of the explosion … and leaving its back exposed again.

Running at full, dead speed, Warren leapt and planted both burning hands into the creature's ammunition box.

Bullets exploded everywhere through him and the machine, knocking themselves away from each other like magnets of the same pole. The concussive force shook Warren's senses like a pint of white lightning while the machine's hands tried to tear out part of its exploding back.

Warren hit the ground, leaking in a dozen directions while the creature tossed the flaming ammunition case in the air and deadly firecrackers snapped to life, scattershot bullets firing in every direction.

Warren rose, hands still burning, and looked back at Alex. He churned like a funeral pyre that would not die, a witch at the stake still fighting for life. On the other side was the rot of Graves. From his chest had sprung a black flower where his heart should have been, with jagged white petals.

Warren wanted to run.

Again. Like always. But run where, in this mustard gas world of monsters and horror?

Only one place made sense in the lunatic fringe they now called home. He dashed toward the wounded mechanical monster, screaming an unholy battle cry from the root of his dead heart. Past and future bled away with each step. Hands burning, dead heart throbbing, and mind dissolving into pure rage, he charged the beast, screaming, and leapt.

CHAPTER THIRTY:

RACE TO THE FRONT

Vasilya had no time to process the horrors she witnessed: the bodies and their jigsaw pieces scattered like a puzzle that could never be solved, the stench of life bled into nature's crippled heart, the ruinous world that had once been alive and fertile. Instead, she ran until her lungs seethed, her heart shook, and her face was burning beneath the rubber mask. She charged into a hazy world of gas, of death and chemical nightmare, of science eating the world instead of building it.

She was dragged by rough soldiers in full chemical gear, ferocious-looking bug men with petrol tanks on their backs and flaming rifles in their hand. Dante himself could not fathom Earth as such a clear reflection of the underworld, a man-made industrial boil on existence that had twisted progress towards its own devilish twin.

Amazingly, the colonel ran without aid, rushing toward the front as if he were still that young private in France in 1871, keeping up with the vaunted stormtroopers whose names were synonymous with the art of carnage. This was his world, even fifty years on, even if he claimed to hate it. This was his natural operating environment and he held himself to the high standard of those that led them into its maw.

The haze was so thick the world was a shadow of soldiers, so she focused on listening. Not with her ears, but deeper. Listening for the monster she had created, that had been fused with Felix. Through the hazy miles, nothing after nothing until … the rest of the world dampened.

A sound trickled against her heart, pulling her across the acrid miles toward the growing sounds of the battlefield.

Chopin.

Nocturnes.

Oh god, she thought … Felix.

She ran, throat clogged with heartbeats, and soon found she was storming into a wall of agony. And the battlefield, despite its cadaverous countenance, came alive.

There was a distant flare. An explosion. In the distance, a shadowy figure loomed like a monster amidst the poisoned air.

The Juggernaut. Whirling as if it had gone mad. A smaller creature cast itself upon its back, hands like burning torches.

"Stay low!" screamed their commander in the murky distance. Random shots of bullets filled the air. But she ran forward, against fear, against instinct.

Felix, she thought, following the sad notes that grew louder. Felix … I'm here. There's a creature on your back, near the ammunition reserves. Reach back.

From the notes came the sound of his voice. Low, exhausted, and tinny. Vas? God, I must be dead already … are you really—

Just do what I'm saying, you idiot! Reach up and grab that soldier before he kills you!

The Juggernaut complied, and wonder overwhelmed Vasilya's eyes to see the hulking monster with Felix in its chest dance to her tune and tear the soldier with flaming hands from his back.

She gripped her chest, terrified she'd been shot. But it was the thudding of her heart. Painful, but steady, and in tune with Felix.

Got him, Vas!

Thank God—

From the distance came a voice. English, followed by an explosion that rattled the air and sent shocks so severe through Vasilya she choked on her own scream.

Her heart beat lonely. She strained her mind to hear the soft touch of fingers on piano, the crackle of static from the gramophone, until her heart doubled … and hurt. Felix was hurt.

His hand had slipped and the soldier he'd held was thrown back.

Felix! Can you hear me?

Vas … it hurts. I taste silver and copper. I can't move. I'm sorry—

She ran as the stormtroopers took positions and leapfrogged between themselves. She focused on the Juggernaut until her heartbeats calmed that of poor Felix, until she could taste him taking shallow breaths, then a deeper one. Relax, Felix. Let me be your eyes, your hands. Let me hold your heart.

She held her fingers in a square, and focused.

In a cold second, her mind rushed across the battlefield and smacked into the cockpit where Felix lay.

Everything ached, with a tiny pain that shot and dropped as he breathed. She stumbled forward, grunting as if each step was stuck in the grave dirt of the battlefield. Moving seemed to disconnect them, so she held fast.

A scream that stunned her filled the air.

In the mustard air, the shadow creature with flaming hands was charging toward the Juggernaut. It was a hideous man, savage, animal, like some unchained creature from the distant past ...

She forced the Juggernaut's arms up to grab him, but he was faster than her brand new reflexes, and the Juggernaut lumbered to catch up to her intent. God, how did Felix even manage to move it, let alone fight in it ...

Because it's not a pure machine.

Part of it is Felix.

The madman gripped on to the top of the Juggernaut and began hammering into the hole in its back.

"Fire!"

The stormtroopers filled the air with searing lead, some of it nailing Felix, some of it the creature. Each shot made her wince, and inside she felt the Juggernaut's exposed patches. Chinks in the armour blown apart by grenades. And the fire-fisted creature kept cracking down with the force of an industrial compressor.

She again attempted to yank the creature off, but the arms were unwieldy, like a puppet made of jelly.

Felix, let go. Just let go and let me move it, ok? I can save you, I will save you, but you have to let go. She tasted blood in her mouth. She swallowed.

His voice was a distant ember in her heart and mind, racing across the chords of piano that acted as a symphony amidst all the destruction. I'll try.

She gasped. Sharpness tugged her nerves and metal and movement became one. The fire-fisted monster continued to pound.

Dark thoughts rose: the assassin on the train, the poison laced upon the workshop wall, her mother's last meal hidden and long since gone, and the insidious face of Monsieur Fabergé as he spoke ill of her.

Spoke for the last time.

They were pinpricks compared to the heinous anger and pain swelling in her rampaging heart as she wrested control of the Juggernaut to face the man with hands aflame.

CHAPTER THIRTY-ONE:

THE HEARTS OF MONSTERS

Cracks formed on the creature's shell with every burning punch, and the beast slowed, even as fresh hails of bullets sang through the air. Enemy soldiers surrounded Warren, more accursed stormtroopers. But he did not care.

He pounded.

He pounded it for the searing agony of his flesh, for being yet another walking nightmare come to life, for what it had done to Alex.

He pounded until his right fist finally snuffed out to the crackling sound emerging from the beast's shell. Bullets burst inside his guts, but he hammered on knowing the satisfaction of killing this son of a bitch was just seconds away—

When life returned to the beast.

It swerved and ran and jolted as if struck by lightning, attempting to grasp Warren while the Germans closed the circle, and Warren gave up his pounding to hold on for sweet life as the creature tried to toss him like a rag doll. Warren knew if he let go, he'd lose the shielding presence of the beast and one of those bullets would have his brain's name on it.

C'mon, Qimmiq. Don't lose your head now, and don't waste my good luck charm.

Holding on like Tarzan taming a mad bull, Warren glared at the shark tooth in his fiery palm. He clenched a fist, driving his fingers into the tooth. Fresh pain awakened a primal scream within him that, for the briefest of seconds, paralyzed the outside world. He swung on top of the beast, saw the crevasse he'd beaten out of the metal and wood, and threw down a blistering punch with the force of a stampede.

The force ripped up his arm, shattering the bone faster than it could mend and slammed into his chest and flared white in his eye. All the pain Warren had thought was only memory followed its path with hooves of nails and broken glass. A splintering whiteness blinded him as he flew off the creature and became unhinged from gravity's embrace, limbs flailing.

When the earth finally claimed him, the sick sensations of self-mending began … slower. He lay like a dead thing, and the creature shook, engulfed in flames.

The faceplate swung once on a single screw, then dropped, burying an edge into the ground. The spider glass was shattered. And Warren saw into the heart of the beast, now exposed.

Inside was something akin to a small room and chair. Sitting in the chair was a boy.

Younger than Alex. Blood had run trenches down his nose and ears. And he was sixteen, if he was a day. Dead eyes wide in a last thousand-yard stare as mustard began to mangle his face.

A new sound drove across the battlefield, worse than the scream of shells or the roar of gunfire.

The painful wail of someone in the distance, someone who had their first taste of agony on the battlefield. A virgin scream that tore a strip off of what was left of Warren's soul, followed by an equally terrifying eruption:

The roar of the mechanical monster's engines.

CHAPTER THIRTY-TWO:

THE ENDURANCE OF ASHES

Soldiers spoke, guns fired, and the world moved on with its spectacle, but all Vasilya could hear were the last chords of a waltz, unfinished and incomplete, longing for the final notes as Felix's soundless words reached out from the heart of the monster she had created.

Vas, I can't shake him, I can't. Oh god, I'm sorry, I love you—

Then the shadow soldier's hand, shimmering electric blue, killed the transmission, and knocked her back to the dead earth.

Colonel Balk was running toward the mechanical husk. But his skills were useless. Sure as the sunrise, and as permanent as time, Felix was beyond even the aid of a talented healer.

She wanted to dig her own grave and fall inside, but could not find the strength to move. Only when the soldier began to approach the fallen shadow, whose fist still burned, was the will to movement restored her.

No, she thought. They will not be the first to touch him. Not him. They can have the rest of their enemies, but this one is mine!

An angry swarm raced from her blood and into the frigid machine.

She took a few steps forward, punching her legs, forcing Clack to scramble. "Rise," she said, voice tasting like the suffocating plastic of the mask. "Rise, goddamn you!"

A spark danced upon the battlefield, a tether of light shooting across the broken ground with the speed of anger, passed the circling Germans enclosing on the fallen man with the torch hand.

"Rise!"

And the husk of the Juggernaut obeyed with the roar of engines. A stormtrooper aimed his rifle at the fallen shadow soldier, but his eyes were on the Juggernaut.

"Burn."

A blast of flame engulfed the German, and the platoon's eyes turned towards the machine.

Until, a second later, they were mowed down and cut in shreds with machine gun fire and flame, until the only things standing were the Juggernaut, Vasilya, and a stunned Colonel Balk. He'd ducked the worst of the attack in a slit trench, but was now racing back to Vasilya.

"What are you doing?" he shouted, gripping his masked head with his one hand. "Felix could still be alive! You have to let me help him."

Help? The word slapped her cold face as blood ran thick and steady down her nose. "Help him? You wanted to help him? You murdered him as soon as you put him in this monster!"

The Juggernaut moved fast and with a mechanical grace she could not help but be impressed by. It snatched the colonel in an iron grip.

"Stop!" he screamed, shaking. "You're crushing … me."

"Look at him!" She shoved the colonel's face into the broken command chamber. There sat Felix, slouched against his restraints, skin churning from the chemicals swimming in the air. In his chest were a series of pipes and tubes that flowed into the Juggernaut's engines. "Look at what you've done to him!"

The colonel gasped as the iron fist of the Juggernaut began to crush his ribs and bruise his organs. "It was … his … choice!"

"And this is mine, Colonel. I wish I could say it was an honour to serve with you, but I'm afraid all that's left is to relieve you of duty."

The other hand of the Juggernaut rose, its thick fingers pinching the gas mask off the old man's face.

"Breath in the deep scent of victory, Colonel," she said.

He shut his eyes and mouth, but the pain released a hideous scream that she relished before crushing him in the mechanical fist. But a hideous "crack" forced her to stop the crushing.

The creature dropped Balk. He hit the ground, and Click bounced out. Eyes dead.

She made no move to save him. Clack ran out of her coat to the broken remains of his dead twin.

Vasilya turned away, hating herself, but focused on her goal. "I'm sorry, friends. I'm so sorry."

She marched toward the soldier, a terrible wind rolling across the battlefield, making the gas wave and sway like a family of sick ghosts.

He was still moving. The flaming hand still burned.

He wore no gas mask, no protection suit, and while his skin was sore to look at … he was not blistering … not like Felix. Beside him lay another body, churning with flame, gurgles of agony cluttering the air.

"I'm … sorry," he said, in English. "I'm sorry, Alex. I tried. I didn't run, I tried."

"Save your prayers for your god," she said in Russian. "I've no use for them. You will burn for what you did." Before her command was a thought, the Juggernaut's fire hose was lit and focused on this strange soldier. "You will all burn."

A whispering word in the distance held her.

Words with a cadence that had almost been lost to her recollection.

It was unbelievable, but they grew in strength like a breeze becoming a gale.

Someone was speaking Russian on the wind.

And, as the words and accent were recognized, a rumble came from the earth.

And the soldier with the burning hands looked at the ground with horror and said a single word. "Charger."

CHAPTER THIRTY-THREE:

MORE THAN DEVILS BELOW THE EARTH

The world around Warren erupted with violence and dirt. From the battleground surged a giant, pus-white worm the width of a hundred-year-old Washington red wood. Like lava surging from a volcano's mouth, its dead white body launched into the air, an infinite snake from below the roots.

The mechanical beast and its tiny handler both fell back in the aftershocks before Charger's head curved, his body became an upside-down U, and revealed its face.

It was an eyeless black hole, surrounded by grey teeth, a hideous maw that dove straight for them.

Warren pulled himself back with handfuls of dirt, tearing at the ground to take him away, when a battle cry came from beyond the mist. It was Rasputin.

"Leave none standing! Drive them into the grave!"

Charger crashed into the mechanical beast, tearing it apart as it burrowed again, shaking everything to the bone.

Another scream filled the battlefield, and this time a discerning word crept out. "Felix!"

Blood filled Vasilya's mask as the giant snake ruptured the earth, crashing on the Juggernaut. Wood broke, metal bent, and gears locked as the shock of impact reverberated from the machine to her.

Lying on her back amidst the carnage, all she could think about was Felix's tough yet frail body, strapped in the command capsule. She shut her eyes, and saw the world in battleship grey and crimson shadows from a dozen vantage points. Eyes like the bastion of periscopes she'd built for the creature, a spider vision of optics.

And all of them registered the plunging worm, its maw ready to tear into all that remained of Felix.

She screamed his name and her hands felt like metal bending in heat into iron fist.

The creature crashed into the Juggernaut, tearing it in half, the legs shooting off into the distance. She screamed the name of her dead love, then plunged the remaining gauntlet into the pus-white flesh, and held on as it dove underground.

The deep darkness of the world flooded her until all she could taste was mud and blood—then fired all remaining weapon systems as if the triggers had always been in her mind.

Flame and bullet and gas and blade cut through the meat of the creature, turning the air to squeals of horror.

The creature thrashed as it burrowed to safety, smashing the Juggernaut against the sides of the hole until it broke free, but not before its wounds spewed forth viscera and gore.

The Juggernaut gripped the side of the hole as the worm charged on into the dirt, leaving a tunnel of ooze.

Within Vasilya's heart, steam hissed, a sick sound of metal pressed to flesh. The gas tanks burned. The engine overloaded. The wires trembled.

The Juggernaut was running out of control on her anger and she could not turn it off. Flames burst around the creature, and the world smelled of burning plastic and searing metal.

A hideous warmth enveloped mind, body and spirit, then ignited like phosphorous and torture.

"Felix!" she screamed before blood clogged her throat, and the splintered sight of the Juggernaut fizzled out.

The butterflies on her back sizzled.

Below the earth, the squeals of the mechanical creature died in the distance and soon a pall suffocated the air. The tiny soldier who seemed to command the mechanical beast fell on his back and twitched as if drunk or sick or both.

And nowhere was the Lost Battalion to be found.

Hand burning, body slowly mending, Warren had heard why. The distant sound of shells. The approach of battle. The grind of tanks.

The British were coming. And the Lost Battalion was not nearly as tough as they claimed. Not yet.

Warren's legs mended, the pain like a constant slap with an iron rod, but he dragged himself, digging in with his elbows, crawling toward Alex's body, which still burned worse than Warren's right hand. "Alex? Alex can you hear me?"

"I can."

But the voice was Russian.

From the haze, Rasputin emerged and stood before them, tattoos dancing across his skin as if Warren were punch drunk on corn whisky and staring at a beehive. Rasputin kneeled before Alex, and whispered low. Patches of tattoos, like fairytale critters, slinked off his skin and on to Alex's, snuffing out the flame.

"How the hell did you do that?" Warren said.

"Hell will not have us, nor Heaven above," Rasputin said, then scooped Alex's smoking body into his arms. His skin was black and red, moving as if all of it were dancing lice and stray burned paper. "We will make our Eden, or El Dorado, by the force of our dead hearts. And avenge what they have done to us on earth." He then turned his back to Warren and marched toward the horizon.

The pounding of artillery, the scream of men in battle, raged to the west.

Warren gripped the air with his burning hand. "Hey! Don't you take him from me!"

"He came to me willingly."

"Rasputin!"

The mad wizard crested a barren knoll. "Alexander is one of us. You should be grateful. He'll live to see Judgement Day and the peace that will follow our ascension."

As he passed into the mustard mist, two soldiers from the Battalion approached, pistols in hand. One Austrian, one French.

Warren scrambled to his feet, and fell on his knees. Pain flush and wild, as his legs strained to work. He screamed, and charged past them, reaching for Rasputin as he and Alex vanished into the grey mist.

They shoved him back to the earth, and before he could muster the strength of a tackle, two pistol barrels pressed against his head.

"*Au revoir*," said the Frenchmen.

Two shots rang out.

Blackness flushed Warren's eyes closed. A crumpled sound ... he opened his eyes. Both men lay flat on their backs, holes through their helmets. Tremors filled their chests before deadroot bloomed above their hearts.

Warren looked toward the fallen soldier who had commanded the beast. He was twitching ... when, like a page torn out of scripture, wings burst from his back.

"Net that bird!" said someone in English, and Warren turned to see a gaggle of soldiers in gas masks. At the lead was a husky man in an American doughboy uniform and full gas gear, but his hand was powder white. "Howdy," he said. "Time for night-night." The white fist drilled Warren and there was a smell of roses burning in his head that turned off the grey twilight of his vision and swallowed him in darkness like the belly of a whale.

CHAPTER THIRTY-FOUR:

HOSTAGE OF WAR

The painful sleep that had embraced Vasilya was only punctuated by a shock of images that branded her mind and made her crave darkness. Felix, falling into a hole in the earth, harnessed inside the Juggernaut. He falls deeper, further away. But before he is swallowed by the hole, his dead eyes flash open—

"Vas."

She screamed and the sound tore away the dark veil of sleep and introduced fresh new horrors.

She was on her stomach, on a raised platform, staring at green tiles dribbled with dark blood. She could not move and her back was itching.

"Is she awake?" said a voice, somewhere above her. English. She shut her eyes. Clack? Clack can you hear me? A thought shot across the room, looking for connection.

"She's awake," a man said.

"How bad are her injuries?" said another, deeper, with a hint of a lisp and sympathy. "How is her heart?" She hated it immediately.

"I've never seen anything like this before."

"I asked you a question. How is her heart, her body and mind? Is she poisoned or ill?"

"Her vital signs are all normal, Sir. I'm rather amazed, since we don't know how she sustained these injuries. It reminds me of some of the tank casualties we had, when the petrol was hit with a shell. She'll live, though as what, I have not a clue."

The other man's voice, the hated voice, had a grim majesty that made her shiver. "When I want your speculations on the nature of human evolution, doctor, I will ask to see your latest paper in *Lancet* or the findings of the Royal Geological Society. Until then, treat her as you would your own child. If I find one brass feather missing, or she so much as leaves with a sniffle she did not enter with, you will be held accountable in full. Let me know when she awakens."

The thick steps of a man in good shoes thudded against the tile until a door closed.

"Fat, bloody toff," the doctor said, "telling me my business, just because he knows the professor—" He cut himself short. "Nurse? I think we should try and adjust her gurney. Sit her up."

She watched two pairs of shoes appear below her. Soft white for the lady, dull oxblood for the man.

"And be gentle," said the doctor, with a conniving tone.

There was a series of snaps and clicks as they prepared to pull her up and the blood rushed back through her head, unsure of which way to go. Dizzy, she caught sight of straps and restraints and flexed against them.

The itch on her back was worse than a harvest of ants marching across her shoulder blades. She wore a medical smock, hanging loose on her sickly, thin body. Yet, while exhausted, and starving, she did not feel weak. She was raised until she could see the faces of her oppressors.

The doctor wore enough cologne to have her wishing for her gas mask. He had black hair and a permanent scowl under tired eyes that hid behind thick, round glasses. The nurse was thin and bony with straw-blonde hair. There was no sound, other than a drip of water coming from somewhere she could not see. The lime green tiles climbed up the walls of the windowless room.

"Good morning," said the doctor. "Or should I say *guten Tag?*"

She stared, deadeye. Don't reveal your heritage. Remain a mystery. This may give you an advantage. But what advantage? She was a prisoner of the British, and that could mean she was anywhere: France, England, even the distant shores of the United States of America.

Wherever it was, she was buried beneath the earth.

And everything was dead.

Felix.

The colonel.

Click. Clack. All of them gone like so much smoke in the wind.

Tears welled.

"Well, I would have thought that being alive would have cheered you up some. That's gratitude, for you. Now, do you speak English?"

She shook her head. The infuriating itch growing out of her back was cold and she focused on its annoying chill while the doctor babbled his condescending remarks. She anchored her thoughts to one of the iced itches on her skin. It wove into another, like braided metal.

"*Parlez-vous* French?"

The metallic pains wove into each other until the itch vanished and what was left was an iced sheen of strength the likes of which she had only felt …

... communing with the Juggernaut.

"Oh god," she said. "The butterflies."

There was a rush of air behind her as the harness around her body shook under the flap of metallic wings.

"Doctor!"

"I see it! Get the chloroform!"

"No!" Her body thrashed and thrashed, spinning in the air, legs whipping hard and knocking the doctor's glasses off.

The restraints snapped.

She was up in the air, the whoosh of air behind her, and for a moment held still in the air as the heat from a bulb covered her neck. Below her, the ground was covered in the black shadow of her wings.

Her fingers wove into her filthy, matted hair. "What have I become?" Blood began to drop down her feet.

"Code white!" screamed the doctor. "Code white!"

She held herself in the top right corner of the room as soldiers flooded the room, but behind them, a large man entered wearing a Tennyson frock coat.

"Sir, you can't," said a soldier, trying to push him back, but the man thrusted forward, shoving the soldier away. "I outrank you by a few leagues, Private." He looked up. "Hello," he said, face full of worry and wonder. "I'm sorry we frightened you."

She held herself in the corner, arms and wings shaking. "Get away!"

"All of you," said the man. "Leave. Now!"

The doctors ran out and the soldiers, amazed at the man, followed, until it was just the two of them.

Her arms and legs shook. "Leave me alone!"

"I'm afraid I cannot allow that," he said, in Russian. With a lisp. The annoying man who had been in the room before. He had a young, arrogant face that screamed of too many cakes past dinner, but his eyes were wide and seemed to take in the whole of the encounter as if absorbing every detail. "You are injured, my dear, and we must administer some medicine or else I fear your new wings will become infected."

Her elbow bent, and she flexed it out in a thrum of pain. "Go to hell!"

"If you wish. But I offer another option. Come down."

"I ... can't!"

He pumped his fist in the air. "Nonsense. You are perhaps the most resourceful and talented creature under the heavens that I have ever heard about in story or witnessed in my own rather exciting life. You are a child of Fabergé, but a creature of your own making, and you somehow managed to survive as a Russian inventor in the heart of the Kaiser's empire. Now, listen to your heart. Can you hear it?"

She shivered, but nodded.

"Good. Follow the thumps. Follow them all the way to your newborn wings. Hear them reach."

The frantic beating of her heart made her shake. Then, sweat slick on her palm, she slid.

"Careful—"

She screamed and fell and dove as the heartbeats thundered into her wings and held her above the ground.

"Splendid!" said the man, both arms high in a V. "My dear child, you are the eighth wonder of the world!"

Each flap hurt worse than the last, but her heart eased some and slowly, awkwardly, she landed on the ground before the fat man. He stank of cigar smoke and something sweet, like plums. Brandy? It had been ages since the scent of Mother's Christmas vice had reached her. The man was not much taller than she, and his kind face made her sick and suspicious. She backed off into a corner. "What do you want from me?" she said, arms folded.

He grimaced. "Your help."

She nodded. "Of course. And what do I get in return? You have nothing I want." Blood pooled and stained her smock, a crushing loneliness icing her heart colder than the metal fused to her back. She stumbled, and he caught her, and she pushed him away. "Leave me alone."

"As you wish," he said, turning to the door. "But please, let the doctors tend to your wounds. You've become something very rare and special, Vasilya. I'd hate to see you destroy yourself before you had a chance to fly home to St. Petersburg."

She shivered, but looked at his wide backside. "You'd ... you'd let me go?"

He turned and faced her. "We do not employ slavery in Britain, my dear. I only came to offer you a chance to help us in return for saving your life. But I will not hold you here captive like some rare specimen in a geological collection. We do not preserve freedom by denying it unless there is no other choice. And when there is not, it is a grave day indeed." He nodded, then turned to the door.

"Who ... who are you?" she said in English.

He smiled over his shoulder, but his kind eyes held worry. "My name is Winston. And I fear I may be the only friend you have left in the world."

CHAPTER THIRTY-FIVE:

CAPTIVE OF WAR

Ice cold water woke Warren from deep hibernation on a stained concrete floor.

"Good morning, champ. Looking a little grey in the face." The voice. The last one he'd heard. It came from a man in a dishevelled uniform, the AEF patch on his shoulder and stupid Marine haircut, and Southern accent making it clear this bastard was an American. He was grey at the edge of his black sideburns and five o'clock shadow, and the bucket in his hand dripped like the smugness on his face. "I'd worried I'd knocked you out for good."

Warren shook his head, pulled his ragged carcass from the floor, and felt something choke him—

An iron collar snaked around his neck. Manacles gripped his ankles and hands. Each set of manacles and braces was linked to chains that ended on locks on the ground. The weight was oppressive at first, then comfortable. Warren didn't know the limits of his strength ... but it was clear they knew that, too, and they weren't taking any chances.

"Thanks for the shower," Warren said, spray trailing his words like weak spit. "You going to wipe my nose, too?"

"Sorry, kid. Not in the contract."

"I see." He hawked a glob of old blood and dirt and spat it on the arrogant shit's well-shined and cleaned boots.

"Nice aim."

"Not really. I was aiming for your mouth."

The American flipped the bucket over, sat on it, and sighed. "Why is it sharpshooters only come in two varieties? The ones who won't so much as fart when they're alone, and the ones who won't shut the hell up no matter where they are?"

"And you know which one I am?" Warren said, snickering, until the American put his hand out in front of him. Dangling from a chain was a shark tooth.

Warren glanced at his hand.

The thick triangle was scarred into the palm and not healed. "Give that back," Warren said, grunting. He strained against the chains and manacles, and then hissed. They hurt. Honest to god pain.

The American tossed the tooth in the air, then caught it. "I think your Indian buddy was the strong, silent type."

"Inuit, you ignorant shit heel." The words sprayed off his lips. "What the hell am I doing here?"

"That's an interesting question, Warren."

Warren smiled, viciously. "I get it. You know my name, you know everything and I'm at your mercy. Could you hurry this little interrogation up so I can get the hell out of here?"

The American shook his head. "Actually, Warren, we don't know everything. And that's the problem. Sure, I know you're Warren Bishop, oldest son of Thomas and Delores Bishop, a career criminal and layabout remittance man until you signed up for the war after your brother's heroic death at Vimy." He hissed inward. "But you see, there be the problem for us, Warren. We have more than one report that your brother didn't die at Vimy. That he ran away after the battle, tarnishing his VC with acts of cowardice—"

"Shut up."

"Desertion."

"Cram it."

"And treason."

The chains shook as anger met resistance from every link, every brace, every lock on his body. "Shut the fuck up!"

The American spun the chain with the shark tooth. "Oh, I appreciate the display of brotherly love. I'd feel the same way if my kin were the one being indicted, but don't hurt yourself. We know all about how strong you are with that strange heart of yours. So we took precautions. Better luck having a flea break out of Fort Knox than you breaking that iron." The chains groaned against the strain, and the American raised his eyebrow. "In any case, even if you do tear through here like a torch through tissue, you're only in chains until this interview is over."

Warren kept pulling. The chains bent.

"And if you do break out of here, you'll never find where that mad Russian took poor Alexander."

Warren stopped, exhaled hard. "And you do?"

"We aim to find him."

"Why do you give a flying fuck about some dead Canadian soldier?"

"I don't. But our governments do. Not because of Alex, mind you, but because of that Russian. He's the key, Warren. A key to ending this war."

"You have got to be kidding me. He's a fucking monster, madder than a hatter—"

The American stopped spinning the tooth. "True enough. Rasputin is one of those rare threats that comes through the tides of history every hundred years. He's our Napoleon, Warren, in a war that hasn't had one. And if we play him right, he'll help us end this war."

Warren laughed and the chains jingled and jangled like industrial Christmas ornaments. "Can you hear yourself? End this war. With Rasputin's help?"

The American snickered. "I'd nail my soul to Lucifer's door sooner than make a pact with that wretch. He's more diabolical, sicklier than you know, kid." He stood eye to eye with Warren and there was not a lick of fear in his countenance. "I've seen his dark art tear apart lives in almost every goddamn corner of the world, chased his sorry carcass from Cuba to China and every banana war in between as he tried to revive his dreams of the army of the dead." He nodded. "Yeah, I know his score, kid. That is no Siberian monk you've been hanging with. He's the bastard son of Rasputin, and no idle threat to this world, and by god I am not letting him out of my sites now that he's at the height of his goddamn powers."

The chains jingle-jangled, but not from struggle. Warren laughed at the gruff Marine, then shook his head. "You're right out of a dime novel, you know that? Lost son of Rasputin. Dark arts. What next, you going to tell me he vacations in Atlantis?"

"You better pray he took your brother somewhere less impossible to find."

The jangling stopped. "Where is Alex?"

The American paused. "With Rasputin. More than that, we don't know. Yet."

"Then get these goddamn chains of me and I'll get him myself."

"Oh, you're in chains more than you know." He removed a key from around his neck. "And I'll let these ones off, even give you back your shark tooth knickknack. But I'll be putting fresh ones on as soon as these are free. You're about the most dangerous thing on two legs on our side of the war, besides myself." He smiled again, fat and ugly. "So, here's the offer. Help us get Rasputin. Help save your brother. And help end the war."

Warren let the weight settle on him like an iron cloak. Freedom was now a dream lost to a dead life. He was a slave to the army, a slave to brotherly loyalty. What was Alex, anymore, anyway? A burned-out husk. His mind no more than worm food. The last image of him, Rasputin dragging his black, flaking body, smoke rising as if he were a living pyre, descending into the earth like the devil returning home.

Fuck him, Warren thought. He dragged me into this war with his death, and didn't have the decency to let me die chasing his ghost. Now I have to go back to that nightmare to get what's left of his corpse? For what?

I'm damned. Heaven won't have me, being some blasphemous creature, and hell's probably full.

"Hey, sleepy," the American said, then snapped his fingers three times. "Don't drift off to the land of nod just yet."

Warren fought the urge to bite the man's hand off.

"Look, I can see that what brains you have are scrambled. So I'll make it really easy. Help us defeat Rasputin, get your brother out of his clutches, or become the world's biggest lab rat."

Just then, two men in surgical masks came into the room from a door that didn't seem to be a door, but just a chunk of wall that swung inward. One pushed a cart stuffed with sharp and jagged instruments.

"Service or torture?" Warren said. "Very noble choices."

"Noble? Son, I'm from Kentucky. I'm a pragmatist. And I don't have much time." He walked to the door. "He's all yours, Doctor. Let me know if he smartens up."

"Yes, Captain Pierce," they said in unison.

"Very theatrical," Warren said, voice getting louder. "But the truth is, you need me more than I need you."

Pierce walked out. "Keep telling yourself that when they tear out your heart."

"Asshole!"

The door slammed shut. The doctors' hands were full of blades. Warren strained against the restraints … when a deep, wormy tremor erupted in his stomach. His mouth was dry as parched dirt. He pulled against the restraints as if it were some way to dial back the sickening hunger in his dry, empty gut. But the doctors looked like they were brimming with water. Juicy, red water …

"Gu … gu … get out."

One of them laughed. "Sorry, son. Captain's orders."

"You don't get it!" he screamed, hunger in his teeth so bad he could almost taste the marrow juice on his breath. "Get away from me, before it's too late."

"Now who's being theatrical," said the other one. "Time to see what you're really made of."

They approached.

"Get back! I can't control this!"

They laughed while he seethed against his braces, against the chains, against the concrete—and the weakest link on the ground snapped.

"Captain!"

Then the next. Then the floor lock snapped.

And now, tied to Warren's wrists, were whips of chain. Mind thick with hunger, he slashed the two doctors to the ground, chains cracking their weak bones on impact. Screaming, they crumpled to the floor and he tore at iron manacles at his ankles when the captain ran in.

"Lock the door behind me!" Captain Pierce screamed.

Anger and hunger tussled through Warren's mind before he resolved to simply eat the bastard who had locked him in here, when he saw Captain Pierce's hand was gloved, and carried a white cloth—

Like on the battlefield.

Warren thrashed his chains like a beast unhinged from captivity, and the old soldier rolled behind the cart, the instruments clattering against the floor before Warren yanked back the chain.

The captain gripped it, and shot toward Warren like a bullet, snaking around his neck, and shoving the cloth over this mouth.

"Night-night," he said, but not before Warren tore him off, launching him against the wall like a rag doll.

Darkness infected his vision.

The broken, sweet bodies of the doctors lay before him. The hunger fought to stay awake, but consciousness faded out. Falling back, Warren saw Captain Pierce above him, huffing. He put a boot on Warren's neck. "I've wrestled critters your nightmares can't even breed, son. Smarten up and get with the plan, or I will snuff you out like a candle."

Warren's hand reached out to strangle him but only reached a murky veil before tottering into oblivion.

CHAPTER THIRTY-SIX:

GROUNDED ANGELS

Vasilya had no more tears. After the doctors were done with their swabs and sutures, sewing her back and disinfecting her wings, all pain became ice, cold as iron in winter. That is what she needed to be. An iron heart to survive any storm, kill every pain. And when your heart is frozen metal, you will not shed tears. Not for the pain of wings. Not for that last dreadful image of Felix plunging into the depths of the earth.

No, she told herself, huddled in the corner of her cell, avoiding the thick blankets they provided, the food on the tin tray, the steaming tea that looked about as weak as she felt.

No. I am iron. I will not break.

Her wings remained folded beneath her nightgown. The urge to trigger them to span out, to stretch proud and flap, was snuffed in her ice heart.

She tussled with the value of tearing them off, destroying every vestige of time she'd spent in the dreaded German workshop … but if that man, that fat Winston, was telling the truth…

She shivered, and tried to swallow the chill. He's a liar. They're all liars. They want one thing from me. Once they have it, I'll be tossed to the wolves or the scrap heap or both, given what I am.

God, what am I?

Is this what Felix felt like, when Balk convinced him to blend his body into the Juggernaut? Did he feel this weak, this lonely?

Felix. You idiot. Why did you leave me like this?

A lock shifted out of place on the door.

He walked in. Ruddy face smiling. "Well," Winston said, "you have a capital look about you compared to when we last spoke."

"I have never felt better," she said, devoid of colour or emotion, perfect for the bland English language she was now forced to speak.

He sat on the cot and it sank some. The tray sat between them. "Feeling too good for food, are we? May I?"

She shrugged.

He took a pale carrot and began to chew. "I see why you avoided it. Ash has more zest."

"Am I free to go today? Or are your words as hollow as the echo of these prison walls?"

Winston nodded, glumly. "Indeed. If you feel up to it, I have provided the means for you to leave here by ship for Archangel, where the White forces are still in command, though the fighting is growing. You also have the choice to go to Vladivostok."

"In Asia?"

"It is more stable from the troubles. And, should you wish to make the rather epic sojourn, I have it within my means to send you to the Caucuses where the Whites have been faring better."

"I see. My choices are really no choices at all."

"It is a world war, my dear," he said gravely. "I can send you to the New World, much further from the troubles of the old." He grimaced.

"What? Are the Germans fighting there, too?"

"No. But they are looking for you. I was informed this morning that two of the stormtroopers who had participated in the battle survived. Which means there is more than a fair chance the high command in Berlin knows you are alive, as well." He sighed. "Given all they had spent to make your weapon work, and the knowledge of its initial success, I fear their network of assassins are priming poison and pistol for you. Their reach is long, my dear. And even should you master your gift, I do not think you can outrun a bullet."

"I see. So I'm dead if I leave your hospitality."

"I am sorry about that—"

"No you're not. If you know as much about me as I think you do, you have only one thing on your mind: how to use me to your advantage to win the war against the Germans. You're no better than they are. And you know what? I don't care." Conviction hardened in her cold heart. "If I am not free, then I will lash out at my tormentors. I will do what you want me to do."

"And what might that be?"

Disgust crinkled her frosted countenance. "What else? You want me to build you the same weapon I did for the Germans." She blinked, and Felix, lashed to the inside of the Juggernaut, fell down, down, down into the dark.

"Actually," Winston said. "What I'd like to do right now is take you for a walk."

"So I am to be your dog instead of your prisoner."

He smiled, sadly. "Guard."

Outside the room, down a ghostishly lit corridor, the hint of salt in the air made her back itch. Outside, beyond the walls, strange birds and a rolling deep echo sang.

"What is it you do for your government?" she said.

"The official title is Minister of Extraordinary Affairs, which is both ponderous and as inaccurate as any name in Parliament." He smiled. She did not. They passed other silent doors with rusty locks.

"And how many others do you have locked up here?"

"Just one."

"Who"

"A rather curious man, one that you will meet in due time."

"He must be more than curious to require an entire prison."

He smiled. "The prison was not for him, or you. Besides you two, it has not seen service in years."

"Why? Are all your convicts serving on the front?"

His voice carried a growl that followed the echo of his quickening steps. "I closed it down because they were abusing the prisoners with straps and the lash and treating human beings like cattle before slaughter."

Her voice remained cool. "I did not realize you were such a humanitarian."

He gave her a stern stare. "If it were up to others in Parliament, you'd be in the belly of Woolwich arsenal being dissected like a Swiss watch."

The rusty itch on her back hurt. She said no more, fearing that unless he had the last word, the conversation would not end. Much like Colonel Balk.

They climbed rough-hewn stone steps to a hallway braced with bars. Through them, she could see the main floor of the prison. A handful of men were scurrying about like mice. There was a massive new structure in the far corner, a cage of some kind, and she could smell the fresh grease and hint of acetylene from it being welded. The main hall was filled with all-too-familiar pieces. Work benches. Electrical equipment. Another bloody prison workshop. She thought of Clack and called out for her last remaining pet. Clack. If you can hear me. Come to me. Blood dripped from her nose, and she wiped it on her sleeve. Nothing. They were both gone.

"Guard! The door!"

A bell chimed with an ugly ring and a grated door opened with a heavy swing. Guards littered the place with the sunken look of the English.

The smell of salt and cold wet air grew as they descended another flight and walked a stony path past a giant doorway that held in its rafters a medieval looking gate and she wondered if it was for keeping criminals in, or barbarians out.

Natural light crossed the floor as they entered a foyer with high ceilings and windows and the world chilled some more.

"Where are you taking me?"

"Just to see some friends."

A bramble of self-consciousness came over her and Winston smiled, that same wretched, kind smile. "Here." He handed her his pinstriped jacket. It stank of smoke and plums. "This should keep you warm. We will only be out for a sliver. Guard! The main door!"

Two guards pulled the double doors inward and light flooded the room. Vasilya gasped, then remembered herself. Steady as steel, cold as iron. The light crept across the floor until it swarmed them and she was blinded. She covered her eyes.

"You've been in the dark too long," Winston said. "Let the fresh air and light brace you."

He walked into the light. Gripping his jacket, she strode out and her senses were overwhelmed. Grass and pebbles stung her feet as she walked. Waves rushed against a rocky shore in the distance, but close enough to see the violent tussle between wet and rock. A rough, hilly terrain rolled out under a white cloud sky, sunlight pale and luminous as it filtered through the clouds to the earth. The air was cold and damp, but alive. Wild and powerful and tousling her hair into a mockery of medusa.

And in the air, birds.

Dozens of them.

Of different shapes and sizes.

Riding the wind from the sea, floating in the air.

"Where am I?"

"Mainland of the Shetland Islands, Scotland."

Her wings itched as they started to move.

"This point is a bastion for birds of all sorts," Winston said. "Those riding the currents have come from all over Europe and the world. Egypt, Russia, Canada, Norway. A resting stop on their great migrations. They do not fight for food, or the affections of a mate, or for primacy of place since the wind is indifferent to their rankings."

"Why do they come here?" she said.

"There are theories, of course. But none so much better than the others that it could be taken as gospel. A prisoner once told me they came to take the prayers of the forsaken to St. Peter."

"What happened to him?"

"I suppose you'll have to ask St. Peter." He took a cigar out of his vest pocket, snapped it to life with a match, and took three long puffs as his thick hands protected flame from wind. "If you look in the pockets, you'll find some crumbs."

She dug in and indeed this strange, proper man had crumbs in his pocket. "Go on. They've been expecting us."

She tossed them and the wings of a dozen birds fought against the current and dove to her feet. She knew nothing of birds. Winston could be lying through his teeth, setting the stage for the metaphor she smelled coming off him like cigar smoke.

The birds were ravenous, and inched closer and closer. She stepped back, toward the prison as the food ran out and one by one they took to the air again.

All but one.

An owl. Its yellow-black eyes hid amidst a cluster of brown and black feathers, though his chest was largely white. He gripped the ground with talons and turned his head at such an awkward angle Vasilya feared his neck was broken.

"Hello, Merlin," Winston said. "He's a bit of a cheeky one. Strange as he is wondrous."

"What does he eat?"

"Mice, if he can catch them." She thought of Click and Clack. They'd make short work of this creature of flesh and feather.

"Why isn't he flying with the rest of them?"

"He can't. His mother vanished after he was hatched, and he got in a rather nasty tussle with a rat when he was young. He hides in the rocks and waits until they all arrive on the ground before appearing as if from nowhere, hence my name for him. He's as docile as a dog to humans, too. Strangest bird I've seen outside of an exhibit." Winston puffed hard on his cigar, smoke vanishing in the hard wind. "I shall make you two promises, Vasilya, the first of which I've only ever made to one other person. I will not lie to you. We do need your help. There is an evil wind on the battlefield. A vile treacherous man who, if unopposed, has within him the ability to make this truly a war without end. Help us defeat him, and the war itself has a good chance of ending."

She watched Merlin struggle against the other birds as they fluttered around his awkward walk. "And your second promise?"

"When we win, I will see to it that you will have free passage to anywhere in the world that you may wish to go. Back to Russia, Asia, the North America, or the hills of Kilimanjaro if you so desire."

The birds fluttered around Merlin, screaming wild songs of disdain and disgust.

"You said you would not lie to me."

"Yes."

"And your spies have clearly done their work on me, on Colonel Balk, on my … on Monsieur Fabergé and my home life?"

He puffed. "Sad affair, having to intrude on people's privacy, but in our case made necessary by our dire circumstance."

"Then I want you to tell me something." She braced her iron heart. "What has happened to my mother?"

Winston gazed into the rocky crags and ashen clouds as winds tried to whip them from the grip of the earth. His face took a grim countenance. "When last I read your dossier, our agent in St. Petersburg had confirmed that your mother had been arrested by the Bolshevik's secret service for her ties to the Fabergé family. We suspect she's being held in Moscow, but we cannot be certain."

The wind tasted salty, foreign, and awful. "Find her." She gripped her hands and inhaled the rotten hair. "Find her and free her and I will make your monster. She ... doesn't deserve to be abandoned." She dug her nails into the palm of her hand, and the mist of her eyes eased.

Winston kneeled down and extended his hand. "Agreed." They shook, and the warmth of his hands was as strong as the smoke of his breath. "And thank you, Vasilya. I do not like the role of prison warden."

"And I grow tired of being a prisoner. Find my mother and we can both be free." She faced the prison.

From the outside, it was a stone and iron castle. A strange fortress of ruined towers and modern construction, grey as the dead faces of the battlefield. The door was but a tiny mouth to a skull-faced hell.

Merlin approached, waddling like a penguin.

"Get away," she said.

He fluttered his wings uselessly.

"Don't be a nuisance."

"I think he's taken a shine to you," Winston said, then began to walk to the grisly grey doors. "I taught him to perch on a hand. Give it a try."

His unblinking black eyes seemed stuck on her.

"Fine."

She knelt, extended her hands, and only then saw how savage and strong his talons were. He gripped her, painfully. She seethed, and he eased his grip.

Slow, she stood, Merlin on her hand. Her voice was low. "Maybe we can learn to fly together?"

She strode back to the door where Winston stood, face milky-white in the dark. "Let us see my materials," she said. Lady Frankenstein had work to do.

CHAPTER THIRTY-SEVEN:

HELL'S GUTS

There was no restraint left when he woke to find the pile of glistening red and black meat in front of him, only a ravenous hunger that stabbed through thought, desire, or will.

Belly full, Warren tried to tear out his own throat. But the new chains were shorter, stronger, and he could not gouge himself to death for the sickness that was his hunger.

Doctors came, a soldier by the door with a rifle at the ready. Warren paid them no mind as they listened to his dead heart and tore off pieces of his grey skin, watching the incisions sew themselves up. He sat, mute, as they twitched with fear and walked away from the blood stained bones at his feet.

They did not talk.

He might as well have been a circus geek, chewing light bulbs or shoving railway nails into his skull to the sound of calliope and steam whistles. Come one, come all, come see the most hideous wonder of the world, the great Grey Shambles! See as we shoot him full of bullets to no effect on his dead, black heart! See as we force feed him the dead meat of a lost soul! See as we strip away everything that makes him human until all that's left is a husk, chained to the floor in misery and defeat!

"I could run and join the circus," he said to the stray meat on the floor. "Think about what P. T. Barnum could do with me." He'd always wanted to run with the circus, the elephants and clowns, the sweet lady acrobats in their slim and glittery outfits, the lion tamers and knife throwers. "They could toss me anywhere." He snickered, tasting the antiseptic air and wondering if his breath would stink up the room with the fetid aroma of mustard gas. "The Human Shambles falls fifty feet on to his neck! The Human Shambles becomes lunch for the lions before his dinner performance! The Human Shambles does the famed bullet-catch magic trick and only loses one eye!"

His laughter dissolved into the hiss and crackle of the room's lighting, shadows became pregnant with memories of all he had lost, all he had become. But the ghosts in the room did not speak. Chained like Quasimodo before the townspeople that detested him. They paced, like vipers about to strike.

Father in his Sunday clothing, drunker than a miner, his quiet face tight with anger and grief and hate.

Tik's face, always grim, had lost its smile, and instead he just shook his head before folding into the dark.

And Alex ...

Wreathed in flame, he stood in the shadow, face disintegrating from the ruddy-cheeked boy who was the first one on the track, the first one to volunteer for service, the last one to call Warren coward ... burning into the grey-faced soldier of the Lost Battalion, grim and serious with eyes wide to the wild talk of the mad sorcerer Rasputin ... into the gibbering mess Warren had carried from the nightmare of Marlow's pit, down the corridor to the vile room of worm magic ... and the simple creature of loyalty that had emerged from that blasphemous surgery ... to the burning corpse whose only remaining features were lidless eyes that glared with indictment at all of Warren's failures.

Death.

The word hung around his head like flies around a turd. He sucked a red piece of flesh from his teeth, and spat it at the broken bone at his feet, marrow sucked dry.

Days rolled. No one came to see Warren, and he could not have cared less. They were leaving him to rot, scheming grand strategies while the chains dug deeper into his flesh and his mind began to fade into veils of sorrows, regrets and failures, guilt and shame ...

It had been years since he'd stayed this still. Whatever happened to that rambling itch, that need to move, to run headlong into the next thing he wanted or desired and running from the price he'd previously paid to have it. Where was it?

Tied to a stake at the bottom of the world.

"So be it," he said.

Doctors came in and spoke to him, but he let his mind wander.

Time was meaningless when you were not of the earth.

The door creaked open. He did not look up, but Captain Pierce's cowboy accent was like broken glass in his ear. "Seems like you're fixing to just lay there. Docs say you won't participate in our tests."

"I'm done, Pierce," Warren said.

"Done what? Moping like a schoolgirl with a skinned knee?"

"Done. Done. Done."

"So you're going to let your brother fry under the guidance of that mad sorcerer?"

"And what do I get if I help you? Will you turn me back into a real boy, Geppetto? Or will your snipers be waiting for the sound of victory bells to blow my brains out of my head. If you win in this war, can you in good conscience allow an abomination like me to live?" Warren exhaled hard, then raised his head.

Captain Pierce stood as arrogant and strong as ever, but behind him was a slight figure in a grey housedress and soldier's coat.

An old wound flared in his dead heart.

Her face contorted between fear and repulsion, and the tone of her voice had the smug yet sad satisfaction of a person who was witnessing a prophecy coming true. "Hello, Warren," she said, voice cold, and determined. Warren recoiled as she stepped closer, hands holding each other in mock prayer or for warmth, face firm as winter winds off Lake Superior. She strode closer and he was shaking despite himself, as if he was still weak under the brutal caress of her correcting hand.

He snorted breath, nerves twitching. "Get out of here. Pierce, get her out of here. Or I'll—"

"What?" he said. "Do more nothing? Time ain't exactly on our side. Go on, Mrs. Bishop. He can't hurt you."

"Warren." The name was said with the deliberateness of a judge passing sentence. "I don't know that I understand all of what is going on. They tell me … Alexander is alive. That you've seen him?"

Laughter cackled from him in time with the shake of his chains.

"What's so damn funny?" Pierce said.

"She finds me chained to the floor, looking like death warmed over, and the first thing she does is ask about Alex."

"But he's missing," she said. "And Captain Pierce says you can help them find him."

"I'm fine, Mum," he said. "Thanks for asking. And how might you be doing down there on the farm? Cows still smell like shit? Rail tramps still needing to be scared off with a blast of shells? Must be hard, all by yourself, without a son to cherish and another to beat!" She recoiled into Captain Pierce's arms as he thrust himself against his chains. "Oh, don't look so angry, Captain. If you knew her like I did, I'd be more careful about showing her kindness unless you absolutely know you can deliver what she needs. The price for failure is a high one, isn't it, Mum?"

She fixed her blouse. "You were wild, Warren." A bitter smugness crept upon her face as she stared down at him. "Too much of your father's Irish in you. I could not allow it to grow. I loved you too much for that."

"Love." The word could not have tasted more rancid on his tongue if his mouth had been full of maggots. "If that's love I'll live off the crumbs of contempt any day."

The captain groaned. "I don't have time … Mrs. Bishop? Tell him what you came to say. I'll be outside."

Then they stood there, two rams glaring at each other's horns. Her thin lip twitched. "I'm ..."

"Disgusted? Disappointed? Disowning me?"

Her face tightened. "Sorry."

Warren stopped straining against the chains. "For what?"

"I feared what you'd become, left to your own appetites, and Alex needed a strong man in the house, a teacher and leader, and the more I tried the more you fought. You set an example, all right, but one he hated and would never want to be." She gripped her nose. "But it didn't work, did it? I mean, here you are and poor Alex is lost in some misbegotten stretch of Europe in the middle of a war."

Slowly, Warren stopped straining his face. "Hated me?"

Thick fingers released her nose and covered her mouth. "You'd gone off in the wilds with that Indian."

"Inuit," Warren grunted.

Mother shook her head. "Alex felt he had to be so much better than you. For me. He excelled, Warren. He excelled because you didn't. He became heroic because you'd gone to the pint glass and saloon instead of the good book or a school yard or an honest day's wage. Always sending a letter for more remittance."

"One." He huffed. "I sent one letter. After I'd been robbed on the way to Port Arthur for a saw mill job."

She held her head back. "For a real man, one was too many. But you provided him an example, Warren. One I could never handle. But it worked. He turned out beautifully."

He wanted to laugh, to spit, to scare her. Instead, he nodded. She turned them against each other ... to make Alexander better? He exhaled fetid breath. "You're welcome, Mum. Especially since you see what good it did him. Do you want to know what has happened to your dear son Alexander? Do you want to know how beautiful he's become?"

"The captain has told me."

"Has he, now?"

"He's ... gone bad. He's doing awful things. I've heard some of this from other wives and mothers, whose men returned home with a wound, but their mind has gone to pot. Shaking like babies in a damp cold room."

Warren blanched. "Shell shock?" Was that the best they could do to assuage her fears? He relished the idea of explaining it to her, of watching the horror tear down her contemptuous visage as he described the flesh-eating, worm-brained, burning critter Alex had become ...

But when he blinked, there was a flicker of flame, of black skin bubbling with the burning jelly, of the whites of Alexander's eyes in full terror as his body burned to a crisp. And the magic of Rasputin sweeping it away, marching him into the grave of the earth …

"Yeah, Mum. Shell shock."

"And he's being held captive."

"Yeah, Mum."

"And that you …"

He rose his neck up. "Oh. Did they tell you what happened to me, Mum? Why they've got me locked to the slab like the Hunchback of Notre Dame?"

"They said you were … experimented on."

He smiled. "You could say that."

"And that you've not said anything about where Alexander was, that you won't help them."

"I've had a bit of a hard row, too, Mum."

"No harder than Alexander, and he needs your help."

"I've helped him more than you could know, and it won't make a lick of difference if I find him or not."

"How can you say that?"

He slouched under the weight of the chains. "Because even if I find him, we cannot win. There's another war brewing, Mum. One from the bowels of hell itself. And it's going to erupt on the earth like the end of days and we'll all be as much as ants against the black flood that's rising. Alex, Me, you. This war may be lost, but the one on its heels is doom incarnate. Better luck building the pyramids with pitchforks and rice—"

The slap that cracked his face was nothing compared to the blows he'd taken since the deadroot landed in his heart. It should not have hurt. It should not have even stung. But the blow carried with it a charge of memory so painful that it sent wildfire through Warren's mind: a moonless night in the cabin, the sound of rage laced with corn whiskey matched by the frantic cry of Mother, the thunder of Warren's own heart as he ran through the terror in his own blood to see Father's hands, like nine-pound hammers, coming down on her slight but strong frame, arms up to block the blow, the heavy thought of knowing he could never tear him off her and the frantic run to the gun case where he plucked out the Winchester, loaded it with a shaking hand, before the wild-eyed jackal that had become his father turned to the sound of the breech being loaded, stalking toward him without fear, Warren's hands shaking, voice cracking for him to get away, and the old man's voice like a rusty door screeching out, "Coward!" before he tore the gun away, the fear that filled Warren like lead as the gun was tossed before he was grabbed and thrown, like a sack of grain from the mill house floor, the shudder of books that buried him, the weakness in his knees as he stood and stared the wild-eyed jackal with strength beyond strength, and those hammers falling down on him, cracking against his nose, his ribs, his head, his jaw, each one heavier than the last until the crack of a rifle shot deadened all sound and Father's body tore itself away from the beating it was delivering ... The smoke leading to the barrel in Mother's hands, Warren finding the strength to stand, to run from the gurgling mess that was Father, running to Mother for protection ... And finding a slap so hard he lost a loosened tooth. "Why didn't you save me?" In the back of the house, Alex cried and she handed him the rifle and so Warren stood unhinged from the world, watching his father slowly leak to death, eyes wide and full of anger until the blood ran toward him, while Mother comforted Alex and said, "Warren did a very bad thing," Father's blood reaching for his feet—

He pulled his head back from the slap and heard his dead knuckles crack hard.

But she stood defiant, eyes as steely as they had been when she'd shot Father. "I am not perfect. I did questionable things. But this is beyond you and me, Warren. I cannot change the past even if I wished to. We go forward, carry our burdens as best we can, and try to make things right before God. You say there's evil in this world we cannot conquer. That maybe we should instead hide in the dark with our fears as a blanket." The stern resolve flickered for one instant. "Do you really think you can endure that kind of silent hell? Do you know what it will cost you?"

A tear, thin as a splinter, cut down her face and left a trail that evaporated under the heat of her face before the drop hit the ground between them. "Do not choose chains if you can be free, and do not dally about the why. You were always a free spirit, Warren. Be one now. And save Alex whatever cruel fate you see with those eyes. Don't let him suffer because you hate me."

She turned away and took three slow steps on the blood-stained tiles before she came to the door, and it opened as if she'd said open sesame.

"Mother."

She stopped. But did not turn.

Grinding, the chains dug in harder as he found it hard to breathe. "Don't expect we'll see each other again, huh?"

She inhaled. "I suppose not, Warren."

Beneath the flickering light, Warren shook and rattled. He cleared his throat, rolling his neck from side to side as best he could within the iron noose. "I'm sorry." His teeth rubbed together. "I'm sorry I couldn't stop him. I'm sorry I couldn't—"

She turned, standing straight, a mirror tear in her once dry. "I know."

When the echo of her boots was gone, Captain Pierce returned and sat on a chair, face so squinted it was as if he was trying to decipher code tattooed on Warren's crinkled forehead. Finally, he said, "Nice lady."

Warren shrugged, chains settling.

"Took a lot to get her here with speed and secrecy, chief. And you can rest assured she'll have protection not only for the journey, but when she gets back to whatever chunk of snow you call home."

"You're a kind soul."

"No, I'm an asshole. And though I'm cruel, I'm also fair. So. What do you say? Will you help us?"

Warren snickered. "Yeah. I'll help you." He stood against the restraints until there was a snap of metal. He followed it with a tearing at the links he'd been slowly pulling at for days and days, until each one of them snapped. Lastly, he broke the chain that tied his neck to the floor all while soldiers rushed in and formed a firing line.

"Hold your fire!" Captain Pierce said. "Hold your fire, goddamn you." He looked back at Warren. "Good god, son, are you the bastard son of Samson or something?"

"I'll help you," Warren said, busted chains like iron snaked around his feet. "I'll help you tear Rasputin apart to each goddamn end of the earth, and I will take my brother back as payment. But no more chains."

Pierce smiled. "You got it, chief." He tossed Warren the large brass key for the manacles. "Men, fall back and give Mr. Bishop here some privacy."

Before the door closed, Warren caught whispers from the men to Pierce. "Sir, how are we going to control him without—"

"Don't worry, private," Pierce said with a chuckle. "He's trading in his chains for a leash."

CHAPTER THIRTY-EIGHT:

OF CURRENT AND CONTROL

The shower room had been cleaned and scrubbed and doused with lemon-stained water, but the aroma of decay and the high ceiling windows with rusty bars made all such attempts at comfort meaningless. The ever-present drip of old pipes cackled in the distance.

A bucket full of steaming water lay beneath the shower, a rag on a stick floating on top. The doctors had given Vasilya strict instructions not to stand under running water, fearing what it might do to her wings. After checking the door twice, she undressed, leaving the starchy blouse and flannel dress they had provided on a dry patch of tile where Merlin sat.

She found it amazing, scrubbing her back awkwardly with the stick, how even with heaven and earth in upheaval in wars of global significance, this minor frustration completely dominated her mind.

"What good are wings if they can't be used and what good is a bath if you can't get clean!"

With beak and talon, Merlin climbed up an overturned oak bucket and blinked at her as if she'd gone out of focus.

She rubbed her under arms, and shivered. "I wonder what it is they will have me make. Is this how I will go down in history, as the Daedalus of war? Or the Icarus, if I try and fly and the wings are torn from my body? Either way, what a fitting place."

Winston had given her a short tour before returning her to a clean cell that had been made to look like a room. As grim as the shower, it was not nearly as stuffy and strikingly small as the halls and cells. Waves of light and murk ran into the room from the impossibly high windows like a luminescent waterfall.

She walked into the shifting sunlight as a cloud claimed it, but it soon returned. It was not warm, but she liked it.

She closed her eyes. The itch of her back eased as she focused on the metallic connection to her shoulders that were cool and slick. There were no mirrors in the room, so she gazed at the shadow she'd cast on the floor.

Come on, she told her wings. Spread out. Come on, easy does it.

A flicker of movement on her back made her wince in surprise, but not pain. And the shadow fluttered.

A knock on the hastily made bath door made them retract on her back with a hiss.

"Miss Savorov?" said a female voice. "Mr. Churchill requires your presence. I've left some fresh clothes for you at the door."

The shadow vanished as a cloud cut the light. "Thank you," she said in English, a stuffy language, but more elegant than German. Softer, anyway. By the time she'd left Colonel Balk's workshop, she'd started thinking in that devil tongue.

And for a moment, there was Colonel Balk on the battlefield … face eaten by chemical gas, shriveling into a bloated mass of sores and abscesses—

She stifled the scream to the core of her iron heart. He kidnapped you, blackmailed you, lied to you, turned you into something you're not. He deserved what he got. And he died in battle, just like he wanted. You must not feel guilt. You must not feel remorse. You must not feel!

Her jaw clamped tight enough to chew through lead. She exhaled hard three times, wrapped herself in a towel gently across her wings, and regained her composure. She opened the door a sliver. On the floor sat a plain blue and grey blouse and dress, clean socks, and polished brown boots with a slight heel.

She shook her head and dressed, wings pressed flat against her back like a metal embrace that gave her an ounce of strength and protection.

Merlin had waddled to a drain and dipped his beak into some pooled water. A trail of pink blood ran through it like a crimson eel. "Come on," she said, offering him her hand. He took it and she brought him eye to eye. "Mother is counting on us."

The clank and thunk of industry filled the halls and the rough voices of rougher men followed as a guard led her back to the main chamber. They swore, and yelled, and made the quiet of the colonel's workshop seem sublime, filled with nothing but automatons, magic, and Felix.

Stop that, she thought. Memories are a trap. We go forward. We do not chain ourselves to nostalgia and pity. Felix is dead. No magic can bring him back. We go forward and try to do right by him and if we can, save Mother from those Leninists.

They were strong thoughts, but barely animated her steps.

In the main courtyard, she found Winston ordering the men to stand straight, then saw her. "Good morning. I hope the accommodations were amiable."

She nodded, then placed Merlin on the rail that ran around this main courtyard while up three-storey-high empty cells stared out at her like grated mouths in an industrial hive. "So," she said. "Here I am. I must warn you that I did not design the Juggernaut you saw on the battlefield where you found me. My imagination does not run into the world of arsenals and death. Though I have a gift for turning such dreams of others into a reality." Then all stood and shifted in their skins as she looked down her nose at them. "Are these the great designers of Britain? They look more like dock workers and union men."

They growled and swore until Winston shot them a glance that impressed her because of its sourness; a look she had not thought his tubby countenance was capable of. He walked to a massive work desk. "Our main designer has not yet arrived because of ... complications due to travel. Your first task is relatively simple." He reached into his pocket and dropped something on the worktable.

"That ... is a collar for a dog?" The men grumbled laughter and she wondered what she'd said wrong and then got angry. "When you speak three languages as well as I do, then you can laugh at me."

"Indeed, a collar," Winston said. "Though for a very large bulldog." The men laughed until he raised his eyebrow. "We need a restraining device that can discharge an electric current strong enough to kill an average man."

"If the goal is to kill, then why do you need to restrain him?"

"You'll understand once you see the man. The problem is, of course, the ability to generate enough current without forcing him to wear a battery the size of a hog. The shock has to be strong enough to prevent him from acting out of turn."

Her voice was tinny and metallic and matter of fact. "So. You want me to create an electric chair that fits around a man's neck. You people are more barbaric than the Germans."

"As opposed to you Bolsheviks?" said a man in the line.

"I am Russian," she said, a razor in her voice. "And no Bolshevik."

"Tell it to the Tzar if you can find his head," said one of the faceless masses before they all laughed.

Winston's angry face burst, but his voice was a controlled growl. "The next outburst and I will see you all serving in the Malaria Brigade and drop you in the heart of Africa until all we find are your chewed bones in a lion's den! Captain Pierce!"

A soldier walked into the courtyard with rolled up sleeves. He was built like an icebox, grey hair at the sides of his oddly cut hair, a strange tropical hat tied around his neck and falling down his back. He walked with hard strides toward them. "Yes, Minister. Sorry I was late. Operation Shackle is almost ready to be deployed top side, just need to clean out the gutters." He spoke English, but with a bizarre accent akin to a broken Irish brogue. He stopped in front of Vasilya.

"Captain," Winston said, "this is Vasilya Savorov. Vasilya, this is Captain Thomas Pierce, United States Marine Corps." He said the last bit as if she was supposed to be impressed. She wasn't. She'd never met an American before. He was taller than the rest, looked as if he had never missed a meal, and was built like a German farmer. Despite the grey whiskers and scars on his face, arms, and hands, he had a youthful complexion, as if he were the taller cousin of Winston, one who boxed more than he smoked cigars.

"Miss Savorov," he said, with a bow. "It is an honour to make your acquaintance. I fear that the hospitality we can provide here at Fort Daedalus is rather weak."

"Charming name," she said to Winston. "An ode to the tower where he was imprisoned with the knowledge of the labyrinth."

"If you wish," he said, "you may call it Winston's Toyshop. And now, Captain, Parliament beckons with news of our efforts. I will wire when I arrive to discuss things with our patron." He faced Vasilya. "If you can, believe me when I say that what I am hoping for is—"

"Peace," she said. The word was bitter ash. "I've heard that before."

He nodded, grimly. "Yes. But no one has yet told you peace from what, or whom." He nodded at the captain, then walked off toward the door. "Do your best in all things, and do them swiftly. The world is in desperate need of miracles, both divine and man-made."

When Churchill, left, murmurs arose from the greasy labourers until Captain Pierce began to bark. "All right, apes. Back to your duties and I want this place so spic-and-span I could eat shit off the floor and think it was beef Wellington. Fall out!" They did, like clockwork, fearing the captain's voice. She was left with the behemoth Marine at a workbench.

"So," he said. "You get your marching orders?"

She crossed her hands. "An electric chair in a collar, strong enough to kill a man, but with no battery."

"Sounds about right."

"I'm sure General Ludendorff is trembling in his helmet."

"Who said we were still fighting the Germans?" He smiled, got up. "I'll be in the medical wing if you need me. Just holler above the noise until we get all the buzzers working in here. You have until tomorrow morning."

She thought she should be surprised, but was somewhat taken aback that such deadlines were now normal. "What happens if I fail?"

He smiled with malice. "Pray your wings are stronger than those of Icarus." He stalked off, and she began scurrying for materials, wondering if he'd hear if she called him a bastard before those buzzers were in place.

Buzzers, she thought. Buzzers.

CHAPTER THIRTY-NINE:

PROJECT DRAUG

They had given Warren another bloody meal, told him to shower, and every step he took there was a sharpshooter somewhere around the bend, ready to take his skullcap off if he decided to go back on his word.

While en route to the shower, he realized where they'd dragged him. A prison.

The walls. The locks. The bars. What nerves were left in his body itched with the urge to run. There'd been few things on this planet that had scared Warren more than tales Tik told of his brother Mikil, caught for stealing a bag of flour and dragged behind the limestone walls of Kingston Pen, the charges somehow getting stained with talk of native savagery and threatening the shopkeeper's daughter. Tik made the pilgrimage to visit him every year, and every visit took a pound of flesh. Sodomy and the lash. Fights in the courtyard and betting at the gallows, the only occupational sports available. Mikil devolved into a beast Tik barely recognized, until he made a break for the walls and a single shot from the guard tower snuffed out his existence. "It wasn't a prison break, Qimmiq. He was running straight out of this world the only route he could see." Tik never forgave the government for what they'd done, turning a hungry man into an animal, and Warren sometimes woke himself from nightmares where he was dragged into the limestone jaws of Kingston Pen.

Suddenly, the No-Man's Land didn't seem so bad.

He let the iced water run off him like a dribbling fountain. The dirt, blood, and stench of war and feeding turned the water at his feet to sludge. But there were no wounds except for the ones he'd come to war with. Nicks on his fingers from Tik teaching him to knife fight. A scar on his inner thigh from too much of a good thing at Lady Regina's whorehouse.

Warren washed his face. And there was his cheek. Still a hint of shattered glass. He massaged it, half expecting to hear the grind of glass dust against his skin from the captain's punch.

When he was soaped and rinsed and dry, he walked out. Weak

sunlight glared down from high windows. Outside, a wind roared with the froth of the sea and he thought of his dispatch from Halifax, all those girls waving to their boys. Tik stared off to sea, only too eager to find a mortal test.

And Warren had stared at the crash of waves, unable to read the Edgar Rice Burroughs book he'd stuffed in his jacket, knowing he was going to visit Alex's grave, and that he was still a coward because it was guilt that drove him. Nothing more.

He dried himself, and let his hand rest over his heart.

Cold and still.

And somewhere out there, Alex was the same way, trapped below the roots.

"Time to get moving, Bishop," said a guard. Warren dressed in fatigues and work boots and a thick wool sweater that would have annoyed his skin had he still been alive. He followed the guards down the hall.

The handful of lights faded in and out of existence as, above them, the air was pierced with a buzz and a scream.

A trickle of suspicion sharpened Warren's instincts as they marched to the growing sound of buzzers, then turned left and up the stairs into grey sunlight, reaching the main floor and what appeared to be an inner courtyard. Above them, in the walkway that traced the cells, snipers stood locked on him. Another buzz, another scream.

"Stupid bitch!" someone yelled. "You could have killed me."

"If I wanted you dead, you'd be dead."

A female voice. Not his mother's. Thank baby Christ for little miracles, he thought. But it was sharp, and with a thick accent he could not place.

Finally, standing before them, was a metal-ringed workroom with a crowd surrounding a young girl. She was a strange-looking one. Not ugly, but Warren wasn't sure if she was pretty, either. She had the bearing of an aristocrat but was dressed in the rough clothes of a scullery maid. And her accent made everything she said sound like an insult from a throne. "The record is now two seconds," she said to the men. "I thought British men were made of sterner stuff. No wonder the Germans have made short work of your army."

The anger in the little mob's eyes was real and palpable. She was playing with fire, but didn't seem to care.

The sound of rifles loading rounds clacked as they cut across the courtyard and Warren saw a bunch of Limey mechanics in greasy overalls holding up a real wide-eyed bastard in a torn work-coat.

All eyes and scopes were on him.

"Why not let the monster of Amiens try," said the wide-eyed Limey with thick mutton chops. And this rang with a chorus of approval until Captain Pierce stormed in from an opposite corridor.

"Shut your shit holes, good God! This is a place of business and I will have order here."

"Fucking Yank," said the grease hound. "Show up three years late and already taking command."

An eerie mood lanced the people. Pierce wiped his face hard. "All right, Migs. Up front."

The Limey swaggered toward him.

"Got a problem with my leadership?"

Migs snorted. "Real brave with a rifle squad at your beck and call."

"They're just aiming for Bishop there," Pierce said. "I'm only going to ask once more. There a problem with me running the operation?"

Migs's meatbone hands flexed. "If I say yes, then I'm locked in a shit cell lower than that … thing over there." He motioned toward Warren. "If I say no, I lose the respect of my unit."

"Then I'll make it easy for you. Save face. If you can knock me down, I'll give you one request."

"Any request?"

"Name it."

While the gang whispered darkly of food and whores, Migs said. "Then we want Princess Anastasia here to work naked."

"You sick shits," Warren said, then felt a gun at his head. "There's a special place in hell for turds like you."

"Watch your mouth, slave," Migs said. "I'm talking to the captain. Well, Sir, what do you say?"

The girl's whole body puckered. "Yes, Captain," she said, an accent not unlike Rasputin's making the words drip dark. "What do you say?"

Captain Pierce smiled at Migs. "I say I'll give him the first punch."

Fuck! Warren thought, watching Migs's fist fly—as if he'd been waiting all day, lining up his shot—and burst out of its spring box and straight for Captain Pierce's head.

There was a horrific snap.

But the captain was unmoved.

Instead, he'd caught the fist as if he'd snatched a speedball with his bare hand. Then there was a sickening crunch and Migs knees hit the floor. Pierce held on to his hand, holding it over his head like a boulder about to drop.

"You sick, little waste of skin and bone," Pierce said. "You think I would have given you a shot if you had any chance of victory? You're as dumb as you are depraved."

"Let go, god," Migs cried, "please, let go!"

"And if you think for one goddamn second you're so indispensable that you can turn my unit into a personal sin palace, boy, you are wrong. Dead wrong. Now, apologize to Miss Savorov."

His face was wet with pain. "Sorry, I'm so sorry."

Captain Pierce's voice was low, but grew with an angry tone that Warren relished. "Good. Now, when you wake up, you'll be working twice as hard because you'll be one-handed. And if I even catch you winking at her in an un-Christian manner, I'll tan your hide and wear it as a summer coat! Do you understand me, maggot?"

"Yes, Sir!"

"Good!"

Faster than a bullet, Pierce's right fist shot down in a straight right punch that knocked Migs out cold on the floor. "And if any of you even think twice about doing anything but treating our guest with respect and busting your hides on the project, I'll drown you in the bog myself. What the fuck are you looking at? Get back to work."

And they did, at mechanical speeds, as Pierce got two guards to drag Migs away. "Not to the infirmary, we need it today. I'm sorry, Ms. Savorov. Our men might be good mechanics and engineers, but some of them come from the wrong side of the tracks."

"Criminals," Warren said. "All the shit heels left behind on the home front while the good and virtuous are stuffed in mass graves in Europe."

"Jesus, Bishop," Pierce said, a sarcastic tone burned into each syllable. "I could not have said it better myself. Get over here."

He marched, the rifle muzzles following him with grey-blue seriousness as he approached the workbench where the young girl sat. A creature fluttered behind her from its still perch on a railing. An owl.

"Vasilya, this is Warren Bishop," Captain Pierce said.

It was a perplexing site: A girl, for she seemed younger than him, and an owl, sitting in a prison. Normal, for Warren, had been shattered corpses and guttural horror, and this sight was almost too pretty to bear.

Not that he thought she was pretty. Not the kind of pretty Warren liked. Thick lips and sinister smiles with laughter so bubbly you'd think it popped from a bottle of champagne. No, this girl was severe. Black hair tied behind her with a rag, rag clothes from the surplus bin, yet her spine was straight as a knife and her bearing was pure aristocrat.

"Vasilya, Warren is going to be your … partner."

"If that is your wish, Captain," she said, accent thicker and richer than that of the Ukrainians he'd known out West. "So long as he does not waste my time. The imps, thugs, and petty tyrants you've hired as my machinists and toolmakers are already setting back what I had hoped would be a simple project. I had to turn it into a game to get anything done and get their prying eyes away from me …" Her face twinged, full focus on Warren. "You …"

"You okay, kid?" Warren said.

She glared, then her back fluttered, as if her dress had been filled with ferrets. "You … bastard," she cried. From her back, tearing through the cloth, were two brass wings.

Like a bullet or a hornet or a damned good knife throw, she shot at him at the speed of malice, tiny hands around his throat, dragging him into the air. "You killed Felix!"

CHAPTER FORTY:

ANGEL OF THE KILL SWITCH

"Don't shoot!" Captain Pierce said, and it was music to her chilled heart. She seethed as crisp pain lanced her back, lifting the dead weight of the soon-to-be-dead man into the air, to the top landing of the prison, ceiling charging toward her.

She swirled in the air, rage commanding her actions like she had commanded the Juggernaut, and she spun, spun, spun until she heaved the heavy man against the top window and her wings pounded the air.

Glass shattered, sending a rain of daggers toward the ground far below. Slick streams of blood ran down her back, chasing the glass like flies before carrion. She snatched a jagged piece before it trailed the others.

Clinging to the window bars hung the maggot that killed Felix.

"That's some trick," he said, pulling himself up so his knee was on the window's edge. "You win those at a carnival?"

"Shut up!" she screamed in Russian, then slashed his back.

The cloth tore open and a scar appeared on his back.

Then sealed up almost as soon as it opened.

"Hey, I just got this shirt."

"Silence!"

She slashed again and again, turning his shirt to ribbons and filling his back with painful scars...

But the only blood that dripped came from her hands, back and feet. And no sooner had she stopped but the wounds on his back sealed themselves.

She fluttered in circles, dropping the blade of glass, then grabbed him with both hands and tore him from the bars. Insanely, he did not resist.

He floated in the air for a half second as she swooped to the top of the building, then dove like a spear, gripping his neck, and pushing harder than gravity. It was swan dive to the shop floor, and she pulled herself out of it as the bastard hit hard concrete.

A hideous crack filled the stunned room with dust and waves of impact.

She grabbed a saw from the work table as Captain Pierce touched her foot, almost grabbing her ankle. She darted out of reach and the big American stumbled. "Goddamn it, Vasilya! Stop it!"

God Almighty could not stop her.

She dropped on the bastard's neck as he struggled to remove himself from the crater he'd created.

She dug the serrated blade into his neck. "Back!" she yelled to Pierce and the guards. The bastard hissed, but froze as she sunk it in deeper. "See if you can attach your head back before I saw it off!"

"Why?" was all he got out before the saw cut in deeper.

"Why?" She grated the blade until it hit bone, and the torn flesh tried to mend itself as if it were made of maggots. "You ... you killed Felix! In that mustard gas nightmare, you killed him!" Blade scraped bone. "And this time ... I will kill you."

The bastard's teeth gritted. "You ... the slip of a thing in the gas mask." Recognition dawned on him, and an anger to match.

A fist shot out, clutched her throat, and tore her hands away from the blade still in his neck.

"You and that goddamn machine damn near cremated my brother!"

The girl struggled, and her brass wings fluttered, but she was locked in his grip tighter than a hung noose. The other hand tore away the saw.

"Bishop," Pierce said, cool and slow. "Let her go."

"That ... mechanical nightmare tortured Alex! And it sure as hell didn't do me any favours."

She squirmed, brass wings fluttering and face going blue, but only Pierce's voice came through. "I know."

"You knew?" Warren grunted. "You expect me to work for this fucking witch?"

Pierce was closing in. "Bishop, let go, or we'll never get Alex back."

"It might be worth it."

A snap movement and the barrel of an officer's pistol rested against his head. "Do you really want to find out?"

Her eyes rolled.

Warren released his grip.

She fluttered away, coughing, then landed hard on the far side of the courtyard. Her flightless owl waddled to her, head turning to keep Warren in its sites as it approached her feet.

He stood, wiped his neck where the wound was gone. "I didn't agree to this, Pierce. How the fuck can you expect me to work with the little monster who made that industrial monster?"

The pistol stayed clear on his head as they stared eye to eye. "If you don't, we're all doomed. Together we have a chance of turning this war into a meeting of the minds."

"Fuck that," Warren said. "And I'm sure she'd say the same, huh, Duchess? You really want to work with the man who killed your toy?"

Her voice croaked out, harsh but firm. "You killed more than that, you colonial peasant!"

A memory flashed like a bulb.

One he didn't want to see.

The creature: a horror of wood, wire, and iron, furnished with more weapons than an arsenal, mechanical movements bringing it to life ... but at the core, where Warren had torn a hole ...

"A kid."

She wiped spit from her gasping mouth, rubbing her neck, and keeping her eyes low.

He rubbed his neck, too. "There was a kid inside that goddamn thing. Wires in his heart like he was ... oh god, was he attached to it? Did you do that to him?"

"I did nothing of the sort!" she screamed. The wings retracted on her back and she hissed while the owl stood guard at her feet. "If it was up to me, I'd be the one dead in its heart at the bottom of the world, not the one left alive to deal with his murderer."

"All right, children, that's enough," Pierce said, taking the pistol barrel from Warren's head. "Truth is, right now, I don't give two shits about how you feel about each other. Vasilya, go to the infirmary. Bishop, you'll go in when she's done and until then, you're going to clean up the mess you two made."

She glared at him as a nurse walked away with her. When she was gone, Warren began picking up pieces of stained glass. "You know she'll try and kill me the next time you blink."

Pierce holstered the pistol. "Noticed that look in her eye, did you?"

"Yeah. Like looking into a mirror."

"You're going to have to be the bigger man, Bishop. You've got hope. Alexander is probably still alive, somewhere in Rasputin's underground liars. But she's got nothing but ghosts, and a mother caught in the fire of revolution. Can you imagine what it might be like for her? She's just a kid."

Warren said nothing as the ghosts around him nodded before wandering back into the abyss from which they came.

"I don't know how to say this, since this is somewhat beyond my training, but you have to stop ... flying."

Vasilya, again belly-first on a medical gurney, stared once more at the dirty tiles of the prison infirmary as the occasional bright drop of blood dribbled down her shoulder and splashed close to the nurse's off-white shoe.

The new nurse spoke with an annoying folksy accent that screamed "peasant" with every word. "You do speak English, don't you?" she said.

"I speak better English than you."

The sting of iodine made her hiss, but the pain was almost a relief. A hot shot of sensation in her otherwise frozen body. The doctor had stitched her up quickly without a word and left, but this nurse, who she'd not seen before, had the nerve to keep talking while finishing up his work.

"I don't doubt you speak many languages well."

She closed her eyes and tried not to think of the horrors compounding on her, just focus on the sting of iodine and not that ... that murderer in the other room. A prison in hell was too good for him. She'd kill him herself the minute she got the chance. She could wait. She could be patient. Her heart and mind were strong and cool as ...

"Iron."

Vasilya opened her eyes. "What?"

"Oh nothing, just wondering what your wings are made of. You're really quite a sight, I'll give you that. When I signed up with the Matrons I had no idea I'd have such an adventure."

She flexed her lightly bandaged hand and a similar warm, blurring sensation came and went. "Are we done? Can I go?"

"Afraid not, deary. Got to gauze your wings closed so they can heal."

"No—"

"Doctor's orders, I'm afraid. You'll just have to get by on two legs like the rest of us, or like your feathered friend. Sit up, and remove what's left of your blouse."

She did, and saw the steel grey hair and green eyes of the nurse. She was older than Mother, and a thousand times her inferior in looks, bearing, and pedigree. She began wrapping the gossamer-web of bandages around her waist while Vasilya pretended not to shiver. When she was done, the nurse held her hands as if in prayer. "You're a brave one, child. You're to go back to your work room. Please ... no flying."

Merlin sat upon a crate of medical equipment, then ruffled himself.

"He's a fine sight. What's his name?"

"Merlin."

The nurse laughed, clapped her hand. "Perfect!"

"I did not name him. Winston did."

"Oh, 'Winston,' is it? Well, I didn't know you and the minister were on such good terms."

"Minister?" The question bloomed and she was amazed that she had not inquired more about who it was that had dragged her here. "He's a priest?"

"Oh, lord, no. Not the way he drinks." She covered her mouth. "I mean to say, he's a government minister."

Vasilya took the fresh grey blouse that was handed to her and put it on, slowly. "And what is he the minister of?" When her head came through the hole, the nurse was looking around the room. "He gave me some ponderous title."

"That's his secret ministry. I suppose I could tell you his normal one."

"I'll find out eventually and, besides, how much of a secret can it be if he's a member of government?"

"You have to promise me you won't tell, all right?"

"I am a prisoner on a Scottish Island, more than two thousand miles from the only home I've ever known, and everyone I love is dead or lost. Trust me, there is no one left to tell secrets to."

The nurse gave her a sympathetic sigh, then nodded. "He's the Minister of Munitions."

"Why is that such a secret? England has been at war for years."

"Well, only he's not just the minister. He's the government's liaison with, well, this is just rumour, you understand."

"If you'd rather not say."

"Well, I'm late, and so are you, with your invention and all that, so maybe later." She gathered her things. "Now remember—"

Vasilya took Merlin from his perch on the crate. "No flying. I heard you the first two times, Nurse … what is your name?"

She smiled. "Nurse Fairweather." She left Vasilya to finish up. When she was gone, and the door closed, Vasilya sat looking at the bloody instruments on the pan beside the examination table. She took a scalpel, cleaned it, and folded it into a cloth in her pocket.

She flexed her injured hand, and let the peace of the pain hold her for just a moment longer. When it had evaporated, she felt … better.

She took the scalpel and placed it in the folds of her dress while Merlin blinked at her. "Come on. We have collars to make to keep that monster in step." A cruel smile broke across her cold face. "Death might just be too good for him."

Warren's body had healed, his hunger wasn't so great as to be a threat, and he was sick of looking at the courtyard, his cell, and the shower and ghosts. He'd asked if the prison had any books, since it was made clear he wasn't allowed outside. Pierce had laughed. "Funny you should ask. First thing Churchill installed when he was Home Secretary before the war was a library."

Walking with a guard in front, and one in back, Warren discovered how huge the prison was. The corridor leading past the rows and rows of cells was long and desolate with the wet echo of their steps ricocheting off the walls into the deeper extremities. The main courtyard was a circle and from it extended these corridors of cells. His room was sequestered below, in a slice of purgatory called solitary. If he was going back, he'd grab as many books as he could before the next stage of Pierce's war plans.

As the ocean roared against the hidden shores beyond the thick prison walls, Warren wondered how he'd die. No doubt, they'd throw him at Rasputin. Even with a killer right cross, Warren doubted Pierce would ever get close enough to the mad Russian to do anything but spit bitter words in his direction.

In a funny way, Pierce reminded Warren of Graves.

In an unfunny way, he wasn't sure who he hated more.

They approached a wooden door with a thick lock. "Blimey," said the one in front. "Heath, you got the key?"

"Yeah, right next to my bonus pay. Of course I don't have the key. It's in the main guard room."

"Jesus, that's a few miles back!"

"Boys," Warren said. "I'm something of a locksmith. Allow me." He approached the door and the pistols firmed their aim. "Don't get your knickers in a twist. I learned this from Tik the Magnificent, the great mage of the Arctic. Watch and be amazed!"

Slowly, hypnotically, he waved his hand in front of the lock, swaying back and forth with a snake charmer's cadence ... then rammed his fist down on the lock, snapping it off, the door swinging gently open.

Both guards laughed, and Warren bowed. "Now, let's see what gems are left here."

They lit a lamp on the office's desk in the centre of the windowless room, and shadows spawned across the walls with a flickering grace.

Near-barren shelves glared back at them.

"Damn, they're almost empty," said the one called Heath. "Jones, did you know?"

"I don't like walking that much for no reason. Well, Bishop. Grab what you can. We've orders to keep you company until Pierce needs you."

Warren snorted, wandering the skeletal shelves for any sign of books. "Don't you mean Captain Pierce? Not a big fan of your CO, huh?"

"We like him fine," Jones said.

"Except that ..." Heath got a stern look from Jones.

Warren collected a few stray books. "Don't tell me. He came here late and took command as if he'd been here since before the Revolutionary War, and he tells stories so outlandish you know they're a crock but all you can do is sit and smile and listen and wonder when the damn blowhard will run out of air. But he seemed to be born with a spare lung and each story gets so much more bizarre and heroic that you wonder if he's not Kipling's long-lost American cousin. Right?"

Heath could have been knocked over with a feather and Jones tried not to look impressed.

"I know, I know. Can't talk bad about him because you fear I'm in cahoots. And I am, until whatever suicide mission they've got for me is done. Then I think Captain Pierce and I might have a conversation about the humanity of chains. Well, I seem to have grabbed all the literature left here."

"Aren't you going to check the titles?"

Warren shrugged. "I'll keep it a surprise until I get back to my cell. Why mope when I can hope?"

The long walk back, he kept his eyes from the shadows at his side.

"Hey, Bishop." Heath said. "Is it true?"

"What?"

"Is it true you're, well, like some kind of creature?"

"Cram that pie hole," Jones said.

Creature? It was a good question. Warren walked on. "I'm just a soldier."

"And the girl with the wings?"

"Beats me. Tinkerbell's big sister?"

They laughed, awkward and cold while waves thrashed the rock outside, the screams of seagulls like the sharp cry of children who've been hurt, a warning bell for loved ones to save them.

Alex, he thought. What are they doing to you now?

He reached his cell. Newly constructed, no doubt to cage one like Warren specifically. Six by seven feet. Concrete walls and a steel door where all the others had been wood and iron. A thin cot lay by a shit hole. The door's lock was hidden inside the steel keyhole.

"There's a lamp, and matches, inside," Jones said. "We'll call when you're needed."

Warren nodded and got into the compressed space, glad he didn't need to breathe because he surely would have gasped until he passed out in the confined, concrete coffin.

"Enjoy the books," Heath said, smiling, then they shoved the door with a grunt. A jagged lock tumbled into place.

Warren sat on the thin cot and lit the lamp on the bedside box. Three books sat on his lap.

A King James Bible. "Surprised I didn't burst into flames when I grabbed it," he said to no one, then feared the laughter of ghosts. He tossed it aside.

Another thick tome. The Harmsworth Self-educator. It promised to be a "Golden Key to Success in Life." Really, it was a dictionary of basic knowledge for folks who really needed to know the inner mechanics of sucker jobs like clerkship. It would have been a cure for insomnia, if Warren could sleep. The bible didn't seem so bad now.

The final one sat on his lap, and he opened the cover and stared at the white stained page.

Kim. By Rudyard Kipling. Once upon a time it was his favorite book

With a care reserved for fine China and tea parties, he closed the book, put it down next to the previous two and prayed he could sleep.

"Good luck with that, Qimmiq," Tik said from nowhere.

Warren rubbed his neck, tracing the invisible cut the kid had carved into him.

CHAPTER FORTY-ONE:

OF LEASH AND MASTER

It took hours, not days, for Vasilya to perfect the collar. "It's made out of telegraph buzzers from the prison's alarm system. It has a lock, but the cord in the choker is so sensitive it can't be torn at without releasing the current."

"And where does the current come from?" said Captain Pierce, a mug of foul-smelling coffee steaming beneath his ugly visage as he stood at her elbow at the work table.

"The charge comes from this." She tapped a large battery on the workshop table.

"A bit clunky to carry around."

"He doesn't carry it. It's got a fixed radius of three hundred yards or so. If he steps outside that zone, the charge jumps. It also fires upon command."

"How?"

She smiled. "It's … in harmony with my thoughts. That's what sent Migs down like a bull in a slaughterhouse when he held on to the initial buzzer design. Only I had not properly secured the charge yet to a large battery. So long as that monster is within eye range, I can keep him in line."

"Don't be so sure," Pierce said. "You don't know what this guy can do."

"Oh, I know, Captain. I've seen him do the impossible with my own eyes. I only ask that you trust me to do the impossible, too."

He put the mug down. "All right. We'll get it on him. But if you try and fry what's left of his brain, you'll end up in a deeper hole than this chunk of rock, kid. Bank on it." He strode off, with an authority that Vasilya did not recognize. She almost hated herself for how much she initially cowered before Colonel Balk in his workshop.

Cowering was dead to her. She rubbed the wound in her palm. It barely hurt anymore and almost too quickly she was thinking about the scalpel, and a medically clean incision, somewhere soft, somewhere that needed a scar, new armour for the new war she was facing.

The ghosts had been kept at bay when Pierce's Exec, a sharp-faced fellow named Lt. Gavin, sat and filled up notebooks by asking questions about every conceivable thing about Rasputin and the Lost Battalion, and the confrontation with the mechanical beast.

Astonishingly, Gavin carried no gun. It was as obvious as the glasses on his nose.

Warren had hoped that by the time they'd got to the point where Pierce had snuffed him out with some dopey chemical rag, he'd feel ten pounds lighter.

If anything, he'd gained twenty.

Each story was tied to even greater improbabilities as if the world was stitched together of madcap stories. He ran his finger through the lamp's flame. "So. What's it all mean?"

Gavin looked up, adjusted his glasses. "That depends on the accuracy of your memory."

"You think I could make this shit up? I wish. I'd rake in more money than Kipling and Burroughs combined." The grime on his finger caught fire and burned, flaring the world with a little more light.

Gavin smiled briskly. "I mean, your brain is likely very different than it was before they administered the ..." he flipped through his pages. "Deadroot?"

"Yup."

"God. This Rasputin has a flair for the dramatic."

"Don't let it fool you. He's got a hold on these men unlike anything we do. They're his brood."

Gavin nodded.

"So? How are we going to stop them?"

"From raising the army of the dead?" He looked up quizzically at Warren's burning digit.

Warren snapped it out. "Yeah."

"Don't think we can."

"Then what the hell am I doing here?"

"Sorry. I meant we, alone. I think we'll likely be the vanguard, but we're going to need some help."

"From who?" Then it dawned on him. "The Huns?"

"I suspect they're more inclined to side with us than the Bolsheviks and Whites, who are too busy killing each other. Maybe if the Whites win their civil war ..."

He spoke so plainly, academically, about the entire four years of war being turned into a carnival freakshow that it was almost sure to be some kind of gag.

"You have the worst sense of humour I've ever heard."

"Captain Pierce says I don't have any. Not sure which is worse, actually."

Warren sniff-laughed and the flame danced. "Seriously, do you have any idea what the plan is?"

Gavin tapped his pencil on his book. "Pretty simple, given Mr. Churchill's intellect. Or maybe that's the genius of it. We're going to unite with the Germans against a common enemy."

"Rasputin?"

Gavin nodded, got up and stretched. "But the only way we'll do that is if we save some German lives from the Lost Battalion. They've retreated, and won't be easy to remove from their hidden nest and we can't divert many resources from the war to do it."

"I suppose that's where I come in."

"You and Miss. Savorov."

"What? Is she going to be my 'Knight of the Sky,' doing strafing runs and dropping grenades from the clouds?"

Gavin smiled without warmth. "No. She's your handler. And the creator of the machine you destroyed."

"She made that hideous contraption? She can't be seventeen."

"Twenty, actually. Though I admit she looks young. And she's brilliant."

"And so what's she making that's going to help turn the Germans against Rasputin and for us."

Gavin turned to leave. "I don't know." He and the guards slowly shut the door, and all that was left was a slit for food.

"Hey, Loo," Warren yelled. "How come you came in here unarmed? You tougher than Pierce? Know some fancy fighting techniques from the mysterious Orient?"

"Hardly." Gavin's voice came through the slit, then footsteps leaving.

Twilight crept into his room, and Warren picked up the bible, as if to ward off the spirits in his head. In the distance, he heard the clitter-clatter of tinkering. Faces emerged from shadows, so he snuffed out the candle, closed his eyes, and lay low.

Moonlight broke into Fort Daedalus like thin sheets of silver that gave everything a fine metallic skin. Vasilya sat in a patch of it, coiling a wire into the buzzer while sounds of drunkenness rose and fell from the distance as a sergeant ordered silence.

Merlin had wandered off into the darkness hunting mice on foot, the tip-tap of his talons a strange sound inside this strange prison. In so many ways, Fort Daedalus was stranger than the peace and quiet of Colonel Balk's workshop. There was a presence of threat. From the workers to the angry sea to the failure of her wings, yet they must be further away from the war than that rail line from Berlin. And so much farther from home.

Home? The word was cold. And Mother, lost inside the bowels of the Bolshevik prison that had become Russia.

She fiddled with the control collar and things tumbled in her mind like the pins of a good lock or the gears of a fine watch, just as Monsieur Fabergé had taught her to do. Each piece has a place. There is a perfect spot for all to work together to become more than the sum of their parts.

She took the tin cover from the floor and placed it over the mechanism, the two prongs that would be in Bishop's flesh. She left them dull.

Petty, she thought. Considering he can't feel much of anything. Yet.

But then what?

I fry his body with more current than an electric chair, enjoy watching his life vanish before my eyes ... then, what? Then they lock me in here forever, making whatever death apparatus they need next in a war that has no end, no doubt claiming the next, the bigger, the worse weapon will bring peace. And Mother will be lost forever inside the iron walls of Russia. Who am I kidding? She's probably long dead.

The gears inside her stalled. She coughed away the pain that misted her eyes.

"Would you like something to eat, deary?"

She was startled to find Nurse Fairweather walking toward her with a tray. A smell came from it that was sickly sweet.

"Chocolate," Vasilya whispered, then swallowed the delicious word.

"We have but a little cocoa here, but given how hard today was I thought it might be best to enjoy now than save for later. There's also a biscuit." She kneeled and smiled. She smelled like lemons, as if she'd been scrubbing herself. "Go on. You deserve a break."

"Tell that to the men running this war."

Nurse Fairweather smiled. "Go on. Take care of yourself. Like a good kitten."

Vasilya took the cup, but it shook in her hand. "Like a what?" The words were familiar. Distant. She gripped the warm mug with both hands and feared her flesh would crack. She put the mug on the floor beside her, and the biscuit.

Nurse Fairweather stood and walked back toward the long hall to the kitchen. "Try to rest some, deary. All wounds need time to heal."

Vasilya waited until Fairweather was gone and the cocoa cooled. Merlin returned, empty-handed, so she broke off half the biscuit and laid it down for him to chew on ...

And within the biscuit was a worn piece of paper.

She tore off little pieces of the biscuit, each for Merlin to eat, until the paper sat in her lap.

On it were four Russian words. "You Are Not Alone."

As Merlin devoured the crumbled biscuits, she held the now cool mug and sipped in cold wonder at what this could mean. A Russian. Here. But what kind? A Tsarist sympathizer … or a cutthroat Bolshevik?

Whatever she was, Nurse Fairweather, like all the rest, wanted her for something. Vasilya would stay cool as iron until she knew what it was, no matter how many kind words and cups of hot cocoa she had thrown at her.

She drank the sweet liquid and tried not to enjoy it. Then focused on the control collar, wishing the rich taste would leave her mouth. As she did, Merlin scurried away into a patch of darkness. Slowly, a mouse appeared, fretting as it approached the crumbs of the sweet biscuit.

Merlin pounced, tearing apart the small creature, thrashing it back and forth until it was dead, then wandering into the dark to finish it off far away from the sweet trap it had set.

Not long after daybreak, Heath and Jones escorted Warren to the infirmary. He walked in to find a sniper in the corner of the room, a doctor and nurse on his right, and Vasilya in the far corner with a box on her lap.

"Well, good morning everyone," Warren said. "Looking forward to today's great adventure? Mind telling me what it is?"

"Lie down on your chest, please," said the doctor. The same one he'd heard that first night he'd awoken in the basement in chains.

"Nice to see you again, Doc." He lay on his chest. "Mind telling me what those samples of my back told you?"

"I'm afraid that's confidential."

"Well, who the hell am I going to tell? Besides, snipers know how to keep secrets. Right, Sharpshooter?"

The sniper was young. Maybe a bit older than Alex. But he had the hard look of a veteran that made him seem twice his age and twice as joyless as any other soldier. "Say. Nice Enfield. Every try a Ross?"

The sniper snorted. "Fucking Canadian death trap, that," he said with a thick Scottish accent. "Rather be armed with a bow and arrow."

Warren smiled. "Only if you can't handle it."

"Please be quiet," said the doctor, and Warren raised his hands in submission before letting them hang like bodies swinging from the gallows as he lay on the gurney.

"Hurry up, Doc. Don't we have a war to win?"

The sniper chuckled. But the girl was silent.

A blade pierced his neck.

It shocked him but didn't hurt. "If things hurt too much, we do have the means to knock you out," said the doctor.

Don't remind me, Warren thought. That black miasma that swallowed him when Pierce shoved that rag in his face was not a joy he planned to repeat. Ever. "Do your worst."

It was a gross hour. Slicing and pulling, slicing and pulling, the doctor had to cut and re-cut his neck, the nurse pulling back his moving skin with pliers, before something cold bit into his neck.

He groaned.

"Are you all right," said the doctor, sarcastically. "Would you like us to—"

"Finish up before I get bored."

Their attempt to sew him up was given up when his skin began to mend itself over what felt like a knot in his neck, an extra rivet in his spine. Both the doctor and nurse stepped back. "There. I think."

Warren sat up, hand reaching for the knot. "What's this for?" Fire lanced through his marrow, twisting his body like a pretzel until he hit the floor on all fours, and a hot scream steamed out of him. The air tasted of burning dirt.

"It is to keep you in line," Vasilya said from somewhere above the ground he was glaring at. "While I enjoyed the sight of you dancing like a puppet with a seizure, I'd suggest you not touch it again. Or else this might happen."

Flushes of current charred his nerves and his arms shot out to the sides as if he'd been crucified by current, smacking the tiled floor with his teeth.

Everything cringed while his body mended, and his teeth gripped their roots. His voice was hoarse and smoky. "Doc ..." He rested on his elbows, fetid smoke rising from his mouth. "Could you tell Princess Tesla to knock it off?"

The grim-faced doctor nodded. "Please, Vasilya. We just got the device in. I'd hate to have to patch it back."

"Your humanity is a credit to your profession," Warren said, then hissed.

Vasilya slid off her chair, battery in her hand like a ten-pound purse, swinging slightly. "You cannot take the device out, and any attempt to run more than a few hundred yards away from the battery will send out a death charge that even your ... brain can't handle. So I suggest you learn to take orders and keep what you consider your wit under wraps, or else you will know suffering the likes of which you cannot fathom."

Anger swelled like a diseased organ in his guts. He got to his knees, wiping his mouth of smoke, words sharp and cold as February ice. "Tell me, Princess. I watched your boyfriend roast my kid brother alive. Sat and watched while that petrol burned and burned his skin as it grew back. On his arms. His lips. His eyelids. Until all he could do was stare at the flames that consumed him." He stood, glaring down at her while the sniper aimed. "Ask me again about suffering I can't fathom." He spat at her feet. "We done? I think the Loo wants a chat with me before the next round of whatever junk experiments you shit heels have planned for me."

Contempt filled Vasilya's face as he walked down the corridor to his cell, pain easing with every move.

But it was amazing.

The pain.

As it vanished like stars in a pink dawn, he realized why it was so wild.

He hadn't felt real pain since Alex had shoved the deadroot in his mouth.

He'd last felt it when he was …

Alive.

Merlin slept, standing up, on a battleship grey army blanket on the floor of her workbench, while Captain Pierce rubbed his neck and sat down. "I hear the restraint was a smashing success." Disapproval dripped off his cut lip.

"Depends on how you look at such things," Vasilya said, caressing the battery with her dirty hand. "It works. He knows it can break him when I want. That is what you needed to get across, correct?"

He lit a gas lamp. "He has a right to be mad, too."

"I do not care."

"You should. We need him, kid. As much as we need you. If this project is going to work at all, we have to see a common enemy and have a common cause." He laid a leather-bound suitcase on the table.

My cause is to save my mother if I can. But there's no way to know if she's even alive. Maybe Nurse Fairweather … no, do not rely on her yet. Or maybe ever. Do not be bribed into a project you know nothing about with cookies and chocolate. "Has Winston sent you the design yet?"

"Oh yeah."

She held still. "May I see it?"

"In a minute. First, I want your word."

"My word."

"That you won't fry Bishop the second you get the chance." He lay his elbows down on the table, sleeves rolled up to reveal thick veins on hard skin, scars and the stains of an old tattoo whose original shape was lost to the ages. "You have a right to be mad, too. But you know it wasn't him that killed your boyfriend."

"He was not—"

"It was that great, white worm."

She tapped the sharp edge of the battery. Steady and slow. As if typing out a code to herself on her skin, each time, closer to puncturing herself.

"You remember that, don't you?"

Tap, tap, tap.

"Well, before we get to Mr. Churchill's design, we should be clear on who you're making this for."

Tap, tap, tap.

He popped open the briefcase. "Story time, but since we have some . . . material finally arriving, I need to make this short."

"How unfortunate." Tap, tap, tap.

He laid down a photograph of an ugly man with no hair and a long beard. The picture was grainy, the man's eyes wild but unfocused, as if the flash had caught him peering places beyond the camera. "This is Rasputin. A Siberian monk. And sorcerer."

She smiled.

"Something funny?"

"The way you said it."

He ignored her jest. "He's Rasputin."

Her smile froze, trying not to reveal a sense of horror at that name. The cursed healer. Monsieur Fabergé had long suspected he was mesmerizing the Tzarina, and had so influenced the court to send Russia into war before they found out and tossed him from the palace. "Where is ... Rasputin now?"

"Last we heard of him, Lenin had him shot not long after the Tzar and his family."

A small quiver ran through her for the old world that was dying, if not dead, in the heart of Russia.

This was the demon the colonel said was unleashed when the Tzar fell. Lenin had not killed him. He'd released him. Against the West. She tapped her finger.

Tap, tap—

The skin snapped.

She exhaled as a trickle of blood ran down her finger. "We have a Siberian monk in command of a great worm, a reject from your Theosophical Society. What do you want me to build? A giant hook to fish it from the sky?"

"Rasputin is no joke, kid. He's a necromancer."

"What is that?"

"A man who can bring back the dead." The captain kept talking while the word kept sinking in. "Not en masse. He's needed to use some pretty rare stuff to do it. Unfortunately, the war has provided pretty fertile ground for deadroot. And he's been growing an army in No-Man's Land ever since he defected from the Russian Expeditionary Force in France in 1916."

The captain sat closer, and she expected his breath to stink of coffee and rot or ale like the worker bees, and she hid her surprise as it stank of peppermint. "He's a zealot. Feels he was chosen by history to end this war by overturning it with dead soldiers."

She closed the bloody digit within her hand. Raise the dead. This is madness, but so was the Juggernaut, so is that damned man Bishop, so are my wings...

Pierce snapped his finger louder than a gunshot and her attention snapped back just as hard. "No time for daydreams today. You still with me?"

She nodded.

His peppermint breath droned on with his backward accent, about Rasputin the Necromancer and his army of the dead, the kind of story Mother would have been aghast at her reading, let alone listening to. Then, she shook her head. "That man, Bishop. He is one of them. Dead?"

"Technically, no. His heart … it's aging, burning quick. Keeping alive by killing his future. But the ones he stood with? They're undead, between here and the afterlife. Thanks to a thing called deadroot, you get it into a dying or dead man fast enough, it becomes his heart, stem grows into the brain, and, for reasons that are beyond this Parris Island grad, he gets, what the hell was the word Wells used?" he flipped through the pages of the dossier until he stabbed the page with his finger. "Right. Re-animated. And they come back tougher and stronger than a herd of wild mustangs. Hence that dent on the floor where you dropped Bishop ass over tit."

"And once they are … re-animated. How long do they live?"

Pierce grimaced. "No clue. Especially with Bishop. The rest? For all I know, they live forever in that weird state so long as they—" he puckered his mouth. "Not sure how to say this to a young woman."

"You can spare me the folk modesty of your backwater country, Captain."

"They're cannibals."

She wrapped her finger with a sliver of cloth.

"Near as we've been able to figure, they eat humans and humans alone. If they don't … you ever see a strongman, like at a circus?"

She had not but didn't feel like speaking and nodded.

"Those guys, the ones who make Goliath look like David, they have special diets. Eat raw meat, eggs, bulgur wheat mixed with grizzly shit."

"Your point, Captain?"

"That's what those guys eat to stay strong. If they don't, they got sick, weak, fat and their hearts give out. It's a one-way ride. But when you starve someone like Bishop … they become something far worse, far more fierce. They're like a rabid dog with the strength of a tank. Almost had to put Bishop down before we … fed him."

"Pity."

"It would be. He's the only one of these sons of bitches we've been able to capture. Let alone Rasputin. The diabolic shit is slicker than a greased bullet."

A hideous mechanical alarm blared out and someone screamed for the captain to come quick.

"What's that?" she said.

The captain stood, and tossed her a giant sweater. "Mail call."

A buzzer died in the distance while Warren fought every urge in his stinging body to touch the lump on his neck.

"You all right?" Lt. Gavin said, sitting on his stool, notebook at the ready.

"Like a new dollar bill. Crisp." He gripped his fingers, massaging his hands. "Guess I don't like the sound of buzzers these days. So, I don't know how much more I can tell you."

"Actually, today I'm supposed to be telling you something."

"I can only hope and pray it's more thrilling than the *Harmsworth Self-educator.*"

Gavin shot a little smile. "I think so. Today, we talk about how you're going to be of service."

Warren clapped. "Joy.""

"We've got a plan so that they'll come to you. After a fashion."

"'After a fashion'? You talk like some snooty book sometimes, Gavin. You know that?"

"We can't all talk like penny dreadfuls, Warren. Or you'd be out of a job."

Warren narrowed his eyes. "Was that a joke coming out of that academic visage? Or an insult?"

Gavin looked up. "Perhaps you are rubbing off on me. I find most of your jokes are insults."

Warren sniffed, then laughed. "Touché, Loo. How the hell are you going to draw them out?"

Gavin put on what looked like a gardening glove and pulled something out of a sack by his feet. "With this."

Horror laced itself across Warren's eye skin as the smell crawled through the air and dug into his nostrils. "Deadroot," he whispered.

"It's a fake. Grown and modified by expert biologists in London under Churchill's watch. Smells just like it, doesn't it?"

Warren nodded. "Shove it back in the sack."

Gavin complied. "One of our advanced commando units has managed to … reclaim some bodies so that we might set the stage of a similar scene that you witnessed with … what was his name? The madman with the rat?"

"Marlow," Warren grunted.

"Right, Marlow. We've attempted to provide the same bait, since Rasputin and the battalion have barely been seen since the battle. And when they arrive to claim their prize, you'll be there to greet them."

Warren's head dropped. "Really?"

"Really."

"With what?"

"Another mechanical beast, like the one that killed your brother."

Going into the grey light of the natural world, Vasilya did not shiver against the hideous spray in the air and the cold that was moist and penetrating. A single automobile approached them. Above, an airplane buzzed as it ran through the dangerous skies. This must be important if they're willing to risk something as expensive as a plane to protect it from the air.

"I suggest you brace yourself for what you're about to see, kid." Pierce said.

I've been braced since I got here, she thought.

The vehicle rumbled like a black mechanical bear that grew as it approached, dragging a carriage of some kind behind it until it stopped, grey and rain-stained before them. Two figures sat in the car, but only the driver got out. His face was scarred with chemical damage, one of his eyes glassy. He wore a British uniform, but no clear signs of rank or nationality. He saluted Captain Pierce, who returned the salute. "Operation Scavenger is complete, Sir," he said. His accent ... Irish?

"Well done, O'Neil," said the captain. "How much was recovered?"

"I hope enough to warrant how many died."

"How many?"

O'Neil grimaced. "Only me and the tank crew assigned for me got back, Sir. Jerries led a riotous counterattack to stop us stealing it from them. I fear this might set back the project."

"That's for Churchill to work out," Pierce said. "Drive it in the main cargo door around the east end. We have a detail to unload it. How about our passenger?"

O'Neil smiled, and it was the hideous, mangled look of a once pretty face now tortured and unsure of its affect. "Intact, despite the rather insane journey she took. You can thank the Czech Legion in Siberia for her survival, and our contact in the Caucuses for getting her to India. Hasn't said a word the entire journey."

"I have enough talkers in this base." Pierce waved at the passenger, who finally disembarked and snapped out a parasol. Vasilya stared as if sunlight had appeared out of thin air. It was a work of art, pink, white and red, with a picture of a cherry blossom, the umbrella shielding away the rain and hiding its owner's face. Then, the parasol lifted.

An Asian woman. Her face was oval, with coal-black hair tied tightly behind her head, all except a silver strand that ran like a scar alongside the right side of her scalp. Her age was curiously hard to define, hidden in the quiet strength of her countenance. "Captain Pierce," she said in perfectly clear English, without a trace of accent. "I am Dr. Rachel

Oshikawa, Japanese consul for the Theosophical Society." She handed him an envelope. "My government and Ambassador Morris have cleared me to work on this project with you. And I am eager to get started." The car rolled off, dragging its draped cargo behind it.

Captain Pierce nodded. "Welcome to Fort Daedalus, Doctor."

She began walking, not paying any mind to Vasilya. "I suppose we have Mr. Churchill to thank for both the name and the selection of our work?"

"Yep," he said.

"For a brilliant man, he can be somewhat childish."

Pierce smiled. "Doctor, I'd also like you to meet your chief assistant, Vasilya Savorov."

Doctor Oshikawa nodded without looking at Vasilya, and kept walking.

"She created the Juggernaut."

The doctor turned sharply. "I do not enjoy jokes, Captain."

"When I'm joking, Doctor, you'll know it."

She looked down at Vasilya. "How old are you?"

"Twenty."

"Where did you study engineering?"

"St. Petersburg."

"They do not let women into their engineer's academy."

"I never said I went there."

"Who instructed you?"

For a moment, Vasilya did not want to reveal the truth. But the quiet but intense glare from this rather austere Asian woman was starting to annoy her. "I am the protégé of Carl Fabergé."

Doctor Oshikawa faced Captain Pierce, who squinted but did not back down. "A jeweler's apprentice? I've traversed the globe, through three war zones, and ended up on a miserable excuse of land to help stop this war from destroying my nation, and you toss me into an abandoned prison with a child who plays with rubies? This is madness."

"And what have you done?" Vasilya said.

She glared at Vasilya. "You will refer to me as Doctor."

"And you will refer to me as Vasilya Fabergé."

"Ladies," Captain Pierce said, scratching his thick, burnt neck. "Cut the vaudeville act. We got work to do."

They returned inside to the courtyard work areas, where three of the labourers were pulling a cart in front of the bench, a tarp over what was a hideous orb.

Vasilya stepped forward, but the orb … grew no closer. Voices faded to the background of her mind like the chatter of hummingbird wings until Captain Pierce's peppermint voice reached out closer and told her to "stop running!".

She leapt over the hole Bishop had made, and ran until she stood before the orb, then tore off the tarp, and whispered.

It was Felix's coffin, his body long gone.

The command chamber of the Juggernaut was cracked and ruined and smelled like grave dirt that had been burned in an oil fire. It was a great cracked egg, a ruined heart of wood and wire, the command chair torn and frayed, ravaged by the war.

"Captain," Dr. Oshikawa said, cool and level. "I must protest. She should be able to control herself."

The command chair's straps were torn, greyish blood speckled the chamber. Her iron heart sank into the floor, drowning in concrete.

"You have to understand, Doctor—"

"I think my abilities of comprehension are more than up to the task ahead," said the doctor, "but they did not include babysitting a spoiled Slavic child. Surely you have nurses for that."

"We do. But she's had a rough go of it."

They want me to turn his coffin into a weapon.

His coffin.

The air crackled with static.

She closed her eyes.

And saw him dead before her, grey eyes open, begging for help.

The battery shook. And an arc of electric current flared, caressing the hide of the chamber. The air tasted like copper.

"Vasilya," said the captain. "Switch off."

She breathed static, hair standing up. "I will fix this, Captain," she said. "Alone."

Doctor Oshikawa walked toward the chamber. A bolt of current lashed the air like a whip as the doctor approached. "The next one won't be so gentle."

The doctor scowled at her. "Power and vanity. You're dangerous."

Vasilya turned, protecting the orb. "Very observant." The captain gripped Dr. Oshikawa's shoulder, but she moved forward out of his hold, hands in her jacket. "And ignorant. You carry the bearing of a peasant who wishes she were in the throne room instead of the kitchens. But you're really just a scared child with a gun."

"Quiet!" A jagged lance of lightning forked from the battery and shot at the doctor.

But the doctor's hands were already out of their pockets.

A fan of metal strips snapped out as the bolt crossed the distance and ricocheted the spike of current straight into Vasilya's chest.

Painful static filled her mouth and nerves and her wings snapped out in full before retracting hard. Shaking, her knees hit the floor like a grounded angel. Dr. Oshikawa's tiny, muddy boots were so tight that her steps were like daggers on concrete, her words hard and sharp. "We do not honour the dead by hiding in their shadow." She offered Vasilya her hand.

Vasilya slapped it away, and pulled herself up, breath ragged. "Spare me your Oriental aphorisms," she said.

"Then appreciate the laws of power," Dr. Oshikawa said. "I do not fear you. You possess no cunning I cannot outmanoeuvre. And despite your hostile intent, I intend to see this project through because it means more than whatever sacrifices we've made to arrive at this crossroad." She leaned down. "If we fail, others will face the same fate as your friend."

Vasilya's hand snapped out to slap her and was caught at the wrist as if the woman had seen it coming.

The doctor bent her wrist at an ungodly angle until Vasilya cried.

"Your anger is misplaced," she said. "Attend to your wounds, and then we shall begin."

She released the wrist and Vasilya dropped, the wetness of blood caressing the base of her wings. She stumbled toward the infirmary. A fresh, hot hate revived her iron heart. Watch your back, Doctor, she thought. I've killed worse than you.

Then she cut the thought, fearing the cunning woman might be able to read her mind. In this scrap of hell, Vasilya figured, anything was possible.

As she walked down the hall she heard the guards on the far wing screaming. "Captain! Bishop's had a seizure."

She laughed to herself, figuring she'd tapped a little hard on the battery and poor Warren Bishop had felt the aftershock. Her dark laughter was cold comfort the rest of the walk to the infirmary.

CHAPTER FORTY-TWO:

THE ELECTRIC KNIGHT OF NO-MAN'S LAND

Warren stood, the aftermath of the seizures having sent wild flushes of pleasure that still rocked his body, as Jones and Heath measured him in the hallway. But his heart felt hungry, the beats like bites from a hungry critter. Each stray one a little bit deeper. And the hunger … Warren knew what it wanted. To eat until it starved. "Something tells me I'm not getting a new suit of Sunday bests."

Heath laughed. "Maybe a straitjacket. Damn near boxed my head off. Good god, man, what was that?"

"Ask the little princess," Bishop said, fighting the urge to rub the bump on his neck. "She enjoys animating her newest toy."

Heath chuckled and called out the measurements as Jones nodded, pistol in hand.

"The front door opened," Warren said, ignoring the ghost of his father who stood on the bed and pissed on the bible. "Churchill back?"

Jones shook his head. "New visitor."

"Any word on the front? Scuttlebutt of value?" Warren said.

"Americans did some fine stuff in Argonne," Heath said, rolling the tape. "But if you listen to them, they haven't lost a battle since 1776."

"Even without mighty Captain Pierce," Bishop said, as the shadow of Alex began to cry. "Even more impressive."

"He kind of is, if even half his story is true," Jones said. "Supposed to be a marksmen unlike any other."

"Bet he eats flour and shits pound cake, too," Warren said.

Heath called out the last measurement. "Well, that's it. Time to go."

"Really? Is Princess Spark ready with my next dose of shock?"

Jones nodded to Heath, who took out his pistol. "Nah. The real work's beginning now, I think. Let's move."

The male doctor's cough was sickening and consumed him as he examined her wings. He finally shook his head. "You can finish her off," and hacked out of the infirmary room.

Nurse Fairweather dressed the wounds as the worst of the static left Vasilya's mouth. Then she stopped, and stood in front of her.

"He'll be coughing for a while," she said with a smile. "How are you, deary?"

"I'll live."

"That's my greatest hope." She held her hands as if in prayer. "You got my note?"

The silence of the room grew as the doctor's cough disappeared down the hall, and their words became whispers. "You are from Russia?"

Nurse Fairweather nodded, then spoke in a language that had been all but dead to Vasilya. "Yes, child. I call Russia home, as you do. And I am here to help you escape this prison. And return to our motherland."

"Return me? Who sent you?"

"Your mother."

Vasilya's back itched. "She …" She shut her mouth. This could be a trick.

"Scared of lies, are we? That's natural. But here's the truth. She was informed of your rather miraculous journey by our scouts."

Vasilya's body retreated, just a little, from the kind face of Nurse Fairweather. "You're a Bolshevik."

"I am. And I am the only chance you have of returning home to your mother and escaping this wretched war, thanks to their capitalist secret society."

"But war consumes Russia."

"Propaganda," she said. "Spread by our enemies. The revolution is complete and we are at peace. Don't be fooled by the slick words of these warring nations, my dove. They would con the devil himself."

Her nerve hardened at the word Fabergé had used for her. "But if the war is over, why would you want me? No government sends spies to do its bidding just because a mother weeps."

"No. But Russia is ravaged, child. We have broken the chains of the past, but we must build the pillars of the future. And you must help us. We need engineers, not soldiers. Builders, not warriors. You can do that, child." She gripped Vasilya's hands in a warm embrace. "Think of it, what good you could accomplish as the builder of a new Russia!" Her face was positively glowing. "Your mother would be so proud!"

"I …"

"And you would ease her mind. She's worried."

Vasilya dug her dirty thumbnail into the bandaged wound on her finger. "She wouldn't have been burdened at all with it if you had not arrested her."

"She was not arrested, deary. She's not locked away in some dungeon. She came to us to find you. To save you." Nurse Fairweather brushed the hair away from Vasilya's eyes, hooking it around her ear. "She asked for our help and we were all too happy to give it. I have arranged your escape tonight, child. When the lights go out, fly to the top of the building, follow the walkway to a ladder to the roof. The hatch will be open. Your freedom will be waiting for you there." She closed Vasilya's hand, holding the tight fist and warming it. "Or do you wish to continue building horrors out of your genius?" Fairweather held her stare. "Can I count on you?"

Warmth flooded her. "Yes."

Nurse Fairweather smiled. "I knew we could."

Bishop threw a look back and smiled at Heath, but was relieved to see there were no ghosts on his trail. "So, off to the roundtable are we? Hope so. I'm getting tired of being buzzed for no reason."

By the time Warren arrived, there was some kind of assembly, and a new woman he did not know. Oriental, with a skunk strip of white through her midnight hair. Pretty, and prettier the more you looked—

But his eyes were hooked to the orb that now hung from a chain above a T section.

The orb of the mechanical beast. The one he'd broken through with a white-hot fist, only to see the face of a dying child inside, slowly eaten by mustard gas.

Next to the battery that made him twitch, Vasilya, the princess, sat with her head down instead of sneering down the side of her nose. Behind her, on a workbench, her owl slept on a crate.

Christ, he thought as he approached. Her boyfriend died in that son of a bitch. And now it's hanging there for her to see, a constant reminder of his death like a ransacked coffin.

Pierce nodded. "Well, family's all here. We can finally get to business." Warren sat opposite the Oriental woman. The guards returned to their posts, but the snipers were still hiding in the walkways above, sights boring into his skull.

Pierce leaned back, hands behind him. "I regret that Mr. Churchill could not be here, but there's a storm coming so all flights and ships have cancelled their connection to the mainland. However, he authorized me to go ahead with this meeting."

"Our loss," Warren said.

The Oriental lady gave him a curious look.

Pierce shook his head. "Today is the culmination of years of effort to convince the authorities of each of our governments that there is a threat in this world, live and active in No-Man's Land, as real and as dangerous as the Germans or Austrians. I've briefed you all on the threat that is Rasputin. And tonight we begin the counter attack to that threat. But first, I'd like to introduce the newest member of our team, Dr. Rachel Oshikawa, Deputy

Master Inventor and Superintendent for his Majesty's Imperial Japanese Government, and liaison with the Japanese branch of the Theosophical Society."

Her deportment was almost mechanical in its exactitude, Warren thought. And she held her gaze on him like a game warden studying prey.

"She will be leading our design team," Pierce said. "The goal here is to create a weapon that can stand up to Rasputin and his soldiers before they can truly make an army that can't be stopped."

"Our secondary objective is a bit more difficult: to enlist the aid of the German army by using our machine to save their soldiers." Warren shook his head, but Pierce ignored him. "By enlisting their aid toward a common enemy, we can end this war at the same time. Mr. Churchill is currently in negotiations with ... elements in Germany that also wish to see the war end."

Warren snorted. "And don't know about Rasputin?"

"Some know," Vasilya said, still staring at the battery. "And I'm sure they've tried to recover the Juggernaut, only to find it missing. Tell me, Captain. Will they look kindly on their property being stolen and reshaped by their enemy, even if it is for a ... greater good?"

Her voice was a threadbare ghost of its former self.

"They will," Captain Pierce said, chin up, "when we give it back to them at war's end as a peace offering."

Vasilya's face puckered as if lemons had been shoved in her mouth. "I see."

"So," Warren said. "You've got the brains—" He pointed at Dr. Oshikawa. "And hands—" He pointed to Vasilya. "Which makes me what?"

"A horse's ass," Pierce said. "But also the perfect candidate for the pilot."

Vasilya's head turned away.

Warren rubbed his face. "Really?" And the flicker of memory turned his senses upside down: to taste the air above the fetid ground of the war, to hear wind made for beasts and gods. "Pilot."

Pierce hardened his stare, but Dr. Oshikawa spoke, clear and sharp. "We've attempted to make war automatons for some time, but while we've made a string of advances in the mechanics and industrial capacities needed to sustain the machine, the weakest element has been the human pilot."

The flicker of joy turned to ash. "Oh?" Warren said.

She leaned back in her chair. "But you are not human, Warren Bishop. We believe we can ... wire you to the machine in a way that would allow you full control of its abilities, weapons systems, and mobility. You should consider yourself fortunate to be given this chance."

His heart took another bite of itself, but slowed as the image of Alex crept in his head: wearing his own collar, dancing to another's tune. He would end his brother's slavery. "Yeah, fortunate." Warren crossed his arms. "You can get off the icicle you're sitting on. I'm all right with a suicide mission."

"That's enough griping from the gutter, Bishop," Pierce said. "We're on a deadline and we need to have this machine up and running in three weeks."

Vasilya chuckled, darkly, her back still to them.

"You don't think this is possible?" the doctor said to Vasilya.

"I'm sure anything is possible if you build it, Doctor."

"We're going to make it possible," Pierce said, leaning with his knuckles on the table. "All of this rests on the feasibility of Bishop successfully being ... attached to the machine. So, Doctor, you and Ms. Savorov will be burning the midnight oil to develop the ... what did you call it?"

"The integration harness," said the doctor.

"Just tell me when." Heath and Jones walked toward him. "Unless you need a hand."

Pierce's smile widened. "Don't tell me the baddest hombre of the Western Front is getting claustrophobic."

Despair clung to Warren's mind and wrapped itself tight. "Just bored. There's got to be something I can do that isn't a risk to the operation. I could clean the shower, the infirmary. C'mon, Captain. Do you really want to give up free labour and the chance to rejoice in my cleaning the bog?"

Pierce's smile eased. Warren didn't like it, but it was as if he could see the fear. Then he looked at Vasilya. "He's still within range of the battery, right?"

She nodded. Warren glanced again at the wreck of the capsule.

"Fine, you're on KP until midnight, then it's back to bed with you." He jutted his chin at Heath and Jones.

He got up, ignored the stare of the doctor, and spoke to Vasilya. "I am sorry you have to live through this again, kid," he said. "It's fucking cruel."

The shock he expected ... never arrived. Instead, Pierce shoved him along. "Hustle before I change my mind."

Warren marched on. Robbed grave in this room, ghosts in mine. I hope the shitter doesn't hold any surprises.

Vasilya tapped the battery, mind unhinged with possibilities. Escaping the war, this prison, these strange and awful people. Going home, seeing Mother. Meanwhile, chatter filled the deep echo of the room

"He is a crude one," Doctor Oshikawa said. "And he is one of your soldiers?"

"Not mine," he said. "Damn Canadian. Fought under Currie before Rasputin got to him."

"Is he?" she said. "I thought Canadians were more ..."

"Polite?"

"Refined. Like the British. But he's more like you."

Pierce snorted. "I'll take that as an insult and carry on." He cracked his back. "You know the objective, Doctor. I expect some results tomorrow morning."

"If it can be done it will be done," she said.

"You all right, kid?" said the captain.

Vasilya looked at his ugly countenance and was surprised to find a glimmer of concern in the pug-like exterior.

"It's a hell of a thing we're doing to you, I know. I won't even pretend to know how you feel. For what it's worth, I'm sorry."

"Sorry for what?" she said.

"For being your puppet master until this war is done. I don't like it, but that's the hand we were given." He turned and marched toward his office down one of the aisles, the echoes of his footsteps like distant rain on a tile floor.

The doctor stood. "We should begin." She walked around the table like a lecturing professor, and talked about animatronics, mechanics, and design specifications required, and the biological complications based on analysis of Warren's undead heart, but Vasilya was miles away already, racing toward home, far away from the industrial death trap that hung off chains like Christ on Golgotha.

"Vasilya? Are you listening?"

"Yes."

"You are a bad liar. We do not have time for me to repeat myself. Failure is not an option."

"I've heard that before," she said, bitterly. "Doctor. And from everything I've seen, failure has been the option of choice for every nation involved in this war."

"Your losses and pessimisms may be warranted," the doctor said. "But they are now irrelevant."

"Irrelevant!" Sparks flashed from the battery. "Irrelevant! Tell me, Doctor, what have you lost to this war? Your youth? You're old enough to be my mother. Your career? You're an engineer to a Great Power and that damn cult that began this war. Your family?"

The slap was hard enough to wake Merlin, who hooted violently but did no more than waddle on his railing perch. Vasilya's knees hit the floor. She gripped her face, shock cutting through her anger.

The doctor stood above her, hands behind her back. "One does not need war to lose family. Or have them stolen. You do not have a monopoly on suffering, simply because the first boy who broke your heart died in battle, fodder for trite songs of romance and tragedy. There are no songs for what I've lost." She shut her slight, oval mouth. "We do not have time for this." She yanked Vasilya up and the battery crackled. In the distance, Bishop cursed, followed by the sound of a full bucket dropping.

"What was that?" said the doctor.

"Bishop," she said. "I … must have jolted him."

Swear words echoed from the hallway, long and fast and filthy.

"His vulgarity is—"

"Boundless."

Doctor Oshikawa smiled, and a quiet sound burbled past her lip. A gentle laugh, distant and tiny as the sound of a falling leaf. "While our objective may not silence his foul mouth, it will give him pause before speaking out of turn." She walked to the front of the capsule and stared into the dark, broken centre. "The pilot who manned your mechanical armour, how did he control the device? What kind of engine did it use and how did he access it? There doesn't seem to be a hydraulic control system…"

Vasilya dusted herself off, then pet Merlin. "I thought you were the smartest creature in the room. Why don't you tell me?"

She turned.

"And if you hit me again, I'll burn this entire room down in hot current. Even if I don't electrocute you, you'll burn to death."

Dr. Oshikawa folded her hands behind her. "You are resourceful and cruel. I'm surprised you're not German."

"Russians have a stronger appetite for suffering."

Dr. Oshikawa had no witty comeback to keep Vasilya in her place. Indeed, she said nothing. Just stared into the jagged hole. "We must focus," she said, voice still and silent. "On the future, not the past."

"Spare me the oracle of Delphi speeches, doctor. Let's just get on with what the captain wants of us and maybe I can get back to making wings for Merlin." She looked at the owl, who clacked and turned his head for her to scratch the feathers behind his head.

A sneeze broke the stillness. Then a sniff. Dr. Oshikawa wiped her nose and Vasilya wondered if she was allergic to owls. It might be fun to find out.

The Doctor took the long way around the table, then stopped, her back still towards Vasilya. "Of course. We should focus on the work."

She gripped a black canvas bag that had been offloaded with the capsule, and grunted as she brought it up to the table. "Bishop's heart will need to be braced to a converter that we can tie to the nervous system of the armour. My branch of the Theosophicals had devised a 'thinking dynamo' as a possible model for the engine."

Dynamo, Vasilya thought. Well, at least she's on the right track.

The doctor produced the "thinking" heart. And Vasilya's breath vanished. Attached to it was something akin to the brain she'd taken from the Turkish Chess Player.

"What do you call that?" she said, the words falling out of her like misty breath in fall. "The … thinking machine you've attached to the dynamo?"

The doctor set it down. "It is an arithmometer. Though of a unique stripe." The way she touched it, the slightness of her caress.

"Did you build it?"

"No. My father did."

"He was an inventor?"

She nodded.

"And did he make the tools for it? The patterns?"

Dr. Oshikawa stiffened. "Why do you ask?"

"If he had, I'm sure you'll know how to fix them. Should anything go wrong."

Dr. Oshikawa bowed her head. "No. But I know how to make them."

"How?"

"His apprentice showed me."

There was a stiff sadness in her words and Vasilya did not press further because the clues were so clear and her conviction so strong she had to retrain herself from blurting out … you're Felix's mother.

They worked, Vasilya keeping herself mouse silent while the hours ticked on and trying not to consider the reality of what she'd discovered. As night consumed day, the doctor left her to gather some food. Leaving her alone with her thoughts. But a sound crept out of the capsule that rattled her nerves so badly she froze—

A ghost, a phantom, a memory arose to plague her—

From the dark interior, Merlin appeared.

"Get out of there!" she said. "How in the world did you climb in—"

The thought snuffed out as she saw the food in his beak.

A silver mouse.

Clack.

Her hands shook as Merlin spat out the morsel that his beak could not crack. She winced, then ran and picked up the small creature. "Hello, my friend." She caressed it, but the sparkling eyes were coal-black, the body crumpled.

And it dawned on her. She must have willed them to save Felix. To run to him, into the hole. And they must have tried. She steeled herself and scurried around the command capsule but no ghosts were waiting, nor Click. Just bloodstained memories and the aftershocks of tragedy.

She opened Clack's chest chamber.

His heart's engine was rusted and busted beyond repair. But the ignition switch was still whole.

Footsteps approached. She wiped tears and closed up the carcass of her dead friend, and placed him deep in her pockets as Felix's mother returned with thin gruel and a sad face.

CHAPTER FORTY-THREE:

ESCAPE FROM FORT DAEDALUS

Still stinging from the uncalled-for shock treatment, Warren scrubbed toilets and shower until they came as close to sparkling as these shit holes were going to look, and his hands smelled like lemon tainted filth.

Heath had even allowed him some privacy because the stench was so bad, and there was no way even Warren could break through these walls in an hour of solid punching.

The filth was fascinating, in its way. A grime made of old blood, mould, and rat turds. The rodents ran silent across pipes and in drains. It was nice to have rats that weren't afraid of humans. Though a shimmer of movement in the shadows turned his sponge hand into a wet fist.

"Time's almost up, Qimmiq." Tik popped out of the darkness, swinging a pocket watch.

Warren eased his wet grip. "Don't you have an afterlife to stink up?"

"They take my chains off on Sundays."

"Very funny."

Tik bowed. "Tick Tock, Qimmiq. You can't stay in limbo forever."

"That's what this place is?"

"Ain't talking about the prison. Talking about your mind. You know it. I know it. Ghosts are just the first sign of things to come, Qimmiq."

Warren washed his hands, unsure if the water was freezing or burning, trying to scratch the grime off his skin. "Yeah. Great to see you."

The watch kept swinging. "This is the last you're going to see of me. Believe it or not, I get in trouble each time I keep you from driving your head into a ditch."

"Thanks for the vote of confidence."

"No jokes tonight, Qimmiq. Your only chance is taking that Russian Shaman and punting his head a good ten miles from his body. And you got to do it faster than you think. There's a nest of sleeping hornets in your mind. They're waking, slow. You're not supposed to be between worlds like this forever. Your heart?"

He nodded. "It's burning out."

"And you won't make it to that battlefield on your will alone. You need a little help."

Warren sat on his upturned slop bucket. "Pierce took your shark tooth. I'll get it back when—"

"You need to get it tonight."

"He won't just hand it to me."

"You may be rotting away, but you're not expendable. He needs you. And you need it. Listen?" Tik looked up and around. "Hear it?"

A buzz. Warren had just thought it was the aftermath of having his bell rung by the goddamn zapper in his neck. But the more he focused, the more insidious it became. "That's the hornets, huh?"

Tik nodded, the spinning watch slowing as he faded into the shadow. "And heads up, Qimmiq. There's a viper in the grass here, waiting to strike. Stay sharp."

Warren sprung up. "Wait, Tik. Who is it? Hey, you can tell me?"

"Oh, you'll know as soon as you see it. Just don't get bit. Good luck, Qimmiq. Let the hornet's sleep."

Then he was gone.

"Mystical, magic riddle bullshit," Warren said, kicking the bucket.

Heath opened, pistol drawn. "What was that?"

"Me. Talking to myself."

"Well, come on. Infirmary's next."

Ignoring the buzz that was in his head, Warren focused on his paranoia as they passed through the thin walls to the infirmary. "Very kind of you to get the bog fit for a brigadier's inspection," Heath said.

"What can I say? I'm a kind soul. Where's Jones?"

"Captain Pierce had some clandestine mission and that's all I ever hear." Heath chuckled but Warren did not. Pierce liked his unit to operate with clockwork perfection.

They reached the infirmary door and the pistol shoved Warren's buzzer. "C'mon, then. On to the next task."

Warren stiffened.

"You're quick, Bishop," Heath said, voice still jolly. "But not bullet quick. Now, let's go see the nurse, nice, quiet and slow."

The entered the infirmary, the door closing soundlessly behind it, the kind of doors meant to keep screams in. The doctor who had dissected parts of him was on the floor, dead eyes wide. Standing by the operating table was the nurse, a grey-haired woman with a warm smile whose name he'd never discovered.

"Well done, Heath," she said like a grandmother. "You're a real tribute to the cause."

"Thanks, Captain Scorpion. All right, bub, on the table."

"Scorpion? God, is everyone reading the same gutter literature?"

"You should feel lucky that you've managed to bring an otherwise gutter life into the tide of progress. Now, would you be so kind as to do what Heath has asked? My understanding is I need you to be alive. But I will take my chances with you dead."

"Chances for what?"

She smiled and took his cold hand. "The revolution needs your heart, Mr. Bishop." Lightning sizzled through him and he fell to his knees.

Outside, a storm crashed against the prison walls, throwing torrents of rain and flashes of lightning, belting it with everything it had and sending shimmers of electric-blue shadows into the commons as lightning forked from the thundering darkness.

Inside, the lights dimmed and then returned as Vasilya listened to Dr. Oshikawa discuss the computational heart she'd brought, too stunned to do much more than steal fleeting glimpses at the woman who had to be Felix's mother.

She nodded when she thought appropriate but couldn't decide what to say. What can I say? I loved your son? I shoved him in that dreaded machine because he wouldn't let me do it myself? That the brute we're working with likely killed him with his own bare hands? And did you know … did you know it was him that had been in the Juggernaut? Who told you? Winston? Pierce? The questions were maddening as was her residual dislike for the woman.

"So," Dr. Oshikawa said. "Do you think it's possible, if his heart works as predicted, to brace it with the computational one? A duel engine for his armour?"

Vasilya scratched Merlin's neck, making him flutter. "I am not sure. The … the first pilot. His heart was wired by use of, well, a healing art, to the Juggernaut. I do not know how it was managed, only that the practitioner of that art is dead."

Dr. Oshikawa nodded. "I feared as such. Mr. Churchill was unclear about the nature of your talents."

"Talents?" she said, hoping it sounded ignorant.

"Your uncanny ability with machines. Most of such talented members have found themselves within the Theosophical Society. But none have ever created anything so daring so quickly. For most, it takes years, and most of what is made has been for …" Dr. Oshikawa caught herself. "I should perhaps not be surprised that a disciple of such an acclaimed … jeweler would be handy with tools and materials."

She swallowed hard. "Daughter."

Dr. Oshikawa considered her.

"I am the daughter of Carl Fabergé. A bastard daughter, but a daughter nonetheless." She approached the dynamo heart. "I do not know how Bishop's heart operates, but if it can serve as an engine, this will work." She touched the mechanical heart. "I can make it work."

"How is that?"

"Like the engine of a Fabergé egg that was never built. A dual motor that was to operate an optical illusion." Her voice quieted, and her breath tasted of Mother's last scrap of cheese and a whiff of gold flakes, and behind her lids the stars sparkled like a diamond encrusted cage around a fantastical creature. "The birth of a phoenix. The engine was to work the illusion as well as generate a diorama. We have no need for such theatrics, but the internal mechanics are such that they can serve as a bridge between his dead heart and the mechanical interface." She coughed. "Though it won't be as pretty."

Dr. Oshikawa folded her hands in front of her. "I see." She looked high up the prison walls to the rain slashed windows. "From the dossier and reports I've read of what ... Bishop is, I think his heart will be an engine unlike that which we might hope for the mechanical armour. It is durable and rather strange and will allow him to do things even your Juggernaut could not." She nodded at Vasilya. "Though this melding of engineering and flesh ... I fear what comes of such a marriage."

Vasilya's wings itched. "Fear? Of what?"

"I fear for those who must carry the burden to be the first of their kind, who may feel alone in the world that made them and will likely shun them. To be reborn orphans in war. We are playing nursemaids to changes beyond Darwin, beyond Newton, and even beyond what the Theosophical Society dreamed. We have no map to guide us but our conscience which is, alas, chained to this never-ending war. I fear we may not do our world justice."

Memory directed Vasilya's words. "But I am a blasted tree; the bolt has entered my soul; and I felt then that I should survive to exhibit what I shall soon cease to be—a miserable spectacle of wrecked humanity, pitiable to others and intolerable to myself."

Surprised, Dr. Oshikawa's held her arms behind her back. "You believe we are Frankenstein?"

"No," she said. "Frankenstein's daughters. We've not begun with the dead, but a monster, using science to push it beyond itself towards what, exactly?" She shrugged.

Dr. Oshikawa's back straightened. "If there is a lesson to be taken from Shelly's Gothic world view, it is that we must not abandon to the world that which we have brought into it." Then, her visage shook. "We must not let the standards of the day destroy our sense of responsibility to life in our hands. No matter how it looks. No matter how much it might be hated." The doctor's lip shook. "No matter..."

The iron in Vasilya's heart smoldered. She reached out her hand to the doctor—

And the lights went out.

Weakness had been as foreign to Warren as voiding his bowels since the deadroot took hold, but he was useless as a baby in a hurricane as Heath tossed his body and fastened the restraints gallows tight, shoved a rag in his mouth, and bound it with a strap of well-used leather.

The nurse sauntered beside him. "I apologize for the gag, but from what we've gathered, you do not feel much pain, so I have no idea if you'll scream as we cut your heart out. Besides, you've got a rude gob and I fear this procedure will turn the room blue." She winked, and picked up the surgical saw he'd seen in the Casualty Clearing Stations, the tiny teethed number they used for cutting up limbs. "But first, Heath, could you be so kind as to crack open his ribs?"

Warren thrashed. She put down the saw, then jolted him harder and all he could do was twitch and think in hazy bursts. Blackguards and betrayers and knives in the back!

Heath stood over, sledge hammer on his shoulder. "So long, Bishop. Nice knowing ya."

The hammer cracked on his chest, bouncing back and sending Heath stumbling.

"Careful!" she growled. "Last thing I need is you knocking yourself out. Now, again, and hurry. Our plane should be arriving."

And heavy blows became as steady as his long dead heartbeat. Warren screamed into the gag as the hammer danced off his chest, bones bending, then reforming.

Heath was sucking wind, sweat crawling out his skin. "It's like they're iron."

"They just need softening," she said. "Stand back. And when I say so, drop that hammer for all your life's worth." She caressed Warren's forehead. "This will be over soon." Eyes shut, she said a prayer in Slav babble. "Now."

The hammer dropped. Again. Again.

Warren bit through the gag and the scream cracked with his bones. Burning hair and flesh filled his flaring nostrils as everything became brittle and frail. Every ounce of him like broken glass that had just settled, and every movement a twist of agony.

Smoke rose from him as a knife plunged into his chest, easy as a needle through paper, and his body was torn open as he choked on the fullness of pain that spiked through his mind, limbs locked in a fatal paralysis. Black blood splashed his face, and internal gore splashed cold on his burning chest as the nurse hacked into him, the sound harkening him back to the hell of battlefield surgery, where men with wounds like this were often shot instead of saved.

Then the hacking stopped and all he could do was shiver.

"What is that?" Heath said.

"This is what we came for. Dzerzhinsky made it clear that this was a key to solving the labour crisis in the army, of protecting the revolution. Don't touch it, just get me those pincers."

The nurse shoved the freezing clamps into the cavity in Warren's chest, and gripped his heart and began to lift it—

Red flexed through his vision as the restraints snapped from his right hand.

"Crack his head! Now!" the Nurse said.

The hammer descended.

Warren caught the wooden handle and drove the hammerhead into Heath's chest, knocking him into a cabinet to the serenade of shattered glass.

He growled at the nurse before gripping her neck.

She growled back, hand in his chest.

Lightning burst and light blinked out of existence.

Vasilya panicked in the fresh darkness. Pieces were now moving she could not stop. Fairweather would be here soon, she had to reach the top of the prison in haste. Her back itched as her wings started to flutter—

A candle flickered into life and she saw Doctor Oshikawa's face. "Are you all right?"

She rested her wings before they sliced through the dress. "I ... I don't know."

"There must be protocols for a power failure," the doctor said. "I'm sure the captain will have—"

Cracks of rifle fire broke through her words.

"Intruders!" screamed a voice. "We've got snakes in the den! Lockdown! Lock—" Another rifle shot.

She ducked, instinctively: snipers. They were everywhere, to keep Bishop in line, but were they all Bolsheviks?

Captain Pierce's voice echoed. "You sons of bitches are all dead men walking. Those loyal to me, Code Raven!"

"Go to hell, Yankee fuck!"

The deadly shots and screams punctured the darkness. Vasilya had to fly. Only death awaited her here, a lonely end if she stayed—

The doctor's hand wrapped itself around hers, voice a whisper of steel in the dark. "Fall back to the wall, and stay close to me."

Her hand was warm, her voice confident. Vasilya did not want to see her hurt. And she would be, if Fairweather saw her shifting alliances. Dr.

Oshikawa would be dead. "I ... I can't." She let her wings cut through the back of her dress and flutter. Painfully, she rose off the ground. "Please hide. They don't want you. Take care of Merlin."

Dr. Oshikawa's face shifted from control to wonder.

"No you don't!"

An icy grip clenched on her ankle and yanked her down with such violence her wings winced. She crashed on the ground. Stunned, she couldn't breathe. Crinkles of pain etched their way into her back like slivers of iron. She tried to move her wings and the pain almost drowned her from consciousness.

Lightning revealed the owner of the hand—

Migs, mutton-chop face ruinous from the captain's beating, a revolver drawn on Dr. Oshikawa, but his grin and eyes focused like a predator on Vasilya. "Gonna pay for what he done to me, Princess." He licked his chops, then glared at the doctor. "And I dare you to do something fancy with that electric eel fan of yours, you yellow witch."

The doctor raised her hands. "As you wish."

She spun out of sight as the pistol fired wildly. And in the flashes of fire, the doctor twisted like a dervish, then gripped the gun with one hand and his arm in another, and tossing him face-first into the capsule, head cracking against the frame. In her hand was his now spent and smoking pistol. She placed it within the folds of her jacket as Migs fell on his back and, then, kicked his face so hard his nose collapsed and his body lay still.

Doctor Oshikawa picked Vasilya from the floor and laid her on the work table on her stomach. "Vasilya? Can you hear me?"

"I'm sorry."

"You ... you're ..."

A monster, she knew. A cowardly, ruinous monster.

"A most wonderful creature." And the doctor smiled. "I'll get you to the infirmary."

"No need for that," said another voice.

The doctor reached for her pistol but she was not as quick as the lightning that tore through the air and dove into her like streams of white-hot daggers emerging from Nurse Fairweather's fingers, her nurse's smock a hideous smear of black blood and gore that would have disgusted even Goya. The doctor contorted and collapsed as she approached.

"Don't worry," Nurse Fairweather said to Vasilya. "She'll live. And we have a plane to catch."

Vasilya shook. "I can't..."

"Wings hurt? Don't worry, deary. I always have a contingency stratagem."

While more rifles cracked out, Fairweather looked up. But at a worm's eye view, the doctor, hand shaking, pushed her fan into Vasilya's hand.

Fairweather whistled. "Charlie? Now!"

From the darkness of the top walkway descended a rough hemp rope. The nurse grabbed Vasilya, tossed her over her shoulder. "Time to go, my angel of the revolution."

Then they ascended into the darkness above while the captain screamed. "Bishop! Somebody get Bishop!"

Every movement singed. Every thought burned. And through all the barbed agony, what made Warren grunt was Pierce's Kentucky voice yelling something about a raven.

Warren watched the slow mending of his ruined chest, but something was wrong. The witch had taken his heart. He was still alive, undead, and healing slow. And though he sensed there was strength in his body, it was leaking out like a whiskey barrel peppered with grapeshot.

Rasputin said a kill shot to the head would take them out ... but he doubted he'd live long without his deadroot heart.

He rolled off the table into the dark as lights flickered but would not stay on, the room weaving in and out of his mind as he scrambled to the door, yanking it open.

He stumbled, bracing his chest with his right arm as the distant hall filled with the nurse's lightning.

Vasilya. The kid was easy pickings. Even hummingbirds can't outrace lightning. He shuffled hard, then broke into a jog, then a weak run, every inch of him like broken glass.

Through the dark, punctuated by natural flashes of lightning, he saw the nurse with Vasilya over her shoulder, ascending to the top of the prison, then Pierce's angry voice. "Bishop, get Bishop."

The kid was scrambling in the woman's grip.

Fighting.

She was going against her will, rising above him.

"Can you reach her?"

It was the doctor, the Oriental one, lying on the ground.

I'm dead if I don't. Real dead.

But Alex needs to die.

C'mon, Qimmiq. This time, there's only one way to run.

Up. "This is going to hurt like a bastard."

He ran, teeth crushing themselves, and leapt up to the first level walkway, gripping the rail and hoisting himself up. On to the next, doing pull-ups and scrambles for a footfall as fast as he could. Then another. Strength bleeding out after his initial jump.

Shots cracked down, skimming his back and taking pieces with it.

Fucking snipers. His arms shook, but he leapt again.

A shot tore into his shoulder, and ripped one hand away from the rail.

Two shots flashed from down below—

Captain Pierce and the doc were unloading fire into the sharpshooter, who careened as he fell to earth. "You're clear," Pierce yelled. "Get her, Bishop! We're screwed if you fail!"

"Sure," he said. His left shoulder lanced with frosted pain, but he screamed as he tore himself up another level. Then another. One step closer, one step harder. Until the storm outside crashed against the prison, cascading the world in blue light.

There, on the top right corner, a trapdoor to the ceiling had been carved and was now torn out. The nurse crept up a rope ladder.

"I've got a shot," Pierce yelled.

"Don't! You'll hit her," the doctor said.

No shot fired as Bishop scrambled onto the top walkway. The trapdoor slammed shut. Growling, he pulled himself up and ran to catch her, slow as molasses, and tired as dead dog.

"Hurry the fuck up, Bishop!" Pierce yelled. "All units, we have a live one on the roof."

Warren gripped the rope ladder, chest in agony, until lightning flashed again and rekindled his anger.

"Witch," he said between his teeth. "I'm going to tear you apart."

In the wilds of the roof, the storm lashed everything with thunder and rain and a taste of electricity in the air. A hellish wind bowled Nurse Fairweather over, spilling Vasilya to the ground on her side, wings still bleeding.

Her arm was yanked. "Get up, deary. I'm not afraid to carry dead weight if I have to."

Vasilya tore her hand away from the rain-soaked grip of the nurse. "I won't go."

Fairweather's grey hair was wild and wet like rotting cloth in the Herculean wind. "You will, or so help me your mother will never surface from the box we've buried her in! Russia needs you. And our escort is almost here." She held her hand up and shot a current of white-hot electricity into the air. "Now watch me finish off the hideous man who tried to strangle me." She headed toward the trapdoor, a gentle hand on Vasilya's shoulder.

She shirked away. "How do I even know my mother is alive at all? Until you can prove that, I am not going."

Behind her back, she gripped the fan the doctor had slid to her.

High above, a black plane circled, riding against the wind like a wild stallion, a rope ladder hanging off its sides. Fairweather laughed, her voice going to Russian. "Oh, deary. You don't make current without that battery. And I broke it before we left." Her fingers flickered with blue lightning.

"But I do. I'm an engine for the revolution, and soon, we'll be making Russia glorious again. Be your mother alive or dead."

The trap door began to open. Bishop's ruined head peaked out. He was slow, torturous in his movements until his mouth screamed. "Don't touch her …"

Fairweather looked at him. "How interesting. I tear out your heart, and you suddenly grow a conscience. I'll bring this up at the next meeting of the Secretariat."

"Run," Bishop said to Vasilya, then charged.

Fairweather's hands crackled and she unleashed electric fury into Bishop … who pushed on. With Fairweather distracted, Vasilya unfolded the fan behind her back as the whole world crackled with lightning.

"Who knew you had a noble heart," Fairweather said. "Too bad it just burned out." A bolt of whiteness charred Bishop and he dropped on knees and elbows, the fetid stench of his body sizzled in the rain. Vasilya hobbled to her left so that Fairweather's back faced the edge of the prison roof.

Fairweather turned to Vasilya. "Stop." She did. "I hate to do this, deary. But you are too troublesome at the moment. You'll be much better when we're back in Moscow." Forks of lightning leapt from her finger.

Vasilya snapped out the fan.

The bolts charged into the metal, and blasted Fairweather into the chest, knocking her over the edge of the roof and into the darkening night, complete with the soiled bag in her hand. The circling plane vanished.

"Jesus Christ!" Bishop said, moving faster but still slow, and leaning over the edge, clutching his chest where a large wound was etched. He was leaking black blood and his knees shook. "Oh fuck, this is going to hurt …"

He dove over the edge.

He shot like a bullet past the prison walls and then the sheer cliff face of the island, toward jagged rocks that waited like the massive busted jawline of a dead giant, chasing the witch nurse as her burned body twitched back to life before—

Thud.

And Bishop thudded next to her, waves lashing them like a cat of nine tails to drag them into the sea. Water filled his chest, making him heavy, but he held on as the nurse was pulled into the waves, fist clawed tight around her black bag.

Bishop gnashed his teeth, then let go—

The sea claimed him, stronger than any force he'd ever felt, and he swam with desperate and leaking strength, hands grasping water as he pushed out to reach the thick ankles of the witch. He gripped her tight—

—and the raging water pulled him deeper.

Vasilya, perched on the roof's edge, heard a shouted, "Don't!" and turned back to see Pierce scrambling through the door.

"He's drifting out to sea!" Vasilya screamed.

"He's tough enough to take it—"

"No … his heart is missing. She took it out."

Pierce's face was ashen. "We'll get a boat."

"There's no time!" Her wings fluttered.

"Kid, you don't even know how to fly."

"Of course I do. It's like falling, but in reverse."

Dr. Oshikawa climbed up the ladder, and stood behind Pierce. She gripped herself. "Good luck."

Vasilya nodded, closed her eyes, then jumped. Her wings shook as the wind tossed her like a piece of felt into the torrent of the storm.

Bishop sank, dragging the nurse with him. He climbed her until he could grip her arm, his own seeming to fill with sand, and pulled at her fingers.

Sparks lit from her eyes as bubbles ran through her grey teeth, hair wild and outstretched like the snakes of Medusa.

Fuck, he thought.

A muted laugh came from the drowning witch before the world turned to white fire.

Vasilya swung in the wind while her wings tried to find themselves and terror surged through her blood. I need to fall first before I can fly, just focus—

A white explosion plumed from the dark depths of the sea, bursting above the surface.

Bishop was thrown out of the sea like an unwanted corpse.

Dive, she told her wings. Dive, my friends, or we're all dead!

And they listened.

She bolted down like a bullet, wings twisting her so she was on target, until she closed in on Bishop's burned body, his arms flailing, and in one hand a rotten sack.

She reached for the other one—

Gripped—

—and slipped.

He fell, the sea ready now to be his grave.

Dive harder!

Her wings were flat against her back as she tore down and with both hands grabbed his left arm, fingers biting into his thick flesh.

Now, up!

Pain burned her shoulders and back as she tried to dive down and pull up. They beat and she whirled, skirting the shattering rocks at the bottom of the shoreline.

The wings hummed like wild hives of hornets, steering her some, as Bishop's legs skirted the water before she finally pulled out of the dive.

Spiraling up, she saw the shadow of a black winged creature in the clouds ... the plane Fairweather had called for.

A burst of killing light snapped across the air as it opened fire with a machine gun and nose-dived toward her on a one-way mission ... until a lonely rifle shot cracked and silenced the machine gun. Another shot followed, and the dreaded hum of a nose-diving plane grew against the cracks of thunder.

Vasilya careened to her left as the plane dove past her. She shot past the edge of the roof and let go of Bishop's incredible weight, shooting into the air like a sling-shot stone. Ecstatic relief washed over her with the rain before exhaustion pulled her from the heavens. The thunderous crash of the plane on the rocks below was matched by the anger of thunder. She landed hard on her knees, and crumpled next to Bishop.

Water coughed out of his black lips, voice a hazy and charred version of its former self. "I always liked you knights of the air." He chortled, then gasped, gripping his chest. His meaty fingers released the bag in its grip.

As the doctor took Vasilya in her arms, Captain Pierce tossed the rifle on the roof, grabbed the bag, then Bishop's left arm and picked him up and lay him across his shoulder. "Quick, we need to get his heart back, now. We don't have time to hunt for another Bishop."

"Thanks for caring," Bishop said.

And then the doctor screamed. Vasilya glared as Bishop's left shoulder came off. Bishop seethed as he hit the ground.

"He's not mending," Pierce said. "Jesus fucking hell, what the am I going to do with him?"

"The heart," Vasilya said, gasping, weak, as the doctor covered her with her body, adding to the warmth that had almost died. "Get it back inside."

Pierce looked at the bag "Damn thing's burned and soaked."

"Try!" Vasilya screamed.

In the infirmary, they stood around the stained table as the medical doctor with lump on his head tried to stifle his horror at the task at hand. Bishop groaned, body moving listlessly as if it hadn't the strength to feel much of anything. Then they waited for a miracle.

His wounds remained. His skin would not stitch itself.

The doctor peered in the hole. "It needs help. Something to stimulate it."

"Like what," Pierce said.

"An ignition switch," Vasilya whispered, holding the towel around her soaked frame.

Doctor Oshikawa placed her hands on the sides of her face. "Like the one in the Phoenix egg?"

She nodded.

"Can you show me?"

"I will try."

The doctor nodded, and her clear voice ran out fast and strong. "Captain, get him down on to the desk and grab every medical person here who isn't a traitor." She gripped Vasilya's hands hard. "Frankenstein's daughters have much work to do."

CHAPTER FORTY-FOUR:

OF MEN AND MACHINES

Warren was not at the bottom of the sea. Not in a prison of lightning. But on his back, glaring into the tower of gloom that was Fort Daedalus's high ceiling. A cloth covered his chest.

"He has awoken."

"About time."

Vasilya's face appeared above him. "Don't move."

"Well, well," he said, ignoring the flares of pain each word poked into him. "If it isn't the angel that kicked me out of hell."

She shook her head, but she was smiling. "You're … not out of hell yet. Though you are healing well."

"Kid, stick to the truth." he said. "Your poker face ain't worth a three dollar bill."

"What was the last thing you remember?" she said.

His face bunched. "The witch in the water. Electric smile that sent my brain burning. But I had my heart in my hand … god, just when being me couldn't getting any weirder." He heard something whirl. "What the hell is that?"

"We have had to make some adjustments."

"To what?"

"Just rest up, Bishop," Pierce's ugly mug completed the bizarre portrait above him. "You've had a hell of a day. We all have. So we're talking it easy until Minister Churchill arrives tomorrow."

Bishop was steamed and the whirling grew. "Hell of a day?" Bishop said. "Pierce, you are the grandmaster of understatement. Now, someone, I don't give a flying fuck who, tell me what's that whirling noise?"

Vasilya vanished, as ashen faces looked back at him.

"Here." She handed him a mirror, face grim. "Look at your chest only."

He reached for it. A low thrum of pain spread as she peeled back the cloth on his chest.

He ignored her and looked at his face first.

An inhuman double glared back. Eyes white and wide, the rest black and red and scarred and moving. "Swell."

But the real horror was below—

A hole in his chest.

He remembered burning current, and hammer strikes.

Inside the hole, something moved.

Faster than his dying heart beats.

Slowly, his hands retracted into claws, gripping the sheet in his hand like a baby with its blanket. "What ... what the hell have you all done to me?"

But the real fear sprang when he lifted his head and saw what was coming out of the gaping hole. Three thin cables led out of chest like snakes. "Oh god," he whispered and reached for the mirror with his left hand ... but it never arrived.

He turned.

All that was left was the shoulder, rounded, as if there'd never been an arm there at all.

"We've got it in some special goo the doctor suggested," Pierce said. "We might even be able to save it."

The mirror cracked on the floor. He followed the snakes from his chest to where they led: straight into the busted mouth of the mechanical nightmare, which now had the semblance of a living thing. Steam came out the back, and lights flickered from its dark, cavernous mouth.

"It was the only way," said the Oriental doctor. "Your heart was barely ... functional. Without the bracing dynamo to inject some current, you'd be dead right now. The permanent kind"

He sat up, against the restraints. "My heart ... the thump," he grunted through angry clenched teeth. "It's gone. It just sits in my chest like a lump of mud."

Pierce pushed him back, and Warren let him. "Maybe that's what it felt like, but it had its own engine, an internal one, that kept you running. But yanking it out? Brother, you don't have long."

"Indeed," said the doctor. "Yours had been badly burned, and soaked in saltwater. We had to ... connect it with a new power supply so that it could keep you alive. A rather miraculous device. Vasilya? I think you should tell him."

He glared at her, and she tapped her lip as she spoke. "The dynamo turns that power into energy your heart can use," Vasilya said, a sad smile on her lips. "It has its own brain. Something I made for a little friend, long ago. A test for making the next Fabergé egg." Her hand dropped from her mouth. "The Phoenix."

Warren shook his head. "So now I'm a cripple, jolted to some steam engine in that ... thing with some kind of mechanical egg inside me?"

"For now," the doctor said. "We're hoping you're natural mending will—"

"We both know I'm not mending anything. I can live, but not heal. Which is why I'm heading for No-Man's Land and not coming back."

Pierce shoved him back. "Hey, these ladies saved your hide, Bishop. Least you could do is be a little gracious."

Warren rose up against his hand, ignoring the desire to use the one that wasn't there. Cold, biting pain flexed in his chest. Warren seethed, then lay back down. "How about you, Angel? How's your wings?"

"Fine," Vasilya said. "Thank you."

"You like flying? I did." He blinked. "I think."

He had flown. But he couldn't see it. Feel it.

He thought of home and Mother and all he could see were a dance of shadows.

The only thing that was clear was Alex.

The only thing.

"We both would have been in trouble if Captain Pierce hadn't shot the airship that charged us."

Warren snickered. "Captain may be a better shot than me."

"Ain't no maybe about it," Pierce said. "Now that we're all bosom buddies, I have some business to attend to." Pierce yelled an order and the three of them watched as a procession of men were marched at gunpoint out of the prison. Migs, face like a broken bottle, was in the rear. When they were gone, everyone stared at something different. And Bishop saw the doctor's hand holding Vasilya's as a voice screamed "Fire!" and rifle shots cracked through the wind's roar. The doctor and Vasilya held each other.

For Warren, there was only the face of Alex.

Shadows marched for that memory, too.

Vasilya vanquished sleep from her mind as she and the doctor worked through the night modifying the command capsule for Bishop, while the wounded man lay there, his skin now a dark grey, the contour of corduroy roads, and the trail of cable from his chest to the old Juggernaut a painful and constant reminder of the price he was paying, a price that Felix had paid.

Dr. Oshikawa said nothing of her son as they worked until dawn, when grey sunlight flittered inside.

"This will work," she said. "If his heart is strong enough."

"And if it isn't," Bishop said, startling them because he'd been so still and silent. "What then?"

"Our original plan required you to be the engine of the machine," Dr. Oshikawa said. "But you are … a hybrid creature now, and the parameters of what we can accept in terms of thresholds will not be the same. We are in uncharted waters."

"Here be dragons," Bishop said, crossing his right arm, then putting it back with a grunt.

Dr. Oshikawa nodded, put down her pencil, hands still. "Vasilya, carry on with the schematics. I must use the lavatory." She walked with perfect pacing away from them.

"If you were not already wounded and weak," Vasilya said. "I'd thrash you myself for being such a brute."

His face was ashen. "Might want to get your licks in before they send me off to the big top they have waiting for me. Because, Angel, I am not coming back."

"Then I suggest you make peace with God, and pray he has room for uncouth bastards."

She stalked off to the guard room's lavatory, Bishop's words low and clear. "God don't want me and I'm pretty sure hell is full."

She pressed open the door.

Dr. Oshikawa was gripping a sink as if the weight of the world had been removed from Atlas and placed on her back.

"Doctor ..."

"Churchill told me. He asked me if I'd heard of Felix Hilt. I'd stopped ... thinking about him." A broken reflection gazed back at her, shards of glass around the sink and her small booted feet. "Focused on my training. Learning everything I could from my father even as he dismissed my efforts. Whenever the wound in my chest ached for him, I took on another impossible mission, another task beyond that of a mere daughter of industry ... and succeeded."

"Then the pain would be back. My darling boy, so majestic and small, such a wonder unknown. My tiny Haruka." Blood flowed down the white porcelain, then hung, like a tear, before dropping.

Vasilya took two steps forward. "That was his name?"

Dr. Oshikawa lifted her head and stared at the broken mirror. "Haruka Felix Hilt. Child of engineers, a motherless son of war."

Vasilya stepped back as the doctor's hands and fist became whirlwinds, targeting every reflective surface, every possible image of herself. The remaining mirror shards broke apart under each blow.

"Stop it!" Vasilya yelled. But the doctor's deadly work continued. "Stop!"

She charged, laying a single hand on the doctor's arm before iron hands seized her wrist and neck, ramming her to the wall. Seething, the doctor's eyes were wide. Blood ran down her hands on to Vasilya. "And you ... you could have stopped him. Could have been the one in that goddamn machine!"

"I tried!" Vasilya said.

"Tried and failed. You let him go! You let him go!"

She stumbled back, hands red claws, until her back hit a stall. "You let him go. You miserable thing, you let him go. You were not strong enough to save him. Weak and rotten. You let him go."

Vasilya gasped, massaging her neck, wings crinkled but not damaged.

"Let him go. You let him go."

Against her own defences, the need for space and privacy that had acted as a barbed wire around her, Vasilya approached the doctor, ready for a kick to the chin or fist to the throat. She approached slowly, arms and palms up.

"Get back."

She closed in.

"Stop. I don't—"

She held the doctor, who shook.

"Get off me, please! I don't deserve—"

Then the sobs took over, and she fell into Vasilya's arms. Awkwardly, she brought them to the ground among the broken glass and porcelain.

Vasilya gritted her teeth until a flicker of warmth in her iron heart eased the tension. She cleared her throat. "Would you like me to tell you about your son?"

The doctor shook, but her head on Vasilya's chest nodded.

"All right. I will." Tears welled. "The first thing you should know is ... he was a marvellous dancer. Though his hygiene left much to be desired." She smiled, and chuckled, though the doctor only gave the barest hint of mirth.

They sat like that for a quiet hour, Vasilya sharing her most precious memories, her buried treasures within her iron heart, as she tore a piece of her dress and tied it around the doctor's wounds, before guards came to see if they needed help. When she was done, most of the tears and the worst of the shaking had stopped.

"We'll be out in a minute," said the doctor. They stood, the doctor helping her up this time. "You ... really loved him."

Vasilya nodded. "And I think he loved me."

"There is no question of it," the doctor said. "His father had a noble heart. Nearly died protecting us when the damned Russians invaded Port Arthur ..." Realization caused her hand to cover her mouth. "I'm sorry."

"Don't be. No nation has a monopoly on cruelty and savagery."

"Nor on hope and courage." She kissed Vasilya's forehead, gently, as if it were as fine as a flower petal. "Come now, musume. The time for tears is over."

Pierce punched Warren so hard it almost hurt, and nearly spilled him off his slab. "All right, shit heel. What did you say to them?"

"The truth."

Pierce scratched his whiskers with a clawed hand. "Boy, we don't have time for you to tear them down like that. Next time you even think of giving them shit, I'm going to tear off that last arm and club you with it."

Warren snickered. "You still hit like a—"

Pain glared through Warren's head as a left cross came at him fast and hot and blaring white. It damn near took his head off. Then he saw a tiny white sliver bouncing in the captain's hand. "You ain't the only one knows how to make a little Eskimo mojo work in your favour."

A heartbeat thudded. Warren pulled against the straps. "Give that back!"

He smacked away Warren's hand. "All in good time," he patted his head like a dog. "But so help me, Bishop, if you don't apologize and then stop giving them shit, I will toss this trinket into the drink."

The two women walked back together, the doctor's hands bandaged. Both their faces were red and raw, but light smiles graced them. Pierce cracked his knuckles, Tik's shark tooth in his palm.

Warren grunted "About what I said. I'm—"

Buzzers sounded.

"Shit," Pierce said, turning on a dime and running for the door. "He's early. Even Rome wasn't built in a day. Everyone!" he screamed. "At the ready! Minister Churchill has returned!"

CHAPTER FORTY-FIVE:

NO BULLET-PROOF BATTLE PLAN

Grim and overcast as the sky, Winston sat next to Pierce at the table, as all around them they waited for the minister to speak. Even Bishop had found the strength to sit with them, though he stared at the old Juggernaut where his wires were tied. Winston gave him a curious look, then placed a large hand on the tin cup of brandy Pierce had provided.

"Ludendorff has died."

Vasilya shuddered at the name and recalled Colonel Balk's comments. That one of the generals of the war had gone mad.

Winston took a sip of brandy from the tin cup Pierce had provided. "Apparently, he died some month ago. There's no word of it in the papers, but our friends in Berlin assured us that he had died in his bed. This is most unfortunate, as our agents have mostly been within his camp. And now we are cut off."

"How?" Vasilya asked.

Pierce gave her an odd look, as if this wasn't the time to ask questions.

"That fine point," Winston said, "is unclear. I suspect he succumbed to the malady that had been infecting him and took his own life, though Berlin would never let such a fact escape their breath."

She recalled Hindenburg. "Could it be he was murdered?"

"Perhaps we could keep the questions until after the minister has spoken," Pierce said.

Winston looked keenly at her. "It is possible, but why do you think it was likely?"

"I ... met Hindenburg. Once."

Winston's face went wide. "This was not in your debriefing."

"So were lots of things," she said, a trace of old bitterness on her tongue. The doctor gave her knee a gentle, but firm, grip.

"He didn't say it, but I thought he'd want Ludendorff out of the war."

"Why?" Pierce said, sharply. "They've been the duo running the war since Tannenberg."

"Because Ludendorff … was thought to be going mad."

A hush came over them, except Bishop, who didn't seem to care one way or the other what they were discussing. Attention firmly magnetized by the old Juggernaut.

"His camp is harder to crack," Winston said. "We had put out feelers for a possible coordination of our plans, to perhaps forestall our original aim. But with who knows what in charge of the war effort, his focus will be on victory, even if Germany starves to shadow."

"He respects strength," Vasilya said. "And sacrifice."

"Indeed. But only for his own men."

"Then we go ahead as planned," Pierce said. "Force Rasputin from the underground to fight German troops. Then, we initiate Bishop and—"

"Give the Germans a noble sacrifice," Bishop said and all eyes were on him.

"That is our course," Winston said. "And it looks like we have little time to change it. Generals Foch and Haig do not care for our venture, and if not for the Society's influence they would have ignored the possibility we have created. They still believe they can win this war without us and are march toward Berlin. Haig tried a final attempt to reach a conclusion. It was victorious, but bloody. The casualties are enormous. In fact, that is the only reason we've been kept alive. The prime minister wants the war over sooner and with less casualties than Haig's vision."

"If the Germans are firmly guided by a true warlord," Dr. Oshikawa said, "then I doubt they will give in until there is no other visible choice. Even if their position is a mere house of cards, they will protect it against all odds."

"These are grim tidings," Winston said. "But I concur, Doctor. Which is why I've begun Operation Phoenix. Today."

"Operation Phoenix?" Vasilya said.

The doctor smiled. "I suggested it might be fitting."

But Pierce bit his lip, shaking his head.

"A problem, Captain?"

"No. A thousand problems. Nothing's been tested. Bishop has never ridden in the damn thing, and we've had to jerry-rig him to the contraption to keep him alive. The doc and the kid haven't even begun work on the armaments, armour, or mobility problems."

"That is why I did not come alone. Help is on the way, shortly."

"Shortly? With the operation already in effect?" Pierce said.

"It would not be the cavalry if it arrived early," Winston said. "He's had to take a special train and vessel, so he did not come with me. He's been working on the issues you mentioned and is arriving with solutions."

"Who is it?" Dr. Oshikawa asked.

"And spoil the surprise?" Winston said, aghast.

"This is hardly the time for childish humour," she said. "If we are to make any progress at an efficient rate, we must be in the know. Sir."

"Fine. I was hoping you'd enjoy the surprise more."

The buzzer sounded.

"Aha!" Winston said, jumping out of his seat, fist jutting the air. "He caught the earlier ship. I shall have my surprise and you shall have your answers. Come now!"

They marched to the door.

Vasilya looked back at Bishop.

"Unless it's the Virgin Mary doing a floor show, I'll stay."

The three adults scampered off.

She sat next to him, the battery between them. "Are you in pain?"

He sighed, face steered toward the Juggernaut. "Nope."

"Do you … do you think you can stop this Rasputin?"

He shrugged. "If the past few months have hammered one lesson into what's left of my so-called brain, it's that anything is possible. But the horrific is almost always more likely." He lowered his head. "Not aching to see who the mystery saviour is this time?"

"I'll find out soon enough."

"And then we'll be on the road to Judgement Day." He snickered. "Or at least I will. Not sure what you ladies will be doing when I stumble back to Rasputin's hive to give it a hard kick, playing some white knight for the goddamn Germans." He shook his head.

"I've also been on the battlefield," she said, walking to face the Juggernaut. "You're going to do something heroic, Bishop. Maybe you can do what we couldn't."

"What the hell was that?"

She touched the jagged mouth. "Stop the war."

"Just get me near my brother, and I'll do what you want, before I go to hell."

"You … believe in hell?"

"I have one foot it in it now."

She touched the seat inside the maw. "And heaven?"

"That's for angels."

The main door creaked open again, and a swarm of soldiers surrounded the team. But at the lead was a massive wheelchair with a small man inside it.

The chair was fascinating: thick rubber tires, and Vasilya could hear the whirl of an engine as the wheelchair approached, and a loud, clear voice.

"It is now or never," Winston said. "We raise the Phoenix tonight and ship out tomorrow or the project is dead."

In the chair sat a frail man in a brown suit and moustache, hands in his lap like a child or an old lady. His eyes were wide and his countenance expressive as they approached, though a scar on his forehead blemished his kind face. "Jane? Is that it? My glasses."

A young woman at his side, with a pretty face but rather ugly hands, placed a pair of glasses on his face, adjusted them, and he gasped. "It is. And it's just as I thought it would look. You can see the automaton parts leaping up at you. Fabergé was a master of deception as well as beauty."

Vasilya's folded her arms. How the hell could he know that?

The procession approached closer. "I knew it," the man said. "I knew Fabergé and Balk would try this approach and I cannot believe it worked with a human heart. It must have cost Balk greatly. It took me years to forge something similar for the Society, and they scarcely had my genius."

Her face went ashen as the man in the wheelchair's eyes flirted to her. "You." He scrutinized. "You must be Vasilya Savorov."

"Vasilya," Dr. Oshikawa said. "This is Mr. Herbert George Wells."

She looked at Bishop, but his attention was still galvanized with the coffin of his future.

Vasilya walked slowly to the man in the chair. Who looked her up and down in a rather ungentle manner.

"Sir," Vasilya said. "But ... you were—."

"Let's just say the assassin's bullet was sharper than his aim, but crueler than his intent." And she saw what he meant. The scar was a bullet wound, just below the hairline. His body was withered away, all but his face and his intense eyes. "So much beauty in the world and I can only caress it with my eyes."

Jane slapped his head. "Don't forget yourself, George."

Winston laughed. "We thought it best to let Berlin think they'd succeeded in full measure, allowing us the advantage of surprise."

"So I've been dead to the world for years," Wells said, pain slowly leaving his face. "But let's get on with the show, right? Pressing business, and all that. Let's take a look at the Juggernaut." The pain of the slap retreated as they rolled toward the machine. "The Germans were right to try and kill me when this war started, child. I once had talents like yours. We are a rare breed. I wished old Darwin was still with us to explain it, though I have my theories—"

"Focus, George," Jane said. "Focus."

"Absolutely right, my love. This is the command capsule. I assume you used the wiring from the Flute Player to hook up your pilot ... Jane, please turn me."

They followed the cables to Bishop, who looked as rotten as he had before Wells appeared.

Wells smiled. "You must be Private Warren Bishop, Canadian Corps."

"And you are?"

"You're a mite young for a private."

"And you're a tad young for a cripple chair."

Wells became stern. "Rather brooding sort, isn't he? But I guess being an orphan of evolution for as long as you have would be. I'm H. G. Wells."

Warren grunted. "Can't remember you. Did you write *Tarzan*?"

"Shut it, Bishop," Pierce said.

Well's face went cold with anger. "Burroughs? That cheap pulp scribbler wrote … fantasy nonsense, children's daydreams and young boy wishes."

Bishop snorted. "You upset rather easy, but I guess being crippled for as long as you have, it's only natural."

Well's face went from white to tomato red.

"Temper, George." Jane said, a smile on her face.

For Vasilya, it was an uncanny and uncomfortable scene. Dr. Oshikawa put her hand on her shoulder. "Gentleman, we do not have time for this game of wits. Mr. Wells, please, continue explaining our course of action."

He stretched out his neck, and looked down his nose at Bishop, who shook his head. "Wise course of action, Dr. Oshikawa. We're lucky to have a level-headed engineer among us. Jane, please, to the front of the table." She wheeled him and they all sat, Winston on Well's right, Pierce on his left. Jane stood behind him. Dr. Oshikawa sat with Vasilya. Bishop was carved of stone, glaring back at the Juggernaut, disembodied from all that was said.

"As I told you, Vasilya," Wells said, "I had a talent like yours. Though much greater." Sadness and not pride twined his face. "I still have it, of course. The bullet in my skull did not … cripple that part of my being. It swells in me like a tempest in a teapot. The headaches of wonder almost consume me."

Jane rested her hand on his shoulder, and he leaned into it for a hard second, then focused. "While I'm a prisoner of this body, I believe my talent might find use in the hands of one as gifted as you. I've been working on a means of transference. Jane?" From the back of the wheel chair she took an iron helmet with no visor and placed it on the table. Then, another with a faceplate. "The metal is from an ore found in a meteorite, brought back from Africa by Sir Richard Burton himself for one of the Society's projects. Its full properties are not known. One is an amplifier, the other a receiver."

"What is it amplifying and receiving?"

His eyebrow raised. "My talent. My thoughts. At least that's what the test subject said."

"And where's he?" Bishop said.

Wells buttoned his lip. Winston walked over to Vasilya. "I will not cast illusions upon you. The boy went mad."

"But he had no talent!" Wells said. "I told you that was the risk. It would be like trying to plug a socket into a man's brain."

"Or heart," Bishop said.

"Last warning," Pierce muttered.

Winston's eyes never left Vasilya. "I told you I would not force you to join us. You can leave. We can try and find another way."

"I'll do it," Dr. Oshikawa said. "I may not have the talent, but I have both the skill and the mind for building the Phoenix."

"How I wish that were true," Wells said, dirty eyes on her until Jane yanked his ear.

"No," Vasilya. "I will do it." She walked over to Bishop and looked down as he looked up. "A rather poor hand has been dealt to you. But I won't let you play it alone. Hold still."

He did.

She caressed the shock button in the back of his neck—

There was a hiss. Smoke rose from Bishop's head.

Captain Pierce stood. "Kid—"

"He may not have the option of leaving," she said. "But I won't torture him."

A small twinge of relief fell on Bishop's face. "Thanks, Angel."

"Excellent," Wells said, bringing attention back to himself. "If this works, we'll do in a night what would take months. My team is already assembling parts of the project, and as soon as they're done, we may begin." He smiled, curling his moustache.

It was lonely, even with the ghosts, though Warren had harboured a secret wish they'd been burned out of him by the nurse's lightning touch. Jones and Heath showed up, then vanished. But the army of shadows grew as his memory sifted away

But if Bishop focused on the black abyss inside the Juggernaut, they stayed on the periphery. Even they wouldn't hazard the space between his eyes and this dark unknown. He just stared as the world made plans around him, until Vasilya broke his vision with a moment of sacrifice he wished she didn't have to make.

Then they were off, making plans elsewhere in a work room, the prison becoming a mechanical clock of men and crates.

A ghost sat down and started talking.

"Captain wanted me to see if you had anything else to add."

It was Gavin. The Loo who'd been debriefing him. He had one arm in a sling, and a shiner the size of a mule kick.

"Jesus, what happened to you?"

"From the jailbreak. Two came at me."

"Looks like you fought like a rabid mongoose."

"Who knew the son of a pastor could be so fierce?" He smiled, but it was void of pride or joy. "So, looks like we're rushing spearheaded toward the operation."

"Yup."

"Did you see our ... guest?"

"The asshole on wheels."

"It's something else, huh? I've read everything he's done. Loved *The Time Machine*. Gives me some hope."

The name of the book was familiar. "Why?"

He looked sheepish at his pad, tapping it with a pen. "There's that scene, where the traveler's gone far into the future, so far human beings are nothing but dust, a wild and strange world of red sand and strange stars."

"Sounds depressing."

"Except of course that it was a man who went to the future to see it, to show us." He stopped tapping his pencil. "Look, they are apparently going to be quick, is there anything else you'd like to add?"

"Like a last will and testament?"

"If that's how you see it."

"No other way to see it." He gritted his teeth then tapped the buzzer in his neck. A slight hiss, but no more annoying than a mosquito bite. "So you're letting me write my own tombstone. Fair enough." He coughed politely into his hand. "Ahem. 'Here lies Warren Bishop. Remittance man and coward.'" He was surprised as hell to find Gavin actually writing it down.

"You're a poet, Warren Bishop." Gavin's boots echoed away as a scurry of more came along, gathered around Wells like a wizard in a storybook. What magic he had, they awaited to see. But instead of excitement, it was fear in their eyes, and Vasilya was sterner than a train wreck.

She approached her owl, Merlin, who was sleeping on a crate but awoke with a hoot as she approached. She lay a tin of bully beef at its talons and said something in Russian that sounded sad, but, Warren thought, most things do.

"So," Bishop said. "Do you want me out of here while you work your magic?"

"I'd prefer it," Wells said, "but you are needed here. When we are done, you'll be one with the machine."

Warren flicked the cables. He stood, saluted Pierce lazily, and then sat in the maw of the Juggernaut. "Let's go win a war."

CHAPTER FORTY-SIX:

BASTARD PROMETHEUS

The helmet was heavy and sat on her shoulder with a pained anchor. Her breath was loud and annoying and tasted of copper, so she breathed through her nose and was already hot and stuffy. But it was extraordinary, to be surrounded by the metal of the stars. What wonders were its properties? she supposed, and knew she'd find out soon enough.

Around them were cartons of materiel, lids freshly cracked, all brought in by Wells's silent men in thick hats and thicker arms, with almost the countenance of Bishop. Everyone eased when they retreated back to their cars outside. Inside the crates lay the armaments

"Ready?" Wells said. Behind him stood ashen faces, but the one that steadied her was Dr. Oshikawa.

You are brave, my musume, she had said when they'd had a moment alone. And strong. And very talented. But do not let this work consume you. I do not fully trust Mr. Wells, nor anyone here save Churchill and perhaps Captain Pierce, not after the break in security. Be cautious. Do your duty. But do not … sacrifice yourself.

Her eyes were sterner still through the visor of the helmet.

"I am ready, Mr. Wells."

"Good child. Stand back, the rest of you. There will be forces unleashed that might hurt if you get too close. Vasilya, close your eyes. And open your mind, like you would reaching out for a current, or a dynamo, or even a simple gear."

She did. The darkness was complete.

But not for long.

A bright spot appeared, a diamond swimming in the midnight depths of the helmet. Then another, then another.

"Do you see the distant stars?" Wells said from outside.

"Yes … it's astounding." They multiplied more until there were a hundred pinpricks of light and she might as well have been swimming in space. There was a depth beyond the metal. Was this the map the meteor used as it traveled the dark heavens?

The white line crisscrossed the heavens and connected the dots of stars, and it coalesced into the shape of a hand. A hand made of stars.

"Now, child," Wells's voice echoed throughout the heavens, kindly but firm. "Make your own. Concentrate."

She did, focusing on a single star that burst like a comet and touched others, weaving a pattern like her hand on drawing paper and blue ink, the design of a hand, just like the one before her.

"Excellent," Wells said. "You're more talented than I could have hoped. Now, take my hand. Let us work together."

The crowd, including Warren, were transfixed by the site. Between the two was a wave of purple light, a shimmering mist that connected them just as Warren was connected to the Juggernaut. Vasilya turned, and her wings snapped out of her back. She hovered before the Juggernaut.

"What an extraordinary creature," Wells's tin voice said from his sightless helmet. "Are you all right?"

"Yes," she said. "I can … see what you want to make."

"Excellent! Then there is no time to waste. We shall make this Juggernaut a Phoenix!"

Static and fear gripped them as machines rose from their crates and floated toward the Juggernauts.

"Telekinesis?" Dr. Oshikawa said, to Churchill, who nodded.

"But a sliver of his old ability," he said, meaning "stopped dead by a single bullet. Until now."

Then, a force gripped Warren out of his wonder and carried him from his gurney. "Easy."

Then it steadied. "I've got you," Vasilya said. "Mr. Wells, we don't need to place him just yet."

"Quite right."

Warren dropped like lead and crashed into the gurney.

The capsule tore itself apart with a crack as new wood, new metal, new screws and servos, wires and cables floated in the air and melded themselves into a new one, almost as if each substance was a different kind of liquor being poured into the other for a cocktail strong as white lightning. The old seat shook out of the capsule, replaced with a larger one, and with it the control sticks and pedals.

A pragmatic thought cut through the wonder swimming in Warren's head: how the hell am I going to steer this boat without all that gear?

Hand in hand amidst the stars, Vasilya and the old man weaved a tapestry like the design Dr. Oshikawa had made. It was less clunky than the Juggernaut, more human and less tank, but laced with all the implements of misery that modern arms could provide. Most were to be expected. Mortars with shells, dual machine guns in the arms, a store of fragmentation grenades, and flame thrower. But the shell of the creature was dull, as if coated in a weird mesh.

"The outer shell and cables are coated with fire retardant salves," Wells said before she could ask about the strange sheen. "So that if our hero does get in trouble, he may douse himself in flame for protection against unwanted attack."

To ward off the swarms of Rasputin's men, Vasilya realized. And there was more. Cables with prongs attached to the electro-generator. For shooting the lightning that could incapacitate Bishop's fellow draugs.

Glittering in the dark heaven, it seemed mythic, a creature torn out of the lost pages of Daedalus or Archimedes himself, some ragged son of Athena or Mars ...

And it was becoming real.

She could feel the harmony of parts welded from blueprint to reality, a complex mosaic twining itself into a whole from a thousand moving parts. An effortless act. So simple and flawless it was intoxicating. Mr. Well's mind was an astonishing thing, gilded genius.

"Oh it is so good to be free again," he said, "to create."

The Phoenix was almost complete.

And she spoke to him with her thoughts, silent to the rest of the waking world. "Mr. Wells ... can they hear us?"

"Not now," he said. "We're communicating through the helmet's frequencies."

Good, she thought. I'd hate to have to explain this. "I'd like to add a compartment."

The star grip on her hand tightened. "No need, young one. It is complete."

"But ... there needs to be a failsafe. A secondary ... pilot. Should Bishop require assistance."

"Tacking on David to Goliath?"

"That would be the goal, yes."

"And who might that David be?"

"Me," she said without hesitation. "I can't let Bishop face this horror alone. No one should."

"Putting yourself in the line of fire would increase risk, weight, and danger to the mission. Besides, you are valuable alive."

Her voice hardened. "It is my life to do as I chose."

"That's what I was afraid you'd say." The grip became ice, silencing her thoughts in pain. "Do know that I am crushed and sorry about this, child. The world needs me. The greater good requires me whole, my abilities intact. While I would have found a man more comfortable, I am intrigued by you. Your talents are strong, if embryonic, but these wings of yours make up for your novice status."

The stars swirled, and a vortex of celestial shrapnel swung around her.

She lashed back with lightning but it scattered across the spinning walls.

"Brave, but futile." Black string webbed around her mind like tar, killing the blast. "This world needs me more than you, but with me taking your body and talent I will give them both. In the end, I'll give them more than you could ever have done. And there is no way I will risk that by being the secondary pilot on a suicide mission."

Arcs of pain cut through her mind, riding the black web.

The blazing set of armour before them stood twenty feet tall, its barrel chest of steel and cable open to reveal where the cables in Bishop's chest were going.

But his eyes were elsewhere.

A stitch of current burst from the battery, Bishop noticed. Vasilya's hands bunched up. Warren kept his eye on Wells.

"Vasilya," Dr. Oshikawa said. "Are you all right?"

Vasilya's wings fluttered but she remained silent, then her hands twitched again. And Wells's immobile hands flickered.

"Son of a bitch," Warren said. "He's doing it. Get those helmets off, now!"

The cable reared up like a serpent, and smashed Warren down amongst the onlookers, then dragged him back to the wall.

Bishop fought with the live cables as if they were black pythons gnawing at his heart, and in a single, brutal jerk tore them off.

Energy sapped out of him like air from a balloon.

Now, go now, keep moving.

He charged over the table as the crowd got to its feet. Bearing down, he flew in the air like Tik had taught him.

"Don't! Stop!" Churchill screamed. "Don't touch him or—"

But Bishop was too far gone.

He slammed into the old man, bones crunching under his weight, toppling him over.

Warren gripped the helmet with both hands.

A blast of infinite rushed through his brain and he saw Wells's black hands strangling an electric angel in the centre of a hurricane. He stumbled into the vortex, and caught his attention.

"Miserable colonial," Wells's steam-like form screamed.

"Dirty old shit!" He charged and slammed into something harder than steel.

"Pathetic as you are inadequate. This war cannot be won by a single act of heroism. It needs men of quality to make it work if you fail, and sacrifices must be made. I'm sorry to do this, young lady. But the time has come to—NO!"

The stars were swallowed by darkness.

Vasilya dropped but her wings came alive before she hit the ground. She tore off the helmet.

Everyone was picking themselves up.

All but Jane.

She had Wells's helmet in her gloved hands.

"Get Bishop hooked up before his heart falls out!" Pierce screamed as two guards dragged his body to the cables he'd pulled out of himself. "You okay, kid?"

Vasilya nodded, but flew over Wells, who was screaming at his wife. "Why the bloody hell did you do that?"

She said nothing, only brought up his chair, fixed his clothing, and endured his screams of rage until he seemed spent. Then she looked up at Vasilya with wonder, who finally landed. Dr. Oshikawa kneeled before Vasilya, checking her pulse and temperature. "Did he hurt you?"

"He tried."

"Fools," Wells said, glaring at his withered legs. "Winston, you and your lot are damned. This mission is useless without me, without what I can bring to the table. When the Queen hears of this, the Society will have you all locked up for crimes against the order of things!"

Winston's face was stern as a bulldog before growling. "What good capital you have with me is spent, and our Queen may owe you much but not a free hand to ruin what we've created. I do not think we will be requiring your services again, Mr. Wells. Plane, boat, or cast him in the sea, so long as his visage is gone!"

Jane nodded, and turned him around.

"How dare you!" Wells shouted. "You've made a dangerous enemy today, Winston. I will remember this!"

"I apologize for my husband's behaviour," Jane said in a nasally voice. "He can be such a baby."

"Don't call me that!" Wells screamed.

"I'll be sure to take care of him. Sorry for the hassle."

They stood in hard silence until Jane pushed him toward the door, Wells's screams ricocheting around the room until the prison door had them stifled. Then Winston strode before Vasilya, anger and bitterness focused on the prison door. He laid a hand on her shoulder, smelling of smoke from distant woods. Then he gazed up at the machine. "I fear I must bear more bad news."

"My mother is dead." She steeled herself. "Because of what I did. Not going with that spy—"

His face tensed. "She died a month ago under house arrest. That Bolshevik who tried to steal you was armed with only lies, and hurtful ones at that. If you had gone, you would have found more of the same. Regardless, I am so sorry, my dear, that a loved one should meet such a cruel fate, so far from the tides of battle." He gripped her shoulder hard once. Then turned to the machine. "My god, it stands as righteous as the armour of a crusading knight. You have done an incredible thing."

"Hardly," Vasilya said, the shock of the moment barely holding her together. "We have. The blueprints were Dr. Oshikawa's. Wells made the most of it, though I could see the pattern before me like a diagram in movement. But the burden is largely Bishop's." She walked toward him.

They'd placed him in a chair, cables in his chest again, eyes fluttering open.

"Sorry," he said.

"For what?"

"For losing your mother. For not killing the bastard. For not saving you myself. Some track record for a war hero, huh?" He laughed.

Vasilya gripped his still smoking hands. "If you hadn't interceded, he would have killed me and taken what was mine. You did save me, Bishop."

He whistled. "Score one for the underdog."

She smiled, then turned to Winston and Dr. Oshikawa. "The Phoenix suit is complete. But I believe it needs an addition."

"What kind?" Dr. Oshikawa asked, and her face turned to sadness when Vasilya told her.

"The kind that will house a co-pilot."

CHAPTER FORTY-SEVEN:

BATTLE'S EVE

Warren was too sick and weak to do much arguing, and knowing the utter conviction in the kid's eyes, it wouldn't have done much good.

Vasilya was going to ride piggyback into battle.

It was entertaining to see Churchill argue with her and lose. More painful was Dr. Oshikawa's quiet compliance.

There was a pain in that woman's face as they built the final elements of the compartment, doubling as an escape hatch, because it appeared Vasilya had done the lion's share of the work while still tied to the wicked bastard Wells.

The doctor treated her not only as an apprentice, as a colleague, but as family. There was a kind authority and concern in her questions and movements that Warren longed to have at a different stage in his life. Instead of memories of broken bottles, harsh discipline, and the sting of constant wraps across the knuckles and bottom.

The rest of the team packed things, organizing for their removal from Fort Daedalus. All Warren could do was wait for the strength to return to his deadroot heart.

"Oh fuck."

Pierce walked over, grabbed a chair, and sat in it backwards, arms crossed on the back rest. "Ready to make history?"

"If this is the opening to a coach's inspirational speech, you can cram it, Cap. I know what I have to do. Vasilya and the doc briefed me. Once they flick the main switch, I'm basically one with the machine. My legs will be its legs, my arms … well, my arm will be there. They said the signals from my brain should still move the left arm, which is pretty much all I could ask for."

"Well, you got it all figured out, don't you?"

"I did read the *Harmsworth Self-educator*." He brought up two fingers. "Twice."

Pierce smiled. "Well, no good deed goes unpunished. Here." He tossed

Tik's shark tooth necklace. "Seemed to come in handy last time you were in thick of it. Would be hard pressed to keep it to myself. Though I suspect I'll be needing luck."

"Oh great, you're coming too?"

"Me and my unit. Half are already in the thick of it. They've been ferreting out Rasputin in the wake of the offensive against the Hindenburg line. Apparently, the Lost Battalion has gathered under the city of Cambrai. And the Germans are poised to counterattack your fabled Canadian Corps. So, we'll be rejoining your unit."

"Huzzah."

"Jesus, Bishop. We're on the eve of victory and you look like I just shit on your birthday cake." If we pull this off—"

"I'm going out there to save my brother, and to take myself out of creation before ..."

"Before what?"

The shadows around him shook their heads in disgust at him.

Warren shook his head.

Pierce nodded. "Suit yourself. I'm a coach, not a nursemaid. Do your duty, Bishop, and I'll do mine." He bowed to the two women, then stopped halfway down the hall. "Call to arms for the First Marine Airborne Division!"

Vasilya inhaled deep and long at the sight of Warren inside the chest of the Phoenix. He sat on a form-fitting chair, hand on a control rod, feet strapped into pedals that would allow his movements to become those of the machine. The Phoenix was more human than the Juggernaut, but armed as it was to the gills and back, it still looked like a titan come to earth to bring God's vengeance. Her hands flexed in and out of fists. "Are you ready?"

"Flick it," he said.

She nodded, and closed the hatch. The gears wound and sealed shut.

Dr. Oshikawa pressed the ignition in his back.

Whirl turned the dust into a storm that cleared as Vasilya covered her eyes.

"Holy shit," Bishop said, his voice a static charged klaxon call.

"Are you ok?"

The machine nodded. "Wait, did I just do that?"

"You're tapped into the main nervous system," Dr. Oshikawa said.

"Damn. This is tripping the light fantastic and no fooling."

"Take a step forward," said the doctor.

The room shook slightly as he did, far more gracefully than Felix had.

"Another."

The Phoenix walked the room like a fairytale giant who'd been in bed too long. Legs stiff, but knowing what it wanted. Not unsteady, like a baby. It was almost too good to be true.

"Excellent," the doctor said. "Now, raise your right arm."

He did, turning it, opening a four-fingered hand of steel and iron.

"Now," Dr. Oshikawa said. "The left."

The head turned; the padded shoulder shrugged.

"Goddamn it," Bishop's mechanical voice said.

"Concentrate," Vasilya said.

"That's what I'm doing! I can feel it … but the bastard won't move."

"This is unacceptable," Dr. Oshikawa said. "The weapon system is designed for optimal use with both arms."

The Phoenix turned and stared down the doctor. "You think I like the idea of going into a gunfight with one hand tied behind my back, then you're nuts."

"Play time is over, kids," Pierce ran down to the commons, dressed with full pack, rifle, and more knives than Vasilya wanted to see on a single person. "We are leaving. Now."

"What?" Dr. Oshikawa said. "Impossible. We haven't even initiated the weapons system."

"Then do it and get that tin man out on the tarmac!" he screamed. "We've got to move. Rasputin's men have just attacked the German army north of Cambrai. We are leaving. Now." He looked at Vasilya. "Last chance to stay home and play with your owl, kid."

Vasilya walked over to Merlin. "So long, my friend. I wish I'd had time to fix you." She blinked. "But you seem pretty happy the way you are, don't you?"

Merlin blinked.

"Enjoy hunting the mice and rats here." She walked over to Dr. Oshikawa, who placed both hands on her shoulder. "To find you and lose you in such a short span … fate often plays cruel, *musume*."

Vasilya's eyes misted. "I'd endure it all again. To meet him. And you."

Dr. Oshikawa embraced her with the kind of warmth and safety only a mother could provide, the kind that breaks your heart to leave. She gave her a fierce squeeze, then broke it. The doctor wiped her face clean of tears, put a warm sweater on Vasilya, then helped her into the iron cabinet on the back of the Phoenix.

Vasilya looked down.

"Good luck, my daughter. Come home to me."

The lid descended with the vent of steam that covered her words. "I'll try."

Dr. Oshikawa pulled the armament switch. Bishop's voice seethed inside the Phoenix like a voice in a tin cup. "Good god, I feel covered in spikes. Jesus."

Vasilya strapped herself in as he moved forward, then reached out with her mind to the machine's nervous system and saw the world from a vantage point both perfect and inhuman.

Pierce's voice crackled inside the Phoenix. "Let's move, Bishop. Any smart words before we hit the battlefield?"

Bishop grunted. "I'm … running out of words."

Pierce opened the loading bay door and washed them in grey sunlight. "Then allow me. 'Cry "Havoc!", and let slip the dogs of war.'"

Bishop walked, only it wasn't him, it was the tin can the size of a house that he'd become. Periscopes for eyes and saw the world in a rounder fashion, yet it was no worse than stumbling home from the tavern three sheets to the wind, and so he'd found each step easier than the last. And each step was majestic for its solidity, its finality. Warren had walked without his heart close, but moved with the strength of a hundred metal men in his limbs, except for his accursed left arm which was as limp as a dead dog. "You all right, Angel?"

"Yes," she said, her voice soft in his ears as if there were one of her standing on each side of him.

They walked out of main doors. The main approach to the prison was now a tarmac where three planes, each almost as big as a blimp, sat with chains attached to their fuselage. Gavin and two crew members held the chains' ends: massive hooks. "You're a real pioneer, Bishop!" Gavin screamed. "Do you know how many records you must be breaking today?"

"The only thing I'm breaking today is Rasputin's neck. Then Alex. Let us finish it."

They hooked him in a triangle formation on his back. Then Pierce and two other men in flight gear, goggles, and backpacks appeared. "We're going to hit the ground hot, understand?" Pierce said. "No remorse. No retreat. We do it, or we don't come back. You see the red lever between your thighs?"

Warren and the Phoenix nodded.

"If they bunch up, tie you down, yank that son of a bitch and get ready for a funeral pyre. Any questions?"

Warren shook his head. Then looked at Gavin. "Do me a favour. Write my mother. Tell her I tried."

Gavin nodded. "Tried what?"

Pierce slapped Warren's dead left arm. "Let's take to the sky. Roll out!" Each of them hopped into the modified two seats of the plane. The propellers hiccupped then sputtered to life.

"I think you'll do better if you kneel," Vasilya said. "Try and skate on your heels."

Warren bent. "Smart kid. You ever gone flying?"

"Only by myself. I don't know if I trust those contraptions." The engines revved and the Sopwith Camels shook.

"Hold on, Angel. I'll do whatever I can to get you out of here alive." The planes shot off dragging them like a boulder to the edge.

The sky was another world.

They tore into the clouds as she held her breath, then held herself in the wool sweater Dr. Oshikawa had given her, for cold bit with the strength of pincers and she cultivated what warmth she could.

The world she had known dissolved below her as a weightless sensation rose. From her own periscope she saw only grey—

Then majestic sunlight!

They had pierced where it had been hidden and here, where the light was both orange and pink, but morning and dawn, she watched the shape of clouds like a sea of gentle cotton, twisting and bending into shapes while the planes dragged them on.

Mother once said we only see what we want to see in such images. That they only reveal what's in the heart.

Vasilya looked away. Her heart had been sore so long … but she peered into the white softness.

Felix and herself. Dancing.

Amidst the wonder, the grandeur of sunshine in heaven, amid the brief respite from the hell they were racing toward, the absence of ghosts that gave Warren peace …

A tremor bit in his heart. Sweat filled his mouth.

And fear was on him like a pox.

Fuck … I'm hungry.

CHAPTER FORTY-EIGHT:

REUNION

Dragged through the sky for buzzing aeons, the clouds finally broke and they could see the battlefields below and Vasilya moved her periscope.

From the sky, it was a sickening sight. Hideous. A dead world of black earth and craters, cracked roads and ruined fields, grey streams, and obliterated forests with the dead husks of their former lush, green glory standing like lonely sentries on the hills of gloom.

Graveyard for a generation.

This is what the survivors will inherit, Vasilya thought. This is what we'll have to build upon. If I survive ... don't think about it. The future is a daydream, and we are too awake to wonder about it. God, here I am, flying above France, and with my own wings at rest ... I have also seen the astounding amidst the ashes. But must it come at such a catastrophic price? Or are those just Tom Swift daydreams before they become modern nightmares?

She watched the trail of battle cut across the earth and hoped she was wrong. That perhaps hope could be built upon tragedy.

The hunger wasn't strong, Warren thought. Certainly not the rabid kind he'd felt before. Maybe it was the machine part of him now. Half a man, half the hunger. It was crapshoot logic, but it was all he had, sailing the sky like a tin can in a crow's grip, dragged through heaven's majesty before being dumped in hell.

Just keep it under control, he thought. I don't even want to think of what I'll do with this body if I need to feed. What the hell could stop me ...

"Bishop?"

"Yes, Angel."

"Look to the north ... what is that?"

It looked like a swarm of ants on a dead carcass above scarred terrain. "The Canadian Corps, I think. Ready for a counterattack."

"What does that mean?"

He snorted. Then tried to move his left arm. Nothing, "It means we're almost there."

The planes weaved hard up into the clouds again, no doubt for surprise. "Better hold on tight, Angel. Not sure how low they're going to dump us but I suspect my landing will not be a thing of art."

"I've taken recoil precautions," she said, and pistons steamed back and forth like an artillery gun. "I will be ok."

Cutting through the air, Warren thought, No you won't, but I appreciate the lie.

Machine gun fire slashed through the stillness and the Phoenix swung in the air like a marionette in the hands of a rummy three days from his next drink.

Black shadows in the air cut through with the sound of hornets.

"German Fokkers!" Bishop said. "And we're swinging here like a sitting duck! Some welcome from the shit heels we're supposed to be saving." The chains jerked them around in every which way, stability giving way to dizziness. "Hold on, Angel!"

They raced through the air, dipping and weaving as the rattling sound of a machine gun peppered the air until it hit metal—

The lead plane.

Pierce.

The old dog had his rifle in hand, and fired at the screaming tri-winged birds soaring away, while the fuselage leaked clear fluids through a pockmarked skin.

Shit, Warren thought. There's no way he can hit—

Another single shot cracked out, and the familiar scream of a downed plane filled the sky as a Fokker spiraled down with a stream of black. The captain screamed something into his pilot's ear, then faced the two side planes as machine gun fire tore through him in a red, misty burst ... but the son of a bitch cracked off one more shot before descending off the plane.

Another scream of a diving Fokker.

The Phoenix fell and tore as the two Camels attempted to drag its too-heavy load.

"They're not letting us go," Bishop said as they swung wild. "Stupid shits, we'll drag them into the ground."

"Bishop! I think I see—"

A sickening subterranean scream flared in the air. He didn't need to be told twice. Ahead of them was the German army, tiny ants being crushed by a thrashing worm—

"That's ... that's ..." Vasilya said.

Bishop gritted his teeth. "Charger. Hold on, Angel. Time for this Phoenix to fight."

At first, she had no idea what he was doing, too captivated by the gargantuan white creature that dove through the Germans like a dead white train the size and thickness of a hundred elephants. Bigger than it had been before and more hideous.

"It just wasted a brigade," Bishop said. "Our good and bad luck is running out."

The gauntleted right hand of the Phoenix rose and crushed the chain in its mitt. They fell, dragging the remaining plane with them.

"Bishop! Your left arm!"

"Still can't move it," he screamed to the pilot through the Klaxon. "Can you?"

A gasp and weightlessness flooded Vasilya and stretched her own wings as the chains snapped free and they fell, a silver torpedo, aimed right at the monster that had taken Felix away from her. Faster than cannon shot, they descended. The recoil gauges went haywire, and she knew … the impact would—

"Angel…" Bishop said. "This landing is going to be ugly if you can't get a hold of this arm. Maybe it's better you should fly back—"

"No. I won't run. I won't fly." She gripped the controls, and reached out to the nervous system of the Phoenix. "I'll be your left arm."

"Ok, kid. Let's try it your way."

"Form a ball for maximum impact!"

Bishop did, and she followed, and the Phoenix plunged.

"God save us," she said. "Because physics will not be kind." She felt the strange link with the machine that was also Bishop, and how the flow and strength ended at an iron rut that was his left arm. She reached out to it, felt its strength, then snapped the chain above its hand.

They fell, weightless, and screaming—

The periscope filled with a white worm. It charged for them before a righteous blow knocked her through windows of darkness.

A horrific yawp filled the air as the Phoenix's arms and side tore into the rotting flesh of Charger, the impact as violent as Bishop had ever faced, but blunted by the solidly built machine and his long dead flesh.

"Angel? Kid?"

They'd torn down the side of it, slicing a grey gash that made the creature belch violently, and landed like a shell into the ground, buried up to his right shoulder. He couldn't move it any more than he could tunnel to the heart of the earth with a spoon. The left arm was sticking out and dead as a coffin nail.

"Angel?" Bishop said, then grunted. "Oh hell, Angel? You awake?"

The worm reared its head up, giant mouth a vortex filled with grey talon-teeth, leading to its gullet. It howled like storm winds in Port Arthur.

"Angel! Wake up! Jesus Christ, snap out of it!"

But she was stone cold out of it.

He tore his eye form the periscope. He was locked in tight, and didn't even know how to get out. All around him electrical equipment sparked at his ear as a cable arced with electric current.

Shit, he thought. Maybe this will work.

He turned his neck quick and jammed the buzzer still under his skin into a protruding, sparking bolt—

White fire ran in his nerves.

"Ffffffffffffuck!"

A noose of current dragged her from the embrace of sleep to hear Bishop screaming. "Arm up! Angel, get the arm up and fire!"

Dazed, she fought to connect with the machine—

"Now!"

She focused, then stared through the bubble world of the periscope: the hideous maw of the beast descended. The connection solidified, and the mighty left arm shot up.

Machine gun bursts shredded through the air with thousands of rounds, forcing the creature's head to dive besides them and burrow a fresh tunnel into the earth, shaking them free before the creature launched up again. Vasilya's guts watered, but she saw the right arm of the Phoenix come free.

"Hold on!" Bishop said, and the iron claw of the Phoenix's right hand gripped the roots of a blasted tree and yanked. The Phoenix emerged from its prison of dirt and mud, scrambled to its legs as the earth shimmied and shook like the earth was birthing a fresh and hellish quake.

"Nice shooting," Warren said. "Get ready though. That bastard's not going to fall in the first round. Hope the Jerries like what they see."

Haze had covered them, made of dirt, debris, and that listless wash of war that turned everything into a dour stain. Bishop moved them away from the fresh crater Charger had made. The air was speckled and thick and the rumbles that had almost crippled his knees subsided down in the deep.

And he saw what had given his legs stability.

A litter of dead soldiers, torn from human form, no more than stains of once-human materials scattered from their original pieces.

All of them German. They'd been fighting the damn creature head-on, its skin like moving battle armour. And they'd be back.

And they looked delicious.

And then he realized how exposed he'd been—

"We're going in the hole," Bishop said, and began running. "Now!"

"Why?"

"Because—"

The scream of shells cut him off as he dove in after the worm and German counter-battery fire wreaked havoc upon their own dead.

Above the lip of the worm hole, a storm of fire raged and the earth rumbled, almost closing its mouth. "What do we do?"

"Hell if I know," he said. "Pierce wasn't exactly a man of detailed battle plans. I do know we can't take on the Lost Battalion and the German army at the same time."

"Should we go after the creature?"

"Down these holes? Not a chance. It will sneak up on us and tear us apart before we can blink. You sprayed its face with lead and that might be the only place it's weak." Jesus, they'd been hitting it with shells and the damn thing was still thrashing them. How the hell are we supposed to lay it to rest?

From the dark corridor, a rumble. "Jonah," she said.

"Kid, my name ain't—"

"Jonah and the whale."

The corridor shook. But his memory was blank. "I don't understand."

"Let it swallow us so we can do a burst of flames on the inside, where the tissue is softest."

"That's insane."

A charging white form came into view. "If you have a brighter idea, Bishop, now would be the time."

From the black corridor, the terrible head of Charger surged from the dark. "All right, but we better make this look good or we'll just die in the crossfire. Ready the damn Phoenix effect you were so proud of and try a blaze of glory."

Bishop stared down the creature, wishing there were another way to save the gas for Rasputin and the boys, but with Charger barreling down on them like a white bullet from the devil's hand, there was no time.

The climbed toward the top of the hole and Charger followed. Bullets crackled against the Phoenix's hide as the wall of fire from the artillery marched beyond them. They gotta see it, Warren told himself, they gotta see this giant mecha man rising from the grave—

And for a second, the peppering of machine guns and sniper shots stopped. Warren gripped the triggers for the gas in his left hand, and the right the sparkers. "Hold tight, Angel. Time to make headlines!"

The white worm roared like a thousand stabbed pigs and chugged at them with the industrial indifference of a runaway train. Mouth wide and gorging, it sprang from the earth and barreled into them—

"Hold on to the lip as long as you can!" Warren said. "They've gotta see us fighting this damn thing!"

Hideous screeches filled the cabin as the razor teeth shredded against the Phoenix's metal, jarring them until the creature swung its head side to side to dislodge them from gripping its mouth and engulf them into the belly.

"I can't hold on much more," Vasilya said while the Phoenix rattled with the cadence of a buggy over a corduroy road. "It's damaging the suit!"

"Let go!"

They were swallowed in darkness and the war muffled beyond the jagged teeth. They borrowed down into the black gullet of the beast, tumbling through thick walls of goo to the echo of hideous gulping that made Warren squeamish.

"All right," he said. "Hitting the gas." Pumps squirted liquid from a hundred holes. The beast shivered. "Time to burn an ulcer into this son of a bitch." He hit the ignition…

Nothing.

They slid further into the creature's belly, toward an oily black chamber. "Hell, no, what the fuck—"

"What's wrong?"

"The ignition switch don't work. The teeth must have shredded it. What about the current? Can't you shock us a spark?"

The black, oily centre of the beast inched closer.

"I'm … trying … no!"

"No, what?"

"It's not connected. Wells … he must have sabotaged it when I fought him."

They lurched further, deeper, lower and the sound of a pulsing gullet reminded Bishop of the fear of the tallow machine the Germans used to turn corpses into oil. He forced the arms of the machine to grip the sides of the beast's slimy flesh. "Then unload the guns, everything we've got that won't bite us back! Go, go!"

Vasilya reached into the machine's central core and rode to the circuit command systems for the weapons. "I'm here."

"Fire!" he screamed.

Both arms burst and shook the Phoenix to the core, unloading storms of led into hideous flesh. The world tumbled back and forth as the beast shook and the cavernous gullet filled with dead meat and fluids, then the corridor went taut. And everything shook.

"He's going to spew us out!" Bishop said. "Hold on!"

A gush of fluid ran from the black centre, firing them out in a fountain of gore. Bishop twisted them so they faced the gooey picture of the beast. "Grenades! Load, now!"

Both arms shot out, facing the creature down as the grenades rolled into their rifle chambers and the beast shot his head up to chomp them again. "Waste him!"

A salvo of grenades rolled out like a stream of tossed apples, some bouncing off his mouth, and some dropping inside.

Vasilya pushed the launcher to move faster, faster, so that all reserves were gone, so the creature who had stolen Felix from her would have one last meal of fire and iron.

"Starve in hell, you monstrous shit!" she screamed in Russian.

Crackling explosions filled the air like a fireworks display as large chunks of worms tore themselves off the hideous hide and the Phoenix descended in a rain of the monster flesh.

Smacking the earth, they bounced twice with a painful, jangling gait before resting on the cracked earth. Amazingly, the impact hadn't killed them: the landing recoiled properly, steam gushing out the vents as the hydraulics in the legs slid and rebounded so they stayed on their feet to watch the death throes of the creature.

"Nice landing," she said.

"Nice shooting," he said.

And Charger thrashed like drunken cobra, black juice spitting from its mouth until it contorted and vomited a grey mass before crashing to the ground before the Phoenix.

For you, Felix, she thought to herself. I hope it brings you some peace.

When the creature finally crashed, a haze of dirt lifted in the air. The smell was like the den of rats set on fire: putrid and unholy "You ok?" Warren said.

"Yes. Are you?"

"Well, we're out of ammunition, and grenades, and are caught between two armies and the bastards who unleashed this critter into the world. But besides that … I'm happier than a pig in shit."

Behind them, the sounds of soldiers on the move. The patter of boots on soggy terrain. And screams not in English. "Here come the goddamn Huns."

They emerged from the haze. Stormtroopers. Flames at the ready, wide-dispersed pattern.

"Let me talk to them," Vasilya said.

"Be my guest. Angel." I hope you know how to move men like you do machines.

She cleared her voice than grabbed the small cone where a microphone lay inside, then willed the klaxon to crackle to life. "Attention, proud soldiers of the Kaiser. We do not come to fight. We have come to help."

The soldiers kept moving, taking positions, but slower.

"Today, we have a common enemy. One that we must unite to defeat. The forces that sent this creature against you, it was not London or Paris, but something more hideous. Something that could destroy us all."

They took positions. He and Angel were sitting ducks. "This isn't working, Angel. We should—"

A hiss of steam, then Warren's jaw dropped as the iron casing that had held her close to the Phoenix's back cracked open. She stood like a target, a microphone held to her lips, spewing out kraut speak he couldn't understand. "Angel. Get the hell back inside!"

If they only saw the Phoenix as a threat, there was no hope. But not if they saw an angel. She ignored the smell of burning flesh and dirt and continued. "Let us be allies. And defeat our common foe, and return to our homes in peace. Follow us to victory." She dropped the microphone, grimaced, and let her wings sprout full in the haze of the morning.

"Angel," Bishop said, "don't do this!"

But it was too late.

She was in the air and every eye was on her. "All right, you superstitious lot," she whispered. "Try and turn down the request of a Valkyrie." She rose in the air as wind swept her hair to the side. "Follow us to victory!" she screamed.

And for the first time, her wings did not hurt, but held her aloft as easy as the wind plays with an autumn leaf—

Until a rifle cracked.

As she thought it might.

And she fell from the sky to the battleground.

"No!" Bishop screamed, swiveling around and covering her with the Phoenix's body.

A hundred yards away, upon a ridge, sat a hideous site.

A row of giant rats, the size of the beast Marlow had kept as a pet, numbering a hundred. Upon them rode the Lost Battalion, helmets dull and thick. Rasputin stood shirtless, the rest in their mosaic uniforms, eyes red as cherries. Hungry and savage. At his right, Alex, a smoking rifle in his hand.

Rasputin's voice was a battle cry that made the rats' fur bristle and the men's wide-tooth smiles inch back into a rictus. "Requiem for this dead world! Let us claim in death what they stole from you in life. United, unchained, this world is ours!"

A horrific cry covered the battlefield, strong and savage and big. Behind that ridge, out of sight, must lay an army.

An army of the dead.

Vasilya lay at his feet trembling, a wet red blossom on her shoulder.

"Do not fret for me. Do … what must be done," she said.

He nodded. "Oh, Angel. I'm so sorry."

She slapped the periscope. "Go, you idiot!"

He faced the horde upon the ridge, his voice a terrifying bellows, an inhuman yell, the last sound he made before he charged, left arm dangling.

And behind him, an echo of his primordial rage, as thousands of German soldiers charged behind him, into the fray.

CHAPTER FORTY-NINE:

RECKONING

The red wound was growing redder, from shoulder to chest, and every pounding step of the marching soldiers sent rivulets of pain through her. It was hard to breathe, harder to concentrate as a stampede of Germans rushed past her, one crushing her ankle with fresh sparks of agony until she heard from the din a hoarse voice screaming "Bearer! Get a bearer!"

A soldier's face appeared and blocked out the spinning sky. "Hold on to my hand, I have some morphine."

"It doesn't matter," she said. "I've done my part."

"Bearer!" he screamed. "You'll be ok. The bullet went right through … oh god, your … you have wings."

They were trembling, trying to flutter up and away. She tried to calm them with her mind. "Oh my. You're that mecha—" He shut his mouth.

The reality of the situation crept on her. She was in German hands. She'd killed Colonel Balk … it made little difference. "Do whatever you want. I'm done with this war."

A stretcher bearer rushed forth and soon she was being dragged in the other direction. "She needs special treatment!" Something stabbed her arm and a euphoric numbness closed around her like a blanket. "Get her bandaged up and to General Vogel."

"Vogel …" the name rose out of her mind as it slipped into sleep … the man in command of Felix's unit … she fought against the numb thickness until another puncture on her arm turned her arms and legs to jelly, and a strap across her chest stopped her wings from being anything but a mere rustle of leaves itching her back.

The earth drummed with Warren's mad dash up the hill, the Phoenix moving as if it were him, as if they were one, as if they were intent on tearing these maggots limb from limb. His strides were matched as the rats of Rasputin dove down. He whipped his body back and forth, driving his right fist into one until its neck cracked, then whipping his dead left arm to scythe another. The beasts trailed off into the fire of flamethrowers and bullets from the stormtroopers as their riders leapt off and engaged in macabre fisticuffs, tearing limbs from bodies as flames covered everyone.

At the top of the ridge, Rasputin and Alex stood back, reining their rats as bullets doused the Phoenix, sparking across its metal surface, chipping loose pieces. Rage fed Warren's momentum and hunger as he punched and slashed his way through the Lost Battalion's cavalry charge, the hell of war behind him as the Germans fought against the impossible and the screams of men torn asunder became a never-ending symphony in the control capsule, Rasputin's tattoos dancing across his form like wild oils, Alex's red eyes as big as tomatoes …

No, not Alex, he told himself as he tossed a rat into a pile of Lost Battalion soldiers. That thing ain't him. Whatever it is, there's only one way to save him.

"Rasputin!" he screamed. "You're a dead man walking!"

Fists of metal and whips of iron, he tore his way through them with the same violent surge that they dispatched the Germans who now lay in clumps, dead, burning, or both, flame throwers exploding as their bodies crumpled against the onslaught, and soon there was nothing but a sea of red and white that Warren waded through against the tide, drilling dead soldiers so hard in the head they could not rise from the grave again, tearing bodies apart so they were useless pieces of a broken toy, crushing skulls with his hand as they tried to climb over him like he had the old Juggernaut.

He could barely move with the weight of soldiers on him. They blocked the periscope and clogged his every step.

"We missed you, Warren" said one.

"Think you're on the wrong side, mein friend!"

"Alex would be so disappointed!"

He grunted. "Fuck you and the rat you rode in on!"

"Rasputin sends his regards."

They tore into the suit, looking for holes, and fished for grenades.

There wasn't any choice. He stumbled, pressing the gas button, until the Phoenix was dripping.

"Alex!" he said, then pounced on a flaming German.

Fire roared and curled fast and thick around him as the men screamed, hands retreating from their grenade sacks and covering their eyes. Warren dove forward before they exploded in a series of hideous pops. The blast cut a hole through a path of other soldiers and he ran through the gap, a thing of fire and metal, hacking and slashing through the soldiers that stood before him with screams and slashes. Moving forward, always forward. No running except up that goddamn hill. Cutting his own path, his mind raced. Kill the bastard, break his hold on Alex, and let him die free.

His hunger grew with the anger, and worse, through the periscope, ghosts cluttered his field of vision while he fought his way through the melee. Each fistful of soldiers he'd crushed crept back on the hill as phantoms on the periphery of vision.

He kept slashing.

Piece were torn with every encounter. It was becoming harder to wade through the sea of combat, and beyond the waves of violence lay the dead, the truly dead, waiting for him to fall ... and then what? Drag him to hell was the most likely scenario.

Fine, Warren said, burning through the crowd, racing toward Rasputin. They can drag me to hell if they want. "But I'm taking that son of a bitch with me."

He surged up the hill, conviction as sharp as bowie knife, and charged forth toward the crest of the ridge while dead soldiers crashed into and past him, into the remaining Germans. But they couldn't win this battle on their own.

He tore through the soldiers in every possible uniform until Rasputin screamed "Path!"

They folded away like the sea before Moses, and kept chugging into the Germans.

Warren braced himself for a leap—

When Alex threw a sack at him with deadly intent, red eyes still wide as his rictus, a bulging form—

Grenades.

A dozen of them.

Warrens smiled. Clever, brother—

The world went boom.

Vasilya gasped out of the darkness to find herself still, and no longer in motion against the tide of charging soldiers. The hellish sound of war was all around her but everywhere were shadows marching behind canvas walls, matched by the fetid stink of infection mixed with the iron taste of iodine. Rows of soldiers on stretchers stood before her while medics attended them with a cold detachment.

"So. The sleeper awakens."

The voice was wretched. Words shredded and gasping as if the lungs were made of tar. Vasilya shivered, then turned to the corner where an old man sat beside her stretcher. His face was hideous, a mutilated mass. A patch held over one eye but the other was clear and angry. One hand lay on her shoulder. The other was missing. "Welcome back," he said, he gasped, "from the dead, child."

She tore herself away from his touch, but struggled against restraints that were tight around her chest, her wings tucked in tight and unable to move. "Balk ... you're—"

"Alive?" He gasped, a rotting smile pulled tight while his eye raged. "After ... a fashion." Each word brought suffering. "Did not ... think I'd live ... to see you again."

"The feeling is mutual," she said, bitterly, but regret seeped into her heart to see his face. "What am I doing here?"

"Breathing ... thanks to me. I hear ... you have rebuilt ... the Juggernaut ..." He leaned closer. "For the British." He shook his head. "Never ... would have believed ... it."

"We have bigger problems than the British," came a voice from the flap door. General Vogel, looking ten years older than the last time she'd seen him, scratched his dark grey and black whiskers. "So, this is the Angel of Cambrai. I would not have suspected a traitor to Germany to be so inspiring to my army."

"Forgive her," Balk said. "She's ... Russian."

Vogel sat on a stool next to Balk. "Well, no one is perfect." Then his hard face was all hers. "My men are getting slaughtered. These are the same men who came after us when we used the Juggernaut?"

She nodded, and told them what she knew.

"Incredible," the general said.

Vasilya struggled against the straps. "But our Phoenix, the new Juggernaut, it was meant to be a symbol, of cooperation. How is it fairing?"

The general leaned back. "Not well. It apparently came close to cresting the ridge where their commander is actually watching the battle like Napoleon at Austerlitz, and bought a respite to my men ... damn thing was apparently a ball of fire before being knocked down."

"Down?" she said. "But not out? General, you must find a way to save it. It's the only way to defeat Rasputin."

He stood. "Out of the question. My men are getting slaughtered and we need to fall back for a counterattack if any—"

"There won't be a counterattack!" she yelled. "They're probably turning your dead into fresh recruits as we speak, if you give them any time to recover it will just overwhelm you."

"What would you have me do? Ask Hindenburg to stop fighting on all fronts to help us? He doesn't believe in monsters and ghosts—"

"No," she said. "But he'll respect victory. You need to contact the British."

"What?" His eyes bugged out.

"The Canadian Corps is not far from here. I saw them when we arrived. They can buy you time."

"And tell them what, exactly? Monsters have sprouted from the ground and we need help defeating them? They'd laugh before firing all batteries on our location."

Her wings wrangled against her back as she strained the straps with her chest. "You must try! There are those in that unit that will know what it means. Tell them this is part of Operation Phoenix! Tell them to engage the common enemy. Tell them the Theosophical Society has found a way to victory!" She glared at Balk. "This ... this is the way to end the war, Balk. Not a decisive blow, but a decisive enemy and a shared victory. Even Hindenburg couldn't argue with that!"

A runner stumbled into the tent. "General—the machine ... it's—" He was gasping, hands on knees.

The general yanked him up. "What about it?"

His head was shaking. "They've ... they've killed it." Vasilya's eyes shut against the shaking tears. "They're carrying it back to the ... madman on the hill."

Vasilya shook her head. "Cowards. If you will not do anything, I will. Let me go."

"Ridiculous!" Balk said. "We ... need her."

"Don't be a fool!" she yelled. "You don't need me, or another Juggernaut, you need another army. And I can get it for you. Undue these straps."

"General, she's a liar ... an ungrateful ... murderer."

Her rage would have frosted hell itself, listening to Balk talk of murder. And the guilt over her actions voided like air in a vacuum. "General. You don't have time. Let me go, send your men into attack, and I will get you the reinforcements you need. Or go down in history as the Jew who lost the war for Germany. I wonder if your people will fare better here than in the pogroms of Russia."

Vogel's face bristled, but the thorn of truth in her words stuck. He took a blade from his belt, silver and clean, a ceremonial piece.

"General!" Balk exclaimed.

He cut her free. "Do you need transportation?"

Her wings fluttered free. "Just don't let your men shoot me and I'll be fine." She faced Balk. "And you..." The fists of her hands relaxed as she exhaled into the ruinous face of her former master. "You saved my life, though you'd do it just to shove me back in chains. So I won't kill you. Today. But come near me again, lay hands on me again, even to save my life, and I will tear out your last eye."

She ran out of the tent into the din of battle, ran harder and harder as her wings fluttered and all around her stopped what they were doing to see the fallen angel of Cambrai take flight and head west on the wind toward their enemy, back itching and wings bleeding.

Beneath the iron hide of the Phoenix, a dozen starving undead soldiers carried the burden up the hill like ants with a dead beetle. Warren moved, but the Phoenix did not respond, and the disconnect now seemed obvious—

The cables from his chest hung out, their torn ends frayed apart and ripped from the main line that went into the machine, the periscopes were shattered and the husk of the Phoenix was heavy and dark. The grenades had dented in the armour on the chest plate of the control cabin, and through a tiny crack of metal the light of gloom flooded in.

I'm trapped in a ten-ton coffin.

He leaned forward and his heart rattled in his chest. Pain, real and deep, bit his gut like sickness, contorting his mouth and biting his nerves.

Each mechanical heartbeat was like a slug to the chest, the final mile before it expired, and he tasted death with each breath. He'd barely lasted five minutes without his heart, and now its sole source of power was starting to fade. How much time had the machine given him?

Whatever I've got, he said. I'm saving.

The marching dead stopped.

"With a hundred hands and five hundred knuckles, crack this armoured giant apart," Rasputin said.

The Phoenix shook, as slowly, piece by piece, armour was stripped, wire was torn, and the hulking mass that they'd spent their blood and sweat making, the effort of all those talents, was destroyed in seconds...

The grey light filled the cabin until the sky was above, interrupted by the triumphant glare of Rasputin. The starving soldiers clacked their jaws and licked their teeth.

"Welcome, Warren Bishop, to your funeral. And a new dawn rising."

High above the battlefield, frigid winds fought Vasilya like invisible octopi. Tears streamed as her hair flowed wild and tangled. With each hard turn, each twist and tumble, her back slicked with blood. And she knew that wherever she was going, she would not be coming back.

Behind her the sounds of battle dissipated, but the images were still fresh in her mind. The cold and the weakness, she told herself, I don't know how much more I can handle ...

And then she thought, not of Felix, but of Bishop.

Foul-mouthed, rude and raw, a savage colonial thing she'd hated on sight as he'd fought her beloved, a rotten human being, worthy of contempt in life and pity in death ... a self-professed coward who had only gone to war out of guilt and had become a monster from a fairy story for his trouble ... the Germans said he'd fought like a beast when she'd fallen.

She would do no less for him.

Her speed was majestically fast, a bullet more than a bird, and she knifed the air as if she'd been doing it all her life, instinct taking control of her commands to the wings.

Pain grew with every mile, but she pressed on. Iron heart holding true, but the mad flap of wings was soon shaking her hard. A trail of blood dropped from the sky as she struggled on against the icy embrace of the wind, on and on until she once again saw the large formation like a gaggle of toy soldiers in a child's playroom floor, hiding in scars cut deep in the earth. Thank god—

The descent was agony. Each flap tore a little deeper. Each wing bled a little more. Each blast of wind shoved her into a spin from which she barely tore herself out.

Screams and glares and the sounds of rifles loading welcomed her as she screamed. "Do not shoot! I have a message from Mr. Churchill!"

As the ground approached, a hideous rip came from her back. Flying became falling as her wings tore themselves off. Her knees broke upon hitting the planks deep beneath the trenches, and lances of pain woke her enough to scream.

Soldiers surrounded her, grubby faced and mutter English. "Take me ..." she muttered through clenched teeth but her voice was drowned out by the crowd.

"It's a girl—"

"Jesus, those wings are still in the air—

"She's bleeding like a gutted sow!"

She gripped one by the shirt and yanked him down. What would Warren say?

"Just take me to your commanding officer, you colonial shit heels!"

He was as useless as a baby in a tin coffin, glaring up at Rasputin's face, swimming with his tattoos. "I am impressed by your attempt at valour, but as your brother would say you are again a day late and a dollar short." The rat that Rasputin rode shivered, teeth like barbed wire. "The war you were in is over. Ours is about to begin."

"Save the speech for the slaves who have no choice but to listen. Alex," he faced his brother. "Don't do this. Don't follow him into the gutter of hell."

Rasputin gripped Alex's shoulder. "Alexander has chosen the righteous side of victory. And neither you, nor a false angel, nor any other trick of mechanical marvels will do anything to change that. My army of draugs is consuming the Germans now, and planting dead root as we speak. Every fallen soldier will rise again to punish those that unleashed this war in the first place, and imprisoned me while birthing mechanical monstrosities when flesh and spirt are the true guides to immortality—"

Warren leaned up from the command capsule, feigning injury, but only just. "Until they go crazy ... start seeing ghosts ... and consume each other in madness. Forget to tell them that?"

"Grab him," Rasputin said.

An iron grip pulled him from the dark of the capsule, and the cable from his chest came with him until it was taut. Alex held him like a criminal in the fist of a noose. Warren grunted, trying to find strength in his arms and legs to thrash him.

"Your brother is beyond your command," Rasputin said. "Crush his skull."

Warren's knees hit the ground and Alex's hands gripped his head as if it were a Christmas nut, fresh out of the fire, ready to be cracked.

"Alex ... don't."

Rasputin nodded. "Now, Alexander. Show him the error of his ways."

"Alex ... you ... always said I was a coward. I was the monster. The one that killed Father ..."

Alex's face snickered.

"And you had every right to hate me. You ... you're the hero of the family."

"Alexander," Rasputin said. "Now."

White cascades of pain shook. A scar of pain crackled across the bone. Warren seethed. "But I came back, Alex. I could have run, but I came back for you. Even ... even when I knew you were dead ... even if it was impossible. I chose to do it. Are you choosing to do this?"

"Alexander, silence him."

Warren's teeth clenched. "I love you, Alex. I'm sorry. I'm sorry I couldn't have saved you from this bastard."

"Now!"

Alex's hands shook.

"Sir!" screamed a draug soldier. "Sir!"

"Kill him," he screamed.

"I'm sorry," Warren said.

"Sir! Tanks! Coming from the west. It's the Canadian Corps!"

"What? Impossible!"

Alex's hands eased, until he wasn't crushing Warren's head so much as holding it up, then gripped it so he rose to his feet, and the brothers were eye to eye. "Let me save you," Warren said.

"War-ren?" Alex said, broken and weak, and for a half second there was a moment of clarity in his red eyes as fresh and innocent as when they'd chased each other to school on rural route one, a brave kid following his cowardly older brother as far as he would take him. "War-ren ... I'm sor—"

The rat charged.

And the world slowed as the steam that was left in his heart sputtered out, the pistol fired. With his right hand he gripped the shark tooth around his neck, letting it bite into his grip as he pulled back for a straight right haymaker—

The sick wet slicing of razor teeth engorged his stomach as the rat Rasputin rode dove into him and tore a good part of his guts away.

The strength of steam power was thinning from the cable in his chest. Rasputin, high atop his rodent steed, yanked the cables, dragging Warren close to the wizard's grip. "You never deserved this gift, and you've made it a technical blasphemy!" He ripped the cables to shreds.

A battle cry silenced the world above Warren as Alex charged, tackling Rasputin from his mount and into the dirt, while all around them soldiers ran toward the rumble of tanks.

But the rat charged Alex, who belted Rasputin once before tumbling down the hill.

Holding in what remained of his guts, Warren stood, weak, and stumbled to see Alex gripping the beast's jaw with his hands. "Stop him!" Alex screamed. "Get him!"

He faced the wizard, who was coughing blood. "Not so goddamn tough when you have to fight yourself, are ya?" White heat filled his right hand, and Rasputin's eyes glazed with something Warren had not seen in the shit heel's face before.

Fear.

Rasputin stumbled back, muttering some words. But Warren charged forward as his heart beat one last monstrous thud. His fist drilled the Russian wizard with a right cross that shone bright and white as lightning and moved twice as fast, cracking the bastard's neck like a twig—

A dark hush washed out of Rasputin as he spun to the ground. The tattoos shivered on his skin, stuck to the dead corpse, and became pus-filled sores that bubbled on his flesh.

Warren hit the battleground face-first, twisting his neck to see the madness around him. Spell broken, the army of the dead went mad, tearing at each other like rabid wolves from the same pack while distant shellfire rained down upon them.

All but one.

The lights were dimming, but Alex's boots came into view, in his hand the jaw of a giant dead rat.

He sat, pulled Warren into his lap, while the world went mad with violence around them.

"I'm sorry," Warren said. "I tried … I tried to save you."

"You can," Alex said, black blood leaking out the back of his neck. "You can."

Warren's hand hugged his brother's neck. Alex nodded.

A dark light covered him and a familiar voice came out of the void. "Not bad, Qimmiq. Not bad at all."

CHAPTER FIFTY:

RESURRECTIONS

Vasilya was astonished how quickly it all ended, sitting with the Canadians in a forward trench as the celebrations rang out. Four years of a war that, once started, few thought could end. The suffering was biblical in proportions and yet now, at a canteen, waiting for the arrival of her patrons with a bandaged leg, it was over. A switch turned on, from dark to light, and while the relief in the faces of the men were heartening, every other thought weighed a ton.

She sipped bitter coffee laced with rum as rumours filled the mouths of those around her about the creatures the Corps had fought, the courageous and stalwart defence of the Germans, and praise for General Vogel who some say might face court-martial or be made chancellor depending on how Hindenburg feels.

But no word of the Phoenix, or Bishop.

That he succeeded, that this victory was in no small part due to his efforts, there was no doubt.

But not to have seen him, not to hear his stubborn, foul-mouthed comments in the wake of victory … it made Vasilya lonely.

The door to the canteen opened and a familiar face brightened her sadness.

Winston—Mr. Churchill—dashed in, face red with joy. "So, how are they treating the Angel of Cambrai? Has it been to your satisfaction?"

"The food's worse than Daedalus," she said. "But other than that, I'm fine."

He smiled. "We owe it to you to make sure you never feel just fine, but exuberant and well-tendered. You can bank on that, my dear."

She smiled. "Sir, have you heard from Bishop?"

His smile took a melancholy timbre. "That's why I'm here, in fact. I've made arrangements. They say you're good enough to walk with crutches. And I think you should be there."

"For what?"

The door opened again. "This place is a maze to confound the Minotaur," said a gentle but strong voice. Dr. Oshikawa was in a nursing sister's thin-waist greys, complete with kerchief, though it made her exotic beauty stand out that much more. She reined in her excitement to a small, but buoyant smile. "They said you'd been hurt—" was all she could muster before tears streamed and she held Vasilya, and then released her quick. "Your wings ... are you—"

"I will be all right."

Dr. Oshikawa gripped her tighter. "You brave, stupid, insolent girl," she said with a muffled voice into her neck. "I'm grateful you're still with us."

Winston stood. "I wish we had hours for a comfortable return of good wishes, but there is a pressing matter. And you are both required. Come. Duty calls."

It was a solemn moment, marked by the silence of war.

First, they went to an American cemetery. They stood amongst a handful of rough and tired-looking Marines as a casket of Kentucky maple was placed in the ground, and Winston gave a short speech on the life and contribution of Captain Waylon Pierce. And as the casket descended, and the trumpets played, all Vasilya could think of was the tough-as-nails American with the strange accent, whose act of courage bordering on insanity likely made victory possible thousands of feet in the air.

"His contribution to peace and justice in this world," Churchill said, "has not been paralleled since the age of chivalry, for without his dogged pursuit of the enemy of humanity, from Caribbean shores to the darkest of Africa, like Percival chasing the grail, we would not have found our course for victory. The Society is grateful for the courage and zeal of Captain Waylon Pierce, though few will ever know his name."

And from there, the occasion sank lower as they rode by car and then horse under full military guard to a crested hill of Cambrai, where Vasilya had last seen ...

"Bishop."

She wanted to run, to fly, but instead she was forced to the slow, painful march on horseback toward the rank and awful scene. Funeral pyres were lit, the bodies of the vile soldiers piled high on them, as well as what she thought were wolves. The stench proved there could be hell on earth, and it was laced with the vile smoke of war.

But from the cleared scene were two bodies, a sad relief on a lonely hill. One man held the other in his arms, a hole in his head and a gun in his hand. Bishop lay comfortably in the man's lap. Body ruined, dead heart still, but his face was serene and relaxed. Beside them was the ruined husk of the Phoenix.

"This is where the war ended," Churchill said. "On that there can be no argument. Where victory was pulled back from the iron jaws of defeat."

Dr. Oshikawa gripped Vasilya tighter. "And Rasputin?"

"A ruinous affair," Churchill said. "His body ate itself as if it were starved for food. All that was left were bones and a broken neck. We've destroyed what was left and cast it into the sea."

"Help me down," Vasilya said. Dr. Oshikawa dismounted, then lifted her down. They approached the two bodies, then stopped, the smell too much. She covered her nose. "Thank you, Warren Bishop." No tears came. Instead, her heart ached. She had never liked him, and indeed hated him, and hoped that being grateful was enough, for she was that. Here sat the man that ended the war that had ruined so many lives. A blowhard, a thief, a killer and coward.

And now. A hero. "Where ... where will he be taken?"

Churchill stood beside them. "Their mother, who was most helpful, wanted us to send them home to Canada. I don't know if the Society will allow that. He still as more to teach us—"

"I'll take them," Vasilya said.

"Pardon?" Churchill said.

"I'll bring them home. If you can support the venture."

Churchill nodded. "I will see what I can arrange." He sighed. "Godspeed, Warren Bishop. Your family and all the human race was lucky to have you."

They walked back as two coffins marched forward.

"When you are done returning them," Dr. Oshikawa said, lightly. "Where will you go? Russia?"

"No, war still rages there, and it is no longer my home."

"Europe or England?"

Vasilya sniffed, and long-lost words from simpler times revived themselves in memory. "No, I'm sick of the precious graveyards of the old world."

"Ah." The doctor spoke carefully as if the words were written in her mind, well-practiced and cautiously rehearsed. "Then perhaps, if you'd like, we could go somewhere together, somewhere far away from the graves of this war, and the prejudices of the old world. Somewhere to start fresh." She lightly touched her back. "Somewhere where you could recover, and learn to be all you want to be. I have a cousin who lives in America, California. She says it's beautiful." Her lips trembled and she stared forward, sternly. "Though that's just an idea."

Vasilya placed her hand in Dr. Oshikawa's "Your *musume* would love that very much."

They rode their horses, coffins in tow, and headed west as the sun kissed the horizon, and the sky stood before them like a promise, tears drying as they made their way forward.

CODA

January 1, 1919

In the deep recesses of Buckingham Palace, the audience chamber for Queen Victoria was lit by a single candle. Six attendants worked furiously against the encroaching darkness, but she knows the candle inside is flickering out.

A knock from the front door.

"Enter!" she says, as black exhaust comes from her pipes. The attendants worked twice as hard, her body no longer able to live without them.

Minister Churchill strides in, face beaming even in her dim eyes. "Majesty. Good news. The Society is reconciled. Hostilities have stopped. Peace terms initiated. I have word from the German Academie Arcane that they have agreed to repatriation if certain terms and changes are made and we have found a talent who could—"

"Enough."

"Majesty?"

"Enough. We end."

He approached, face taut. "We have spent the past four years keeping your empire alive, keeping the Society from a civil war. You must live to see—"

"I've seen. Too much. Death. That is all."

"But what if I told you that we could return you to your ... most human form?"

Her gears shook. "No." A dream that could not be rekindled. She welcomed the blanket of darkness. "We are finished."

"Or perhaps, reborn?"

He clapped. The door opened. Chains scraped the ground as two large officer dragged a bald man with corpse flesh into the room and dropped him before her feet.

"Majesty, I give you the war criminal Rasputin."

The broken man lifted his head, and within each socket were the toys of mesmerists.

"He is three hundred years old," Churchill said.

Victoria blinked.

Churchill clapped again. "And we have studied him. And what he can do. And why."

The two officers dragged him to his feet, his arms locked in place with bracelets etched from gold and covered in arcana. When he screamed, it was wordless … for the ragged meat in his mouth was evidence of a slashed-out tongue.

"Death is your prerogative, of course," Churchill said. "But know that you are turning down life for another age. One of prosperity. Of peace. Of the Society maintaining the balance."

An officer reached behind him and took out a serrated blade.

Fear tingled through her dying wires, but none of the "counter measures" of Mr. Wells came alive to save her: she was naked before men of violence, pitiful creatures of lesser blood, those who were meant to be ruled.

"But you can have it now. All it costs is his heart."

And her candle flickered, a world without Victoria bloomed before her eyes, of madness and rutting and the poor reaching for the stars on a hill made of bone, of the Society's talents and gifts turned loose like monsters in daylight, eclipsing the horrors of the war … a world where there is no balance of Houses upon the earth.

Rasputin screamed and gagged, trashing uselessly against the restraints.

Victoria flicked her glance to Churchill. Her metal teeth clacked. "Prevail."

"Of course, Your Majesty."

And the dim lights went red.

AFTERWORD

I started out in horror fiction, and still love it, but I adore mash-ups and smashing genre conventions almost as much. When I was a kid, a magazine described John Carpenter's *Big Trouble in Little China* as a "Kung Fu, horror, action-comedy ghost story." And it was! And it was marvelous! So, when I became a writer in 1999, I promised myself to embrace mash ups, too. So—here is my Frankenstein/steampunk/Great War novel. I wrote it at maximum speed for pulp authenticity and to maintain enthusiasm for the world, the characters, and the high stakes and deep horror of the story. It also rests on years of deep reading of the literature of Great War veterans, many of whom would no doubt agree that war is a horror story made real.

It was a long road to publication. Since the idea first germinated I've immigrated, lost both my parents, was near homeless, rebuilt my life and created a loving family. Many close calls came and went until the day you found it in your hand or on your screen. I think it was worth the wait. I hope you do, too.

Jason Ridler
Parts Unknown, CA
www.jasonridler.com

ACKNOWLEDGMENTS

Thanks to Nick Mamatas, David Wilson, David Dodd, and all the people at Crossroad Press for helping me get this beast back into the world. And to Professor Thomas Vincent at the Royal Military College, who's teaching about "the world of war" informed much of this work

ABOUT THE AUTHOR

Jason Ridler is a historian at Johns Hopkins University and the Official Writing Instructor for The Arts at Google through Greater than the Sum vendors. He has published nine novels, including The Brimstone Files series at Nightshade Press, over eighty short-stories, and many historical books, academic articles, essays and columns. His writer's guide Undefeated: Stay a Writer Against the Odds was called "essential reading for working writers and those who hope to join them." Visit him at www.jasonridler.com.

OTHER BOOKS BY JASON RIDLER

The Brimstone Files Series
Hex-Rated
Black Lotus Kiss

The Spar Battersea Series
Death Match
Con Job
Dice Roll

Standalone Novels
Rise of the Luchador
A Triumph for Sakura
Blood and Sawdust

Works of Nonfiction
Maestro of Science
Mavericks of War
FXXK Writing: A Guide for Frustrated Artists
Undefeated: Stay a Writer Against the Odds

Curious about other Crossroad Press books?
Stop by our site:
https://www.crossroadpress.com
We offer quality writing
in digital, audio, and print formats.